Praise for Linda Lael Miller's national bestselling series

SPRINGWATER SEASONS

"A DELIGHTFUL AND DELICIOUS MINISERIES. . . . *Rachel* will charm you, enchant you, delight you, and quite simply hook you. . . . *Miranda* is a sensual marriage-of-convenience tale guaranteed to warm your heart all the way down to your toes. . . . The warmth that spreads through *Jessica* is captivating. . . . The gentle beauty of the tales and the delightful, warmhearted characters bring a slice of Americana straight onto readers' 'keeper' shelves. Linda Lael Miller's miniseries is a gift to treasure."

—*Romantic Times*

"This hopeful tale is . . . infused with the sensuality that Miller is known for."

—*Booklist*

"All the books in this collection have the Linda Lael Miller touch. . . . "

—*Affaire de Coeur*

"Nobody brings the folksiness of the Old West to life better than Linda Lael Miller."

—*BookPage*

"Another warm, tender story from the ever-so-talented pen of one of this genre's all-time favorites."

—*Rendezvous*

"Miller . . . create[s] a warm and cozy love story."

—*Publishers Weekly*

"Heartwarming. . . . Fans of Miller's Springwater Seasons series will not want to miss this enjoyable tale."

—Romantic Times

"An author who genuinely cares about her characters, Miller also expresses the exuberance of Western life in her fresh, human, and empathetic prose and lively plot."

—Booklist

"I loved this book! Ms. Miller touches our hearts again in a very special way. Do not miss this wonderful story!"

—Old Book Barn Gazette

"[A] triumph. . . . *One Wish* is an entertaining Americana romance that shows why Linda Lael Miller has remained one of the giantesses of the industry for the past decade. The story line is crisp and filled with family conflict."

—Harriet Klausner, Barnesandnoble.com

TWO BROTHERS

"A fun read, full of Ms. Miller's simmering sensuality and humor, plus two fabulous brothers who will steal your heart."

—Romantic Times

"Linda Lael Miller has gifted her fans with a book that is in actuality two novels in one. . . . Fans of Western romance will devour this 2-for-1 gift package from the ingenious Ms. Miller."

—Compuserve Romance Reviews

Also by Linda Lael Miller

Linda Lael Miller

Springwater Seasons

Rachel Savannah Miranda Jessica

POCKET BOOKS

New York   London   Toronto   Sydney   Singapore

POCKET BOOKS, a division of Simon & Schuster, Inc.
1230 Avenue of the Americas, New York, NY 10020

Savannah copyright © 1999 by Linda Lael Miller
Miranda copyright © 1999 by Linda Lael Miller
Jessica copyright © 1999 by Linda Lael Miller
Rachel copyright © 1999 by Linda Lael Miller

These titles were previously published by Sonnet Books

ISBN: 0-7434-0362-2

First Pocket Books paperback printing November 2000

10 9 8 7 6 5 4 3 2 1

POCKET BOOKS and colophon are registered trademarks of Simon & Schuster, Inc.

Cover art by Robert Hunt

Printed in the U.S.A.

QB / X

June of 1998
Port Orchard

Dear Friends,

Welcome to the Springwater stagecoach station, which will grow before your very eyes, into a thriving community, complete with a saloon, a schoolhouse, a church, and a newspaper, among other things. There are six books in the Springwater series, although I may do more. I love the idea of writing a long, involved story and watching this fictional town full of delightful people come to life. I hope the many and varied characters will become as dear to you as they are to me.

Let me know what you think, and to receive a copy of the *Springwater Gazette*, Springwater's own newspaper, please send a business-sized stamped, self-addressed envelope, with your address clearly printed. We'll add you to the newsletter list automatically, thus giving you advance notice of every new release, whether it is part of this series or not. The address is:

Linda Lael Miller
P.O. Box 669
Port Orchard, WA 98366
e-mail: lindalaelm@aol.com

God bless and keep.

Warmly,

Linda Lael Miller

Contents

Rachel

For Amy Pierpont,
with love and appreciation

Spring

Near Springwater,
Montana Territory, 1874

CHAPTER

1

TREY HARGREAVES HAD BUSINESS to attend to that chill and misty day in early spring; he was dressed for courting and in a fair-to-middling hurry, so he very nearly rode right on by when he spotted the stagecoach bogged down square in the middle of Willow Creek. The driver, a strapping, ginger-haired young Irishman by the name of Guffy O'Hagan, was fighting the mules for all he was worth, but the critters had gotten the better of him and there was no denying it.

It wasn't that the creek was exactly dangerous, Trey thought, reluctantly drawing the black and white paint gelding to a halt on the bank to survey the scene proper-like. The water was fast-moving, what with the thaw and all, but it was no more than four feet deep, and a person would have to be downright stupid to drown in a trickle like that.

He sighed. The problem was, there were a surprising number of stupid people, even in these isolated parts, out beating the brush for a chance to get themselves killed. While he had no real worries about Guffy, the man being no sort of greenhorn, he wasn't so sure about the woman. First of all, she was wearing a blue feather on her hat, a bedraggled, plumelike thing, bent at one end—by the ceiling of the stage, no doubt—and second, she was halfway out the window, fluttering a handkerchief at him like some duchess summoning a servant.

He sighed again.

Her voice rang out over the rush of the stream, the infernal splashing and the bellows of the balking mules, not to mention Guffy's loud litany of forbidden Anglo-Saxon words. Clearly, he'd forgotten that his passenger, traveling alone as far as Trey could tell, was a lady.

"Sir!" she cried, with more waving of the handkerchief. "Pardon me, Sir? Are you an outlaw?"

Trey allowed himself a semblance of a smile; perhaps the woman was more perceptive than he'd first thought. Did they show, all those years when he'd been a wanderer and a scoundrel, making his living mostly by gambling and serving as a hired gun?

He ignored her question, sighed once more, and sent the paint wading into the icy water. His pant legs were soaked through by the time he reached the door of the marooned stagecoach, and his boots were full. He'd be lucky if he didn't lose a couple of toes to frostbite.

Close up, he could see that the stranded lady was young, barely out of her girlhood, probably, and more than passingly pretty. Her hair was auburn, a billow beneath that silly feathered hat, and her eyes were someplace between gray and green. She had good skin, long lashes, and a soft, full mouth that made Trey ponder on what it would be like to kiss her.

"As you can see," she said primly, in starched Eastern tones, "we are in need of assistance. First, though, I should like you to answer my question. Are you an outlaw, Sir?"

Trey wanted to laugh, but he didn't. He was afraid she'd stop being funny, out of sheer cussedness, if he gave in to the urge. "Well, Ma'am," he said, "I reckon that depends on who you ask." He touched the brim of his hat when he saw the flicker of alarm in her eyes. "Name's Trey Hargreaves and, for the most part, I've contrived to stay on the right side of the law. I reside at Springwater," he cocked a thumb over one shoulder, "back that way a few miles."

At the mention of Springwater—he didn't flatter himself that his name had wrought the change—her eyes lit up and some color came to her cheeks. "Thank heaven," she said. "It has seemed to me that we would never arrive. Especially since we've run aground here in the middle of this . . . this river." She nodded to indicate the roof of the coach, where a great deal of baggage was affixed with rope. "If we should overturn, the books would be lost, and I don't need to tell you, if you come from Springwater, what a dire event that would be. Without education, the children will be left to the influences of places like the"—she lowered her voice confidentially here, and lent the words a dire note—"like the *Brimstone Saloon.*"

It was all Trey could do, and then some, not to laugh out loud when she said that. As it was, he felt the corners of his mouth twitching dangerously, but he managed to retain a somewhat sober expression. "God save us all," he said, with fervor, and laid one hand to his breast.

Her eyes narrowed for a moment; she was bright, that was clear enough, and she'd discerned that he was pulling her leg a little. She put her hand out to him. "My name is Rachel English," she said. "I've been engaged to teach at the new school in Springwater."

The coach swayed dangerously, nearly turning onto its side, and Miss English drew back the hand she'd offered to hold her hat in place. With the other, she clutched the window's edge, and the expression of thwarted fear in her face tugged at Trey, in the empty place where he'd once kept his heart.

"I can wade ashore," she said. "I can even swim a little, if need be. But those textbooks mustn't be ruined. Please, Mr. . . . Mr. Hargreaves, lend us your assistance."

"Sit tight," Trey counseled her. Then he reined the paint toward the front, where the mules were still carrying on fit to whip up a froth on the water. "How-do, Guffy," he greeted the youthful driver, with a grin and a tug at the brim of his hat.

"Not real well," Guffy ground out, cordial enough, considering he had both hands full of reins and fractious jackass. "If you'd kindly . . . get the lady on solid ground . . . I'd have less . . . on my mind."

Trey made another motion, as if tipping his hat, and rode back to the door. Bending down, he turned the latch and pulled—no easy task, even with his strength, with the rushing water working against him.

"Come on," he said to Miss English, and curved one arm to reel her in.

She drew back, and it struck him that she could probably show those stage mules a thing or two about digging in their heels. "The books—" she said.

Trey was wet and he was cold and he was hopelessly late. He was not, therefore, of a mind to argue. "I'll get the damnable books," he said. "But only when you're out of this coach and standing on the bank over there."

She grabbed a small, tattered handbag and something that looked like a plant cutting from the seat beside her. "Very well," she said, "but I will hold you to your word, Sir."

Trey hooked an arm around her waist—she was hardly bigger than a schoolgirl and weighed about the same as a bag of horse feed—and hauled her, her unwieldy plant stem, tiny handbag, and all, up in front of him, just this side of the saddle horn. She smelled of roses after a rainfall, Trey thought, in a fanciful fashion that was utterly unlike him. She might have just climbed out of a bathtub and dried herself off, instead of traveling three-quarters of the way across the country. If she was the new school-marm, she was Evangeline Wainwright's friend, sent for from Pennsylvania, and the topic of such interest around Springwater that even he had heard of her. From his daughter most especially; Emma eagerly anticipated her arrival.

Holding her fast, lest she slip away and float downstream like so much flotsam, Trey squired the new teacher to the Springwater side and set her on her feet. She clutched her bag, the plant cutting wrapped at the roots in damp cheesecloth, and her dignity, and there was a plea in her eyes as she looked up at him.

"The books, Mr. Hargreaves," she said.

"Trey," he replied, sounding foolish even to himself. He turned the paint away and the two of them splashed quickly back to the coach.

"I could use some weight up top," Guffy said, breathless from the battle. "You mind climbin' up, Trey? Go round the other side, so you don't tip the damn thing over."

Any fool could have seen what needed doing, but Trey overlooked the unnecessary specifics of the suggestion, given the state of Guffy's nerves, and made his way to the far side of the coach. There, grasping the framing of the baggage rack, he raised himself to stand in the saddle, then scrambled upward. The stage swayed perilously for several moments while Trey spread his weight as best he could, like a high-wire artist seeking balance.

The rig finally settled, though, and the animals calmed down a little. The paint plodded his way back to the shore and up the bank, reins dragging, and shook himself off like a dog, thereby baptizing Miss

Rachel English in the ways of the wild and wooly West.

"Come on down here and take the lines," Guffy shouted back, over one meaty shoulder. "I'm going to see if I can persuade that knucklehead out there in the lead to point himself in the right direction."

Trey nodded and made his way carefully to the box, where he took up the reins, watching as Guffy climbed nimbly over one mule's back and then another, until he was mounted on the animal in front, on the left.

"Mr. Hargreaves!" he heard a voice call. "Oh, Mr. Hargreaves!"

Exasperated, Trey turned his head and saw the schoolmarm with her hands cupped around her mouth. He was too annoyed, and too busy with the reins, to reply.

"Don't forget about the books!" she called, and pointed with one hand to indicate the roof of the coach.

He heaved yet another sigh and ignored her. She was as exasperating a female as he had ever come across, and he felt sorry for the man who would eventually marry her. Someone surely would though, trial that she plainly was, for women were scarce in those parts, especially passably pretty ones, like her.

Suddenly, miraculously, the wheels of the coach grabbed and lurched forward, and the eight mules pulled as one, rather than in all directions, as they had before, nearly pitching a distracted Trey into the water. At a careful pace, the stage gained the bank and lumbered, dripping, up over the muddy slope, onto the grass.

The mules stood shuddering, wet through to bare hide, and looking even more pathetic than mules commonly do.

Miss English picked her way toward the sodden coach, stepping daintily over mud and stones and slippery grass. The feather on her hat looked somewhat the worse for wear, but it still bobbled foolishly in the breeze. Trey couldn't help noticing her womanly shape as she approached, though; perhaps because of the hectic nature of their encounter, he'd somehow overlooked that particular aspect of her person, despite the fact that he'd practically carried her from the stage to the shore just a few minutes back.

"I suppose I should thank you for your assistance, Mr. Hargreaves," she said, with restraint, clutching her plant cutting in both hands. "Alas, you did not heed my instructions concerning the crate of books."

He secured the reins and climbed down from the box to execute a sweeping bow and open the door of the coach. Only the most extreme forbearance kept him from telling her what to do with her books. "I seldom heed instructions, Ma'am," he said, "unless, of course, they're called for, which yours were not."

She blushed and clambered into the dripping rig, fussing with her skirts in a hopeless effort to keep the floor from wetting her hem. Guffy, meanwhile, had gotten back to the box and taken the reins in hand.

"I see you have no appreciation for the value of an education," she said.

Trey suppressed a grin. "On the contrary, Ma'am," he countered good-naturedly, but with a sting, "I hold the skills of reading and ciphering very dear. If that coach had turned onto its side, though, I reckon most everything would have been lost—the rig itself, the freight, and half the mules. You might not have fared too well either, and Guffy, well, he could have gotten himself crushed without even trying. So good day to you," he made to tug at his hat brim, but the hat was gone, probably a mile downstream by then, "and think nothing of it. You're mighty welcome."

She flushed all over again at that, and a pretty sight it was, too. Almost fetching enough to make Trey forget that he'd never make it over to Choteau, some twenty-five miles away, in time to stop Miss Marjorie Manspreet from getting onboard an east-bound stage and leaving his life forever. He'd gotten a late start as it was—maybe he *had* dallied a bit, back at Springwater, though he had a whole string of excuses at the ready—and now it was downright hopeless. He'd have to ride the rest of the day and much of the night to get there before Marjorie lit out, and he just didn't feel up to making the effort.

He whistled to the paint, which ambled toward him in obedient response, while Miss English put her head out the stage window. "I apologize," she said briskly. "You *were* quite helpful, and I should have thanked you."

"Not at all," he said, and that time he did grin. There was just something about her that drew that response from him. He turned his attention to Guffy, who was beaming down on him from the box, the spring sun shining around his big frame like an aura.

"Much obliged, Trey," he said.

Trey mounted the paint and leaned down to gather the reins in his hands. "Come by if you're staying over. We'll discuss the trials and tribulations of skinning mules."

Guffy laughed and nodded, setting the team in motion again, making for Springwater, and the stagecoach station that had given the place its name. Another team would be waiting there, and maybe even a relief driver, if the gods were smiling. With luck, the boy might get himself a night's sleep in a clean bed, some of June-bug McCaffrey's legendary cooking, and a few well-earned shots of whiskey down at the Brimstone—on the house, of course.

Since Emma, Trey's eleven-year-old daughter, was visiting the Wainwright ranch for a while, in order to help with the housework and the little boy and keep her good friend Abigail company, Miss Evangeline being exceeding pregnant these days, he decided to follow the stage in, dry off a little, and take a meal at the station himself. If there was any justice at all in the world, Miss June-bug would have made up a batch of her baking soda biscuits to go with supper. Trey had a powerful yearning for biscuits and besides, he'd lost a perfectly good hat and a prospective wife helping Guffy get the coach across the creek. He deserved *something* as a reward, and the taste of Miss June-bug's cooking would serve for now.

* * *

Rachel was sick unto death of that dratted paeonia cutting, which she had nursemaided all the way across country, forever taking care that it wasn't crushed, that it didn't dry out, that it wasn't left behind on some sooty train seat or in some rustic station along the way. She probably would have flung the thing out the stagecoach window long since if it hadn't been for Evangeline's wanting it so. Dear Evangeline, her good and trusted friend. She could hardly wait to see her again, to look into her eyes and find out if the happiness glowing in her letters was shining there, as well.

No one on the face of the earth, Rachel firmly believed, was more deserving of marital bliss than Evangeline Keating Wainwright. Not that Rachel was even remotely interested in marriage on a personal level. No, there had been but one man for her, Langdon Pannell, and he had died in the war, so horribly, so senselessly. She could not and would not take the risk of loving so thoroughly again; her grief over Mr. Pannell had shaken the very depths of her spirit. Besides, in a rash and reckless moment, she had given herself to him, the night before he rode away to fight, and he had given himself in return. Their communion had been so complete, a fusing of souls really, that for Rachel, even the prospect of lying with another man seemed a travesty.

She was thinking these thoughts as the stagecoach rolled and jostled over the last few muddy miles to Springwater, where the stream called Willow Creek had its beginning, according to Evangeline's letters.

She was honest enough to admit that she was watching their erstwhile rescuer, riding along beside the coach, while she reflected. He was a handsome man, in a rakish sort of way, with dark hair tied back at the nape of his neck, and eyes the color of mercury. She hadn't been able to help noticing his eyes; she'd never seen any quite like them.

There was a scar, long healed, along the edge of his jaw, and he was big; to Rachel, who was diminutive, he seemed almost as large as the horse he rode. The man and his mount gave the impression, in fact, of a war monument come to life, all brick and bronze and stubborn majesty.

She sat back and closed her eyes, but the image of Trey Hargreaves and his warhorse stayed with her. That set a vague sense of panic astir in her, for in those moments, Langdon was but a shadow in her memory, without face or feature. She sat rigidly upright, and fixed her eyes on the opposite wall of the coach, upon which someone had posted a tattered bill that read, "Repent or burn. Thus sayeth the Lord."

"Thus sayeth you," Rachel grumbled, and ripped the bill down. She'd been looking at it ever since she'd left the last coach, at Choteau, and boarded this one. She crumpled the warning and tossed it onto the floor. Dear heaven, but she was weary of traveling—she longed for a hot, savory meal, a night of sound sleep, and the near-forgotten pleasure of getting about on her own two feet. Rachel was a great walker, and she had sorely missed that pastime over the weeks she'd spent in transit.

At last, she heard the driver, Mr. O'Hagan, hail someone from his perch in the box of the rig, and the vehicle itself sprang violently from side to side as he hauled back on the reins, shouting to the mules, and set the brake lever. "Springwater station!" he called out, with a jubilant note in his voice.

Rachel slid across the hard, narrow seat of the coach and peered out at the station house. It stood on the far side of what looked like a full acre of mud, and someone had laid down rough-hewn boards as a sort of walkway. A beaming woman in a calico dress and an apron stood on the step, waving, while a large man of somber countenance made his way along the zig and zag path of planks. Here, of course, were the McCaffreys, the town's founders and leading citizens. It had been Jacob and June-bug McCaffrey who had seen that the schoolhouse got built, according to Evangeline, and they'd rounded up the funds to send for her and a supply of primers as well.

"Hello, Miss English," Mr. McCaffrey said, in his impossibly deep voice, opening the coach door and putting out a work-worn hand. "Welcome to Springwater, such as it is. We were beginning to fret about you."

"We run into some trouble at the creek," Guffy put in, before Rachel could reply. "Hadn't been for Trey here, we'd still have trout swimmin' betwixt our spokes."

Jacob concentrated on helping Rachel down before acknowledging Hargreaves with a noncommittal nod of his head. "Obliged," he said.

"Don't mention it," Trey replied, his tone as clipped as Jacob's. "You have another driver here? Old Guffy's had a hard day. I promised him some consolation whiskey."

It seemed to Rachel that Jacob bristled beside her; not surprising, she thought. After all, Evangeline had told her a great deal about the McCaffreys in her letters, for she considered them dear friends. Jacob was a preaching man, as well as the stationmaster, and therefore liable to take a dim view of whiskey drinking. As Rachel did herself.

In the end, though, Jacob simply shrugged and said, "You look a mite used-up yourself, Trey. You're welcome to stay for supper if you'd like."

Trey grinned full out, a devilish, boy's grin, and Rachel was dumbstruck by the change it wrought in his face. "Nobody but a fool would turn down one of Miss June-bug's suppers," he said.

Miss June-bug was waiting on the porch, her eyes shining. The woman was close to sixty, Rachel knew, but there was a glow about her that made her seem twenty years younger. "We're mighty glad you've come to us," she said, and embraced Rachel warmly.

It brought tears to Rachel's eyes, that simple human contact. She did not think anyone had embraced her since Evangeline and Abigail had set out, four long years before, on their splendid adventure.

"The girl is plumb tuckered," Jacob observed. "You look after her, Miss June-bug, and I'll spoon up some of your chicken and dumplin's for Guffy and Trey."

"You bring a plate for Miss English first," June-bug

said, taking Rachel by the arm and leading her over the threshold and into the fragrant warmth of the station. There were long tables set throughout the room, six in total, and a blaze crackled merrily on the hearth of a great stone fireplace. "Guffy and Trey will manage just fine on their own."

With that, Mrs. McCaffrey squired Rachel to a room at the very back of the station. It was a small chamber, with a high window, and the bed looked inviting, plain though it was. Just an iron frame, two pillows, and an old, faded quilt. Nearby was a table, with a freshly filled kerosene lantern and a box of matches close at hand. There were pegs on the walls for Rachel's clothing and a pitcher and bowl of plain red and white enamel stood on a rickety washstand in the corner.

"We can heat up some water for a bath once you've eaten, if you'd like that," June-bug said quietly.

Like it? Rachel's eyes stung with tears of joy and relief at the mere idea. It would be her salvation, after all those days and nights spent traveling, first on various trains and then on stagecoaches. She had managed only furtive washings along the way, and she needed a bath as much, if not more, than she needed sleep and food.

"You're very kind," she murmured, with an accepting nod. "Thank you."

Mrs. McCaffrey cast an eye over the paeonia cutting. "I could put that in water for you, too. Looks like it's lost most of its starch."

Rachel smiled at the idiom and handed over the cutting. "Evangeline asked me to bring it," she said, "and I don't mind admitting that I've grown tired of babying the thing. No doubt I'll forget what a trial it was, when I see the first blossoms."

June-bug looked at the start with such longing then that Rachel found herself wishing she'd brought two, difficulties be damned. "That will be a sight to see," the older woman said, on a long breath.

"The blooms are this big," Rachel replied, making a plate-sized shape in the air with both hands. "I'm sure Evangeline will be happy to give you a cutting, once the plant's established."

June-bug beamed. "I reckon you're right," she said. "I'll be sure to ask her soon as I get the chance." With that, the stationmistress left Rachel to look at her accommodations—she would be boarding with the McCaffreys for the foreseeable future—and the other woman had just left when Guffy knocked at the still-open door, bearing the satchel and small trunk that held her personal belongings.

"Ma'am," he said, eyes averted, and blushed as deeply as if he'd found her naked in that room, instead of just sitting on the edge of the bed, trying to gather her wits.

"Thank you," she said, and meant it.

No sooner had Guffy gone than Jacob appeared, carrying a wooden tray filled with food. He brought a bowl of chicken and dumplings, steaming and fresh, and a cup of coffee besides. In addition, there was bread and a weathered-looking apple.

Rachel moved the lamp and matchbox to the washstand, and Jacob put the tray down on the bedside table. It made her feel a bit guilty, being waited on, as though she were playing the invalid to avoid having to do for herself. A farmer's daughter, the youngest and only girl in a family of four, Rachel was not unaccustomed to work.

"I could have eaten at the table," she protested gently.

Jacob treated her to one of his rare smiles; Evangeline had described him very well in her letters, so well that Rachel felt as though she already knew him and Mrs. McCaffrey. Odd, she thought, that there had been no mention of Trey Hargreaves, either for or against. On the other hand, Evangeline was no gossip, for all that she professed to enjoy a generous serving of scandal with her tea—that was one of her finest qualities, her willingness to believe the best of people until they proved her wrong. Rachel wished she herself were half so charitable.

"You've had a long trip," Jacob said to her. "You take your rest while you can get it. You won't have too many pupils at first—only a dozen or so, from the ranches and farms near enough for the children to make the trip—but you'll have your hands full all the same."

Rachel wanted to ask about Mr. Hargreaves, who he was, where he'd gotten that scar on his jaw, and a hundred other things, but she knew her curiosity wasn't suitable, so she quelled it. She could and would ply Evangeline for whatever details might be forthcoming.

Having served her meal and offered his plain counsel, Jacob left the small room, closing the door behind him. Rachel devoured the delicious food—June-bug's reputation as a cook was wholly justified—and continued to assess the room as she did so. Having been a schoolteacher since she was sixteen, nearly ten years now, she reflected with disbelief, Rachel had boarded with all sorts of families. As humble as this chamber was, she'd never lived in a better one—the log walls were thick, and there was an inside shutter for the glass window. The mattress felt as though it were stuffed with feathers, instead of straw, and the floor was made of solid planks, planed smooth and set tightly in place, so the draft wouldn't seep between the cracks. There were no visible mouse-holes and no spider webs. Furthermore, the bedding smelled of spring sunshine and laundry soap, and she ventured to hope that the sheets were fresh.

Even on the few nights when the stagecoach had stopped for a night, she'd slept sitting up in the dining room, for it was common practice in hotels and way stations for several guests of the same gender to share a bed, with no allowances made for matters of hygiene or term of acquaintance. Privacy was, of course, impossible in such circumstances, and in any case Rachel was not willing to close her eyes in the presence of a stranger. She was, as a consequence, utterly exhausted.

She ate as much of the food as she could, then carried the tray out to the kitchen area herself. Junebug was already heating bathwater in a number of kettles, and she smiled, pleased that Rachel had eaten well.

"You go on in there now and put your feet up.

Jacob will tote in the tub in a minute, and then I'll carry the water. It's nice and hot."

Again, Rachel's gratitude was such that she could barely keep from embracing the woman and slobbering all over her with wails and sniffles. "Thank you," she said, with hard-won dignity. She was a grown woman, after all, and should have been past such wild swings of emotion, whether she was tired or not.

An hour later, she was climbing out of her bath, scrubbed clean and smelling of the rose-scented soap she'd bought before leaving Pennsylvania. Rachel was a great believer in the restorative powers of perfumed soap; hadn't Evangeline mentioned, more than once, how much the cake she'd given her as a farewell gift had meant to her, out there on that isolated ranch?

After drying off with a towel from the wooden rod above the washstand, Rachel took a nightgown from her satchel and shook it out. The garment was chilled, and slightly damp, from the creek crossing, no doubt, but it was a great improvement over the clothes she'd worn for the better part of a week. She got into bed, stretched, and tumbled into a fathomless sleep, never stirring, even when Trey and Jacob came in to carry out her tub.

Chapter

2

THE SCHOOLHOUSE, hardly more than a glorified chicken coop, might have been a profound disappointment to Rachel if she'd had any choice but to dig in and make the best of the situation. It measured no more than twelve by twelve feet, that little structure, and the floors were bare dirt. The stove was roughly the size of a milk bucket and could not be counted upon to heat even so small a space as that one in the midst of a Montana winter, nor did it seem particularly safe. There were no desks, only three short rows of benches, hewn from logs and still splintery at the edges. Birds were nesting in the rafters, and there was just one window, behind the crudely made table that was to serve as her desk, and in any case it was dirty enough to filter out any available daylight.

For all its shortcomings, Rachel realized, the Springwater school represented a concerted effort on the part of the locals. Clearly, folks had scrounged and salvaged what they could, and valuable time had been taken from ranch and farm work in order to put up the building.

Grateful that the school term would not begin until the last part of August, Rachel set herself to preparing, sorting the primers brought from Pennsylvania—the pages were only slightly warped from the dampening at Willow Creek—sweeping the floor and routing an assortment of critters, planning lessons for pupils at various levels of education. She composed letters to certain charitable organizations back East, prevailing upon them for slates, maps, a chalkboard, and other necessary items.

All this took a week, and then Rachel found herself in unfamiliar straits: She had nothing to do. Junebug would not allow her to help with the cooking and spring cleaning at the station, and although she was most anxious to be reunited with Evangeline, the Wainwright ranch was a good distance away. Certainly too far to walk and, according to Jacob, too dangerous a trip for an unaccompanied woman.

At first, Rachel spent a great deal of time standing in the bare-dirt dooryard of the schoolhouse, looking across the road at the Brimstone Saloon and fuming at the injustice of it all. The place was not at all what one would expect of a frontier establishment of that nature, neither ramshackle nor rustic, and certainly not weathered. In point of fact, it was downright fancy—whitewashed, with a row of trimmed windows across the second floor. There was grass growing out front, and every day the portly bartender came out, persnickety as an English butler, and picked up any

empty bottles and cheroot stubs that might be lying
about. It galled Rachel not a little that such an insti-
tution should thrive, while the school, the very future
of the town and the territory, went begging. It had
galled her even more to learn, on her second day in
Springwater, that Trey Hargreaves, the man who'd
rescued her and the town's schoolbooks, owned half
interest. Furthermore, there were regular brawls at the
Brimstone Saloon, and the place drew every repro-
bate who chanced to be passing by. Not to mention
attracting drovers and, with them, their herds of
bawling, dust-raising, long-horned cattle.

Fretting, of course, was a fruitless enterprise, and so
in time Rachel decided to ignore Mr. Hargreaves *and*
his business enterprise entirely. She got a list of the
six families who would be sending their children to
the school come fall, borrowed a retired coach horse
from Jacob, and set out to visit each home.

The Bellweathers, Tom and Sue, lived at the edge
of a clearing, some two miles from the schoolhouse, in
a well-kept cabin. Their ten-year-old daughter, Kathleen, was a lively, spirited child, plain as the proverbial mud-fence and totally unconcerned by the fact.
Rachel liked her straight away.

Tom was a lean and wiry man, with friendly eyes
and coarse black hair that hinted at Indian heritage,
while Mrs. Bellweather, Sue, was timid, with a look of
bleak bewilderment lurking behind her shaky smile.
"I don't see where Kathleen needs fancy schoolin',"
she said, seeing Rachel off at the end of the visit. "She
can read some—Tom taught her from the Good

Book—and all she's likely to do is get married and have young'uns anyhow."

Rachel had faced this philosophy before, in the East, and it never failed to rankle. Long experience had taught her, however, to look past this ill-founded belief, for there were nearly always deeper reasons for such prejudices. She suspected that, in this instance as in many others, there had been other children in the family once, some older than Kathleen, very possibly, and gone from home, and some younger, and no longer living. The loss of one child, let alone several, usually made a woman more protective of those remaining. No doubt Mrs. Bellweather was simply afraid to let her daughter make the two-mile trek to and from school each day, and Rachel could sympathize.

Standing beside the borrowed horse, reins in hand, she assessed this earnest and careworn woman with gentleness and respect. "It's important for Kathleen to learn as much as she can," Rachel said cautiously. "And to be with other children. Perhaps Mr. Bellweather wouldn't mind riding with her in the mornings, at least part of the way, and coming to meet her in the afternoons."

"There's no time for such as that," Mrs. Bellweather scoffed, though mildly. Something—irritation, perhaps—flashed in her eyes, and was quickly quelled. "We're plain folks, Miss English. We work from sunup to sundown just to keep body and soul together. We need Kathleen right here."

Rachel held her ground. "I've no doubt that Kathleen is a great help to you. Perhaps, though, for her sake, you'll find a way to spare her, just during the school term. I promise you, Mrs. Bellweather, that your daughter will have a better life if she attends class regularly for the next few years."

"Tom's set on it," Mrs. Bellweather confessed, with a long sigh. Then she gestured to a little grove of trees, birches and cottonwoods mostly, some distance from the house. Squinting, Rachel saw what she had half-expected to see—grave markers, tilting wooden crosses set into the ground. "We had two little boys, once," Kathleen's mother went on. "They died right after we settled here, of a fever. There was three little girls, too, all of them come after our girl, Kathleen. One of them wandered off one day, her name was Betsey, and got herself drowned in the pond back there in the woods. Little Anna, she fell underfoot when Tom was workin' with some horses and was trampled afore he could get to her. Then there was Mary Beth. The fever got her, like it did her brothers." The woman paused, let out a shuddering breath. "Kathleen's all we got left to us."

Rachel wanted nothing so much as to put her arms around the other woman and weep with her, weep because life could be so hard, so brutally hard. She'd learned for herself, though, that the shedding of tears was a waste, and besides that, Mrs. Bellweather had little enough besides her dignity. She wasn't likely to welcome a display of pity. "While she's with me," Rachel said, "I'll take care of her."

"I reckon that has to be good enough, the way Tom

feels on the matter," Mrs. Bellweather answered, resigned. "But I'm still agin the whole idea. I don't mind tellin' you that much."

There wasn't a lot Rachel could say in response to that; she thanked Sue Bellweather for the tea and hospitality, said she looked forward to seeing Kathleen at school on the last Monday in August, and mounted Jacob's old horse to ride off.

By then, it was mid-morning, and Rachel, having breakfasted early with June-bug and Jacob, was hungry. She waited until she was out of sight of the Bellweather place before ferreting through her saddlebags for the fried egg sandwich she'd made before leaving the station. She consumed half of it in a few distracted bites, put the rest away, and rode on, musing over the directions Jacob had given her when she set out.

She would visit the Kildare place, a small ranch owned by a widower, who had, according to the list June-bug had made out, two sons, Jamie, eight, and Marcus Aurelius, age ten. She was still smiling over Marcus's lofty name as she guided the horse up a steep sidehill and into the woods. A good part of her mind remained with little Kathleen Bellweather and the burdens being the only surviving child had placed on her. Due to these distractions, she was upon the makeshift camp before she even suspected that it was there.

A fire burned in a circle of stones, and there was a wheelless Conestoga wagon, with a rough lean-to woven of branches beside it. Rachel was just about to call out, announcing her presence and apologizing for the intrusion, if the inhabitants proved unfriendly, when a small, freckled face peered around the back end of the wagon.

"Who are you?" the child demanded. A boy, Rachel saw, nine or ten at most, with straight fair hair that continually fell into his eyes, bare feet, and rags for clothing.

"My name is Rachel English," Rachel answered, climbing down from the horse and feeling the corresponding sting in the balls of her feet. She walked most places, and though she was a competent rider, she was not used to the saddle. "What's yours?"

"You'd better git before my pa comes back," the boy warned.

Rachel looked around at the small, forlorn camp, which showed little or no sign of an adult presence. There seemed to be no food, and there was no livestock, either. "Tell me your name, and then we'll talk about your father," she said, making no move to mount up and ride away.

"Toby," the boy spat. "Toby Houghton. You happy now?"

Rachel merely smiled, for she saw through Toby's bravado. He was small, he was hungry, he was alone, and he was afraid.

"My pa's gonna be back any day now," Toby insisted. "Any minute, mostly likely."

Rachel nodded sagely. "I see. How long has he been away?"

Toby dragged fine white teeth over his lower lip while he considered his reply; his blue eyes were sharp and slightly narrowed as he studied Rachel. She added intelligence to her assessment. "A long while, I reckon," he admitted, at great length. "But he's comin' back. I know he is."

"When was the last time you had something to eat, Toby?" Rachel asked, careful to keep the pity she couldn't help feeling out of her voice and her expression.

"I shot me a squirrel just yesterday," he said. He was as grubby an urchin as Rachel had ever laid eyes on, and she felt a deep and immediate connection with him. They had something in common, the two of them—they were both essentially alone in the world, strong people set on making a place for themselves. His father had abandoned him, and his mother was probably dead. Rachel's family had been splintered— her three brothers permanently divided by the war and scattered all over the world by then, her parents long since gone on to whatever reward awaited them, worn out by their struggles to keep a struggling farm in the black.

Rachel turned and raised the flap on her saddle-bags, taking out the other half of her sandwich, still wrapped in one of June-bug's cloth napkins, and offered it in silence.

Toby withstood the temptation as long as he could, but in the end pride gave way to hunger, and he darted forward, snatched the food out of her hand, and gobbled it down with a desperation that would have brought tears to Rachel's eyes, if she'd allowed them leave.

"I think you'd better come to town with me," she said, when the brief frenzy was over and Toby was fit to listen. "Just until your pa gets back, I mean." God knew where she would put the child—she could hardly promise the McCaffreys' hospitality, without even consulting them—but she couldn't just leave him there, either.

Perhaps he might find a place at the Wainwright ranch with Scully and Evangeline and earn his keep helping out with the chores, she thought. If Evangeline had said it once, she'd said it a hundred times, and always with that special, joyous exuberance Scully had brought to her life—there was no end to the work on that place. Spring, summer, winter and fall, day and night, there was always something needing to be done.

Toby looked eager, but at the same time, troubled. "What if my pa don't know where I got off to?" he worried aloud.

"He'll know," Rachel said evenly. He'd know a few other things as well, this irresponsible, vanished man, when she got through pinning back his ears for him. "Get your clothes, Toby. We're going to town."

He hesitated, then went back to the dilapidated wagon, crawled inside, and came out again a few minutes later with a small bundle. He waited, gentleman-fashion, until Rachel was mounted, then put his foot in the stirrup and clasped her hand so she could pull him up behind her. His skinny arms rested gingerly around her waist.

"My pa's gonna be real mad," he warned.

"Don't worry about your pa," Rachel replied. "I'll deal with him when the time comes."

Half an hour later, they were at Springwater, approaching the station. To Rachel's consternation, Mr. Hargreaves was there, one shoulder braced against the frame of the open door, a match stick between his teeth. Guffy O'Hagan was sitting on the step, ready and waiting for the next stage to come in. When it arrived, he would help Jacob exchange the team of horses or mules for a fresh one, then take over for the other driver.

"Who do we have here?" Jacob asked, with one of his slow grins, coming around the corner of the station and seeing Toby slide to the ground, clutching his bundled belongings. Jacob's sleeves were pushed up and his clothes were dirty; it was plain that he'd been working in the stables out back. The stage line owned some forty horses, and caring for them required a lot of hard effort.

The boy stood stiffly, his head tilted way back so he could look Jacob in the face. Toby introduced himself.

"Well, howdy," Jacob said, shaking the lad's hand. His eyes met Rachel's, questioning. "Why don't you go on inside and tell my wife—her name's Miss Junebug—that I said to feed you as much as you can hold?"

Toby took to the offer and went inside, casting tentative, cautious glances at Trey and Guffy as he passed them. It was almost as if he expected one of them to reach out and grab him, drag him back, send him packing. Most of his life, Rachel suspected with a pang, Toby Houghton had been unwelcome wherever he went.

"Where did you find that poor little mite?" Jacob inquired of Rachel, his voice quiet. His rugged, timeworn face was full of compassion and some old and private grief.

"He was alone in a little camp, not far from the Bellweather place," Rachel said. She was still standing beside the horse, reins in hand, and when Trey came toward her and Jacob, her heartbeat picked up speed, a development that pleased her not at all.

"That would be Mike Houghton's boy," Trey said. "There's never been a man more useless than Mike is."

"That's so," Jacob agreed, in his taciturn way. It was a damning statement, coming from him, for in the short time Rachel had known the McCaffreys, she'd learned that they were warmhearted people, inclined to think well of their neighbors, even when they didn't approve of their actions. Trey Hargreaves, with his half-interest in the Brimstone Saloon, was a prime example. They spoke highly of him, and evidently made him welcome whenever he chose to come calling.

"Toby swears his father will be back for him," Rachel said, but with little conviction. Even as she uttered the words, she knew it wasn't going to happen, at least, not anytime soon. Houghton had forsaken his son, simply left him to fend for himself, in a wilderness that had been the breaking of many a full grown man, and strong ones, at that.

"I reckon Miss June-bug would like a lad to feed and fuss over," Jacob mused, gazing toward the house now, with a faraway expression in his deep brown eyes. "She's missed our own boys something fierce. We both have."

Rachel knew a little about Will and Wesley McCaffrey, both of whom had fallen at Chattanooga, again because Evangeline had written her about them. Like most of the other soldiers, on both sides of the conflict, they had been far too young to go off to the fighting, leaving families and sweethearts and un-finished lives behind them.

Rachel was saved from replying by the distant sound of an approaching stagecoach, driver shouting and cursing, harness fittings jingling, hooves pounding on hard-packed ground. Guffy bolted eagerly to his feet and Trey caught hold of Rachel's arm and pulled her out of harm's way, the elderly horse natu-rally following.

"Best to stand aside," Trey said.

Rachel met his eyes squarely. "No doubt you know Toby's father quite well. He would be the sort to fre-quent a saloon, wouldn't he?"

A small muscle flexed and unflexed in Trey's jaw, just above the long scar. "That was unworthy, Miss English," he said tautly. "My saloon is a place of busi-ness, not a den of iniquity, and I'll thank you to remember that."

"Nothing good can come of whiskey drinking and carousing, Mr. Hargreaves," Rachel responded, in chilly tones, but she'd lost some of her sense of conviction. As far as she knew, there was no gambling at the Brimstone Saloon, and certainly no trading in flesh. On the other hand, with a name like that place had, it was probably only a matter of time before sin and depravation broke out on every front.

Hargreaves leaned in closer and spoke in a hoarse whisper. "I hope you won't let your blue-nosed, back-East disapproval of me spill over onto my daughter, Miss English, because if you do, you and I will have words. Loud ones."

Rachel stared at him, amazed. "You have a daughter?"

He smiled. "I'm quite capable of making babies," he said. He paused, plainly enjoying Rachel's reaction to that forthright statement. "Her name is Emma, she's just about to turn twelve, and right now she's staying with the Wainwrights. She'll be back any day, though, soon as the baby is born and the missus is up and around again, I suppose, and she'll want to meet you. She's been real excited ever since she learned you were coming to Springwater, Emma has, and I *do hope*, Teacher, that you will not disappoint her."

Rachel was flabbergasted, and not a little troubled by the knowledge that if Trey Hargreaves had a daughter, he probably had a wife, too. She didn't want him to have a wife, though she couldn't have explained why, even to herself. "Mrs. Hargreaves?" she inquired, in what she hoped was an ordinary tone. "Where is she?"

"Dead," Trey answered flatly. His face had gone

hard all of the sudden, and he turned without another word and walked away, toward the Brimstone Saloon, leaving Rachel to stare mutely after him.

In the meantime, the stagecoach had arrived, disgorging a flock of hungry passers-through, and Miss June-bug was busy inside the station, serving fried chicken, mashed potatoes, gravy, and corn fritters. Toby sat at one end of the table nearest the cookstove, eating with both hands, while the passengers scattered themselves about the room, probably as glad of a few solitary minutes as they were of a hot, nourishing meal. As Rachel well knew, the inside of a coach could be a cramped and most uncomfortable place, where some loquacious travelers had been known to hold forth on every sort of subject for mile after mile.

"You be wanting that old horse again today?" Jacob asked, at her elbow, coming over the threshold with hat in hand. He gave a half smile, seeing Toby tucking into his food.

"I suppose it's too late to get to the Kildares' and back before sundown," Rachel mused.

"That it is," Jacob agreed. "Best save that errand for tomorrow, unless you're a hand with a shootin' iron." His expression didn't change, but the light in his eyes might have been mirth; it had the sunny effect of a broad, mischievous grin.

Rachel laughed. "I ride well enough," she answered, "but I don't shoot. I'll stay right here and try to persuade Miss June-bug to let me help her with the washing up."

"She might just give in," Jacob speculated, watching his wife bustle happily between the tables with a large blue-enamel coffeepot in hand. "Knowin' her, she's probably already worked out where to get some clothes for that boy and how to wrassle him into a bathtub. That'll occupy her for the better part of the night, I reckon."

"Is there a place to buy clothing?" Rachel asked, puzzled. As far as she knew, there wasn't a store in miles.

"My June-bug is a wonder with a needle and thread, and every time the peddler comes through, she buys a bolt of cloth. Time that boy gets up in the morning, she'll have made him trousers and a shirt, sort of like them elves in that fairy tale about the shoemaker."

Rachel was touched. "She's a wonderful woman," she said.

Jacob's gaze was tender as he looked upon his wife. "None better," he agreed.

Rachel thought to herself that if she could be loved like that, and love as fiercely in return, she would reconsider her position on marriage. Then, oddly choked up by this observation, she slipped off to her room to wash and exchange her dusty riding clothes for a crisp black sateen skirt and a white shirtwaist with a high, lace collar. She didn't have to relax her standards, she concluded, just because she was living in the untamed West now.

By the time he went to bed that night, Toby had not only been bathed, but measured for new clothes, and June-bug was busily laying out pattern pieces, cut from old sheets of newsprint. Rachel, long since finished washing the dishes, sat at the end of the same table, a book before her, watching the other woman work. Sewing was a skill Rachel had never truly mastered, and therefore her clothing was all store-bought, and correspondingly expensive. Living on a schoolteacher's salary, she had a very limited wardrobe, and she was full of admiration as she looked on.

Lantern light, added to the glow from the fireplace, gave a cozy air to the large room and caught in the silver strands glimmering in June-bug's thick brown hair.

"Tell me about Trey Hargreaves's wife," Rachel said, and was as appalled as if someone else had made the audacious request.

Mrs. McCaffrey looked up from her labor of love. She'd taken to Toby right off, that was obvious, and he'd taken to her. Rachel just hoped the alliance wouldn't end in heartbreak for June-bug, somewhere down the road, when and if Mike Houghton returned to claim his son.

"I didn't know her, though I've pried a few things out of Jacob. Trey lost her afore he settled out here— died in his arms, or so the story goes. She was shot when some no-goods robbed a general store in Great Falls—there to buy sugar, she was, poor thing—and after she died, Trey wasn't good for much of anything for a long time." She paused, remembering, then brightened and went on. "That's a fine girl he's got, though, that little Emma. Smart as they come, and pretty, too. Right pretty." She sighed and began cutting out the small pair of trousers.

"And?" Rachel prompted, sensing something left unsaid. She'd already gone barging into the subject; no use sparing the horses now.

June-bug's expression was rueful in the lamplight, and she was still for a long while, as though looking back over time. Finally, she met Rachel's gaze and spoke. "I reckon Emma's going to have a hard time of it all her life."

"Because of her father and the saloon?"

June-bug smiled sadly and shook her head. "No," she said. "Trey was a rogue and a rounder for a long time. Lot of other things, too, I reckon. But he loves that child, and he'd do just about anything he had to do to protect her and keep her happy."

Rachel waited, knowing there was more. Being a motherless child was very difficult, but this, she sensed, was an even greater challenge, whatever it was.

June-bug's hair, worn down around her shoulders in the evening, fell over one shoulder as she worked, but she raised her head when she finally went on. "Emma's mama was a full-blooded Lakota Sioux. Trey called her Summer Song. Must have been a beautiful woman, if that little girl's looks are anything to go by, but out here—well, everyplace, really—folks don't look too kindly on . . . on—"

"Half-breeds?" Rachel said, to get them both past the ugly word. "Are you saying that people around here don't accept Emma Hargreaves as one of them?"

"There's them who will refuse to send their young-'uns to school if she's there. It ain't right, and it makes Trey mad enough to bite nails, but that's the way of it. And her such a precious little thing, too, with a fine mind and a gentle heart."

Rachel wanted to weep. Poor Emma! Not only did she have to deal with ignorance and prejudice, but she had a saloon-keeper for a father. It was in that moment, Rachel would later reflect, and often, that she had decided to make a special project of educating Emma Hargreaves. She knew of a certain Quaker school in Pennsylvania, where children like Emma were welcomed, and taught to rise, through learning and confidence in themselves and God, above things that might otherwise have held them back. Still, to gain admittance, not to mention a scholarship, Emma would have to score very highly in her studies and prove herself deserving.

"You look so sad," June-bug said, with a tender smile. "It ain't all sorrowful, you know. That little girl is happy, for all of it. Maybe it's them Indian ways of hers that see her through—she's got a knack with animals, for instance, like nothin' you've ever seen. And she listens to the wind and the rain, even the snow, like she can hear it sayin' somethin' to her." June-bug put down her scissors and came to sit on the bench, facing Rachel. "Don't make the mistake of feelin' sorry for Emma. You'll wound her for sure if you do."

Rachel smiled. It was good advice, and she meant

to take it. "I think I'll turn in," she said, with a sigh. "It's been a long day."

"You lookin' in on the Kildares tomorrow?"

Rachel nodded. "Maybe the Johnsons, too, if I can manage it."

June-bug was pleasantly skeptical. "Them Kildare boys will probably wear you plumb out. Full of the devil, they are, and their daddy don't say much to 'em about the way they act. Yes, Ma'am, you're going to have your hands full with them."

More good news, Rachel thought, but she was a person of almost boundless energy, and she would be more than a match for two little boys, no matter how wild they turned out to be. Perhaps, she reasoned later, it was her preoccupation with Emma Hargreaves that made her overlook the fact that she was tempting fate, and sorely.

When she arose the next morning, dressed in yesterday's riding clothes, which she'd shaken out and brushed carefully the night before, she found Toby already up and around, clad in his new shirt and trousers. He was coming through the doorway with an armload of kindling when Rachel first spotted him.

"Good morning," she said, with a smile.

He beamed at her. "Mornin'," he replied, and sniffed. It was probably wrong, but Rachel found herself hoping his father would never return. She wondered if the boy had a mother somewhere, but did not consider asking. "Miss June-bug's makin' biscuits and sausage gravy for breakfast!" he announced.

Rachel laughed. "That is good news," she said. It

was barely dawn, and there were a few lamps burning, as well as a leaping fire on the hearth. The delicious aroma of fresh coffee filled the air, though there was no sign of either June-bug or Jacob.

So intent was she on the pleasures of awakening in the midst of a cozy household that she didn't notice the man lying on the bench, sleeping, and nearly sat on him. She jumped up with a start and a gasp; her heart feeling as though it had stuffed itself into the back of her throat.

Toby laughed. "Don't mind him. He's just an old drifter that had a few too many shots of whiskey down at the Brimstone last night. Jacob let him bed down here, 'stead of the barn, case the old coot should want a smoke and set the hay on fire."

Rachel peered at the man, a grizzled fellow, redolent of liquor and sweat and general fustiness. He looked harmless enough, but startled her again by letting out a sudden, loud snore. "Good heavens," she said, alarmed.

The door opened and Jacob came in, with an armload of firewood. "Not much of heaven about poor old Sibley," he commented, but kindly. "He brung news from the Wainwright place, though. They've got a new baby out there, as of yesterday. A little girl they mean to call Rachel—after you, I reckon."

Rachel was overcome. She had never aspired to such an honor, never dreamed of one, and her knees went so weak for a moment that she almost sat on Sibley for certain. "I must go and see Evangeline," she decided aloud. "Now, today."

"Nobody around to go with you," Jacob pointed out.

Rachel headed for her room, to fetch the paeonia cutting and her cloak. "Then I'll go by myself," she said, and when she came out again, with her things, nobody raised an argument.

CHAPTER

3

RACHEL SADDLED the same ancient draft horse she'd ridden the day before, there in the misty dimness of the station barn, and led the creature out into the early morning. Jacob soon appeared, standing with arms folded.

"Ain't you even going to ask the way?" he inquired in measured tones.

She was occupied with the logistics of transporting that infernal paeonia cutting, but she'd been watching the stationmaster out of the corner of her eye and bracing herself for a more forceful protest than the one he'd offered earlier, inside the station. "No need," she said lightly. "Evangeline and I have been corresponding regularly ever since she and Abigail came out here. She drew me a map once, and I've looked at it so many times over the last four years, I've got it memorized."

"There's Indians out there, unfriendly ones," Jacob said, presumably describing the territory between

Springwater and the Wainwright ranch. "Bobcats and wolves, too. Miss Evangeline had herself a couple of different run-ins with wolves. She ever write you about *that?*"

A shiver wound itself along the length of Rachel's spine. She had indeed received a thorough accounting of those encounters, and she'd had nightmares about them on and off, ever since. Her reaction to that was to strengthen her inner resolve. "Yes," she admitted. "But if I let such things daunt me at every turn—well, I might just as well have stayed home if I was going to do that."

At the sound of an approaching horse, they both turned, and there was Mr. Hargreaves, mounted on his paint gelding. "Mornin'," he said, to all assembled, with a tug at the brim of his hat. "Young Toby tells me you mean to ride out to the Wainwright place, Miss English. Since I'm headed that way anyhow, to fetch my daughter back home, I thought you might allow me the honor of keeping you company."

Rachel couldn't help being glad of an escort, though she was entirely too stubborn to let on. She gave Jacob a narrow look, well aware that the arrangement was a contrived one; obviously, the older man had sent Toby to the Brimstone Saloon, there to prevail upon Mr. Hargreaves to arise from his bed and accompany the reckless tinhorn schoolmarm on her journey. That was, she reflected, if Mr. Hargreaves had ever gone to bed in the first place. He was in need of barbering, as a dark stubble covered his jaw, and his clothes looked rumpled. Carousing was apparently untidy work.

"I could not possibly refuse such a generous offer," Rachel said, ungenerously.

Trey smiled, showing perfect white teeth, and touched his hat brim again. He might as well have said, straight out, that if she wanted to play games, he would make a worthy opponent. "Here," he said, riding forward a little and extending a hand, "let me hold that seedling, or whatever it is, so you can get into the saddle. I'm expecting more drovers to come through tonight, and I want to be back in time to see they get their whiskey and I get their money."

Rachel glowered at him, but she let him take the paeonia cutting and hoisted herself onto the borrowed horse's back. As the fates would have it, it was an utterly ungraceful effort. When she was settled, with her skirts arranged and her dignity in place, though still faltering a bit, she took the paeonia back. She would be almost as glad to get rid of the thing, she expected, as she would be to see Evangeline again.

"Heaven forbid," she said, "that *anyone* should be deprived of their proper share of the devil's brew."

Trey rolled his eyes at that. "This might be a long day," he said, addressing Jacob.

"No doubt it will," Jacob agreed. "Give the Wainwrights our best, and tell 'em we'll come by for a look at that new baby soon as we have the chance."

Trey smiled and nodded, but without the insolence he apparently reserved for Rachel. Then he spurred the paint into a leisurely trot, and Rachel had to scramble to keep up. Her own elderly mount would never be able to match his fancy gelding's pace, and she figured he well knew it.

He reined in at the edge of the woods and waited with an indulgent expression that made Rachel want to slap him. She had never done another human being violence in her life, and she didn't intend to start then, but the temptation was a sore one all the same.

They passed the first half of the trip in silence, Trey keeping the paint to a reasonable pace with, she suspected, some difficulty. She could see that the horse wanted to break free and run, and she didn't blame it.

"I won't mind if you want to ride on ahead," she said, somewhat stiffly, when they stopped alongside Willow Creek to rest for a few minutes and let both animals drink. "Poor old Sunflower here can't move very fast."

Trey patted Sunflower's neck as she drank, but he was looking up at Rachel, who stood higher on the grassy bank, wishing she'd taken the time to pack some spare clothes. She had nearly two months before classes were scheduled to begin and, while she still wanted to visit all the families of her potential students, there was no reason she couldn't spend a week or even two with Evangeline, if she wouldn't be intruding. Doubtless, her friend could use the help.

"Maybe you and I ought to strike a truce," Trey said, catching her totally by surprise. "I have a few redeeming qualities, you know."

Rachel arched an eyebrow. Truth be told, she thought it would be unwise to get too friendly with a man like Trey Hargreaves. He nettled her, but it was deeper than that. He was the most, well, *male* man she had ever encountered, and he stirred sensations in her that she'd thought were buried forever. Buried with Langdon.

"Such as?" she asked, but she felt a smile play at the corners of her mouth.

He laughed and swatted one thigh with his hat. "Well," he said, "I can beat most anybody at arm wrestling. I've never lost a horse race or a fist fight in my life, and for all that, I have good table manners."

Rachel had to struggle not to smile outright. She folded her arms. "Most impressive," she said.

He stretched out his hand. "Shake?"

She hesitated, then moved forward and reciprocated. "For Emma's sake," she was careful to say, but at his touch, innocent as it was, a rush of heat surged up her arm and raced through her system to spark at every nerve ending. He went on holding her hand for a moment too long, and for a fraction of that time, she honestly thought he was about to kiss her.

It was both a disappointment and a relief when he did not.

"We'd better get rolling," he said, letting his hand fall to his side.

Rachel nodded and turned away, embarrassed by the color she knew was throbbing in her cheeks.

It was mid-afternoon when they climbed a steep track onto the high meadow Evangeline had written about so often, and Rachel got her first glimpse of the rambling two-story house. Constructed of logs, it boasted glass windows and a shingle roof. Smoke curled from one of the three chimneys, and before Rachel and Trey could even dismount, the front door sprang open and two young girls erupted through the opening, running wildly, gleefully, toward them.

One—good heavens, she'd grown so much that Rachel barely recognized her—was surely Abigail, ten now, and by all accounts a great help to Evangeline. The other, slightly older and taller, had to be Emma. Her blue-black hair flew behind her as she ran barefoot over the stoney grass, and Trey swung down from his horse just in time to catch her up in an embrace. They whirled, and Emma's lovely hair swung around her luminous face like coarse strands of silk glinting in the sun.

Abigail, an uncommonly pretty child herself, with ebony hair and eyes as blue as cobalt, looked up at Rachel with a pleased expression. "You're Rachel, aren't you? Mama's been waiting for you ever so long."

Rachel got down, clasping the paeonia cutting in one hand, and hugged her best friend's daughter warmly. "Yes," she said, blinking back tears. "I'm Rachel. And you're Abigail. How big you've gotten!"

"We have a new baby," Abigail said. "A girl named Rachel Louisa. Papa says we'd better call her Louisa, because things are confused enough around here as it is."

Rachel smiled and turned, one arm around Abigail's shoulders, to look at Emma, who was huddled against Trey's side, watching her with shy curiosity. Perhaps even—or was she merely imagining it—a certain hopefulness. Rachel put out a hand. "Hello," she said. "I'm Miss English. I'll be your teacher, come the last of August."

Emma ventured out of the loose curve of her father's arm, but only tentatively, offering her own hand in return. "How do you do?" she said.

"Very well, thank you," Rachel replied. "And you?"

Emma looked back at Trey, as though in silent consultation. Plainly, she distrusted strangers, and perhaps she had good reason to do so. He nodded, very slightly, in encouragement.

"I like to read books," Emma said staunchly. "Did you bring any new ones with you?"

"I did," Rachel told the child. Abigail was tugging at her hand by then, pulling her toward the house.

"Come in and see Mama," said Evangeline's daughter. "She's just *perishing* for the sight of you. She likes my papa a whole lot, but he's a man and she misses being around women."

Trey and Rachel accidentally glanced at each other then, and something indefinable passed between them. Something that made them both look away.

"Where is your pa?" Trey asked Abigail. "I'd like a word with him."

"He's down at the corral, breaking horses," Abigail answered, still tugging Rachel along in her wake, but looking back at Trey. "Mama won't let Emma and I go down there and watch, either, even if we promise to stay behind the fence. She says he swears too much, but I don't think it's true because Papa is real gentle with horses. I think she's afraid we'll get stepped on some way, like Kathleen Bellweather's baby sister did—"

The chatter went on until they'd reached the front porch, Trey leading both horses behind him. "You get your things ready, if you've a mind to come home," he said to his daughter. "We'll head for town in an hour or so."

Rachel looked up at the sun, troubled, and dug in her heels against Abigail's pulling. "Will you get back before dark?" she asked doubtfully. She told herself the concern she felt was all for Emma's sake; Trey Hargreaves was a grown man, after all, well able to look after himself.

"An hour or two after, I reckon," Trey answered. There was a grin lurking in his eyes. "You worried about me, Miss English?"

She might have said what came to the tip of her tongue—*Not in the least, Mr. Hargreaves*—if Emma hadn't been watching her so intently. "Yes," she said. "And about Emma, of course. It's no mean distance back to Springwater."

One corner of Trey's mouth tilted upwards. "Well, me and Emma, we don't travel quite so slow as you and that old nag of Jacob's. We can cover twice as much ground in half as much time—can't we, Songbird?" He ruffled his daughter's hair with obvious affection.

Emma beamed up at him and nodded. "I wish we could get a baby, though," she said. "Like the Wainwrights have. Could we get us a baby from someplace, Pa?"

It was Trey's turn to be unsettled; he flushed, along the underside of his neck, looked away, and cleared his throat once before looking back. "Get your things," he said, but gently. "The paint is rarin' for a good run."

Emma dashed to do his bidding, and Rachel let Abigail pull her over the threshold and into a spacious, open parlor, where a massive stone fireplace dominated one wall. There were several good pieces of furniture in view, and the rugs, Rachel knew, had been imported from San Francisco. Evidently, though Evangeline had not said so outright, Scully Wainwright had prospered well beyond his wife's modest claims, raising cattle and breeding horses.

Evangeline herself came slowly, but not painfully, down the stairs, just then, her face wreathed in smiles. She glowed with a happiness that went far beyond the bearing of a healthy child and Rachel, for just a fraction of a heartbeat, envied her friend for all that she had.

"Rachel!" Evangeline gasped, half laughing and half sobbing, as she reached the bottom of the stairs and held out both arms in welcome. She was wearing a pretty blue wrapper with white piping and velvet slippers to match.

The two women embraced, both of them weeping for joy, and then Evangeline held Rachel away from her, for a good look. "You can't imagine how I've longed to see you again!" she cried.

Rachel laughed, and cried. "Yes, I can," she protested, with a sniffle, "because I've felt the same way." She remembered the paeonia start, which had nearly been crushed in all the fuss, and now looked somewhat travel-worn and bedraggled. "Here," she said, thrusting it at Evangeline, "is your blasted cutting!"

Evangeline laughed—and cried—as she accepted the stem Rachel had carried so far. "Abigail," she said to her daughter, holding it out. "Put this in water, please. And be very, very careful with it."

Abigail nodded and rushed off to do her mother's bidding.

"Sit down," Rachel exhorted Evangeline. "You mustn't tax your strength."

"Nonsense," Evangeline said, with a wave of one hand. "I think it's a mistake for a new mother to lie about in bed. Better to get up and move around. Heaven knows, there's plenty to do. Oh, Rachel, Rachel—what a joy it is to see you!"

They embraced again, and then went into the kitchen, where an elaborate black cookstove stood, chrome gleaming. Abigail had put the paeonia cutting into a fruit jar full of water and set it in the sunny window over the iron sink.

"Shall I make you some tea, Mama?" she asked.

"That would be wonderful, sweetheart," Evangeline responded. "Thank you. Then go upstairs, if you would, and look in on your brother and little Rachel Louisa. If they're awake, then you can bring the baby to me—very, very carefully—and see if J.J. doesn't need his knickers changed."

Presently, the tea was brewed, and it tasted better

to Rachel than any she'd had since the day her friend had left Pennsylvania for the Montana Territory, intending to marry her late husband's cousin, a rancher named John Keating. To Evangeline's surprise and, she'd confessed to Rachel in more than one letter, her relief, Keating had been away when she arrived. She'd been met at the Springwater station by his partner, one Scully Wainwright, who brought her and Abigail to the ranch—they'd lived in a cabin down the hill back then—and over the course of that long, difficult winter, Scully and Evangeline had fallen deeply in love. They'd been prepared to part, however, Evangeline being promised to Big John Keating, but then Big John had come back that spring with a bride in tow, and Scully and Evangeline had been free to marry. The match was a good one, and the two had been happy together.

It was a romantic story and just thinking about it made Rachel sigh.

Emma came in lugging a sleepy, blond imp—J.J., of course—on one hip, while Abigail brought the new baby, carrying her with a gentleness that touched Rachel's heart. There was a great deal of love in this house; the Wainwrights were fortunate people.

Rachel wondered, just for that one admittedly maudlin moment, if it would have been like this for her and Langdon, had he survived the war and come home to marry her, as they'd planned. Once, she'd hoped to have a houseful of children herself, just as Evangeline did, but now she was resigned to putting all her maternal energies into her teaching. It was better that way, she told herself. Look at poor Sue Bellweather; being a mother was dangerous business, emotionally. Maybe as perilous, in this wild and perilous place, as entrusting a lover to the whims of war.

And if she was protesting too much, well, she didn't know quite what to make of that possibility.

"Rachel?" Evangeline said, and Rachel realized that her friend had been trying to get her attention. "Would you like to hold your namesake?"

Some powerful, primitive emotion swept through Rachel as she took the infant from Abigail's arms and held her against her bosom; she was almost overcome by it. The baby girl was incomprehensibly beautiful, with an aura of fine golden hair and ivory-pink skin, and she blinked up at Rachel with an endearing expression of bafflement, her tiny fingers grasping at air. "Her eyes are blue," Rachel said, somewhat stupidly.

"All newborns have blue eyes," Evangeline reminded her, but gently.

Rachel had to swallow hard not to weep, partly in celebration of this new and wonderful little life, and partly in mourning for the children she herself would never bear, never hold against her heart, never nurture at her breast. Suddenly, she wanted desperately to have a home of her own, a flock of lively children. Which meant, of course, she'd need a husband.

"I've got my things ready, Pa," Emma said, startling Rachel into looking up from the baby's face. She saw Trey standing just inside the kitchen doorway, hat in hand, staring at Rachel as though he'd never seen a woman holding an infant before. "Just let me get J.J. a piece of sugar bread, and we can go."

Evangeline looked from Trey to Rachel, and back to Trey. Her expression was a puzzled one, at first, but then a slow smile blossomed on her mouth. "You ought to stay for supper, Trey. Or even spend the night. It's a long way back to Springwater."

Trey hesitated, then shook his head. "I don't guess we'd better do that," he said. "But thank you for the invitation. Thanks too for takin' such good care of Emma."

Evangeline smiled fondly at the child. "She's a treasure. We'll miss you very much, Emma. You've been a great help."

Emma looked pleased. "I like babies," she said. "I want to get one."

Evangeline stopped smiling, but Rachel could see that it was an effort. Her friend's gray eyes were bright with tender amusement. "What you need," she told the child, though she was watching Trey the whole time she spoke, "is a stepmother." She let that sink in for a few moments, then addressed Trey directly. "Those rooms above the saloon could surely use a woman's touch."

Rachel thought a round of cannon-fire would probably be more in order, given the way most men kept house, but she wouldn't have said so, not in front of Emma and Abigail, at least. She turned her attention back to the baby and immediately found herself enthralled all over again.

Trey and Emma said their good-byes and left, and

Evangeline stood up to start supper. Rachel sat her back down again, gave her the baby to nurse, and went about preparing the meal herself.

Scully came in from outside when the food was ready. He was just as Evangeline had described him, handsome, in a rugged and somewhat alarmingly masculine way, with turquoise eyes and sun-bronzed skin. The way he looked at Evangeline revealed the depths of his love for her, and that endeared him to Rachel as nothing else could have done.

"Rachel," Evangeline said proudly, the baby sleeping on her shoulder, "this is my husband, Scully Wainwright. Scully, here is my Rachel, at long, long last."

He smiled, moved to offer his hand, and then drew it back again. "I reckon I ought to wash up first," he said. "We're pleased to have you, Miss English. I hope you can stay awhile, as Evangeline has surely missed your company."

Rachel flushed. Scully was a charming man and he, like Trey Hargreaves, made poor lost Langdon seem, well . . . bland, by comparison. "I'll stay a few days, if I won't be in the way," she said, feeling uncommonly shy.

"I won't let you go before a week is out, at least," Evangeline told her, as Scully left the room, presumably to wash. "I'm sure it will take you the better part of the week to tell me all about the last four years, and besides that, I did up the spare room with you in mind. The least you can do is put it to use."

Rachel laughed. "You've always been one to make a strong case," she said.

Scully returned, shining with cleanliness. "Eve would make a fine lawyer," he said, and bent to kiss his wife's glowing cheek. "If we could spare her, that is. Which we can't." Why did the sight of him, the sound of him, make Rachel wish that Trey Hargreaves had stayed, at least for supper? It made no sense at all, given that she didn't *like* Mr. Hargreaves even a little.

Well, maybe a little.

Supper proved to be a lively event in the Wainwright household, with the baby gurgling and Abigail chattering and young J.J. waving a spoonful of mashed and buttery turnips in a precarious arc around his head. Evangeline oversaw the whole meal with ease and once again Rachel found herself envying her friend, as well as admiring her.

What would it be like, she wondered, to live so richly, so fully, so well? Inwardly, she sighed. She might never know, and she'd better accept the fact with as much good grace as she could muster, make the best of things, and get on with her life. As a teacher, after all, she was in a position to make a genuine difference to a great many children, and she wanted to pursue that end as much as she ever had. The problem was that she wanted so much *more*, wanted things she hadn't allowed herself to dream about since the news of Langdon's cruel death had reached her.

That night, alone in the lovingly prepared spare room of which Evangeline was justifiably proud, the house dark and quiet around her, Rachel wept.

Perhaps she truly *might* have a second opportunity

to find happiness—Evangeline, after all, had once counted her own life as over, at least in terms of loving and being loved by a man. Then she'd met Scully.

On the other hand, Rachel reminded herself, with a soft sniffle, hers was a slightly different position than Evangeline's. Her friend had been a widow, an honorable state of being. Unmarried women, however, were expected to be virgins, and Rachel wasn't. She'd lain with Langdon, and she could not rightly say she was sorry, for she had cared for him deeply. Still, a great many men, even ones with reputations of their own, like Trey, would not even consider taking a bride who'd known another man first.

Just the thought of being shamed and rejected like that made Rachel's cheeks burn with humiliation.

She must get a hold of herself, stop fussing and fretting and carrying on like some actress in a bad play. It was only that she was overwrought, finally seeing her friend after anticipating the event for so long, holding the baby that was her namesake in her arms.

Nothing to do with Trey.

But it was more, and she knew that, and furthermore, she knew it had *everything* to do with Mr. Hargreaves, which was the most disturbing realization of all.

He developed a habit, over the eight long and enlightening days of her absence, of standing at one of the upstairs windows, usually the one nearest his desk, and staring down at the empty schoolhouse and waiting. Watching, like some kind of addlepated fool.

And when he wasn't watching and waiting, he was thinking about her. Not about the wife who'd died so tragically, not about the lost years he'd spent mourning her, hating her killers, searching for them. Finding them.

Not about what he'd done, to avenge his wife.

The impossible had happened: Trey had found space in his heart for Rachel English—in fact, he loved her as he had never loved any other woman, including Emma's mother. Wanted her for his own. She was, he reckoned, the first female he'd *ever* wanted that he couldn't have, just by asking.

Not that mapping out the true landscape of his soul for the first time made any real difference; Rachel had made her opinions clear, where he was concerned. She wouldn't have a saloon-keeper for a husband, let alone one with a past like his. He wished, in those moments, that he could go back and change almost everything he'd ever done, make himself into a different, better man, one worthy of a prize like Rachel.

It made his gut grind, just to imagine her going away, or marrying someone else. She was meant to be his—he knew it. The question was, did *she* know?

To distract himself from thoughts of Rachel, from the memory of the revenge he'd taken on Summer Song's murderers, he turned his mind toward his daughter. Emma, who had reshaped his life around just by needing him, who had clutched at his sleeve when he presented himself in Choteau for Miss Ionie's funeral and begged him to take her home with him. That was when he'd settled down; he'd had to make a home, before he had one to offer Emma, but he'd done it. Such as it was, he reflected, glancing around ruefully.

She'd heard about Miss English's visit to the Bellweather house, Emma had, and she was hankering for a social call of her own, complete with tea and cookies. At first, Trey had been at his wits' end, thinking about that—he didn't have the first idea how to make tea, and he'd sooner have wrestled a grizzly than try to bake up a batch of cookies. Emma, for all her brains and her book learning, spent every free hour outside, running the countryside like a wolf cub, and she was probably a worse cook than he was, if that was possible. Generally, the bartender, Zeke, made their vittles, but he wasn't up to anything fancier than cornbread and fried meat.

It caused Trey no little bit of anguish to know his daughter wanted something so much, something he might not be able to give her. It probably signified approval to her, a fancy visit from the schoolmarm, and she asked for so little, Emma did. The thought of disappointing her made him ache.

It was a while before it came to him to approach Miss June-bug with the idea of doing up the fixings, when the time came, so that Emma would not be shamed. Not, he thought, that Miss Rachel English was one to embarrass a child—no, sir, she reserved her humiliations for grown men.

Miss June-bug agreed to the cookie-baking and tea-brewing, for she was a kindly and charitable woman, for all that she would have burned his saloon right down to the ground if she could have gotten leave from the Lord, and that was a weight off Trey's mind. It was odd, then, that he went right on fretting about the matter and watching at the window for Rachel to return. He'd go and speak to her about Emma as soon as he got the chance.

On the afternoon of the eighth day, she turned up, escorted by Scully Wainwright. She was traveling aboard the pitiful old nag Jacob had given her the use of, while Scully rode that fine Appaloosa gelding of his. They dismounted in front of the schoolhouse, tied their horses to the teetering hitching rail, and went inside.

Trey watched for them to come out, and when they did, Miss Rachel standing on the step smiling and waving, Scully swinging back up onto the Appaloosa's back to ride away, he practically killed himself bounding down the stairs and through the saloon proper to burst out through the swinging doors like a man with a mighty purpose.

Rachel, still standing on the schoolhouse step, looked a little startled, as though she might be considering dodging inside and latching the door after her. Trey slowed his steps, for the sake of his own self-respect as much as her reassurance, or so he told himself.

"You're back," he said, and silently cursed himself for a raving fool. Of *course* she was back. She was standing right there in plain sight, wasn't she?

She smiled, and there was something soft in her face that nettled even more than the usual mockery.

Trey resisted an urge to take a step back, like some kind of yellow-belly. "I had a wonderful visit," she said, "but I've got things to do here. Evangeline is up and about and so full of energy, you'd never know she just had a baby." Color flooded her face the instant the words were out of her mouth; no doubt, for an Eastern schoolmarm, it wasn't proper to mention such things in mixed company.

Trey decided to let the misstep pass, since he was so nervous himself and besides that, he wanted something. He stood just outside the fence, a little to the left of her swaybacked horse, both thumbs hooked in his belt so she might not see his hands shaking.

"My daughter Emma heard about your visiting the Bellweathers," he said bluntly. Might as well just spit it out and get it over with. "She's got her heart set on your coming to call on—on her." He'd almost said "on us," instead, but he caught himself just in time. He saw her eyes rise to take in the saloon, looming like Judgment Day itself behind him. He swallowed, thinking he'd be at a loss for what to do if she refused. Emma would be crushed.

"I'd be happy to visit Emma," she said.

He stared at her. Having been braced for a rebuff, he was unprepared for an acceptance. "Oh, well, when?" he stumbled out, once his own face had had time to turn good and red.

"Whenever it's convenient," she answered blithely. "Tomorrow afternoon, perhaps?"

Trey swallowed, thinking of the rough accommodations he and his daughter shared. There was only one bedroom, and that was Emma's. He was usually downstairs half the night, and when he did sleep, he just stretched out on the old couch next to the stove. They had no fancy dishes, and no pictures on the walls, unless you counted the page Emma had torn from a wall calendar, a few years before, a simple rendering of an Indian girl on a pony, watching the moon rise. "Tomorrow afternoon," he echoed, and damn near choked on the words.

"Two o'clock?" she prompted. He couldn't tell if she was laughing at him or not, behind that placid schoolmarm expression on her face, and at the moment he didn't care. She was coming for a visit, and Emma would not be let down. For the time being, nothing else mattered. Nothing in the world.

"Two o'clock," he said, and turned to go so fast that he damn near stumbled over his own feet and landed face down in a puddle of rainwater, mud, and horse-piss. As it was, Jacob McCaffrey almost ran him down with a buckboard.

CHAPTER

4

RACHEL HAD DONNED her best clothes—the black sateen skirt and snowy white shirtwaist—for the call on the Hargreaves household. Her hair was done up in a tidy chignon and she walked proudly, briskly, as was her normal way, with her chin up and her gaze fixed straight ahead.

In front of the Brimstone Saloon, she stopped and debated her means of entrance. Odd that she hadn't thought of this before, she reflected uneasily. Visiting a student was one thing, but walking straight through the front doors of such a place in the broad light of day was entirely another. Schoolteachers were held to exceedingly high standards of morality and personal decorum, and many had been dismissed for far lesser infractions. Perhaps, she thought, chewing her lower lip, there was a rear door.

"Changing your mind?" Trey asked, nearly startling her out of her skin. He stood just inside, and held one of the swinging doors aside for her. "This is mighty important to Emma."

Rachel was indignant at the mere suggestion that she would have been so rude as to turn around and flee at the very threshold of a pupil's home. "I was merely wondering," she said, keeping her voice low in case the child was nearby, "if there was another way in."

A grin spread across Trey's face. "Well," he said, "as it happens, there is. You might have found it, if you'd bothered to look behind the saloon. It's been my experience that rear doors are almost always situated in the back of a building. However, since you've already made a spectacle of yourself, you might as well come right on in."

Rachel passed him with a regal stride, which was not easy, given her rather unregal size of five feet, two inches. She glanced about curiously, once inside, for of course she had never set foot in an establishment of that sort before, and she collected and treasured new impressions the way other people gathered postage stamps or pressed flowers for their scrapbooks.

No lamps were lit, and the shadowy dimness lent the long room an air of mystery, not unlike the innermost parts of a harem, or the secret chamber in some fairy-tale castle. There were two large tables, for billiards or pool, along with a number of smaller ones, some with bare tops, others covered in felt. A roulette wheel took up a good part of one wall, giving the lie to Rachel's own naive assumption that there was no gambling going on beneath Trey's roof, and the bar itself seemed as long as a boxcar, with a glistening mirror behind it. Although she naturally had no standard by which to judge it all, Rachel was sure that the Brimstone was especially well-appointed, for a Western drinking hall. A few customers, careful to keep their heads ducked and their hat brims pulled low, lingered here and there, in isolated silence, nursing their drinks.

Out of the corner of her eye, Rachel could see that Trey was enjoying her discomfiture, try though she had to hide it from him, and that stirred an irritation in her that she wouldn't even have *tried* to master, if she hadn't known how very important this visit was to Emma. June-bug had been baking all morning, and just over an hour ago she'd sent Toby to the Brimstone with her only tea set, as well as enough molasses-oatmeal cookies to feed the nearest cavalry regiment. Toby's reward, upon returning from this errand, had been a feast of sweets that had left him rolling on his cot and holding his belly. Jacob was planning to lecture him on the virtues of moderation, and the McCaffreys themselves had had words over the incident, Jacob maintaining that encouraging greed was no favor to the child, June-bug retorting that the poor little scamp probably hadn't had anybody to fuss over him in the whole of his life.

Just as Rachel's eyes were adjusting to the light, she caught a glimpse of Emma, standing at the top of the stairway at the back of the room. The little girl had tied a blue ribbon in her hair, to match the pretty calico dress she'd worn for the occasion, and her smile was so tentative, so eager, that Rachel immediately put aside all her differences with Trey and focused her attention on the child.

"Emma," she said, "you look *very* lovely."

Emma's long, raven-dark eyelashes lowered, just for a moment, in shy pleasure. "Thank you, Miss English," she said. "We've got cookies. And tea, too. At least, we will have, once I pour hot water over the leaves of orange pekoe in Mrs. McCaffrey's china pot."

Rachel went willingly up the stairs, Trey close behind her. "I have been anticipating this visit ever since your father invited me yesterday," she said. "Tell me, Emma, what is your favorite subject in school? I know you like to read—you told me that when I first met you, at the Wainwright ranch. But what else do you enjoy? History? Geography? Ciphering?"

Emma's dark eyes were alight. "I like writing, Miss English. I want to make books someday."

Rachel reached the landing, and barely stayed herself from embracing the child. It was important to tread carefully, when meeting with new students, especially sensitive ones, like Emma. She might misinterpret an overly avid interest as condescension or pity, and if that happened, the delicate rapport between teacher and pupil could be damaged beyond repair. "What sort of books?" She laid a hand on Emma's shoulder and allowed the little girl to lead her into the living area she and her father shared. "True ones, or stories?"

Emma fairly glowed. "Stories," she confided, with a note of wonder.

"Then we must center our efforts on your composition skills," Rachel said. "Though, mind you, arithmetic and history are important, too, as is geography. We can't give those subjects short shrift."

"Short how-much?" Emma asked, brow furrowed.

Rachel explained the meaning of the phrase, and found herself in the midst of a pleasant if simply furnished room. Three chairs had been drawn up to a worn but solid-looking oaken table, and June-bug's cheerful tea service was set out with such care that Rachel's heart tightened for a moment, just to look at it. A plate of the savory cookies was on prominent display as well. There was no cookstove—merely a potbellied affair with a black kettle on top—and no settee or decorations of any kind, save a tattered calendar page showing a young Indian girl on a spotted pony silhouetted against a giant moon.

It wasn't difficult to work out why Emma would favor such an image, of course; she was proud of her heritage, and Rachel was glad to know it. Too many children of mixed ancestry, and adults as well, were treated as if they were inferior to others. The decision of whether or not to accept that assessment of one's self, however, in Rachel's considered opinion at least, remained a matter of personal choice.

Trey cleared his throat, and Rachel turned to look at him. He was obviously uncomfortable with the whole fuss—her presence, the china tea things borrowed from June-bug, perhaps even the cookies—but he was willing to endure it all for Emma's sake. Knowing that made Rachel think better of the man—

though only slightly, she decided. If he was really as interested in giving his daughter a normal life as he made himself out to be, would he be willing to raise her over a saloon?

And were those bullet holes, there in the wall next to the stove? Rachel squinted, uncertain.

Emma dragged back one of the chairs, the place of honor, Rachel suspected. Her small face was bright and earnest. "Sit down, Teacher." She glanced up at her father, whose face Rachel could not see, since he was standing just behind her. "I mean, *please* sit down."

Rachel made something of a show of settling herself in the chair; it was an occasion for Emma, and for that reason she would savor every moment, every sip of tea. She would certainly consume at least one of the cookies as well, even though they were the size of saucers and sure to spoil her supper. "Thank you," she said.

"Now you can sit down, Pa," Emma told Trey. Some of the child's anxiety had ebbed away, but her eyes were still bright with pleasure.

"Thanks—er, thank you very much," Trey replied, with an elegant bow to his daughter, who beamed in delight. What an engaging child Emma was, Rachel thought, with yet another twinge in her heart.

When Trey was seated, Emma got the tea kettle from the stove, using both hands and a dish towel to grasp the handle, and lugged the steaming water over to the table, there to fill June-bug's china pot. Rachel sensed that Trey was poised to leap, in case the child's hold should slip, as she was herself, but in the end it was a good thing neither of them moved. Emma managed the task on her own, with an awkward competence.

Although Rachel would often, over a period of many years, try to recall the conversation that followed, somehow it always remained elusive and somehow magical, like the shadow of a unicorn, barely glimpsed at the edge of a moon-splashed clearing. She remembered that they laughed, the three of them, and surely they must have talked about school and lessons, but Rachel could never call the precise words and topics back to her mind.

At the end of the visit, she and Emma were fast and lifelong friends, although she still had her reservations about Trey. He was an enigma, a purveyor of whiskey and the lord of a gambling den, and yet he was plainly an attentive parent. Few men of his inclinations, Rachel knew, would have endured a tea party on any account.

Good-byes were said, and Rachel rose to leave, this time by the rear door, belated as that effort seemed. Emma, humming under her breath, carefully cleared away the remains of the cookies and tea, while Trey escorted their guest down the back stairs.

"Mr. Hargreaves," Rachel said, when they reached what would have been an alley, had there been any other buildings around, "you have raised a remarkable daughter."

"Thank you."

"I don't mind telling you that it still worries me,

though, her growing up in a saloon." She was thinking of the bullet holes again, the ones in the wall by the stove. If indeed that was what they were.

Trey's eyes narrowed a little, and some of the luster went off his grin. "We live real simple, Miss English," he said, "but Emma's getting a decent raising. You don't believe me, you just ask Miss June-bug. She's no great admirer of mine, Jacob's missus, but even she will tell you that I look after my little girl. For one thing, maybe you didn't notice, but Emma's got shoes on her feet, good ones, and when your pupils start trailing in toward the last of August, you'll find out that's uncommon out here. Most of those kids will be lucky to have shoes before it snows."

Rachel rested her hands on her hips. "I'm not implying that you don't provide for Emma," she said, in a conscientious whisper, "nor do I doubt for a moment that you love her. What concerns me is," she gestured toward the hulking saloon, "this . . . this *place*. Mr. Hargreaves, I am admittedly a greenhorn, but I do know bullet holes when I see them. Surely you can imagine the danger to Emma—"

Trey's jaw clamped down hard, and she watched, fascinated and a little unnerved, as he made a visible effort to relax it. "Emma did that herself, playing with one of my pistols six months back. It was the first and last time I ever paddled her. Good God, do you think I'm just going to stand there and let some drifter empty a pistol into the place where my daughter lives?"

Rachel drew a deep breath and let it out slowly.

He'd convinced her by the sheer righteous indignation of his response. "Perhaps I have been a bit unreasonable—"

"A *bit* unreasonable? You practically came right out and said you don't trust me to take care of my own child!"

Rachel closed her eyes for a moment. "I'm sorry. I didn't mean—" she paused miserably. "It's just that—"

Trey released a sharp sigh and looked exasperated, though whether with her or with himself, she couldn't quite tell. Maybe it was a little of both. "I guess I might have reacted a mite too strongly myself," he surprised her by admitting. "It's just that usually, when folks feel called upon to express an opinion about Emma's raising, they say I ought to send her away again, to some school, maybe. I don't cotton to that kind of interference."

Rachel, calm again, back in control of herself, held up a hand to snag a certain phrase from the stream of what he'd just said. "Just a moment. What do you mean, 'send her away *again*'? Are you saying that you didn't raise Emma?"

He looked away, then back again. "Up until she was eight, Emma lived with my mother's people, over in Choteau—specifically her second cousin Jimpson's widow, Miss Ionie. Miss Ionie was old, though, and she passed on four years ago, so I brought Emma home. She's been with me since then."

Rachel stood there, absorbing all that she'd just heard. Perhaps she'd been too hasty in giving Trey credit for his daughter's intelligence and good manners, she concluded. Perhaps it was the late Mrs. Jimpson who had deserved the acclaim. "I see," she said.

"No," Trey argued quietly, sharply, "you *don't* see. You probably figure I wanted to be shut of Emma so I could have myself a high old time building my saloon. The fact is, she was only a baby when her mother died, and I was out of my mind with grief. I asked Miss Ionie to take Emma in and she did, God rest her soul. But there was never a day of the time we were apart, Emma and I, that I didn't think of her and wish I could bring her here to be with me."

"But you didn't," Rachel said, without rancor. "Not until Miss Ionie died and you had no other choice."

"It wasn't like that, damn it!" Trey snapped.

"I believe you!" Rachel snapped back, and was surprised to realize it was true. Which wasn't to say she didn't still have concerns for Emma's safety and well-being. It might be prudent, she decided, to alter the course of present conversation. "Perhaps you could build a house, just a small one—"

Trey made a move to snatch his hat off and slap it against his thigh, something Rachel had already cataloged as one of the gestures he made when he was exasperated, but the whole exercise was futile because he wasn't wearing a hat. "I'm not Scully Wainwright," he said. "I've got practically every cent I have tied up in that saloon!"

Rachel frowned. "What on earth does Scully have to do with this?"

"He's got a fine, fancy house. Horses and cattle. Money."

"And?"

"And I don't have any of those things. Not yet, anyway, though I mean to get them, you can be sure of that. Until I do, Teacher, Emma and I are going to go right on living in those rooms up there." He cocked a thumb over his shoulder without looking back. "If you've got any other opinions to offer, I'd appreciate it if you'd just keep them to yourself!"

"You really are irascible," Rachel said, her hands back on her hips. "I'm sorry we started this conversation at all." It had, after all, gotten them nowhere.

"So am I," Trey bit out. Then he turned on one boot heel and stormed away, and so ended the first and almost certainly the last tea party ever held within the walls of the Brimstone Saloon.

"Well?" June-bug demanded eagerly, the moment Rachel set foot inside the station. "How did things go, over there at Trey's place?"

Rachel frowned, wondering what her friend expected of a simple student-teacher visit. She'd seen something of the same attitude in Evangeline, on that first evening at the ranch, a watchfulness where she and Trey were concerned. A subtle but still unsettling interest in the lively dynamics between them.

Rachel shrugged, although she did not cherish a single hope that the gesture would circumvent June-bug's curiosity. "It all went very well," she said, approaching a table set square in a spill of daylight from a high window, where the other woman was busy cutting out another pair of boy-sized trousers. "You were right about Emma. She really is a special child—the sort a teacher comes across only once or twice in a career, I suspect."

June-bug nodded. She wasn't dismissing Emma's exceptional qualities by refraining from comment, Rachel knew; the other woman had accepted them as fact, long since, and probably saw no need to elaborate. "And Trey? Did he stick it out, or head for the hills?"

At last, Rachel smiled. "He *wanted* to run like a rabbit," she confided, "but he stayed for Emma. It was a little like watching a man try to sit still in the middle of a bonfire."

June-bug laughed. "He's a hand with the women, Trey is, but I reckon it's been a spell since he sat himself down to take tea and cookies with a pair of respectable females. My goodness, I'd have given a good laying-hen to see that."

Rachel glanced toward the closed door of the small room behind the cook stove, where Toby slept. "How is the boy?"

June-bug gave a fond smile. "He'll be all right. Just et too many cookies, poor little feller. Now that he's done chuckin' 'em up, he ought to get better right fast."

Shaking her head, Rachel proceeded to her room, where she changed out of her good clothes and into a plain calico dress, suited to working around the station. When she was at her sewing, which was often now, June-bug was willing to accept a helping hand.

The following morning, directly after breakfast,

Rachel packed herself a sandwich and a bottle of tea, saddled Sunflower, and set out on her visiting rounds, choosing the Kildare place for her first stop. Mr. Kildare was a widower, she recalled, consulting the notes she carried in the pocket of her riding skirt, with two young sons. Someone, precisely who she could not then recall, had warned her about the Kildare boys, but she was not concerned. In a decade of teaching, Rachel had encountered a great variety of children, and she'd never been bested by a single one of them.

She was thinking not of her future pupils, but of Trey Hargreaves, when the Kildare ranch house came into view. It was a small place, but more prosperous looking than the Bellweathers', with a painted barn and two horses, one black with three white boots and a blaze on its nose, the other a smaller sorrel, prancing in the corral.

Her heart nearly stopped beating when two lithe little shapes dropped from the branches of the leafy birches she was passing between, shrieking like wild Indians on the warpath. The boys were the spitting image of each other, covered with freckles, their hair carrot red and shaggy. They wore nothing except loincloths improvised from flour sacks, and they had painted themselves with streaks of what Rachel devoutly hoped was berry juice. War paint, no doubt.

"Halt!" commanded the smaller of the pair. The difference in height was so marginal as to be barely discernible. "Who goes there?"

Rachel took a few moments to school her mouth,

which wanted to laugh, now that her heart had settled back into its normal place. She introduced herself, as seriously as possible, adding, "I'm the new schoolteacher."

The larger savage spat with truly splendid contempt. "Pshaw!" he cried.

Who goes there? Pshaw? What sort of Indians were these? Again, Rachel had to work to contain her amusement. There was nothing to be accomplished, ever, by making a child feel foolish. "Nonetheless," she said, with all the dignity of a noble captive facing certain death at the hands of barbarians. For all she knew, they meant to lash her to a tree and build a bonfire at her feet. "You will be attending class as of the last week in August. I'm afraid you'll have to wear trousers and shirts, though. Loincloths are not acceptable."

The savages looked at each other in plain consternation.

"I would like to speak with your father," Rachel went on, when the silence lengthened. "Is he here, please?"

The smaller Indian gave a despondent wave toward the barn. "He's out back, shoeing a horse," he said, sagging at the shoulders.

Rachel got down from Sunflower's back and held out a hand. "How do you do," she said, addressing the nearest boy. "Would you be Jamie, or Marcus Aurelius?"

One of the lads burst into such raucous laughter that he doubled over with it, while the other blushed furiously behind his freckles. The laughing boy was

Jamie, then, Rachel concluded, and the embarrassed one was Marcus Aurelius.

She was proved right in the next instant. The redfaced Indian stepped forward to accept her hand, however tentatively, and give it a brief shake. "Just Marcus," he said.

"All right, then," Rachel said, still keeping a straight face, "so it shall be. Marcus, I am pleased to meet you." She turned to Jamie. "And you, as well," she added.

Jamie remained where he was, hands clasped behind his back, eyes narrow and suspicious. "I don't need to go to school," he said. "I can already read and write and count to a thousand. Ma taught me." He glanced at Marcus. "Taught us both."

"Ma's gone," Marcus pointed out to his brother, none too gently, "and there's a heap we still don't know. I stand in favor of it. Going to school, I mean."

"A wise choice," Rachel said sagely. Looking up, she saw a man coming toward her, a broad smile on his face. He was dressed in work clothes, of course, and perhaps thirty years of age, with twinkling hazel-colored eyes and a headful of thick brown hair, lightly streaked by the sun, as if he often worked without a hat.

"How-do," he said. "I'm Landry Kildare. These galoots, I guess you know by now, are my boys, Jamie and Marcus—"

"Just Marcus," the latter put in quickly, pointedly.

Mr. Kildare's very fetching smile widened. "Just Marcus, then," he agreed.

"Rachel English," Rachel replied. "I hope I'm not intruding. I've just come by to introduce myself and to tell you that classes will begin on the last Monday in August."

"It would be an honor if you'd step inside and have some coffee, Miss English," Kildare said, in his cheerful and mannerly way. Rachel wondered where he came from originally, for she could not recognize any particular accent to his speech. "We don't get too many visitors out our way. Hope these little scoundrels didn't scare you out of your hide. They've got a bad habit of dressing up like African cannibals and jumping out of trees when somebody comes toward the house. Like to have sent poor old Calvin T. Murdoch, the peddler, splashing over the Jordan River into the arms of his Savior."

Leading Sunflower by the reins, Rachel found herself walking alongside Landry Kildare. It was a wonder, in this wild and desolate place, that such an attractive and personable man should go unmarried. June-bug had told her little about him though, merely saying that he was friendly enough when a person met up with him but kept to himself most of the time, so for all Rachel knew, he already had a lady-friend somewhere.

The inside of the cabin was surprisingly tidy and well-furnished, given that this was a household of men. The wooden floors were not only planed smooth, but polished, and there was a colorful, if very worn, scatter rug in front of the hearth. Closed doors indicated several bedrooms, and the area surrounding the cookstove was as clean as if it had been scrubbed down with soapy water and a hard-bristled brush.

"Have a seat, if you'd like," Landry said, indicating a sturdy rocking chair facing the fireplace. Beside the chair, on an upturned fruit crate, was an open book— *Curwen's the Husbandry of Horses*—a cherrywood pipe, and a small tin of tobacco. "Might be you'd rather stand, after riding out from Springwater."

Rachel did prefer to stand; her legs *were* a little cramped.

"I could make some coffee," Landry offered once again, washing his hands at a basin near the stove.

Rachel was about to refuse when she realized that it was important to him to offer hospitality. Visitors, as he'd said, were rare. "I'd like that," she said.

He dismissed the boys, who were plainly eager to get back to their marauding, and made himself busy, putting a small amount of water in the bottom of the large enameled pot, measuring in some coffee grounds, and setting the concoction on the stove. When he was finished building up the fire, he crossed the room and drew up the only other chair to sit astraddle of it, his arms resting easily across the back, looking up at Rachel with those strangely guileless eyes.

If she had to be drawn to a man, if she had to endure all the sweet, secret stirrings, the conflicts and heartaches, why couldn't it have been someone like Landry Kildare, instead of Trey? There was certainly nothing romantic about her instant affection for Kildare, however—it was strictly that of a friend for a friend or, at most, a sister for a brother.

"I reckon you've already discerned that you're going to have your hands full with my boys," Landry said, with a twitch at the corner of his mouth and a light in his eyes. In a flash of insight, Rachel knew that he'd been exactly the same sort of rascal when he was young as his children were now.

Rachel permitted herself the particular smile of amusement she could not have indulged in front of Jamie and Marcus. "I'm up to the challenge," she said, but modestly.

Landry's eyes clouded briefly with memories. "They run wild around this place, I've got to admit that. Since their mother passed over, well, I haven't had the heart to rein them in much. The devil of it is, Caroline would strip my hide off if she saw how they are now, with no manners and all."

"They're good boys," Rachel said quietly.

Landry nodded. "That they are. But what kind of men will they grow up to be, with no proper churching, and them just starting to go to school at eight and ten years old? Caroline always schooled them, and she taught them well, but I don't know that there's another human being in all God's creation who could get those two to sit still and listen for the better part of a day, let alone 'most *every* day, and for months at a stretch."

"We'll manage," Rachel assured him. She felt slightly less confident, however, than she made herself out to be.

The coffee began to boil, richly fragrant, and Landry got up to add cold water and a dash of salt, to settle the grounds. When that was done, he poured them each a cup, adding generous portions of fresh cream and brown sugar, with Rachel's permission, before serving the brew. It was delicious, and Rachel was glad she'd accepted Landry's offer of refreshment, for the concoction braced her up a little. When she left the Kildares, she would visit the Johnsons, the last and most remote family, living in a hollow higher up, in the hill country. The household, like that of the Bellweathers, had just one child, a girl called Christabel according to June-bug, a shy and skittish little thing, with one club foot.

After saying her farewells to Jamie and Marcus, as well as to their father, of course, Rachel mounted Sunflower again and set out. She ate the sandwich she'd packed at the station as she rode up and up, deeper and deeper into the wilderness, home of wolves and grizzly bears and mountain lions.

The silence was underlaid with a hundred different sounds—birds, small animals rustling in the brush, twigs snapping. She strained to hear each one, to separate it out from the others and identify it. By the time the Johnson shack came into view, Rachel was full of foreboding.

CHAPTER

5

A SHOTGUN BLAST rent the air, loud enough to split the sky. Sunflower tossed her head and pranced in agitation, while Rachel struggled to rein her in. In the process, the bottle in which she'd carried her tea fell to the hardscrabble ground and splintered. A crone-like woman stood on the slanted stoop of the Johnsons' tumbledown shed of a house, shotgun in hand. Smoke curled blue from the barrel.

"That's jest about fer enough!" yelled the old woman.

Rachel's initial fear had given way to supreme irritation by the time she'd calmed the horse. Fretful that the animal would step on the shards of glass and cut one of the soft pads inside her hooves, she got down and tried to kick and scuff the remains of June-bug's bottle aside as best she could. That done, she faced the welcoming committee with hands on hips. "Put that thing away," she commanded, in her most authoritative schoolmarmly tone, "before someone gets hurt."

Evidently Mrs. Johnson, or whoever she was, had never been to school, for she did not seem intimidated. In fact, she balanced the considerable weight of that shotgun as easily and as expertly as any man Rachel had ever seen. "Nobody bound to get hurt but you, Miss. Now you take that sorry excuse fer a hoss and git."

Rachel tethered Sunflower to a sturdy bush, well away from the place where the bottle had landed, and took a few purposeful steps forward. "You just go ahead and shoot me, then. I'm not leaving until I've done what I came here to do!"

For an interval that might have been the length of either a heartbeat or a season, the two adversaries just stared at each other, each one waiting in vain for her opponent to back down.

"What do you want, then?" the old woman finally demanded. Her hair was snow white, her eyes brown, and all but lost in the loose and weathered flesh of her face. She was small of stature, and probably didn't weigh much more than a wet barn cat. "Spit it out and git."

Rachel cleared her throat and squared her shoulders. She'd made a lot of home visits in her time, but she'd never been met with a shotgun before. She wanted to choose her words carefully. "My name is Rachel English, and I'm the new schoolteacher. I'd like to see Christabel and her mother or father."

The old lady spat. "Her pa got hisself hanged over in Virginia City five years back. God only knows where her ma might be by now. Probably took up with another waster by this time, if she's still breathin'.'"

Rachel was careful not to let the rush of pity she felt show in her face or countenance. "And you must be—?"

"Her granny. I got me a Christian name, like everybody else, but you don't need to know it."

"But you look after Christabel?"

"Christabel looks after herself. Sometimes me, too, when my rhumetiz kicks up. Anyways, she ain't got no yen nor need for schoolin', so you jest git back on that old nag and point yerself toward home, wherever that might be."

By now, Rachel's irritation had given way to an interest and amusement she wouldn't have dared to reveal. "I'd still like to speak with Christabel herself, if possible."

As dry and brittle looking as an old grasshopper, Granny Johnson spat again, a stream of what appeared to be tobacco juice this time, into the dooryard, scattering a flock of ropy chickens in every direction. She had yet to lower the shotgun. "It ain't possible. Now, git."

Just then, the cabin door creaked open and a girl about Emma's age hovered on the threshold, squinting against the glare of daylight. She was a plain little creature, with ragged clothes and stringy, unwashed hair of indeterminate color. Even at that distance, the stench from inside that shack struck Rachel hard enough to rock her back on her heels. She hoped her nose hadn't twitched, and pretended to sneeze, just in case.

"Don't go shootin' the schoolmarm, Granny,"

Christabel said. "You'll bring the law down on us for sure."

Granny spat yet again. Rachel had never known a person who could summon up so much saliva, seemingly at will. "I done told her to git, but she don't seem to hear too well. Tell her you don't want no book learnin' and maybe we'll git shut of her."

Rachel folded her arms. "Is what your grandmother says true, Christabel? Wouldn't you like to learn to read and write and speak like a lady?"

The yearning in Christabel's dirt-smudged face was clear to see, and it squeezed hard at Rachel's heart. "What use would that be?" she asked. "Ain't no books out here. Nobody but Granny to speak to."

Rachel gestured toward the timbered country falling away behind and around them. "There's a whole world out there, Christabel, and a lot of it is pretty wonderful. An education can take you places."

Again, it showed in Christabel's expression and every line of her body, that desperate yearning to be so much more than she was, have so much more than she had. In the end, though, she merely shrugged. "Who'd tend to Granny if I went galivantin' off somewheres?"

Granny said nothing, and she even lowered the shotgun, though the stock made a sharp thumping sound where it struck the warped boards of the porch.

Rachel drew a deep breath and plunged. "With all due respect," she said evenly, "your Granny won't live forever. And even if you stay right here until the end of your days, if you just go to school, you'll have books to keep you company ever after."

"Don't need no books," Granny grumbled. "We got by jest fine without 'em all this long while."

Christabel took a step forward, her gait awkward because of her twisted right foot. The child was a bed-wetter, that could be told from the miasma surrounding her, but the knowledge only made Rachel all the more determined to rope her in. Of all the pupils who might come within her charge, with the possible exception of Toby Houghton, this one was most in need of her attention and care.

"I could learn to read?" Christabel asked, in a tone of muted wonder.

"Folks would jest laugh at you," Granny put in, helpful to the last. "They'd call names, too."

Rachel bristled. "No one will laugh, unless they've a mind to pass the rest of the day with their nose stuck in a corner. Name-callers will meet with the same fate."

Christabel limped another step forward. "I ain't got a decent dress to wear," she said. "No shoes, neither. Come winter, it'll be a long cold walk down this here hill to Springwater."

Rachel had brought a few yard-goods with her from Pennsylvania, and she suspected that her Sunday shoes might come close enough to fitting Christabel. She and June-bug could put their heads together and come up with a way to get the child into a tub of hot water. Plenty of soaking and scrubbing and combing would do wonders. "I'll sew a dress for you myself," Rachel said, with resolution and reckless optimism, "and I've got an extra pair of shoes."

"We don't take no charity," Granny put in. Her berry-bright eyes were snapping, and her scrawny hands looked fidgety where she held the shotgun, as though she'd like to raise it up again, and draw a bead on the center of Rachel's forehead.

Christabel made her way down the single step and hobbled slowly toward Rachel, her moon-shaped face revealing a careful, tentative hope. "It ain't charity, Granny," she said, without looking back at the old woman or pausing, though it seemed to Rachel that walking on such a foot must be painful. "Not if I make it up in work. I can scrub floors and windows, Miss Rachel, and sweep, too. I can round up stray cows and saddle mules and pitch hay. Ain't much of anything, work-wise, that I don't know how to do. I'd admire to come to school, if there's a way I can make it right to you."

Up close, the odor of that poor child was enough to make Rachel's eyes burn and water. She did not react, however, but simply laid a hand on the girl's shoulder, trusting in the Lord, June-bug McCaffrey, and her own devices to make Christabel presentable. "Lessons begin the last Monday in August," she said. "Do you have a calendar?"

"Don't need one," Christabel said, with the first glimmer of a smile. It changed her plain appearance quite dramatically, that smile. "Granny and me, we can tell what day it is by the signs." At Rachel's puzzled expression, she added, "You know, the rings around the moon and the color of moss and the like. We mark it off on a bit of paper."

Rachel, while still nearly overwhelmed by the pervasive stench, felt a sudden desire to embrace the girl. Would have done so, in fact, if she hadn't been so innately conscious of Christabel's fragile pride. "I'll be watching for you," she said. "You come to the Springwater station, a few days before school starts. In the meantime, I need to take some kind of measure if I'm going to make that dress." No need to mention her private doubts concerning her sewing skills and discourage everyone.

In the end, they used string, unwillingly fetched by a sullen Granny, and Rachel took Christabel's measurements, cutting a separate length for each. Then, sensing that Granny's patience had worn dangerously thin, Rachel said her farewells, extracted another assurance of attendance from Christabel, and mounted her horse.

She waited until she was well out of sight of the Johnson shack before giving way to tears of sorrow, frustration, and pity.

Midway down the mountainside, with the smoke of June-bug's cookstove chimney curling visibly against the pale blue of the sky, Sunflower came up lame. Rachel dismounted and raised the mare's left foreleg to examine the hoof, and sure enough, there was a raw place in the fleshy portion, though she couldn't tell whether a shard of glass had gotten inside or not.

"Poor darling," Rachel said, and patted the animal's neck. Then she proceeded toward home, on foot, moving slowly and leading Sunflower by the reins. Jacob could treat the mare's wound, she was certain, but in the interim there was no choice but to keep going.

It was sunset when they reached the edge of the timber and lamps were burning in the windows of the station. There were a dozen horses out in front of the Brimstone Saloon, and it sounded as if a brawl was taking place inside.

Worried about Emma—or so she told herself at the time—Rachel left Sunflower's reins dangling at the side of the road and clomped up onto the wooden step in front of the saloon to peer in over the swinging doors.

Trey sat, hatless, with the sleeves of his white gambler's shirt rolled up and a cheroot clamped between his teeth, at a small table in the center of the room. Seated across from him was a man roughly the size of a one-hole privy, and the two of them were engaged in an arm-wrestling match. The noise came from the half-moon of spectators who looked on from the rear, thereby affording Rachel an unobstructed view. Emma sat on the stairs, watching through the lathe-turned rails, her chin propped in one palm.

Rachel might have gone on about her business if it hadn't been for the sight of that child. Even though Emma didn't look at all disturbed, but merely interested in the proceedings below stairs, the scene, coupled with all she had witnessed on the mountain, brought out the crusader in Rachel. Full of reckless indignation, she shoved the swinging doors open with both hands and stormed into the Brimstone Saloon like a blue norther.

Trey was obviously startled at the sight of her, and relaxed his arm just enough to allow his opponent to slam his hand down onto the tabletop and win the match. Cheers went up all around—except from Trey, of course, who was flushed to the hairline and looked as though he could chew up a stove poker. The winner and his supporters shouted for whiskey, at the same time watching Rachel's steam-engine approach with expressions of eager dread.

Trey rose slowly to his feet to face her. "What the devil—?" he sputtered. Then, evidently too angry to speak, he fell silent. His fists clenched and unclenched at his sides.

Rachel could not have cared less that she'd spoiled the foolish competition for him; she was only worried about the child watching, wide-eyed now, and plainly breathless, from the stairway. Emma gripped a rail in each hand and seemed to be attempting to press her face between them.

Now that she had braved the lion's den, Rachel wasn't entirely certain what she should say or do. She'd entered the Brimstone on the power of an indignant impulse, but some of the locomotion went out of her when she came to stand before Trey, looking up into those furious silver eyes.

She fell back on bravado. "Are you aware," she demanded, in a fierce undertone, "that your daughter has witnessed this entire sorry spectacle?"

Trey raised an eyebrow. He looked slightly calmer,

though his eyes were still flashing with sparks. "Which one is worse, Miss English?" he shot back. "That spectacle—or this one?"

Rachel was chagrined because, damn him, he had a point, but she wasn't about to back down. Not in front of Emma and all those seedy drovers. "If you care one whit for that child, you'll send these drunkards away and put an end to this vice once and for all!"

Trey too had his hands on his hips now, and he was leaning in, so that his face was uncomfortably close to Rachel's. "If I close this place down," he retorted, in measured tones, "*that child* will go hungry. Thanks to you, I just lost the first arm-wrestling match of my life, and a five-dollar gold piece along with it!"

Rachel wet her lips with a hasty pass of the tip of her tongue. "Perhaps, then," she responded, "you will think twice before wagering such a sum on a scurrilous contest again!"

One of the onlookers laughed. "This mean you ain't gonna take part in the horse race come Sunday afternoon, Trey?"

Trey silenced the man with a wave of one hand, never so much as looking away from Rachel's face. She felt pinned, even entranced, unable to go forward or backward until he deigned to free her, and that made her angry as a swarm of bees whipped to a frenzy in a butter-churn.

"What horse race?" she demanded.

"The one I mean to win," Trey growled.

"There's a race after Jacob's preachin' and the picnic this comin' Sunday," put in some intrepid and interminably helpful observer, from the humming void that surrounded her and Trey.

Rachel frowned, confused. "A picnic? I hadn't heard about that."

"That," drawled Trey, "is because it was supposed to be a surprise, it being in your honor and all. Miss June-bug's been planning it ever since you agreed to come out here and save us all from our sin and ignorance."

Rachel blushed, and only partly because of the forthcoming picnic that was supposed to be a surprise. She looked around self-consciously, but carefully avoided meeting Emma's gaze, though she felt it like a beam of strong sunlight, full of curiosity and confusion. "I don't know what to say," she said.

"How about 'good-bye'?" Trey asked. "We're conducting business here, in case that's escaped you." He raised a pointer finger and dared—*dared* to waggle it in her face. "Furthermore, Miss English, I plan on winning that race. I've got a sizable amount of money riding on it. See that you don't go interfering again, because if you do, I will not take kindly to it."

Rachel opened her mouth, closed it again, completely at a loss. He was just lucky, she told herself, as cold comfort, that she hadn't bitten his finger off at the middle joint. "My horse is lame," she said, in a corresponding tone of voice. "She needs tending." Having so spoken, she turned, with all the dignity she could muster, and walked out of the Brimstone Saloon with her chin high. It was only when she got outside, her head spinning with a welter of confusing emotions, none of which could be fitted with a particular name, that she dropped the facade.

The confrontation with Trey Hargreaves had not been an amicable one, and yet she was filled with a strange, tentative sense of celebration, quite unlike anything she'd ever felt before. Underlying this was a dark and utter despair that brought an ache to her heart and tears to the backs of her eyes. On the one hand, she wanted to dance in the street, but her desire to fling herself down on the nearest piece of flat ground and cry herself blind was equally strong.

She tried to remember, as she walked toward Springwater station through a purple twilight, so busy with her thoughts that she was barely aware of her surroundings, poor Sunflower ambling along behind her, whether Langdon had roused such conflicting reactions in her. He hadn't, she concluded; this was all new, and at once as frightening as meeting a grizzly bear in the woods and as splendid as dancing with an angel.

June-bug was seated in her rocker, near the empty hearth, her sewing in her lap. The needle in her hand flashed silver as she worked, but when she looked up and saw Rachel standing in the doorway, she left off her stitching. "My heavens," she said, "what's happened to you?"

Jacob, smoking a pipe next to an open window, regarded Rachel in thoughtful silence. In their own way, Jacob's silences were as eloquent as the words of any bard.

Rachel remembered that the door was open behind her, letting in flies, and closed it with a groping motion of one hand. "Sunflower's got a sore foot," she said to the stationmaster, sounding strange and helpless even to herself, as though someone else had spoken through her vocal chords. "There was broken glass—I'm afraid she might have picked up a piece or bruised herself somehow, the way she's limping."

Jacob nodded and crossed to the fireplace, tapped his pipe against one wall of the hearth, placing it neatly on the mantel, and went out to see to the injured horse. Toby was already there beside him; Rachel heard his excited voice even through the shut door.

"I believe I asked you a question, young lady," June-bug said, with pointed good humor and a gentleness that made Rachel want to fall into the other woman's arms and wail like a distraught child.

"Something terrible has happened," Rachel said, slowly pacing the length of the long room now, hugging herself as she walked. "Something utterly unexpected and all wrong."

June-bug didn't prod; she simply waited, placid and steady, another shirt for Toby lying half finished in her lap.

"I think—" Rachel lowered her voice, "I think I . . . *care* for Trey Hargreaves."

The vivid blue eyes smiled, even though June-bug's mouth merely twitched. "No!" she said, in a tone of mock horror.

Rachel came to an abrupt stop in the middle of the room, hugging herself even more tightly than before. "You don't understand. He's all wrong for me, and I'm all wrong for him."

"I see," June-bug said, with a solemn nod.

"He's . . . he's a saloon-keeper!" Rachel cried.

"Yes'um, that's so."

"And I'm a teacher!"

"I reckon you are indeed."

"He hates me!"

"I don't believe that," June-bug said, with the first real conviction she'd shown since the conversation began. "The pair of you have been strikin' sparks since the first day, when Trey fished you out of that bogged-down stagecoach and helped Guffy get the rig to shore. Some of the best matches start that way, with fireworks and plenty of 'em. Why, me and Jacob, we like to have stripped each other's hide right off afore we figured out that we was courtin'."

Rachel covered her face with both hands. "Why? Oh, why?"

"No sense in askin' that," June-bug said wisely. "Ain't no earthly answer, when it comes to such matters."

Rachel peeked between splayed fingers, not quite ready to face the world. June-bug was sewing again, at a quick, contented pace. "I shouldn't have come here."

"Nonsense," June-bug replied, without looking up from the green cotton fabric of Toby's new shirt. "The children need you. And so does Trey. One of these days, he'll reason it through and come a-courtin' proper-like, with flowers and pretty words."

The image made Rachel laugh out loud. It was as incongruous as—well, as Trey at a tea party, sipping from a delicate china cup and nibbling at a molasses-oatmeal cookie. "Even if he did—which is about as likely as St. Peter coming in on the next stage-coach—I couldn't marry him. Our principles and values are at variance to say the least, and besides, I will never give up teaching."

"Hmmm," said June-bug, rocking and stitching.

Rachel slumped onto a nearby bench and leaned back against the table's edge, suddenly spent. She had to change the subject, or lose her sanity. "I visited Christabel Johnson today," she said.

June-bug nodded. "You told me you was a-goin' to."

"Granny offered to shoot me—in case I was tired of living, I guess."

At that, the stationmistress chuckled. "That's Granny. She's nobody to trifle with. Why, one time some cowboys got drunked up—just kids really, passin' through and meanin' no real harm—and went up there with a mind to tip over Granny's outhouse. She put so much buckshot in them boys that it took Jacob and me half the next day to pick out the lead." She winced a little at the memory, shook her head and chuckled again.

"Naturally," Rachel said, simply not up to dealing with the image of a lot of cowboys with their drawers pulled down for the procedure, "it's Christabel I'm concerned with. I think I've persuaded her to come to school when classes begin, but there are a couple of problems. She has no clothes or shoes to speak of, but I can make her a dress or two from the yard goods I brought and give her my extra shoes. She'll still need a coat, though, and then there's the sorry state of her hygiene."

June-bug made a *tsk-tsk* sound with her tongue. "That poor little snippet," she said. "You just bring her to me, and I'll get her bathed. Maybe I can move Granny to let her board here, just through the winter."

"I don't think the old woman will agree to that," Rachel replied, with a sigh. "She says she needs the girl to help around the place, and it's probably true."

"Bullfeathers," said June-bug. That was as close as she ever came to cursing in all the time Rachel knew her. "Granny Johnson ain't helpless. She's just got that little girl buffaloed, that's all. I'm going to hitch up the buggy and drive up there and pay her a call first chance I git. Maybe tomorrow morning, in fact, if the stage comes in on time and I can get everybody fed afore it's time to start supper."

If anyone could reason with Granny, June-bug could. Rachel's spirits, chafed raw by the events of the day, rose a little. "I'll see to tomorrow's supper," she said. "You see to that incorrigible old lady."

"Fair enough," June-bug agreed, with a small smile. "I don't reckon Granny'll shoot at me, but you never know."

Rachel headed for her room, there to wash, change her clothes, brush out her hair, and pin it up again. Attending to her personal grooming invariably made her feel better, and the delicious scent of something roasting in the oven had gone a long way toward restoring her as well.

The cleanliness remedy did not fail her; when she returned to the main room, Jacob and Toby were back, standing side by side, scrubbing their hands and faces at the washstand. Toby looked at Rachel with a light in his eyes.

"Sunflower's gonna be all right, Miss English. It was just a little scratch. We cleaned it good and put on some medicine. Jacob put her out to graze in the pasture for a while, so she'll get a chance to heal up."

Jacob merely smiled and placed a big hand on the boy's shoulder, in silent verification of his words. Somehow, it seemed like more, that simple gesture, a confirmation of Toby's very being, the masculine blessing Mike Houghton either could not or would not give.

"That's wonderful, Toby," Rachel said, dropping her gaze from Jacob's face to the lad's. "Perhaps you'll grow up to be an animal doctor."

"I want to run a stagecoach station, like Jacob," the boy said, with a shake of his head and a look of determination.

"Might not be much call for that, with the railroads comin' on the way they are," Jacob observed, but Toby was undaunted.

"I ain't leavin' Springwater," he said. "Not even if my pa comes back meanin' to fetch me."

At that, Rachel and Jacob exchanged another look. If indeed Mike Houghton returned, he could reclaim his boy and there would be nothing anyone could do to prevent him, and they both knew it. The fact that Houghton neglected and probably abused his son meant little in the eyes of the law; children, like women and dogs, had only the most minimal rights.

Jacob squeezed Toby's narrow shoulder. "I reckon we'd better deal with that when and if it happens," he said. "In the meanwhile, we'll just do the best we can. How's that?"

Toby turned and looked up at the older man with something resembling adoration. "That's just fine," he said, in complete trust.

The following morning, the stage arrived right on time, and the three passengers alighted to stretch their legs, take hot meals, and attend to other personal needs. All of them were moving on, and as soon as the coach was loaded up again, June-bug removed her apron and handed it to Rachel.

"Jacob," June-bug said, "I'll need the buggy and a shotgun. I'm goin' up the mountain to pay a call on Granny Johnson."

"You mean to shoot her?" Jacob asked, with the merest twitch at the corner of his mouth.

"I don't require no shotgun to deal with Granny. If 'n I were to meet up with a mama grizzly, well, that would be somethin' different entirely."

"Maybe I ought to go with you," Jacob said, looking uncertain.

June-bug shook her head. "You've got that worn-out team of horses to feed and water and rub down," she said, referring to the eight animals that had drawn the stage west to Springwater, from over Choteau way. As always, Jacob and the driver had hitched fresh horses to the coach and led the tired ones away to the stable. "You see to them poor critters. Rachel's goin' to wash up the dishes, sweep the floor, and start supper for me."

Jacob raised his eyebrows at that, though he offered no comment. It was unusual for June-bug to let anyone take over the tasks she saw as hers to do, and one didn't have to be married to her for forty-odd years, like Jacob, to know that.

"I'd better take along a few of them cookies," June-bug mused, bustling toward the pantry. "Some eggs and butter, too, I think. I know they ain't got no cow up there, and with winter just past, them chickens of theirs are probably as scrawny-lookin' as Granny herself."

Rachel couldn't help laughing a little. June-bug had a pretty good handle on Granny Johnson and her environs, for someone who claimed not to know her well. Clearing up and sweeping was good therapy for Rachel, and she was humming under her breath by the time June-bug set out for the little shack tilting up there on the mountainside, like a climber hanging on for dear life.

"Maybe I should have gone along to protect Miss June-bug from Injuns and the like," Toby said, watching from the front window.

Jacob had resumed his pipe-smoking on the opposite side of the room. "Don't you fret," he said, with a twinkle in his dark eyes. "If it comes down to a squabble, it'll be the Indians that need protectin', not Miss June-bug."

Jacob's trust in his bride was well-placed, as it turned out. Four hours later, the buggy clattered back into the dooryard and there was Miss June-bug, safe and sound, with a wide-eyed Christabel bouncing on the seat beside her.

CHAPTER

≈ 6 ≈

TOBY LOOKED Christabel up and down, squeezed his nostrils shut with a thumb and two fingers, and keened, "Phew! You stink bad as an outhouse!"

"That will be enough," Jacob said gravely, from behind the boy. They were all three standing outside the station entrance, Rachel and Jacob and Toby.

Miss June-bug waggled a finger at the lad. "You jest git yourself into your room, Toby Houghton, and work out why it was wrong to say a thing like that. When you've got it clear in your head, you'll be ready to apologize to Christabel."

Toby looked up at Jacob, as if expecting intercession, but the man only gestured toward the house and ground out, "Go."

Flushed and probably already repentant, if unprepared to say as much, Toby took his leave.

"Who's that?" Christabel inquired, looking to Rachel as though she might bolt and flee back into the hills. Her eyes accused, *You said nobody would be mean to me. You promised.*

"His name is Toby Houghton," Rachel said. "Don't you worry about him. He's a good boy, and he'll turn out to be your friend, you just wait and see."

Christabel looked doubtful; she'd most likely never had a friend, unless you counted her grandmother. "I don't reckon I do smell much like town-folk do," she said sorrowfully.

"We'll attend to your bath straight away," Miss June-bug said, as though proposing that a guest take a bath were the same as offering tea or a place in the shade on a hot day. "I believe I've got some things you could wear while Miss English here is stitching up a dress or two."

Rachel had not even begun the sewing project, as she hadn't expected June-bug to succeed so quickly in her mission of bringing Christabel Johnson down from the mountainside. She was anxious, even excited, to proceed, despite her dubious abilities as a seamstress. Her heart swelled as she put an arm around the young girl; she knew well what courage it had taken for her to break away from familiar miseries and step into an uncertain future.

They set up the big washtub out in the high grass behind the station, and Jacob, June-bug, and Rachel all carried hot water until it was brimming. The job of scrubbing Christabel from head to foot fell to the women, of course, and when it was over, both Rachel and June-bug were as wet as their beaming charge.

When at last Christabel's hair was clean enough to suit June-bug—a tendril of it had to "squeak" between her fingers at a gentle tug—they helped her out of the big tub and wrapped her in a blanket, to keep her from taking a chill. It was sunset by then, and everyone was thinking in terms of supper, a pot of baked beans Rachel had put into the oven earlier that day, to be accompanied by slices of leftover cornbread and some canned carrots from the pantry.

Christabel ate as though she'd never tasted such food before; maybe she hadn't, given the poverty she and her grandmother lived in. Toby came out of his room behind the stove, looking chagrined, in the middle of the meal.

"I reckon I'm sorry for what I said," he told Christabel, in staunch tones. "It weren't mannerly." He rustled up a game smile, even as his stomach rumbled for all to hear. " 'Sides, you cleaned up right nice."

Jacob, June-bug, and Rachel all made a shared effort not to show their amusement, but the sternness of their expressions lacked some element of true conviction.

"Thanks," Christabel said. Her eyes were watchful. Her fine, thin hair, which had turned out to be a pretty shade of brown, gleamed in the lamplight, still moist from washing and ridged from June-bug's comb. Her borrowed dress, oversized but clean, was worn with a certain wary pride. "You better set down and have yourself some of these here beans. They ain't as bad as they look."

Rachel bit her lower lip and did not dare to look at

Jacob or June-bug, lest she burst out laughing after all.

Toby peered over the girl's shoulder to inspect Rachel's baked beans. "I reckon you're right," he said, and took the place that had been laid for him, on the other side of the table, next to Jacob. Both children consumed second and then third helpings of the main course, and together they finished off the cornbread.

All and all, it was a companionable meal, though mostly passed in silence.

Christabel's eyes were especially large as she got up from the table at last and reached for her empty plate. "I'll wash up the dishes," she said. "Then I suppose I ought to lay myself down and sleep, since I'm plum tuckered out."

June-bug rose gracefully from her own seat and took the plate out of Christabel's hands. "You'll have your chores to do, that's for sure and certain. But you can start in on them tomorrow."

"I guess I don't know where you mean to put me," Christabel confided, with painful shyness. "I don't see no loft nor pallet nor anything like that."

"Fact is, we do rent out what rooms we've got to travelers, whenever the need arises, but in the meantime, you're welcome to whichever bed you want," June-bug said, laying a hand to the child's thin shoulder. "And don't you fret, neither. We'll make a place where you can stay, permanent-like, if that's what you want to do."

Christabel looked amazed. "A whole room? All to myself?"

June-bug smiled. "Come along, and we'll make up

the bed with fresh linens and all." With that, they left
the dining room together, June-bug slowing her steps
to match Christabel's more labored pace.

Rachel, long since finished eating, got up to clear
away and wash dishes, while Jacob and Toby went out
to attend to the evening chores. Standing at the work
table in the kitchen, gazing out the darkened window,
Rachel could see the lights of the Brimstone Saloon,
glowing in the darkness. Her thoughts traipsed in that
direction, seeking Trey. Finding him all too easily.

Sunday morning, after breakfast and chores, Jacob
announced that he felt called to preach a rousing sermon. He put on his good black suit and string tie for
the occasion, once the barn work was done, and got
out his ancient Bible. It seemed that his very decision
to conduct a service had stirred the surrounding
countryside to life, though of course Rachel knew
that the day had been planned for some time.

The spring sun shone extra-bright, the breeze was
fresh, and the wildflowers covered the fields like
threads in a colorful patchwork quilt.

With help from Toby and Christabel, Rachel
moved the tables to one side of the room and set all
the benches in tidy rows, facing the fireplace, for
June-bug said that Jacob liked to do his preaching in
front of the hearth. He'd acquired the habit over the
course of several Montana winters, she confided,
when the whole territory turned to ice and crystal.
June-bug herself was occupied with frying up chicken
and boiling potatoes and eggs for a massive salad.

Slowly, as noon approached, Jacob's parishioners began to appear—Landry Kildare and his two boys, both void of war paint and with their hair combed down, were the first to arrive, then came the Bellweathers, followed by a few old bachelor traders, all of whom looked as though they hadn't been out of the woods in twenty years. They were all shy, these mountain men, but their eagerness to be part of the gathering showed plainly in their eyes. There were cowboys, too, spruced up and on their best behavior, passing through Springwater in advance of one of several large herds of cattle being driven up from Denver and points further south. Rachel recognized some of them from the arm-wrestling contest at Brimstone Saloon, though she had to admit they didn't look like the same fellows at all, with their clean hair and stiffly new dungarees.

Emma Hargreaves came in, somewhat timidly, wearing a bright yellow Sunday-go-to-meeting dress that fit her, unlike the borrowed garb Christabel had on, and the Kildare boys' of nearly outgrown trousers and button-stretched shirts. Kathleen Bellweather ran to greet Emma, being about the same age, though she had given Christabel a wide berth, and Rachel held herself back from stepping in. If she pressed the children to be friends, she knew, she might well create a permanent breach between them, but it was hard not to intercede all the same.

The noisy arrival of a buckboard drew her attention away from the children, and she gave a gasp of joy when she looked through a front window and saw the Wainwright family, all dressed up and ready for preaching and a party. Rachel ran outside to greet them, and embraced first Abigail, then Evangeline. Scully was holding the baby in the crook of one arm and little J.J. in the other, grinning at his wife's delight.

"I didn't dare to hope you would come all this way!" Rachel cried, holding Evangeline by the shoulders.

Evangeline smiled. "We wouldn't have missed it. Besides, Scully wants to see the horse race."

Rachel was reminded of Trey Hargreaves, and she felt a mild ache in the depths of her heart. There was no sign of him, and if they met, they were likely to have words, but still she kept watching for him, at the edge of her vision. "You don't plan to enter?" she asked Scully, reaching out for the well-bundled baby. He surrendered the child and used both arms to keep a fidgety J.J. in check. "I should think that Appaloosa of yours could run like the wind."

"He can," Scully said, with a mischievous light in his eyes, "but I'm an old married man now, and henpecked into the bargain. My dear wife is of the opinion that I spend enough time in the saddle as it is, owing to my profession, without making a sport of it."

Before Rachel could shape a reply, June-bug erupted from the station doorway, both arms extended.

"Let me see that baby this minute!" she demanded joyously.

Evangeline laughed, as did Rachel, who surrendered little Rachel Louisa into her friend's embrace.

The blue sky seemed to cast a blessing over them all, and there was laughter and conviviality spilling out of the station itself, ambrosia to the spirit.

"Oh," cried June-bug, having unveiled the baby from her blanket, "she is the *loveliest* little thing—fair as an angel!"

It was merely what people routinely said about new babies, but in this case, it was also the purest truth. The Wainwright infant was pretty as the cherubs in the paintings of the Old Masters, and Rachel was certain she would grow up to be a legendary beauty. Evangeline thanked June-bug for the compliment with a certain pleased modesty, and they all went inside to settle down for Jacob's sermon.

He'd chosen the 91st Psalm as his text, and he was indeed a gifted orator, but Rachel only heard about half of his message because Trey Hargreaves slipped in, midway through the rustic service, to take a chair at the back of the room, next to the door, the benches being full.

Rachel had glanced back when she heard the hinges creak and caught sight of him. From that moment on, her concentration was shattered and she could think of nothing but Trey. In the brief look she'd taken, she'd seen that he was wearing a nicely fitted suit of clothes, with one of his white ruffled shirts and a well-shined pair of boots; his dark hair was clean and brushed, and he'd shaved for the occasion as well.

When the preaching ended, after some two hours, everyone was ready to stand outside under the two shade trees, the women fanning themselves, the men talking of horses and cattle and the weather. All the ladies had brought food to contribute, and there was plenty to set out on the long tables inside, now moved back to their proper places. June-bug was in her element, overseeing it all, just as her husband had been earlier, when he stood before his motley congregation, Bible in hand, deep voice ringing with conviction.

The children, relieved to be released from their injunction to sit quietly, raced all around the station, shouting and laughing. Only Christabel was left out, perched quietly on the edge of a chair someone had brought out and set in the shade of the building, watching the happy foolery with carefully expressionless eyes.

Rachel was about to break her own rule and have a word with the others about including Christabel in their games, when she saw Trey, standing in a circle of men, reach out and snag his daughter as she ran past. He bent and spoke to her, nodding subtly in Christabel's direction.

Rachel stood still, watching, as Emma walked slowly over to Christabel's chair and spoke to her. Christabel smiled, then shook her head and ducked her face shyly.

Emma took hold of her arm and tugged, and soon, miraculously, Christabel was a part of things, if still somewhat on the fringe of it all. Given her crippled foot, it was nearly impossible for her to keep up, but she tried valiantly, and Emma often stopped and came back to encourage her.

Rachel closed her eyes for a moment, so moved that she did not think she could have spoken, had there been anyone at hand to speak to, that is.

As it happened, there was someone close by. Trey Hargreaves had materialized at her elbow, hat in hand.

Rachel blinked, taken by surprise. "Mr. Hargreaves," she said, somewhat squeakily, by way of a greeting.

He nodded. "Afternoon," he said. There was a grin lurking behind that serious expression of his, and though he was making a fine job of holding it in restraint, now and again it peeked out of his eyes. "There'll be dancing tonight," he informed her. "Old Zeb Prudham brought his fiddle."

Rachel's heart beat a little faster, though she couldn't think why that should happen. Heaven knew, she'd certainly danced—though not since Langdon went away to war, of course. If she were called upon to participate in the festivities, she'd manage to keep from tangling her feet. "Yes?" she said.

She thought she saw the faintest flush of color under Trey's tan, but she couldn't be sure. "I reckon every man here is going to want a whirl around the floor with you," he said, and it looked as though every word was costing him dearly. "For the sake of peace between us, you understand, well—" He looked away, looked back determinedly. "I'd like to be the first. To dance with you, I mean."

Rachel was taken aback by the request, mightily

so. Of all the men in and around Springwater, Trey was the last one she would have expected to approach her with such a request. She wasn't exactly his kind of woman, was she? Her heartbeat stepped up again.

"I'd like that," she said, with no more grace than the average smitten schoolgirl.

Trey tilted his head toward her and spoke in a confidential fashion. "Just between you and me, I think that Kildare feller means to court you for a wife. He's good-looking, I guess, and he's got himself a good piece of land and some fine horseflesh. Solvent, too—he's been trying to buy my old homestead up behind his place for a year. Offering cash, too." He paused and frowned, as though aware that he might be making his friend look too good. "You hitch up with him, though, and those kids of his will have you in an asylum before a year's out."

Rachel wanted to laugh, out of nervousness and exultation, but she controlled the urge. "I see," she said. "I'll bear that in mind."

"Good," Trey replied, in earnest satisfaction and what appeared to be a measure of relief.

Before the conversation could proceed, June-bug informed the gathering that the midday meal was a-wasting and they'd better come inside and help themselves before the flies got it all. The response was enthusiastic, but Jacob lead a short, rumbling prayer before the first fork was raised.

Rachel had the fanciful feeling that she was in the midst of a homecoming; it was as if she'd belonged in Springwater all along, without knowing of its existence, and had at last found her way there, having traveled over a long and winding path.

The meal was delicious, a rousing affair, during which Granny Johnson caused a stir by arriving on the back of a brown mule, wearing a calico bonnet with her old dress and carrying the ever-present shotgun across her lap. "Did I miss the preachin'?" she asked, when Jacob helped her down off the animal's back.

"Yes, Ma'am," Jacob answered soberly, "you did at that."

"Dern it," Granny said. "I ain't heard a good sermon in twenty years. I had my brain all set for fire and brimstone."

Jacob's mouth twitched, but he had the good grace not to smile. While he'd certainly driven home the power of the Lord in his message, he hadn't stirred the embers of hell into a roaring blaze, the way a lot of preachers did. Privately, Rachel thought better of him for it, although she knew that many people didn't count themselves forgiven if they hadn't felt the sharp prongs of the devil's pitchfork.

Now, he stood with his hand resting lightly, in a gentlemanly fashion, on the small of Granny's back. "There's still a good bit of food left, Mrs. Johnson," he said. "You go right on in there and fill yourself a plate."

Granny nodded and handed him the shotgun. "If you'll look after that for me, young feller, I'll be obliged," she said. Then she tottered toward the door of the station, stopping briefly to speak to Rachel. "I jest came here to see how you're treatin' my gal," she announced. "If she ain't happy, I'm takin' her right home agin."

Rachel smiled. She was pleased to see Granny attending the festivities, testy though she was. It had troubled her not a little to think of the old woman out there in that shack, all alone, and she dared to hope Granny might actually become a part of the community. Not only would that make the elderly lady's life easier, but it would be a boon to Christabel, too.

Soon, Rachel spotted the two of them, side by side on a sawhorse, Granny with a plateful of fried chicken, potato salad, and pickles in her lap, Christabel chattering earnestly and gesturing with one hand. Rachel smiled and sought out Evangeline, who wanted a look at the inside of the schoolhouse.

By the time they returned from that, the horse race was about to begin. The course was to cover the stagecoach trail from the station to Willow Creek and back, and everybody was on their honor not to take any shortcuts. The prize was a twenty-dollar gold piece, raised by the entrance fees, and there were seven contestants, including Trey, horses prancing at the rope Jacob had laid across the road to form both the starting line and the finish.

The rules were announced—no kicking, punching, or spurring of other riders, and no cutting across the meadow. Cursing was allowed, since there were no ladies entered in the race, and spitting was all right, too. If any fights broke out, everybody concerned would get themselves disqualified.

Having stated all this, Jacob raised his pistol into the air and fired. The racers took off, streaks of man and horseflesh, pounding toward the first bend, raising dust. Rachel was secretly pleased to see that Trey was already in the lead, but it wouldn't have been diplomatic for the schoolmarm to single out one rider over the others, so she just watched until they'd all disappeared from sight. Toby and the Kildare boys chased across the meadow, to keep the horses in view, all of them yearning, no doubt, for the day when they might ride in such a race as well.

It was several miles to the creek and back, but the excitement of the spectators was not dimmed by the fact that the horses and their riders would be out of sight for a long time. There weren't many such gatherings in that isolated place, so this was high adventure for most everyone there, especially the children.

Nearly forty-five minutes later, the first rider reappeared, far ahead of the others, and Rachel had a hard time keeping herself from jumping up and down when she saw that it was Trey. When he shot across the finish line, his horse barely winded, cheers went up and loud congratulations were offered. Had it been any day but Sunday, Rachel thought, most of the men would probably have adjourned to the Brimstone for a celebratory glass of whiskey.

Amid the handshakes and back slaps, Trey looked up, found Rachel, and winked. It was an outlandish thing to do, sure to start talk, but she was pleased all the same.

Through the afternoon, the men played horseshoes

and the women gossiped at one of June-bug's tables, inside the station, while the smaller children napped on various beds and other acceptable surfaces about the place. The older children seemed to have inexhaustible supplies of energy, and played outdoor games that kept them busy until sunset, when the lamps were lit and the food was brought out again. These were the leftovers from dinner, and yet, like the loaves and fishes in the Bible, there was plenty for everybody, with some to spare.

When the meal ended, the women cleared away and washed the dishes. Each family had brought their own plates, cups, and utensils, as well as something to add to the meal itself. The men moved the tables again, this time out into the dooryard, where a crisp spring breeze was blowing, to make room inside for dancing.

Zeb Prudham brought out his fiddle and took up a place before the fire, where a cheerful blaze was crackling, making a great show of tuning each string to within a hair of the note. His antics were, Rachel knew, an integral part of the merrymaking, and she enjoyed them wholeheartedly.

As they had agreed, Trey, who had been keeping his distance since winning the horse race, strode across the room to claim the first dance. As he swept her into his arms, Rachel caught a glimpse of Evangeline's beaming smile, but her attention was soon firmly fastened on Trey and only Trey. She could not seem to look away from his face, and after a while they might have been alone in that large room, for all the notice they spared for anyone else.

Rachel was blushing when the song, the sorrowful ballad *Lorena*, at last came to an end. Being held so close to Trey had had a very strange and flustering effect on her; she felt as though she would surely faint if she didn't get some fresh air. The whole of her person was a single, thrumming ache, and the blood rushed through her veins to set every nerve to pulsing.

The night was deliciously cool, and the stars were out in legions, though the moon was but a sliver. Rachel walked rapidly, fluttering one hand in front of her face in lieu of a fan, and wondering what precisely she was going to do. She was wildly, desperately attracted to Trey Hargreaves, that much was obvious, but she couldn't have made a poorer choice if she'd tried. Men like him didn't marry and settle down to raise families—Emma had probably been an accident. He might want Rachel—he might want a lot of women—but when the conquest was made, he would tire of her and move on.

She was thinking these troubling thoughts, and dashing unconsciously at her cheeks with the back of one hand, when she realized she was nearly to the schoolhouse, and someone was behind her. She turned, hoping to see Evangeline, or perhaps one of the McCaffreys, but instead, there was Trey.

He fell into step beside her. "That was a fine dance, Miss English," he said. "Thank you for doing me the honor."

She turned, fists clenched, and glared up at him. "Why are you doing this?" she cried.

"Doing what?" he asked, and though he sounded

puzzled, she could see by his expression that he knew precisely what she was talking about.

Rachel sent her arms wheeling out, wide of her body. "Being nice to me!" she snapped. "Just yesterday we were shouting at each other!"

"I think we're shouting at each other now," he pointed out reasonably, but he didn't raise his voice, and his eyes were full of gentle humor. "Well, *you're* shouting," he clarified.

They were standing in the middle of what everyone hoped would someday be a street, though at the time it was merely a cattle trail. Rachel shook her finger under his nose. "Maybe I'm not a virgin," she hissed, "but I am no loose woman!"

Trey furrowed his brow, but the humor was still dancing in his eyes. "You're not a virgin?" he echoed. "Teacher! That's a scandal."

Rachel was mortified; she could not believe she'd said such a thing, and yet she had. Heaven help her, she had. Well, maybe that would solve the whole problem. Maybe now that he knew she wasn't pure and untouched, he wouldn't want her anymore. Maybe he wouldn't make *her* want *him*.

He took her shoulders in his hands when she would have turned and fled. "Rachel," he said, "listen to me. Something important is happening here and we'd damn well better find out what it is before it drives the pair of us crazy."

She blinked. She'd expected him to spurn her— most men thought the world ought to contain a perpetual supply of virgins, and only virgins, for them to deflower at their discretion, but it did not seem to bother Trey that she'd been with another man. "We don't need to know," she blurted. "What's happening, I mean. We can just go on, both of us, and pretend nothing has changed."

"Maybe you can," Trey said, frowning and giving her the slightest shake, "but *I* can't. I have to know."

"But why?"

"This is why," he said, and then he hauled her close, bent his head, and covered her mouth with his. Rachel struggled a moment, more against herself than him, and then sagged against him with a murmur of bewildered pleasure. He prodded her lips apart and entered her with his tongue, and the contact was like trying to climb a pole made out of pure lightning. Finally, he held her at arm's length again, his silvery eyes glittering like shards from a broken moon. "I reckon I have made my point," he said, somewhat breathlessly.

Rachel was standing there, trying to will some starch into her knees, one hand splayed across her bosom to keep her heart from beating its way right out of her chest and flying off like a bird. "What are we going to do?" she asked, after a long time.

"I know what I'd *like* to do," Trey said ruefully, thrusting a hand through his hair. "But that's out of the question. Fact is, if we don't get back to that dance right now, there's bound to be gossip. That's nothing new for me, but it might be the ruin of you."

Rachel knew he was right, though the last thing she wanted was to walk back into that station and face all those people. She was sure Trey's kiss had set something ablaze inside her that would be visible for miles, let alone in the confines of a fairly crowded room.

He took her hand, very gently, and slipped it into the crook of his elbow. "Come on, Teacher. There's only one way to spare your reputation, and that's to dance with every man who asks you for the rest of the evening."

She nodded, sniffled once, and allowed him to escort her back into the station. The light of the lanterns, dim though it was, seemed blinding after the darkness, and the music stopped the instant they crossed the threshold, though that was surely an accident of fate.

Jacob, ever the gentleman, presented himself immediately and offered a big hand to Rachel. "May I have the honor of this dance, Miss English?" he asked.

Rachel could have kissed him, for as Jacob went, so went the general populace of Springwater and the surrounding environs. She took his hand, nodded, and let him whirl her into a lively reel. Soon, the floor was a-spin with dancers and she lost sight of Trey entirely. Evangeline passed her, in Scully's arms, and even Granny Johnson was kicking up her heels with one of the mountain men. The girls, Emma and Abigail, Kathleen and Christabel, danced with each other, while the boys stood on the sidelines, looking stubbornly terrified. No doubt they feared being dragged into the fray by that most dreaded of creatures, a *girl*.

By the end of the evening, when folks began to gather up children and picnic baskets and start for home, it seemed that everyone had forgotten how the new schoolmarm had gone outside alone with the owner of the Brimstone Saloon, thereby committing an impropriety that would have gotten a lot of teachers dismissed from their jobs. Everyone had forgotten, that is, except for the new schoolmarm herself.

CHAPTER

7

A WEEK AFTER THE DANCE, Rachel was at the schoolhouse, rearranging the few things there were to rearrange. Emma and Christabel had been helping out all morning, but she had sent them down to the station on an errand, only moments before, when the ground began to tremble and a horrendous roar shook the walls.

Cattle, Rachel realized—apparently, she had been so engrossed in her efforts at organization that she hadn't heard them approaching. Now, the herd thundered into town, accompanied by whooping cowboys firing pistols into the air. Furious, she hurried across the room and flung open the door.

The cacophony was rivaled only by the dust, which veiled the sky and sent gritty gusts of wind rolling over her. The time Rachel had spent outside earlier, teetering on an upturned crate while she washed windows, was all for naught.

Emma and Christabel.

The realization that the children might well have stumbled straight into the melee seized Rachel suddenly, forced the very breath from her lungs. Dashing toward the street, she searched for them, frantic with fear, but she could see nothing, but for the surreal, shadow-like shapes of cattle and horses and cowboys.

She screamed the girls' names, but could barely hear her own voice over the din.

The herd, already frightened and confused, proceeded to panic, and became a great, swirling knot of hoof and horn, virtually filling the small settlement from one end to the other.

Again, Rachel cried out, but by that time she was coughing. Gaining the road, she plunged into the center of the madness, desperate to find the children before they were run down or gored. She felt the heat and brawny substance of the beasts, smelled their rough, dusty hides. She struggled to stay on her feet, but soon enough she was down, surrounded, smothered, blinded.

This was how it would end, then, she thought, with what struck her as a ludicrous sense of equanimity. She would be trampled to death. So much for the old dream of dying in her sleep, ancient of days.

In the next instant, however, she glimpsed a hand reaching down toward her, and out of pure instinct, she reached back. With a wrench so fearsome that she thought her shoulder had been dislocated, she was pulled upward, and found herself on the back of a horse, Trey's horse, specifically, with Trey at the reins, furious and covered in yellow-brown dust.

"The girls!" she gasped, when the shock of being alive subsided a little, looking wildly about, seeing nothing but dirt and cattle and cowboys.

"They're all right," Trey yelled back, over the uproar, expertly guiding the horse through what seemed to Rachel like a medieval battle.

Soon, they were safe in the dooryard of the station. Two sheepish cowboys rode in behind them, but Rachel had eyes only for Christabel and Emma, who were standing at the edge of the road, faces pale and solemn with alarm. Thank God, Rachel thought, thank God. They'd been here all the time, the girls had, with the McCaffreys to look after them.

"We're mighty sorry about the boys carryin' on the way they have," one of the drovers said, to the general assembly, with a tug at the brim of his hat.

Trey's jawline looked as cold, hard, and smooth as creek stone; Rachel wanted to stay just where she was, safe in the circle of his arms, but of course that couldn't happen. He leaned down and set her carefully on the ground, directing his words to the man who had spoken, probably the trail boss.

"They're welcome in my saloon," he said evenly, his silver eyes glinting bright as knife-blades in the sun. "All the same, they damn near killed somebody. You've got a quarter of an hour to settle those jackals down and get the cattle out into the countryside before I get my rifle and start shooting. I won't be too choosy about what I aim at, I warn you."

Nobody doubted that he meant exactly what he was saying, especially Rachel. He was as outraged a man as she'd ever seen, and for the first time since she'd met him, she realized that he was indeed capable of following through with just such a threat.

It chilled her, knowing that. She stared at him, stunned, and he must have sensed that she was watching him, because he met her eyes squarely, and the truth passed, unspoken, between them.

June-bug came forward, *tsk-tsk*ing, while Jacob took a steadying hold on Rachel's arm, for which she was infinitely grateful. As the reality of what had so nearly happened struck her for the second time, her knees turned to water and she probably would have collapsed without her friend's support.

Trey glanced at his daughter, then Rachel again, and reined his horse away, toward the Brimstone. Rachel stood, leaning against Jacob and watching him go. Something broke inside her, a dam of some sort, behind which she'd hidden all her most private and troublesome emotions. Her sorrow over Langdon and her guilt because she could not save her heart for him after all, her long-suppressed yearnings for a husband and a home and children of her own, her ill-advised but unquestionable love for one particular, impossible man. A man who carried a terrible secret. Spinning like flotsam in the onslaught, she turned to Jacob, laid her head on his shoulder, and wept inconsolably.

He just stood there, God bless him, steady as a tree, holding her with one arm and patting her back with the other hand. "Here now," he said, over and over again, "here now." And somehow, it was infinitely comforting, that simple, meaningless phrase.

Within an hour, everyone was composed again—June-bug had taken the girls in hand, soothing and reassuring them in her cheerful fashion, and Rachel had retreated to her room long enough for a sponge bath and a change of clothing. She brushed the dust from her hair, put it back into its customary loose chignon, and marched herself out into the center of things again. She'd feared that if she stayed in that room too long, she might just crawl under the bed and refuse to come out.

"Those tears," June-bug asked gently, pouring tea the instant Rachel reappeared, "what were they all about?" There was no sign of Jacob or Toby, and Emma and Christabel were in the latter's small room, talking excitedly.

Rachel sighed and let her shoulders slump. "I think you could guess," she replied.

"You're in love with Trey Hargreaves," June-bug said, "and you don't think there's any hope of things workin' out for the two of you."

Rachel nodded and sagged onto a bench at the table, heartily grateful for the steaming cupful of fresh tea set before her. She felt strangely fragile, she who had been so strong all her life, so independent, and dangerously near another useless fit of crying. "I've been lying to myself," she confessed miserably. "Saying I didn't need anyone else. But I do, June-bug—I do. I need the wrong man."

June-bug sat down across from her and poured a cup of tea for herself, adding two lumps of coarse sugar and a dollop of milk before she spoke. "Maybe Trey *ain't* the wrong man. That ever occur to you? Maybe he's the right one, put by for you back when the stars was set in their places."

Rachel felt a surge of affection for this dear friend, who spoke in so homey a fashion and was so very wise. She would have liked for June-bug to be right, but she still had grave doubts. "It won't work. I can't live over a saloon—and not because I'm too fancy and think too highly of myself, either. It's because I don't believe such places are good for people. I know without even asking that Trey won't give up his interest in the Brimstone, any more than I'm willing to stop teaching. How can problems like that ever be solved?"

June-bug shrugged, looking placidly confident, and took a sip of her tea. "I reckon you and Trey would have to decide on the solutions between yourselves. Folks have worked through a lot worse, I can tell you that much."

"It seems impossible."

"So do lots of other things that get done every day."

Rachel sighed. "I'm confused," she admitted. "I had the distinct impression that you didn't approve of Trey Hargreaves."

"I don't like that saloon of his, and that's a fact. I don't reckon I'd spit on the place if it took fire. But I've got nothing agin Trey. Fact is, I respect him a lot, for the way he looks after that little girl in there, if nothin' else," June-bug answered, with a nod toward Christabel's closet-sized room. "That says a lot about a man, to my way of thinkin', his bein' willin' to take responsibility for his child. A lot of them don't—like Mike Houghton, for instance. Trey could probably have found another relative to take Emma in, but he didn't. When she needed him, he made a place for her."

Rachel couldn't refute any of that, but then, Trey's morals weren't the cause of her dilemma in the first place. Had he been a different man than the one she'd glimpsed behind that incorrigibly stubborn exterior, she would never have fallen in love with him. No, it was more than the smaller differences that had worried her all along—the saloon and the gambling, her desire to keep teaching. He was going to tell her something about himself, she sensed that, something she didn't want to hear, didn't want to know. She'd seen it in his eyes, out there in the road.

Not unexpectedly, Trey came to call that night and solemnly asked Rachel to go out for a walk with him. Although his expression was grim, he was slicked up like a man headed for his own hanging, and he carried a bunch of wildflowers, obviously just gathered, in one hand.

She accepted the blossoms with a certain poignant sorrow and put them in water, after quietly accepting his invitation. She borrowed a shawl from June-bug before leaving the station, for the breeze was crisp, despite the fact that summer would be soon be upon them.

"You must know that I care about you," Trey said, when they were beside the springs that gave the place its name, the water of the flowing pool musical and dappled with starlight. "That's why I've got to tell you something I've never told anybody except for one judge, down in Colorado."

Rachel waited, barely able to breathe, her arms wrapped tightly around her middle.

He met her eyes. "My wife—Emma's mother—was killed when a couple of outlaws robbed a store in Great Falls," he said. She saw the memory of that day in his face, and grieved with him and for him, but she did not speak.

He thrust out a sigh. "I shot them, Rachel," he said. "One between the eyes, one through the heart."

Rachel swallowed. "In cold blood?" she whispered. She had no real sympathy for the dead outlaws; they were killers, after all, and thieves. But neither did she believe in taking the law into one's own hands.

"I didn't ambush them, if that's what you mean. Legally, I suppose, it was a fair fight. But yes, my blood was cold when I did it."

"Are you wanted?"

He considered the question. "No," he said. "I turned myself in to a marshal, down Colorado way, in a fit of good conscience. He refused to press charges and that was the end of it, as far as the law was concerned."

She just stood there, at a loss for what to say. Right or wrong, she loved him, and it wasn't her place to sit in judgment of what he'd done. She might, in fact, have done the same thing, in his place. "Then it's over," she said softly.

He took a step toward her, then stopped, plainly uncertain. "You've got to understand, Rachel," he said. "I'm not sorry for what I did. I'd do it again."

She bit her lower lip. "Fair enough," she said.

There was a long silence. Then he favored her with a tentative, lopsided grin. "If that's the way of it, Miss English, I'm through biding my time. I want to know what I have to do to make you my wife."

Rachel stared at him, her heart soaring. Although she'd been certain of her own feelings, she had, of course, not been entirely sure of his. "You want to marry me?"

Trey cleared his throat. He was holding his hat in both hands, turning it slowly between his fingers. "Yes," he said, after a long time. "I love you, Rachel. I wouldn't have chosen to, but I do."

Rachel wanted to fling her arms around his neck in pure jubilation, but she held herself back. There were too many things still unsettled. "I can't give up teaching," she said, after a very long time. "I won't."

Trey threw her own words back at her. "Fair enough," he said, with surprising readiness. "I don't mean to close down the saloon, so I guess we're even."

Rachel drew a deep breath, let it out slowly. "You must know it isn't a proper place to raise Emma or any other children who might come along," she said, in a nervous rush of words.

"I'll build you a house, if that's what you want. Hell, I'll sell my homestead to Landry Kildare and take out a mortgage at the bank over in Choteau.

Send for one of those mail-order places like Miss June-bug's always talking about, with the bathtubs and the hot water and all."

Rachel laid a hand to her heart. "You'd do that?"

"I told you," Trey said gravely. "I love you. Besides that, Teacher, if I can't bed you pretty damn soon, I'm going to have to start spending half my time sitting in the horse trough."

She laughed at the image, though his declaration had brought tears to her eyes. "There was someone else," she reminded him. "His name was Langdon and we were in love . . . we thought . . . we—"

He laid a finger to her lips. "That's past. All it means is that our wedding night will be a bit easier for you. Besides, Rachel, I'm not exactly pure myself, you know. There was Emma's mother, for one."

She swallowed. "I'll marry you, then, Trey Hargreaves. I'll raise your daughter as my own, and I'll bear your children, as many as you give me. I'll even live above that dratted saloon of yours—but only until our house is finished."

He pulled her close, grinning, and arranged her head for his impending kiss, the kiss that would seal their bargain. "Deal," he said, and brought his mouth down on hers.

The wedding was held a month later, by which time Trey had put in the order for a small house, which would be sent west from Chicago by rail and then freight wagon, to be erected on a plot of land well down the road from the Brimstone. School would start in just two weeks, and so far, no one had

objected to having a married teacher in the schoolhouse, so classes were to begin on schedule.

Folks came from all over to attend the ceremony,
everyone from Granny Johnson to the Wainwright
family. Evangeline had agreed to stand up for Rachel;
Jacob would perform the service itself, of course, and
June-bug was to sing.

Because it was a beautiful day, full summer now,
the marriage party assembled in the grassy sideyard of
the station, where tables had been set out and ribbons
hung from the trees. Rachel wore June-bug's wedding
dress, a lovely confection of ivory satin, dripping with
lace, while Trey, looking nervous as an unshod horse
on rocky ground, donned his dark suit.

Christabel and Emma had erected a bower of sorts,
using wildflowers and foliage gathered in their wan-
derings, under which Jacob would stand, facing the
bride and groom.

June-bug's song had all the women in tears right off,
Rachel included. Trey tugged at his shirt collar with
one finger, obviously wishing the whole thing were
over and done with. It would be a long time before he
got his wish, though, because after the ceremony there
was a community meal, everything from roast beef to
wedding cake, and after that was another dance. While
Rachel was equally anxious that they be alone together, it was after all her wedding day, the only one she
ever intended to have, and she meant to savor every
moment, be fully present for every joy. The pleasures of
the night to come would take care of themselves.

The exchange of vows was relatively short, and

within a few minutes, Jacob had pronounced Trey and Rachel to be man and wife. Trey turned to Rachel, wrapped both arms around her, and lifted her clear off her feet for his kiss. Hurrahs went up all around.

The meal followed—Rachel, now Mrs. Hargreaves, nibbled at a few things, but she had no real appetite. Trey, on the other hand, seemed ravenous, and consumed a plateful of fried chicken, sliced beef, deviled eggs, potato salad, and pickles. After that, he had cake, and while the women presented Rachel with intricately stitched quilt blocks cut from flour sacks and other yard goods, Trey hung his jacket on a tree limb, pushed up his sleeves, and proceeded to beat every man present at a game of horseshoes.

Rachel tried not to watch her new husband, but her gaze kept straying off in search of him, and she supposed her longing showed as plainly as her love. Although she was hardly experienced, she was no shrinking maiden either, and she anticipated the consummation of their marriage as much as Trey did.

The afternoon seemed endless, the hot, slow hours rolling by like whole days, but at last the evening came, and there was more food, and paper lanterns suspended among the ribbons, from the tree branches, were lit. Old Mr. Prudham produced his fiddle again, and the dancing began.

The first dance was, of course, a waltz, and Rachel and Trey moved together, into each other's arms, slowly whirling round and round beneath a summer moon. The grass smelled sweetly and Rachel's heart was full.

"You are very beautiful, Teacher," Trey said softly, looking down into her eyes. They were dancing alone, for this was the wedding waltz, reserved for the bride and groom. "I can't wait to have you to myself."

A sweet shiver went through Rachel, and she batted her eyelashes, pretending to be coy. "Why, Mr. Hargreaves, are you making improper advances?"

"Oh, yes, Mrs. Hargreaves," he answered. "Most improper." He kissed her lightly, quickly on the mouth. "I mean to have you carrying on something awful, and right soon now."

Rachel trembled; he felt it and smiled again.

"You have a lot of confidence in your abilities as a lover," she teased.

"All of it justified," Trey boasted shamelessly, "as you shall soon learn. Though not soon enough, I'm afraid, to suit your long-suffering husband."

She laughed. "Poor darling," she said, and stroked his smoothly shaven cheek with the back of one hand, "how will I comfort you?"

He made a growling sound and spun her around once, off her feet, before resuming the waltz. The wedding guests, hearing nothing but probably suspecting a great deal, laughed and applauded.

In time, as all things do, the wedding dance ended. Those visitors who weren't passing the night at the station, as the Wainwrights were, offered their last congratulations of the day and departed in wagons and buggies, on horseback and even on foot. Emma, plainly pleased to have Rachel for a stepmother as well as a teacher, was to board with the McCaffreys for a while, so the newlyweds would have the rooms over the saloon to themselves.

They walked through the sultry darkness together, Trey and Rachel, her hand clasped firmly in his. When they reached the bottom of the rear stairs, he suddenly swept her up into his arms and carried her. Reaching the door, he pushed it open with one foot, and then they were inside.

Rachel, who had been so cavalier before, was suddenly nervous. Teasing Trey at the party had been one thing, being alone with him in a darkened room, where they would soon make love for the first time, was quite another. Her heart began to race with a strange combination of anticipation and pure terror.

Trey kissed her, so deeply and so thoroughly that she stumbled when he set her on her feet and might have fallen if she hadn't reached out and grasped hold of something that turned out to be a bedpost, when he struck a match to a lamp wick and she could see her surroundings.

She stared at the magnificent carved bed in amazement. She hadn't noticed it when she had last visited the Hargreaves home, that day she'd taken tea and cookies with Emma and Trey, but then, she hadn't been out of the general living area.

Trey apparently read her mind. Shedding his coat, he nodded toward the lovely piece of furniture. "Pretty grand, isn't it?" he said, with a flashing grin. "I had it sent over from Choteau, and if you don't think I had a devil of a time keeping you from hearing about it, you'd best think again."

Rachel felt the mattress with a tentative push of one hand and found it firm but very inviting. For a major piece of furniture to arrive at Springwater without her seeing or getting word of it was indeed a remarkable thing. The arrival of the stagecoach was an event, let alone that of a freight wagon. "It's . . . lovely."

Trey unfastened his collar and tossed it aside. "Not so lovely as you are," he said, and his voice sounded husky, masculine—hungry. He approached Rachel and, standing before her, slipped his fingers into her hair and let it down, disregarding the many pins that tinkled to the floor. He kissed her again, and the contact left her drunk with wanting, actually swaying on her feet. On some remote level of her mind, she was wondering if she really had made love with Langdon, or only imagined that she had, for this was something altogether different.

When the kiss was over, he ran his mouth lightly along the edge of Rachel's jaw, igniting a thousand achy little fires under her flesh. "Do you know when I fell in love with you?" he asked, in a gruff whisper.

"W-When?" Rachel managed. She was fairly crackling with sensation by then, and hardly able to keep from flinging herself at Trey like a wanton.

"When you poked your head out of that stage window, with that stupid feather on your hat bobbing in the wind, and inquired if I was an outlaw."

Rachel might have laughed, if she hadn't been in a state of sweet agony. "I fell in love with you," she said, "when you pulled me out of the coach and up onto your horse."

He nibbled at her mouth again, fairly driving her wild. "What took us so long to get from then to now?" he asked, unbuttoning the bodice of her borrowed dress, smoothing away the lovely old fabric, revealing her camisole and petticoat. He put his palms over her breasts, holding them gently but at the same time claiming them, and Rachel moaned as her nipples pressed themselves against him.

"Don't make me wait," she pleaded.

He lowered his suspenders, unbuttoned his shirt, took it off, and tossed it aside, all with maddening slowness. "I won't," he said, "not the first time, anyway. I don't have that kind of patience."

Rachel laid her hands to his chest, fingers splayed, and gloried in the feel of his warm, muscular flesh, the mat of dark hair, the hardening of his nipples. While they were kissing, he unlaced her camisole, baring her breasts, and fondled them until Rachel was half frantic to be taken.

Trey finished undressing her, then undressed himself, and eased her backward, onto the new bed, shipped all the way from Choteau. Onto the bed where their children would be conceived and born, where they themselves would die, one and then the other, when they were very, very old.

He stretched out beside her, took long, leisurely suckle at her breasts, and then moved over her, keeping most of his weight suspended on his forearms and elbows. She could see him plainly in the lamplight, though it was dim, see the love and the passion in his eyes, and the question.

She nodded, and he parted her legs gently, with a motion of one knee. She felt him at the entrance to her body, hard and impossibly large, and for a moment her eyes widened and she was afraid.

He paused, waited.

Rachel nodded again, and he was inside her, in a single deep, smooth thrust; she felt herself expand to accommodate him, felt the breath flee her lungs as she was swept up on a wave of desire so high, so hot, so intense that her reason was left behind, spinning in a tidepool.

She cried his name, and scraped his back with her fingernails, and he moved faster, and deeper, ever deeper, until they were both on fire. Then, in a long, undulating flash, the world ended in a cataclysm of fire and light and ferocious pleasure that had them both shouting in release.

When it was over, and their bodies were still at last, and spent, Trey fell beside Rachel, gasping and holding her tightly against his chest. They were both damp with exertion, and she could feel his heart pounding beneath her cheek.

"If I'd known just how good that was going to be," he said, when he found his breath, "I believe I would have been scared."

Rachel laughed, though her eyes were brimming with tears—tears of homecoming, of joy, of restored hope. "I thought I was dying," she said, in all honesty. "I couldn't see, I couldn't hear or think—all I could do was feel."

He rolled onto his side and kissed her, very lightly,

but with the promise of much more. "Give me a few minutes," he said, "and I'll take you back up there, to the other side of the stars."

She stretched, wondering when her melted limbs would be solid again. "Maybe we'd better wait a little while," she suggested, "just until all my pulses settle down."

He bent his head, took her nipple in his mouth and drew it into a primal dance with the tip of his tongue, causing her to moan and arch her back slightly. "Not a chance," he said, after long moments of brazen enjoyment. "Tonight, you're the student, and I'm the teacher, and the lessons have only begun."

Rachel whimpered. She felt as though she'd just been hurled to the top of a mountain and then sent careening down again, and she was still wobbly at the knees. Now he was telling her that there were still more sweeping pleasures ahead. "Suppose I can't bear it?" she fretted.

He found the hollow of her throat and nibbled there. "Oh, you can bear it, all right," he promised, and proceeded to prove it. And prove it. And prove it again. By the time they finally slept, well toward morning, Rachel was exhausted, but she dreamed. She dreamed of silver-eyed babies and a mail-order house with a white picket fence out front and flowers growing in the yard. She dreamed of Emma, grown and beautiful, wearing a wedding dress of her own, and of a busy, thriving town, and a brick schoolhouse, and a white church with a belltower.

In Trey's arms, in his bed, it was so easy to dream.

* * *

Rachel was nervous the day school started; her pupils watched her with mischievous eyes and whispered behind their hands when they thought she wasn't looking. She couldn't imagine what they were discussing, and wasn't sure she wanted to know, but order had to be restored.

She clapped her hands together twice, and sharply. "That will be enough giggling and talking!" she said, in her best schoolmarm tones.

Marcus Kildare waved one hand in the air, and Rachel called on him to speak, even though she knew he was up to something. "Emma says she's going to get a baby brother or sister soon. Is that true?"

Emma folded her arms and lifted her chin, her eyes bright with certainty.

Rachel felt color flood her face, but she did not allow her shoulders to droop, nor did she avert her gaze. As it happened, she suspected that she was already in the family way, but she had told no one but Trey and June-bug. The physical part of her marriage was intense, but Emma couldn't have known that, since she was staying with the McCaffreys until the mail-order house arrived and was set up.

"Mr. Hargreaves and I hope to have a child soon, yes."

Emma looked vindicated. She turned to Marcus Kildare and put out her tongue. He responded in kind.

"Enough," Rachel said. "We are here to learn." With that, she began her first day of classes. When school let out at three o'clock, she made a point of not hurrying across the street and around to the rear door of the Brimstone Saloon, lest that raise undue speculation.

Trey was standing at the stove when she came in, sipping coffee, and he'd already turned the bedclothes back. "Hello, Mrs. Hargreaves," he said. "How was your day?"

Rachel closed the door and lowered the latch. "Long," she answered, but she wasn't the least bit tired and they both knew it. She started to undress, but Trey crossed the room and stopped her, taking both her wrists in his hands and bending his head to kiss her. It was a ravenous exchange, no tamer on Rachel's part than his.

"Just let me get out of these clothes," she murmured, barely able to speak, when he withdrew his mouth.

"No," he said, and raised her skirts to unfasten her drawers and peel them down over her hips. She stepped out of them, never looking away from his eyes, and he sat down and drew her with him, causing her to sit astraddle of him. She flung back her head in an agony of exultation when he unfastened his trousers and then entered her, filled her.

He opened her bodice then, to tongue and suckle her breasts, all the while raising and lowering her along the length of him, his hands firm and strong on her hips. They climaxed together, and Rachel fell forward, to let her head rest against his shoulder. She could still feel him pulsing within her.

"How long can we keep this up?" she asked, when she could manage even those simple words.

"Oh," he drawled, "for a long, long time, Mrs. Hargreaves. Maybe forever." With that, he stood, carried her to the bed, and made love to her again, even more thoroughly than before, and far more slowly.

Neither of them heard the stagecoach thundering into town, right on schedule, the driver shouting, the hooves of the horses pounding on the hard ground, the wheels squeaking as if all the demons of hell were in close pursuit. They had other concerns, Mr. and Mrs. Trey Hargreaves, and for them, the outside world was a very distant place.

Savannah

For Kate Collins,
always gentle, always sweet, always *there*.
Thanks.

CHAPTER

∽ 1 ∼

Summer 1875

THE GIRL MOANING on the opposite stagecoach
seat was painfully young, by Savannah's astute reckoning, not more than seventeen. She was probably
very pretty under normal circumstances, with her
thick chestnut-colored hair and wide-set violet eyes,
but for now, with her belly swollen nearly to the
bursting point under the front of that tattered calico
dress, and her face contorted in an agonizing effort
not to scream, she just looked small and scared and
very much alone.

Savannah nudged the dark-haired, beard-stubbled
man slouched on the seat beside her, gazing out the
window as if he were trying to will himself away to
someplace far from the interior of that smotheringly
hot, cramped, and bouncing stagecoach. He wasn't
much past thirty, but he might have been
Methuselah's older brother if you went by the look in
his eyes. "Do something," she commanded, in an
impatient whisper. **She** knew he was a doctor of some

sort, for all that he'd spent most of his time in the smokier recesses of the Hell-bent Saloon, having turned up in Choteau a week or so before. He'd promptly lost his horse in a faro game, and Savannah had taken it as a bad omen when he'd suddenly boarded that same stage. She'd planned on having it to herself, at least as far as Springwater station.

He smelled of whiskey, old cigar smoke, and a soul-deep sorrow, his dark hair was rumpled, and he was sorely in need of a shave, as well as clean clothes, a decent meal or two, and a good night's sleep. He'd taken the seat across from Savannah and kept his thoughts to himself, at least until the driver had stopped the rig somewhere along the trail—quite literally in the middle of nowhere—to pick up the pregnant girl. He'd moved to Savannah's side then, with a desultory sort of courtesy, to make room for the newcomer.

Savannah nudged him again, for she was used to having her orders obeyed, and promptly. "Did you hear me?" she whispered, though there was, of course, no hope that the girl wouldn't hear as well, jammed in knee-to-knee with her fellow passengers the way she was. "This child needs your help!"

"I'm not that kind of doctor," he ground out, with a long breath. He carried a time-beaten medical bag at his feet, his only visible baggage, a flag of his profession, though his clothes were sorry indeed—scuffed boots, Army issue no doubt, dark trousers worn to a shine, a once-white shirt of good linen, and black leather suspenders. He had especially fine teeth,

Savannah noticed, for the first time, and, under all that self-absorption and debauchery, his features were aristocratic ones, finely carved. His jawline was strong and square, his mouth sensual and expressive.

"I don't care if you're a *horse* doctor," Savannah snapped back, ready to elbow him again, and with a lot more force, if necessary. In fact, she was quite prepared to open her beaded drawstring bag and ferret out her derringer, should matters come to such a pass, and insist that he do his duty as a physician. "Either you look after this girl or you'll have me to deal with."

"She's going to have a baby," he answered, as though this clever diagnosis should suffice to settle the entire matter once and for all.

Savannah might have struck him with her derringer-weighted bag, if there hadn't been such a dire need for him to remain conscious. "Jupiter and Zeus," she swore, "any fool could see that!" She paused, trying for a semblance of diplomacy. "She needs some help getting it done, Doc. And we're all she's got at the moment. You and me."

The girl sank her teeth into her lower lip, gasping and clutching her protruding stomach with a pair of grubby hands. She looked as though she'd just come from weeding some vegetable patch or mucking out a pigpen, and she didn't smell a whole lot better.

The doctor sighed and sat forward. "What's your name?" he asked, with a sort of gruff gentleness that raised Savannah's opinion of him, though only a little, and briefly.

"Mir-Miranda," she said. "Miranda Leebrook."

He reached down for his bag, lifted it onto his lap, and rummaged inside. Taking out a bottle and a bit of surprisingly pristine cloth, he doused his hands with a pungent chemical of some sort, and wiped them clean. "Where did you come from? I understood there weren't many homesteads out this far."

It seemed to Savannah that Miranda attempted a smile, though it might have been a grimace of pain. "My pa and me had words, and he put me out to make my own way. We was headed toward Butte in the wagon, me and Lorelei and him."

"What about the father of this baby?" the doctor asked crisply, but without judgment or rancor. "Where's he?"

Tears glistened in Miranda's expressive pansy-purple eyes. "He's a long time gone," she said. "Won't never be back, neither."

Savannah's heart constricted at this, but she was used to hearing stories, all sorts of stories, and she'd learned a long time ago that it didn't pay to go wading too deep into other folks' troubles. She said nothing, but simply pounded hard on the roof of the coach with the handle of her parasol.

The driver brought the coach to a bone-jostling stop, while the conversation between doctor and patient continued, quiet and calm on his part, breathless on hers, and interwoven with frantic cries.

A broad, dusty face, rimmed in an aura of ginger hair, appeared at the window opening. "There a problem back here, ma'am?" the young driver asked.

Savannah held her temper. "Yes," she said, putting

a fine point on the word nonetheless, and aiming for a soft spot. "One of us seems to be giving birth. The doctor here is prepared to deliver the child, but it would certainly help if the coach weren't rolling and pitching the whole time."

The driver looked regretful, and tugged at the brim of his disreputable hat. "We ain't but three miles from the station, ma'am. It's just the other side of Willow Creek." He glanced in a westerly direction, tracking the sun. "We got to keep goin'. It'll be dark soon, and that's no time for decent folks to be out and about."

Savannah was beyond exasperation. "Can't you see that this girl—?"

The young man shook his head and settled his hat again. "I'm sorry, ma'am. Miss June-bug McCaffrey, up ahead at Springwater, she'll take good care of the whole matter. We got to press on." With that, he was gone, the coach bouncing on its springs as he climbed back into the box to take up the reins again.

The doctor was already engaged in a thorough if awkward examination of his patient. Savannah looked away quickly, but not quickly enough to spare herself a burning flush of embarrassment. For all her reputation, she was not a loose woman, and she had the appropriate sensibilities.

"Can't you say something to the driver?" Savannah demanded. She had little to contribute at the moment, but for her opinions, which seemed unwelcome.

The physician shrugged one sturdy shoulder. "Sounds to me like he's got his mind made up," he said, and gently covered Miranda's legs with her skirts again. He got out the chemical and another cloth and began to wash his hands once more. "Besides, I think you've said enough for all of us."

"Is my baby going to be all right?" Miranda asked, in a tiny voice.

He pulled the stethoscope from around his neck and tossed it back into the ancient bag. Then he flashed a smile, so unexpectedly, ferociously charming that Savannah was taken aback, though for just the merest moment. "I'd wager a good deal that that child is just fine," he said. "Eight pounds, maybe ten, with the constitution of a mule."

Savannah recalled the perfectly good horse this man had lost at faro and refrained, for Miranda's sake, from pointing out that wagering was clearly not his greatest talent. The stagecoach lurched forward again, pitching and rolling over the rocky ground, nearly sending both Savannah and the doctor hurtling across the small gap between seats onto the girl.

"Can we make it as far as the stagecoach station?" Savannah hissed, though there was, of course, no hope that Miranda hadn't heard.

He raised one dark eyebrow. "We can," he said, "but there might be four of us by the time we arrive."

Panic roared into Savannah like floodwaters into a gulch, swirling and splashing and tearing things up by their roots. In her eventful lifetime, she'd helped her father, a barber and erstwhile undertaker in Kansas City, Missouri, to remove everything from common splinters to bullets, arrows, and buckshot from human flesh, and her grandmother had been a midwife of sorts, full of tales and legends. For all that, the idea of actually *witnessing* childbirth made her light-headed.

She swayed slightly, and pressed the fingertips of her right hand to one temple.

The doctor's face darkened. "I'm fresh out of smelling salts," he told her, in a sharp whisper. "So don't you go falling apart on me."

Savannah was incensed at the suggestion, even though there had been some merit to it. She stiffened her spine and shot him a look fit to pierce a dartboard. "I am quite all right, thank you," she said.

Miranda, perspiring profusely now, began to whimper. "It hurts," she said. "It hurts real bad."

He shoved a hand through his mussed hair. "Yep," he said, resigned. "I imagine it does."

Savannah was once again seized by the desire to strike the man with something heavy; instead, she moved over to sit beside Miranda, draping one arm around the poor little creature's thin and quivering shoulders. "We'll be at the stagecoach station soon," she said, and though she was speaking gently for the young woman's sake, she was gazing at the doctor, and she knew her eyes were snapping with fury. "There'll be a nice clean bed for you to lie down in. Everything will be all right, you'll see."

"Where were you headed, anyway?" asked the doctor, ignoring Savannah's displeasure to watch Miranda's face with narrowed eyes.

"No place in particular," Miranda gasped out, her

back arching, seemingly of its own volition. "I reckon me and the babe would've died out there, if it weren't for this stage coming along just when it did."

Savannah spared a bitter thought or two for Miranda's uncaring father, but the present situation was far too desperate to allow for much distraction.

"What about your mother?" the doctor pressed. "Didn't she try to intercede for you?"

"I don't guess I know what that means," Miranda confessed, pressing each word, separate and distinct, between tightly clenched teeth. "For somebody to 'intercede,' I mean. Anyway, my ma's been dead a long while now. The woman my pa took up with— her name's Lorelei—doesn't have much use for me."

"Take it easy," he said, giving the young woman both his hands, which she squeezed fiercely against the pain. "Breathe slowly and deeply. We're going to look after you, Miss—er—well, this lady and I."

"It would comfort me some to know your right names," Miranda said.

"I'm Savannah Rigbey," Savannah responded gently, wishing there were something, anything, she could do to ease the girl's suffering.

"Parrish," the doctor added, and though his tone was cordial enough, the glance he spared Savannah was a mite on the grudging side. "Prescott Parrish."

The coach hurtled downhill, careening wildly from side to side, fit to fling open both doors and toss them out; and then it splashed into axle-deep water. Savannah peered out at Willow Creek with alarm, half-blinded by the late-day light dancing on the water.

She might have prayed then, if she hadn't given up on God a long time before. It wasn't deep, that stream, but she had a swift and terrifying vision of the coach turning over, trapping all of them inside.

"We're almost there," Dr. Parrish said, while the girl continued to grip his hands.

Miranda flung back her head and shrieked like a mountain cat. Her teeth were bared and she writhed, as leanly muscular as any lioness. When she got her breath, she cried out to God for help and mercy, and Savannah and the doctor exchanged yet another look, not heated this time, but somber.

The team scrambled up the opposite bank of the creek, dragging the half-rolling, half-floating coach behind. The ride was so rough after that that Savannah half-expected the baby to shake loose of Miranda's insides and bounce right out onto the narrow floor.

The mother-to-be alternated between screaming her lungs out and making a pitiful, keening sound, something like a long, unbroken sob. Her colorless dress was nearly wet through now, though when Savannah gave Parrish a questioning glance, he shook his head.

"Water hasn't broken," he said.

Savannah hoped that was a good sign, but she didn't think so. She recognized the quiet worry in Prescott Parrish's dark eyes, even if Miranda couldn't.

At last, at last, the driver shouted something to the horses, a coarse and unintelligible roar, and the brakes screeched against the iron-rimmed wheels, grinding the coach to a halt in a great surging billow of gritty, yellow-brown dust.

"Springwaaaater staaation!" he called out, as though there might be some confusion on the part of his passengers.

Dr. Parrish thrust the door open and jumped down, pulling Miranda off the seat and into his arms. "Bring the bag!" he commanded, and Savannah complied, hurrying after him through the roiling dust.

A tall man with very dark hair and kindly eyes awaited them on the porch of the station house, arms folded. "Best get her bedded down right quick," he said. "Straight through the dining room, at the far end of the hall."

Parrish nodded and strode on, and Savannah followed, coughing from the dust. Springwater station was her final destination, for the moment, since Trey Hargreaves and his new wife were already occupying the space over the Brimstone Saloon. She would rent a room and stay on here until she and her business partner could work out some other arrangement.

"Jacob McCaffrey," said the tall man when she was inside. He offered a large, work-gnarled hand in greeting.

"Savannah Rigbey," she responded, watching out of the corner of her eye as Parrish disappeared down the indicated hallway. "I understand your wife might be able to assist the doctor—"

McCaffrey shook his head. "She's on the mountain, my June-bug, tendin' to Granny Johnson. The old lady's laid up with rheumatiz."

Savannah felt her knees go weak. "Isn't there someone——?"

"Miss Rigbey!" Parrish bellowed, from somewhere in the back of the station. "Kindly get your bustle in here!"

She looked desperately up at Mr. McCaffrey, but he merely shrugged.

"Jupiter and Zeus," Savannah muttered, unpinning her hat and setting it aside, then shaking the dust from her skirts as best she could. "I'm coming!" she called back and, after straightening her spine and squaring her shoulders, she marched toward the distinctly unsettling sounds of childbirth, bringing the doctor's bag along with her.

Parrish had laid the girl on the pristine sheets of a wide bed, and was shoving up his sleeves as Savannah entered the room. He didn't spare her so much as a glance. "Get me hot water, and all the clean cloth you can find," he commanded, his voice a brusque bark.

Had things been different, Savannah would have told him what to do with his orders, but this was the exception. Whatever her private views might be regarding Parrish, he *was* a doctor, and therefore badly needed at the moment. She set the bag down within his easy reach and hurried out to obey.

The baby, a strapping boy with bunched fists and pumping feet, was delivered less than half an hour later. Parrish cut the cord competently, washed and bundled the infant, and handed him to his breathless, beaming mother.

"He's right handsome, isn't he?" she said.

Savannah, still struck by the messy splendor of the experience, couldn't help wondering what would become of the two of them, Miranda and her brand-new baby, alone in a remote place like this, with no money and no prospects. She blinked back uncharacteristic tears and averted her eyes.

"I told you he'd be big as a mule," said the doctor, scrubbing his hands at the basin by then. He nodded to Savannah, indicating that he wanted the linens changed on Miranda's bed, and she proceeded to comply, skillfully managing the task without disturbing mother and baby overmuch.

He went out then, without another word, and Savannah supposed he'd board the next stagecoach, come the morning, and move on to wherever he'd been headed in the first place. She certainly wouldn't miss him, but she was grateful that he'd delivered Miranda's baby, however unwillingly, and she wished him well.

When both Miranda and the baby were sleeping comfortably, Savannah left the room and asked to be directed to her own chamber, which turned out to be a small nook behind the kitchen stove. Two buckets of hot water awaited her there, along with her few bags, and she undressed behind a scarred folding screen and washed herself from head to foot, then put on fresh clothes, a blue bombazine skirt and white shirtwaist, deceptively prim. Gazing into the small, cracked mirror affixed to the inside wall, she arranged her mass of red-gold hair in a neat cloud around her face, and pinched some color into her wan cheeks. For all her effort, her light blue eyes revealed her weariness, and a lot more besides.

She made herself leave the tiny room and join Mr. McCaffrey and Dr. Parrish at the table nearest the fireplace. They were drinking coffee and talking in low tones, but when Savannah appeared, they both stood, McCaffrey readily, with the easy, practiced grace of a gentleman, Parrish causing the bench legs to scrape against the floor as he thrust himself to his feet, a moment too late for good manners.

"Evenin'," Jacob McCaffrey said. Only then did she notice the fair-haired boy and the beautiful Indian girl playing checkers on the hearth nearby. Both of them looked up at her in mild speculation.

"Good evening," Savannah said. She played at being a lady whenever she could, but it was a facade, with no substance behind it, and she suspected everyone else in the room knew that as well as she did, even the children. She'd stepped off the narrow path—or, more properly, been dragged off—a long time before.

"Toby," McCaffrey said, in his rumbling, summer-thunder voice, "fetch Miss Rigbey some of them dumplin's and a little chicken. I reckon she's hungry by now."

Savannah hadn't eaten since the night before, having left Choteau very early that morning, well before the woman at the rooming house where she'd stayed since her arrival in the territory was willing to serve breakfast, but she found she had no appetite.

She shook her head. "I'll just brew a pot of tea, if that's all right."

The Indian girl scrambled to her feet. "I'll do that for you," she said, with cheerful resolution. "You must be my pa's partner."

Savannah smiled, finally realizing that this was Trey's daughter, the child he had spoken of so often during their long association. "Yes," she said. "And you're Emma!"

Emma nodded. "I don't think he's expecting you," she said. "He got himself married a while back, you know. A year ago last spring."

"I had word that he meant to take a wife," Savannah said, well aware that Parrish and the stationmaster, and probably the boy, too, were watching her with new interest. "I hope they'll be very happy together."

Emma was intent on ladling water into a big kettle with a spout and setting it on to boil. With the easy skill of a grown woman, she built up the fire and adjusted the damper. "They're happy, all right," she said. "Pa's going to build us a big house, the kind you send off for. The boards and windows and things are supposed to get here any day now. Then we'll all live together, me and Pa and Rachel, like a real family." Her smile broadened. "We got us a mortgage!"

Savannah laid a hand on the girl's shoulder and smiled gently. "You must miss living with your father," she said.

Emma looked up at her with shining eyes. "I don't mind staying here. Me and Toby, we play checkers most all the time, and do our schoolwork together. Besides, I see my pa every day, and Rachel's our teacher—she's my stepmother, but I have to call her 'Mrs. Hargreaves' at school—so I don't get lonesome for her, either." She lowered her voice confidentially. "Except sometimes late at night, when I can't get to sleep."

The men had gone back to their quiet talk, making Savannah feel less self-conscious. "I'm sure it won't be long," she said to Emma, "until you're all together again in your big new house."

Emma's brow crumpled with concern. "That lady in there was screaming a lot, while she was having her baby. It must have hurt something powerful."

Savannah saw no point in lying. "That's so," she admitted. "But it's over now, and she's got the child to show for her pains." For all the good that would do a scrap of a girl, alone and penniless in the wilds of Montana Territory, she added to herself.

"Miss Rachel—I think she's going to have a baby, too," Emma said, in that same confidential undertone. "I don't reckon me or my pa could stand seeing her hurt like that, though."

Savannah gave the child a gentle squeeze around the shoulders. "Don't you fret," she said. "It's a natural thing. Your stepmother will be just fine, and so will the rest of you." She couldn't imagine what made her speak with such authority, given her utter lack of experience with such matters, except that she liked Trey's daughter and didn't want her to worry.

"You'd better have yourself some of these chicken

and dumplings," Emma said wisely, lifting the lid of a cast-iron pot and peering inside. "Jacob made them, but they aren't halfways bad."

Savannah laughed, more relaxed than before. "Maybe I'm a little hungry after all," she admitted, and soon she was seated at one of the tables, far from the men, consuming a plateful of food. When she'd washed her dish and utensils and put them away, she went in to check on Miranda and the baby.

The girl was awake, admiring her little son, and her eyes shone with a queer mingling of pride and sorrow when she looked at Savannah. "He's the image of his daddy, Jack Worgan."

Savannah drew a deep breath and let it out slowly, searching for words. In her line of work, she'd heard just about every story there was, and she figured that Worgan was either dead, married, or just plain gone. She had a personal rule against prying, so all she said was "That's nice."

Tears pooled along Miranda's lower lashes. "I don't have the first idea what we're going to do, my baby and me. I been asking God for help right along, but there sure hasn't been any clap of thunder nor burning bush."

Had she been a religious woman, which she wasn't, Savannah might have pointed out that some folks would construe the stagecoach's coming along when it had as an answer to prayer. The same might have been said of Dr. Parrish's help, too, slow as he'd been to give it, and of the waiting shelter and safety of Springwater station. "We'll think of something," she said, and it was bravado, pure and simple, for Savannah knew full well just how limited a woman's choices really were.

There was teaching, and even if that appointment hadn't been held by Trey's wife, Rachel, Miranda clearly wasn't qualified. There was marriage—prospects seemed a bit scant, Springwater being smack in the middle of the wilderness—or household service, which wasn't so different from being a wife, except that a body could expect to be paid for her drudgery. No grand houses around, either, in need of servants. The last choice was whoring, in all its many forms. That was how most people saw Savannah's way of earning a living, as a form of prostitution, even though she'd never in her life slept with a man for money.

"I can work hard as any man," Miranda said anxiously. "If somebody'll just give me half the chance—"

Savannah looked away. She could have offered the girl a job of work herself, entertaining the men at the Brimstone Saloon—but of course *that* would be no favor. And what would become of the child, growing up in such a place? She forced herself to meet Miranda's gaze again. "Let me make a crib for that baby of yours," she said. Then she removed a drawer from the bureau, set it carefully across the seats of two straight-backed chairs, and padded the inside with a blanket. That done, she gently took the sleeping infant from Miranda's arms and laid him down in the improvised cradle. "What are you going to call him?" she asked, hoping, for a reason she couldn't explain, that it wouldn't be "Jack," after his absent father.

"I want to give him a good, solid, Bible name," Miranda said, settling into the fluffy feather mattress with a yawn. "Isaiah, maybe. Or Ezekiel."

Savannah smiled. "Shall I bring you a plate? Mr. McCaffrey made chicken and dumplings."

Miranda shook her head and yawned again. "No, thanks, ma'am," she said. "More than anything, I want to sleep a spell."

"A good idea," Savannah agreed gently, and started toward the door.

"Wait," Miranda said quickly, and with a note of soft urgency in her voice.

Savannah stopped. The room was filled with twilight now; soon, it would be pitch dark. She expected the girl to ask for a lantern.

"I'm grateful," Miranda said. "To you and to the doc and to that stagecoach driver, too. I guess me and little Isaiah or Ezekiel would be in a grievous plight by now, if it weren't for you folks."

Savannah merely nodded, not trusting herself to speak, and slipped out, closing the door softly behind her.

"You look mighty sorrowful," Mr. McCaffrey remarked, when she turned to find him leaning against the mantel of the big fireplace, drawing on a pipe. There was no sign of the children or, for that matter, of Dr. Parrish. No doubt he'd already struck out for the Brimstone Saloon, there to spend whatever money he might have left on liquor and games of chance.

"I'm worried about Miranda," she admitted, though not until she was well away from the doorway leading to the hall, lest the girl should overhear. "She's got no folks to look after her, no man either."

"I kinda figured that," McCaffrey remarked. "I've got an idea my June-bug will be able to come up with a solution or two, though. She has a way of makin' places for lost sheep. You may have noticed we've got a stray or two around here already."

Savannah sagged onto one of the benches and rested her elbows on the tabletop, propping her chin in her palms. "Emma and the boy—Toby?"

"I wouldn't consider Emma a stray, exactly. Her papa loves her somethin' fierce. But Toby, now, he was alone in the world, for all practical intents and purposes, until we took him in. And then there's Christabel—she's with June-bug, lookin' after Granny. She's got one lame foot, Christabel has, and a heart that's bigger than she is. Anyhow, I don't imagine Miss Miranda and her baby will be that much more trouble."

"You mean, you'll just let them stay here, indefinitely?"

"I don't see what else we can do. Wouldn't be right nor proper to turn them out, after all."

Savannah dashed at her eyes with the back of one hand, much heartened by the man's kindness. She hadn't seen much of that kind of charity in her own travels, had almost given up hope that it existed. "Thank you, Mr. McCaffrey," she said, with a sniffle. She was just tired, she reasoned to herself, that was all. She'd long since corralled and tamed all her emotions—it was safer not to care too much about anything or anyone.

"Jacob," he corrected her, with the slightest shadow of a smile. She hadn't known him long, but it was clear that when Jacob smiled, it was an occasion in itself.

She put out her hand, as though they were meeting for the first time. "Savannah, then," she insisted, and sniffled again.

He set the pipe on the mantel and came to sit down across the table from her. "You don't look much like a saloon-keepin' woman," he observed. "More like a schoolmarm, or the lady of a big, fancy house."

Coming from anyone else, the remark might have stung, but Savannah knew Jacob was merely curious. Although she suspected he could be stern when the situation called for it, his was a benign and gentle spirit. She heaved a sigh. "My story is a long one, Jacob, and it's complicated. I'm not sure I'm ready to tell it just yet."

"That's fine," Jacob answered easily. The station door opened just then, spilling a shadowy chill across the smooth plank floor. "We all got our secrets."

Dr. Parrish came in, looking sober if no neater than before. He pushed the door closed behind him. What secrets, Savannah wondered, what scandals and sorrows, had made him what he was?

CHAPTER

2

T HE FLICKERING LIGHT of the evening fire made
Savannah Rigbey look more like a ministering angel
than what Pres knew her to be—a saloon-keeper and
quite possibly something a whole lot less respectable.
She'd handled herself admirably well during the de-
livery earlier—it had been untidy work, though tame
compared with what he was used to—and he'd
noticed her pallor and the grimly determined set of
her chin and shoulders. Every time the girl, Miranda,
had screamed, she'd flinched, as though feeling an
echo of the pain in her own body.

Now, coming upon her unexpectedly, in the main
room of the stagecoach station, he thought she
seemed smaller than before, more fragile. And, somehow, lit from within.

"Evenin'," said McCaffrey, sparing him a nod.

Pres thrust splayed fingers through his hair and
then inclined his head in response to the other man's
sparse greeting. He wasn't drunk, though the inside of

his head still felt scraped and hollow from the last bout of elbow-bending in Choteau, but all of the sudden he was aware of his seedy appearance in a way that had not troubled him for a very long time. He yearned for a bath, a shave, fresh clothes, and a place in polite company.

"Didn't see where you had any baggage to speak of, Doc," McCaffrey observed, while Savannah just sat there, at one of the long tables, watching Pres in silent speculation. "You just passin' through, or meaning to light right here at Springwater? Town's growin'. Folks have bought land for a newspaper office and a general store, and the Territorial Governor has promised to appoint a U.S. Marshal to keep the peace. We could use a doctor, too."

Pres had just come from the spring that gave the place its name; he'd gone for a walk after seeing to the girl and her baby, to stretch his legs and calm his nerves. As far as he was concerned, Springwater didn't qualify as a town, with just a stagecoach station, a schoolhouse and a saloon to call its own, but he saw no point in saying so. He broke the trance that had held him in place, just inside the doorway, and shook his head, proceeding toward the cookstove at the far end of the room.

"I'm moving on with the next stage," he said, taking an enamel mug from a shelf and filling it with strong black coffee from a pot on the back of the range. He'd know the place he was meant to wind up when he got to it and, once there, he expected to settle in and drink himself to death, swamped by his own demons. Matter of fact, he'd been slowly killing himself for a long time, and most days it seemed he was succeeding.

Turning around, mug in hand and raised halfway to his mouth, he caught Savannah looking at him, though her expression was unreadable in that light. She glanced away quickly, if not quickly enough. "I'm not the sort of doctor you need, anyway," he felt obliged to add. An odd thing in itself, that inclination to expand on the matter of his general insufficiency, as he'd long since decided that his life, his preferences, and his problems were nobody's business but his own.

McCaffrey arched a dark, bushy eyebrow. "We ain't real choosy, to tell you the truth," he said. "If you're better with horses than people, that's all right, too."

Pres laughed at that, and the response was so unpracticed, so unfamiliar, that it came out as a sort of rasp. This time, he saw a quick, glittering flash of annoyance in Savannah's eyes; it pleased him to know he'd nettled her, if only a little, though he wasn't sure why. "I am—or was—a surgeon," he said, drawn into the circle of firelight, almost against his will. He took a seat across the table from Savannah, while Jacob McCaffrey remained standing, one elbow raised and braced against the pinewood mantel.

Savannah spoke at last. "You 'were' a surgeon?" she asked; her voice was soft, but not pitying. "What happened?"

He saw it all again, the blood, the mangled limbs and scattered parts, heard the canon fire and the shrieks. Worst of all, he heard the pleas, for mercy, for death, for an end to the pain. The pleas he couldn't grant. Some of the coffee spilled over as he set the mug down. "The war," he ground out. "The war happened."

"We lost two sons at Chattanooga," McCaffrey said. "Will and Wesley were their names. Twins." He paused, and his voice seemed to come from long ago and far away. "They were good boys. Friend of ours saw them fall, one and then the other. They were born together, and they died together. I guess that's fittin', but it like to have broke their mother's heart, and I don't believe I'll ever put the grievin' entirely behind me, either." The big man sighed and then returned to himself. For him, Pres knew, the story constituted an oration. "I reckon they're buried in unmarked graves, but at least they're in Tennessee."

Savannah was watching McCaffrey with her heart in her face, and Pres was watching her. He couldn't seem to help it. She looked so different in her prim, schoolmarmish clothes, somehow even more alluring than in the bright, flouncing silks, satins, bangles, and feathers she'd worn to sing and peddle drinks at the Hell-bent Saloon, back in Choteau. He wondered what sort of past had brought her to such a present.

She was a soiled dove, a lady of the evening, Pres reminded himself, and he was a used-up, throw-away drunk, friendless, and literally down to his last nickel. What a sorry pair they made, misfits, both of them. Lost souls.

Again, he shoved a hand through his hair.

"I'd better show you where to bed down before you

fall over," Jacob said. "You want any supper? Hot water, maybe?"

Pres couldn't have forced down so much as a bite of food, but the offer of clean water had a distinct appeal. "A bath wouldn't hurt me," he allowed, and caught Savannah with a look of devout agreement on her face. He almost laughed again, but he was too tired, too dispirited, too long out of practice, and his throat still hurt from the last time. For a moment, he wanted very much to stay in Springwater, to find himself again, to build a simple country practice, like the one his father had had, at home in Maine. He'd found a semblance of peace, standing by that spring and watching the first stars rise against the wide sky, had even thought he might be able to lay himself down and sleep through a whole night, here in this quiet place. A grand illusion, all of that, he'd reminded himself then, as he did now. It was the waking nightmares that were real, the screaming and incessant carnage, the black flies and the putrid stenches. He had to keep moving, stay a step ahead of the memories, lest they pull him under like quicksand.

"Come along, then," McCaffrey said, matter-of-factly. "I'll see to the water and find you some fresh clothes for tomorrow."

Pres finished his coffee, stood, and carried the cup over to the cast-iron sink, near the cookstove. That done, he followed the stationmaster to a small room at the back, hardly bigger than a closet, but blessedly clean, with the distant sound of the springs coming in through an open window. The bed was narrow, and covered in an ancient, neatly pieced quilt with a date—1847—and a partial Bible verse embroidered in the center panel. *Seek ye first the kingdom of God . . .*

"I don't have the money to pay for this room," Pres said, moved to confession by the other man's quiet generosity, "or for the bathwater and soap, either. I've got five cents and a stagecoach ticket to my name and I need them both."

"I didn't figure you was real flush," Jacob replied, obviously a master of understatement. "We got water and soap aplenty, and the room's just settin' here, empty as the Lord's tomb, so you might as well be in it as out there in the barn or on the ground someplace. I'll fetch the tub while you're making yourself comfortable."

Comfortable. When had he last enjoyed that blissful state? At home in Rocky Cove, eating his mother's cooking, sleeping in the sheets she kept clean and crisply pressed, accompanying his father on rounds. It all seemed so distant and unreal that he might have been reflecting on the life of some long-dead stranger, rather than his own innocent youth.

Jacob McCaffrey had slipped out sometime during this revery, closing the door behind him. Pres went to the window, more because he couldn't stand still than because he thought there was anything to see. His hands shook even when he grasped the sill to steady them, and he felt a pinch in the pit of his stomach as he stared out on that moonless night. It was an excellent metaphor, all that dark nothingness, he thought, for the ruined and desolate landscape of his own soul.

He rubbed his beard-roughened jaw. It seemed a supreme irony, craving whiskey, for he truly despised the stuff, but crave it he did, especially in still and lonely moments like these. In spite of the way it branded the inside of his belly at every swallow like molten steel.

Without it, though, there wouldn't be the remotest chance of even closing his eyes, let alone sleeping. He had not, in fact, enjoyed a night of natural rest without the aid of whiskey or laudanum since before his enlistment in the Union Army, in the summer of 1862. He'd been full of ideals then, fresh out of medical college and damnably certain of his ability to save the world.

Mercifully, Jacob returned in the midst of these ruminations, forcing back some of the gloom by the simple but palpable force of his presence, carrying a sizable round washtub, lined with copper. After that, he began lugging in water, with the boy, Toby, helping him. Towels were provided, along with a bar of rough yellow soap, an extra bucket of water, a straight razor, and a leather strop. The promised change of clothes appeared, too—a loose, butternut-colored shirt, worn to a chamoislike smoothness, and a pair of rough-spun trousers, black like his own.

"Will's things, or Wesley's," Jacob said, by way of explanation. "Miss June-bug looked for our boys to come back for a long while—I guess she hoped the reports were wrong—and kept a lot of their belongings lest they be needed."

Pres felt his throat tighten and go painfully dry. He

might have seen the McCaffreys' sons in his travels, might even have treated one or the other, for he'd tended Union soldiers and rebels alike, during his term of service, scrambling from one battleground, one field hospital, one ambulance wagon to another. Never doing anybody a damn bit of good, no matter how hard he worked.

"Thanks," he ground out, and took the clothes. "Maybe I ought to look in on the girl and her baby once more."

"Miss Savannah's with them just now," Jacob countered easily. "You have your bath and get yourself some sleep. There'll be another stage through tomorrow afternoon sometime."

Pres nodded, and then McCaffrey and the boy were gone. He peeled away his clothes—couldn't rightly remember the last time he'd changed, let alone scrubbed himself down—and stepped gingerly into the tub full of water. It was cooling by then, but it still felt good.

He soaked awhile, then scoured, soaked, and scoured again. Finally, he stood up and poured the bucket of now-tepid water over his head, for good measure. The floor was awash when he stepped out and reached for the towel; he dried himself and wrapped the bit of cloth around his middle. Except for the glow of the kerosene lamp burning on the bedside table, the room was black.

He wouldn't sleep, of course, with no whiskey to numb the edges of his mind, and he still wasn't hungry, but he did feel a little better all the same.

Downright inspired, he sharpened the razor against the strop, lathered his jaw with soap suds, and shaved. Time he got done, he was out-and-out handsome, in a rascally sort of way.

The bed looked inviting, all of the sudden. He tossed aside the towel, put out the lamp, threw back the covers, and lay down, just to feel the clean sheets against his bare skin. The next thing he knew, sunlight was drumming crimson at his eyelids.

The homey sounds of clattering stove-lids and a woman's voice, singing softly, awoke Savannah on that first morning at Springwater; for the briefest of moments, she thought she was back home in Kansas City, before her long fall from grace, that it was her grandmother on the other side of that wall, working her way through a vast repertoire of hymns and spirituals while she made breakfast. Then, of course, she remembered that she was far from that time and place, and blinked rapidly a couple of times before she got a hold on her emotions. Then she rose, put on her skirt and shirtwaist from the night before, along with a pair of soft kid slippers, and went out to face the day.

A pretty woman with silver-streaked brown hair and bright blue eyes was standing before the stove, spatula in hand, and her smile washed over Savannah like a spill of bright sunlight. "Mornin'," she said. "You must be Trey's friend Savannah."

Savannah nodded, knowing without being told that this was June-bug McCaffrey, back from her mission of mercy to Granny Johnson's place up in the foothills. June-bug told her who she was anyway, and Savannah was charmed; it was easy to see why the stationmistress was one of Trey's favorite people. There was a gentle competence about her, an innate grace, that warmed and welcomed.

Mrs. McCaffrey laughed. "Set yourself down and I'll pour you some coffee. Whew, but I had to hit the floor a-runnin' this mornin', we've got us such a houseful, 'tween the kids and the doc and that poor girl in there with her baby!" She seemed pleased to be cooking for a crowd, for her eyes were shining and her lovely skin was flushed with exuberant color.

"How is Miranda? Has the doctor been to see her yet?"

"Doc's still sleepin', far as I know," June-bug confided, flipping half a dozen flapjacks in rapid sequence with a skillful motion of her wrist. "Miranda's just fine, though. She's already had some breakfast and her milk's in, too, so little Isaiah-or-Ezekiel is right contented. You set down, now. I don't want to have to tell you again."

Well aware that she would lose any argument, Savannah sat down, and allowed June-bug to serve her coffee and then a plateful of pancakes swimming in brown-sugar molasses and fresh butter. She ate with her usual good appetite, and was just finishing up when Dr. Parrish appeared, looking clean and rested and therefore quite unlike his former self. He'd even shaved, and his clothes were a great improvement over the garments he'd been wearing the day before.

He looked faintly surprised to Savannah, as though

he'd expected to wake up somewhere else, or not to wake up at all. Like her, she deduced, in a flash of insight, he was used to being an outsider, never quite fitting in anywhere.

"Morning," he said, somewhat sheepishly, nodding to Savannah and then to June-bug. "I'm obliged for the use of these clothes."

June-bug's expression was pensive, just for a moment or so, though there was nothing grudging in it. "I made that shirt for our Wesley, Christmas of '59," she reflected. "He took uncommon pride in his appearance." She sighed. "It's good to see somebody wearing it again."

There was a brief, weighted silence, then the door opened and Jacob came in. The children, apparently, had already left for school, as there was no sign of them anywhere about.

"Well, now," the stationmaster said, looking Parrish over, "you cleaned up beyond my best expectations."

Savannah laughed, though secretly she was thunderstruck at the change in the doctor's appearance. He was devilishly good-looking, for one thing, and carried himself with a sort of unconscious confidence in his own strength and abilities, a quality she had not seen in him before. Although she was still wary of him, she could admit, at least to herself, that she might have underestimated the man.

June-bug rounded him up and shooed him to the table, like a mother hen gathering in a stray chick, and he sat down, remarkably, and looked at the plate of flapjacks she put in front of him.

"Eat," June-bug commanded. "You look peaky."

Savannah was past due at the Brimstone Saloon, where she hoped to meet up with Trey and hammer out some sort of work schedule, and she imagined Jacob had plenty of chores to do, yet they both lingered, curious about this stranger. It was almost as though someone vaguely resembling the doctor had slipped in during the night to take his place.

Parrish sighed, picked up his fork, and took a cautious bite. Then he took another, and another one after that. It was somehow a momentous occasion, although Savannah could not have said why such a thing could be. When the doctor became aware that everybody was watching him, he looked a little indignant, and both Savannah and Jacob averted their eyes.

Determined to put the day to good use, Savannah went into her rented bedroom to reclaim her handbag, then set out resolutely for the Brimstone Saloon. It didn't take long to reach the place, since it was only a hundred yards or so down the rutted track that passed as a road. The brave little schoolhouse stood just opposite, reminding Savannah of an underling pitched to fling itself upon some brutish bully.

She wondered whose brilliant idea it had been to build two such institutions face-to-face that way, and decided within the confines of that self-same thought that it didn't matter to her. After all, there they were, set solid on their foundations, each one holding its ground.

It was both a disappointment and a relief to Savannah that there were no children playing in the overgrown grass surrounding the school. She loved kids, but she'd learned a long time ago to be careful about speaking to them, at least in the presence of their parents. Too often, the mother or father would drag the child back from her, as though she were some sort of monster, ready to pounce, or the carrier of some dread disease.

So, with a faint and familiar sadness weighting her heart, Savannah turned her back on the school and stood looking up at the building into which she'd sunk every cent she'd saved over the ten years since she'd sung her first song in a saloon. She was good with money, and not overly fond of trinkets and gee-gaws like a lot of the women she'd known, and for those reasons, she'd managed to put by a good deal. She'd made wise investments, too.

She rested her hands on her hips, surveying her plain clapboard purchase, with its swinging doors and hitching rails and the glass windows that were bound to be broken in the first good brawl. What, she wondered, in a state of sudden and keen despair, had she been thinking of, tying up her life savings in such an enterprise?

Savannah sighed. It hadn't been Trey Hargreaves, though God knew, he was everything a man ought to be, and then some. No, try as she might, she'd never come to care for Trey, except as a friend, and that had probably been fortunate, since he'd felt pretty much the same way about her.

Just then, the doors swung open and Trey came out onto the wooden **side**walk, grinning that grin that had set so many female hearts to fluttering, from there to Choteau and probably well beyond.

"It's about time you got here, pardner," he said. He wore a tailored coat, even though it was full summer—a hundred shades of green and yellow were daubed against the distant timber like paint—and the temperature was someplace north of hot. There wasn't a drop of sweat on him. His shirt was white and fancy, and his vest was a rich blue brocade, with a gold watch chain dangling from the pocket. Black, well-fitting trousers and shiny boots completed the picture. "I pour a good glass of whiskey, but my singing voice ain't exactly memorable."

Savannah smiled at her friend. "On the contrary," she retorted, "nobody who heard you sing would ever be able to forget the experience, try though they might."

He laughed as he crossed the sidewalk, his boot heels resounding against the new, raw wood. Reaching her, he took her shoulders in his hands and stooped to plant a brotherly kiss on her forehead.

"Come and meet my wife," he said, and started to pull her toward the schoolhouse.

Savannah balked. "Now?"

"Yes, now," he replied, with mock impatience.

"Won't we be interrupting?"

Trey narrowed those legendary silver eyes of his. "What burr's gotten under your saddle?" he wanted to know.

Savannah's throat ached. She looked up toward the station and then toward the springs, which lay in the other direction, and saw that no help was likely to come from either. "Trey, I'm a saloon woman," she reminded him, in an anxious whisper. "There are folks who'd be real upset to learn I'd been in the same room with their children—"

Trey gave her arm a gentle jerk to get her moving again. "Well, to hell with them, if that's their attitude," he said. "Come on. You're going to like Rachel. Just a little bit of a thing, but she's sure got me buffaloed."

Savannah bit into her lower lip, but she allowed herself to be pulled across the road, through the deep, fragrant Montana grass, up the step to the school-house door. Trey knocked lightly, and all too soon, the rough-board panel swung back on creaking hinges, revealing a small, dark-haired woman with exquisite features and a gleam of intelligence in her eyes.

"Rachel," Trey announced proudly, "this is my partner, Savannah Rigbey. Savannah, my wife."

To say that Rachel was surprised would not have sufficed to describe the expression that crossed her face, however momentarily. Trey, damn his insensitive masculine hide, had neglected to tell his bride that his business associate was a woman, that much was vividly clear. Savannah was mortified; her knees felt watery and conversely, she wanted to turn and flee toward the hills, which was downright silly since she'd done nothing wrong. Not where Trey Hargreaves was concerned, at least.

"Hello," Rachel said, and put out one small, cool hand.

Savannah nodded. "Hello," she said lamely. "I know you're busy with your students, so I'll just go—" She turned on her heel, but Trey took another hold on her elbow and held her fast.

"I hope you'll join us for supper tonight," Rachel Hargreaves said. "Say, six o'clock?"

Savannah's breath had gone shallow. She was not used to being invited to supper, and had nearly forgotten how one responded to such requests. "Well," she murmured.

"She'll be there," Trey told his wife, with a smile, and a look passed between the two of them that fairly crackled. Even Savannah, a mere bystander, felt the flash of heat.

Rachel gave her husband's partner one last thoughtful glance, nodded, and closed the door.

"You didn't tell her!" Savannah accused, in an angry hiss, as the two of them crossed the street again, headed for the saloon.

"Tell her what?" Trey asked, and he looked and sounded genuinely confused.

"That I'm a woman! Damn it, you lunkhead, you don't just spring something like that on a person!"

Trey chuckled, but he still seemed mildly baffled. "I told her I had a partner, coming in from Choteau. She didn't ask any questions."

"That's because she naturally assumed I was a man," Savannah sputtered. "She was probably expecting some portly fellow with a gold incisor, a big cigar, and a bald spot!"

Trey laughed at that image and, since they had

gained the doors of the saloon, reached out to hold one open so she could step in ahead of him. Although there were no horses or wagons out front, the place was doing a surprisingly good business, especially for so early in the day. Savannah didn't know whether to feel chagrined or encouraged by the fact.

"You're worried that Rachel will be jealous of you," Trey said, in a booming voice that made everyone from the bartender to the brooding drifter by the back wall look up, and thus brought stinging color to Savannah's cheeks. "Don't give that another thought. She knows I'm downright foolish over her."

Out of the corner of one eye, Savannah saw the hefty bartender, who was busily wiping out a glass, indulge in the sparest of smiles.

She flung out her hands and let them slap against her sides in exasperation. "I give up," she said. "Just don't blame me if she starts peeling the hide off you the minute she gets you alone."

Trey looked damnably confident of his wife's adoration. "It isn't my hide—"

Savannah cut him off. "Don't you dare say it."

He laughed again, and let his eyes drift over her prim shirtwaist and skirts. "You aren't planning to sing and socialize in that outfit, are you? Seems to me it would be better suited to pouring tea."

Savannah lowered her voice, and her hands found their way back to her hips. "I don't need you or any other man to tell me what to wear when I conduct business, Trey Hargreaves. Furthermore, you'd better remember that I'm not selling anything but whiskey!"

Trey raised both eyebrows and both hands. "Whoa," he said. "All I meant was, I've been running this place by myself ever since it was built, and I've got a house to put up before it snows." He grinned, cocky with pride. "It's one of those sent-for places. Coming by train and freight wagon, all the way from Seattle."

Again, Savannah felt a strange stab of something she wasn't sure she wanted to identify: sorrow, loneliness—envy?

"Soon as the house is finished," Trey went on, when she didn't speak, "you can have the rooms upstairs."

Savannah raised her eyes to the ceiling. Oh, joy, she thought ruefully. An apartment over a saloon in a three-building town. In one and the same moment, though, she wondered what she'd expected. This was her life—saloons and rooms above them, gaudy dresses and singing to the strains of tinny pianos, sawdust on the floors. Nothing was ever going to change, not for her.

Jacob McCaffrey set the checkerboard down in the middle of one of the tables with a thump that should have served as a warning to Pres, but it didn't. "What do you say we make things interesting?" the older man asked, taking a seat on the bench opposite. "Play for pennies."

June-bug was rolling out piecrusts nearby, her shining eyes watchful and intent. "Jacob McCaffrey, you know very well that I don't hold with wagerin'. And here you are, a man of God."

Jacob passed Pres a humorous, beleaguered, and masterfully subtle look. "Now, June-bug," he replied, already lining out the round, red checker pieces in front of Pres with a rhythmic clatter reminiscent of horses' hooves on cobblestone. "It's just a sociable little game, between me and the doc here. The good Lord don't take issue with the like of that."

"We'll see what you have to say when you find yourself playin' checkers with the devil himself," June-bug huffed, using extra force as she wielded her wooden rolling pin, although both her tone and countenance fell a little short of full conviction.

"If the Lord's going to throw a body into hell for bettin' pennies on a round of checkers," Jacob reasoned philosophically, aligning his own pieces on their proper squares, "then He and I probably wouldn't get on together anyhow."

Pres stifled a smile. He'd long since decided that God was either hostile or totally disinterested in His own creation, if indeed He existed at all, but Jacob's homespun faith was a lot easier to take than that of the Bible pounders and raging exhorters he'd encountered in other places. He laid the last of his money on the table, fool that he was, and after an hour or so of long, ponderous silences between careful moves, Jacob had relieved him of that *and* the stagecoach ticket.

The stationmaster wasn't about to offer a rematch. He just put away the red and black pieces, folded the board, and gave Pres what was probably meant to pass as a grin.

"Guess you'll just have to stay on here at Springwater," he said. Then he got up and walked off, and all Pres could do was stare after him. Damned if he hadn't been had.

CHAPTER

3

SAVANNAH WAS ALONE in the little room behind June-bug McCaffrey's cookstove, a colorful tangle of silks and satins covering the bed before her like flowers tumbled from a garden basket. None of the gowns was suitable for dinner at Rachel Hargreaves's table, even if the woman *did* live above a saloon, and yet Savannah chafed at the idea of playing the lady by attending the meal in her tidy skirt and shirtwaist. Her sins were many, by her own assessment, let alone that of society in general, but an attitude of pretense did not number among them.

She frowned, tapping her chin as she considered the garments. The blue one was probably the most innocuous, with its wild spill of ruffles and rhinestone buttons, though the neckline was too low and the skirt hemmed only to midcalf. If she wore that, Rachel would think she was after her husband for certain, and that would not serve. The yellow was bright to the point of being brazen, the green flattered her hair and complexion, but left her back bare, except for a lattice pattern of grosgrain ribbon. The garnet plunged in front, and though the resulting V was filled in with black lace, the outfit seemed to bring out the worst in even the best of men. Whenever Savannah wore it, she made a point of carrying the derringer as well, tucked away in a hidden pocket.

A light tap on the framework of the door caused her to turn, a little startled. Emma was standing in the opening, her brown eyes wide as she took in the dresses. The child let out a long, wondrous breath. "Silk?" she whispered, as though barely daring to murmur the word.

Savannah nodded. Emma, like most frontier children, had probably never seen anything but buckskin, rough-spun woolens, and calico. "Satin, too," she said. "Would you like to touch them?"

Emma came forward tentatively, stood for a moment with the color of the dresses seeming to reflect off her face like light from a stained glass window, then stretched out a small brown hand. Her fingers were trembling slightly as she drew back, in a sudden motion, well short of the glimmering fabrics.

"You won't do them any harm, Emma," Savannah said, putting an arm lightly around the child's erect, solid little shoulders. "Go ahead."

With renewed courage, though visibly holding her breath, Emma reached out again, caressed one dress and then another, with a slow reverence that touched the warm, bruised place at the very center of Savannah's long-hardened heart.

"So pretty," Emma marveled, in the tones of one offering a solemn prayer. "Like a cardinal's feathers, or a blue jay's . . ."

"Indeed," put in a masculine voice from behind them, "the plumage of a veritable bird of paradise, brightly colored, singing the sweetest of songs and none other."

Savannah whirled, though she had known that it was Dr. Parrish she would find, looking on. He was leaning with one shoulder braced against the door frame, his arms folded, his expression one of kindly disdain. She felt blood rise into her face and damned herself for reacting to him at all. "I do believe there is an insult hidden away in that statement somewhere," she said, keeping her tones even for the sake of the child. "What a pity that I care so little for your opinion, sir."

He did not move from his indolent position, but merely raised his eyebrows. "An insult? Perish the thought," he said. "Methinks you are too prickly by half, Miss Rigbey. That is the proper form of address, isn't it? 'Miss Rigbey'?"

She'd never married; the scandal had ruined her chances. Burke Eldon—well, she didn't even like to think about him, about what a mistake it had been to believe in him. About what she'd sacrificed.

Still, all of that had happened so long ago, so far away, and it wasn't as if she'd been the first woman to be badly used. It was past time to forget and move on, though it wasn't easy doing that. "Yes," she said, with all the dignity she could summon. " 'Miss' will do just fine."

Emma, emboldened by Savannah's invitation to touch the dresses, had taken up the blue one and was holding it in front of her flat little bosom, clearly trying to imagine herself grown up and clad in something so grand. Savannah grabbed hold of the present moment and held on, but the pit of her stomach was quivering and she wasn't entirely certain she wouldn't be sick. Forgetting wasn't so easy, of course—the pain, the shame, the fear, the fury, all of it was still with her. "Do you make a practice, sir, of entering a lady's private refuge without so much as a by-your-leave?"

Emma watched with new interest, though no discernible alarm, looking from one adult to the other.

Parrish inclined his magnificent head in a sham of abeyance. "My apologies," he said. "Miss June-bug sent me to ask if you'd like to take a bottle of her elderberry wine along to supper tonight. She'd have come to make the inquiry herself, I expect, but she's busy outside, helping Jacob put salve on a lame horse."

Savannah considered, then nodded in the affirmative. She did not indulge in wine, indeed did not take spirits of any kind, but without June-bug's offering, she would have to present herself empty-handed that evening. She hated being obliged, even for something as ordinary as supper.

The doctor's gaze strayed over the jewel-toned tousle of dresses on the mattress. "Wear the red one," he had the audacity to suggest. Then, while she was still foundering and flailing, awash in a strange, sweet aggravation, he pushed gracefully away from the woodwork, turned, and strolled off.

"I like him," Emma confided.

Savannah sighed. "That brings the count to one," she said wearily.

"Oh, no," Emma disagreed, her dark eyes serious and bright. "Jacob likes him, and so does Miss June-bug. They say he'll be living at Springwater from now on—he just doesn't know it yet."

Savannah couldn't help smiling at that, though Dr. Parrish had left her feeling like a bird flapping its wings under a bonnet. She hoped it didn't mean what she thought it did, because after Burke, she'd sworn never to trust, let alone care about, another man.

In the end, she wore the skirt and shirtwaist she'd had on all day, somewhat to Pres's disappointment, actually, since he'd hoped for at least a glimpse of her in that red confection with the black lace. Instead, though, she went hurriedly through the main room of the station, a basket over one arm, a loose-yarned shawl around her shoulders. In the basket, of course, was June-bug's elderberry wine, discreetly covered by a checkered table napkin.

"Trey'll walk you back home, I reckon," June-bug commented. She was standing beside the front door as Savannah advanced upon it, and looking a bit fretful. You'd have thought Springwater was the heart of some crime-ridden metropolis instead of a mere wide spot along a remote cattle trail. "I don't think you ought to be out alone after it gets dark."

Savannah smiled and at that Pres looked away quickly, annoyed at what it made him feel—like

Lazarus coming awake in the tomb. He'd deadened
his emotions on purpose, after all, and he wanted
them to stay that way. His gaze immediately locked
with that of Jacob, who was standing in his usual post
before the hearth, unlighted pipe in hand. Miss June-
bug did not allow the use of tobacco in her presence,
though she had been known, it was reported, to take
a measure of dandelion or elderberry wine on the
occasion of communion or if her arthritic knees got to
paining her beyond bearing.

Pres brought his mind back to his own problems.
He was effectively stranded, thanks to Jacob
McCaffrey's cutthroat skill at checkers, with nothing
to call his own except the battered leather bag his
father had left him. Even the proverbial clothes on
his back belonged to someone else—his own had disappeared mysteriously, to be burned, he suspected, in
Miss June-bug's cooking fire. His money was gone,
and so was the stagecoach, which had passed through
on schedule early that afternoon, and set out again as
soon as the driver had partaken of a meal and Jacob
and Toby had exchanged fresh horses for spent ones.
Up until the moment the coach thundered off over
the rutted track, Pres had half-expected the old man
to return the ticket so he could move on. Instead,
he'd made a subtle show of tearing it up and tossing it
into the cold grate.

Pres pushed away from the table, agitated almost
beyond his endurance, and began to tread back and
forth like a fidgety horse looking for a break in the
fence-line. By that time, Savannah had gone, taking

those vague, joyful stirrings she'd roused in him away with her, mercifully. The children, Christabel, Emma, and young Toby, were outside, playing some noisy game. The Leebrook girl and her baby, both restless through the day, were resting quietly, and June-bug had returned to the stove, now wholly absorbed in preparing supper for her acquired brood. Many women would have been frazzled in her position, and justifiably so, but she seemed to thrive on cooking and generally "doing for" a houseful of people.

"Good thing we ain't got a rug," Jacob observed. His mouth was as somber as ever, but there was a glint of humor in his eyes. "You'd wear a hole right through it, pacing to and fro that way."

Pres stopped, his hands resting on his hips, and glowered. "I suppose you've got a better suggestion?"

Jacob actually smiled, though so briefly that Pres almost wondered if he'd imagined it. "Matter of fact, I do. You could ride up to the Johnson place and have a look at Granny's rheumatiz. Miss June-bug says it torments her night and day."

Rheumatism. After the things he'd seen, after the battles and their horrendous aftermaths, such a trifling malady would be a lark. "Hot packs," he said distractedly. "All she needs are hot packs and maybe a little—a very little—laudanum."

"Havin' a real doctor come to call would probably go a long way towards making Granny feel better," Jacob persisted, as though Pres hadn't already outlined a method of treatment for the old woman's affliction. "The idea of it, you know."

Pres thrust out a long sigh. In the first place, he didn't know where the "Johnson place" was, and in the second, he didn't have a horse. He'd lost a first-rate gelding at faro, back in Choteau, further proof of his sorry situation. *Pres*, he thought, furious with himself, with fate, and with Jacob McCaffrey, *you've done the home folks proud.*

"I'll take you up to Granny's shack tomorrow," Jacob announced, when Pres didn't speak. "Provided things are under control around here, that is."

"I suppose it's too much to hope that you'll give back my money if I agree?" Pres ventured.

"Way too much," Jacob replied with what passed for affability. "Takes a long while to earn even that much around here. Even for doctorin', you're not likely to get cash money very often. A chicken, maybe, or a mess of trout. A bag of turnips or pota-toes. Yes, sir, it could be some time before you've got the wherewithal to put Springwater behind you for good. Course, June-bug and I will have to charge for your room and board, but you can work that off here at the station, grooming horses and the like. I ain't as spry as I once was."

Pres's jaw clamped down so hard that relaxing it again took a concentrated act of will. It wasn't being expected to earn his keep that irritated him—he'd done that, one way or another, ever since he left home for medical college—no, it was the way Jacob had gotten the better of him with hardly any effort at all. Inside, Pres was chasing his tail like a fox stitched up in a burlap sack. He had that Lazarus feeling again, and his spirit was raw, having been atrophied for so long. "I can manage that," he said. "I'll sleep in the barn, though, and I don't eat much."

Jacob assessed Pres's lean frame and then focused that dark, somber gaze on his face again. "The loft's still warm enough for a man to take his rest in of a night," he allowed, "though the first frost could come at any time, summer or none. As for the food, well, it takes victuals to run a man's body just the way it takes coal to power a steam engine. I reckon most of your sustenance has been comin' out of a bottle, the last little while. Time that stopped."

While Pres would not have brooked such familiarity, such downright presumption, from anyone else, he had little choice in this instance. He was broke, literally and figuratively, with no horse, no stagecoach ticket, and no particular place to go anyway. Inside, he was one big bruise. He might as well come to final ruination in Springwater, he figured, as anywhere else.

"You may come to regret forcing me to stay here," he said evenly.

Jacob spared what might have been a smile on a less craggy and austere face than his. "I don't reckon I will at that," he said. "Come along. I'll show you to the loft and lay out your chores while Miss June-bug finishes makin' our supper. First thing in the morning, we'll head up to Granny Johnson's."

Pres wanted to pick up something heavy and throw it, but he didn't give in to the impulse. Instead, he just followed Jacob out of the station and around back, to the stables, where it looked like he would be sleeping and working for the rest of his natural life.

Rachel had gotten out her lace tablecloth for the occasion of Savannah's visit, and there were tapers flickering in the pair of brass candlesticks set on either side of a bowl brimming with fresh, fragrant wildflowers. Various lamps had been lit as well and the place smelled pleasantly of roasted fowl of some sort, turnips mashed with butter, and fresh biscuits. All of it would go well with the wine.

Trey, proud as any peacock, welcomed Savannah, taking the basket and her shawl, and Rachel, his schoolteacher wife, smiled as she untied her apron and came away from the small potbelly stove where she had evidently prepared all or most of the meal. There was not so much as a trace of dislike or disapproval in Rachel's eyes as she approached; happiness overflowed from her, an excess of the stuff, warm as firelight. Savannah had a desolate, shut-out feeling, just for a moment there.

"Do sit down," Rachel said, taking both Savannah's hands in hers and clasping them warmly. "It is such a treat to have a guest!"

Trey had already opened the wine bottle and set it on the table, between covered dishes with fragrant steam escaping at their edges. He drew back Savannah's chair, and then his wife's. Only when they were both settled, with their napkins in their laps, did he take his own seat. Savannah was secretly amazed at the changes in him, and meant to nettle him a little for his pretty manners, once they were out of Rachel's hearing. The first time Savannah had met Trey, he'd gotten himself hauled off to the hoosegow for riding his horse right through the front doors of the Two-holer Saloon in Missoula and nearly trampling two Temperance workers there to turn the revelers from their wicked ways. Now, he was almost a gentleman.

"Trey's going to start on the foundation for our house tomorrow morning," Rachel confided, when they were all enjoying the succulent food. There was a flush in her cheeks and a glow in her eyes when she looked at her husband that bespoke tender affection and, at the same time, an almost ungovernable passion. "What a fine thing it will be, to have Emma living with us again. We'll have a proper kitchen, too, with a proper stove, and a genuine bathing room—"

Savannah envied Trey's wife, envied her mightily, and not just for having such a grand house forthcoming. No, it was the prospect of a *home* that Savannah coveted, a family, a life that might be considered at least remotely normal. Back east, it would have been highly indecorous for a married woman to hold a schoolteacher's position, and Trey, as a saloon proprietor, would have been assigned a very low social status indeed. Here, though, in the west, where new traditions were taking shape, Trey and Rachel might well be considered respectable.

Quite a contrast, Savannah thought, with her own future. She, who could expect to be viewed as a prostitute unto the end of her days.

The injustice of it made her want to weep, but there was no profit in that. She couldn't go back, after all, couldn't smooth out the twists and turns in the path she'd trod, nor level the steep decline that had brought her to this time and place and state of affairs. She was what she was, and she'd make the best of it, just as she had always done.

"I'll take over here tomorrow," she said, when the evening was nearly over, referring, of course, to the saloon business downstairs. Trey had done his hitch and more, and deserved the necessary time to dig the foundation for the house he would share with Rachel, Emma, and the other children that were bound to come along sooner or later.

Sooner, Savannah thought, if she wasn't misreading that certain ephemeral quality in Rachel's eyes. She'd seen it before, though mostly in far less pleasant circumstances—her midwife grandmother had taught her what to look for, when they'd both hoped Savannah would follow in her footsteps—and it always meant there was a baby brewing, whether the mother had been so advised or not.

"Trey will see you safely home," Rachel said, when the dishes had been cleared and they had sat awhile, sipping coffee. At the door, when Trey was halfway down the outside staircase, she laid a hand to Savannah's arm and spoke in a soft voice. "I'm so glad you've come to Springwater, Savannah. I know we'll be friends."

Not for the first time since her arrival, Savannah felt tears of emotion threaten. She'd acquired numerous male confidants throughout her life, Trey being the best of them, but women tended to dislike and distrust her. She didn't blame them—surely they could not be expected to invite a saloon woman into their homes for tea parties and quilting bees—but she had suffered for her exclusion. Now, here was Rachel Hargreaves, a schoolteacher, educated and gently raised, wanting to befriend her.

She sighed inwardly. Rachel might be of a very different opinion, once she'd seen her husband's business partner in one of her jewel-colored dresses, all of them scandalous by anyone's reckoning, with her hair done up in beads and feathers and her face painted. No doubt the words of her songs would drift up through the floorboards as well, borne on the tinkling notes of the cheap piano below, naughty tunes, designed to inspire devilment in dry-throated cowboys, and maudlin ones, offering cheap solace to the lonely, the bereaved, the defeated.

"I would like that," Savannah said, in parting. "To be your friend, I mean." She meant it, every word, but even then she held out little hope that it would ever be so.

Trey took her arm and guided her down the steep wooden steps behind the saloon. Through the thin plank walls, they heard the click of billiard balls and a swell of rough talk. A half dozen cowboys had ridden in, late that afternoon, and Trey had left them in the care of the bartender.

"I could change my clothes and come back," Savannah suggested, feeling guilty for leaving so much of the burden on him. He'd built the place, after all, and run it almost single-handedly ever since.

"Tomorrow'll be soon enough," Trey said. There was no moon, just the faintest curved etching against the dark sky, and he carried a kerosene lantern in one hand. "Rachel was glad of your company," he went on. "She's been fussing over that pitiful little stove of ours since she closed down the schoolhouse for the day. It's lonely out here a lot of the time, especially for a woman."

"Surely June-bug has been cordial."

Trey chuckled. "Miss June-bug is always cordial," he answered. "She's busy, though, forever cooking or sweeping or looking after some spindly-legged chick she's taken under her wing. Rachel's closest friend, Evangeline Wainwright, lives about ten miles east of town, but they don't see each other very often, given the distance."

Savannah kept pace with the edge of the circle of light cast by Trey's lantern. "I like your wife, Trey," she said truthfully. "Rachel is a fine person, bright-minded as anybody I've ever come across. But I'm not the sort of woman she's looking to keep company with. She was only trying to be polite, that's all."

Trey stopped, raised the lantern, and peered down into Savannah's face. She blinked, bedazzled, in the wash of light.

"Just what sort of woman do you reckon yourself to be?" he demanded. He didn't know about the night she'd run off with Burke, thinking they were going to be married and live out a happy succession of golden days and weeks, months and years, as true partners. What a naive little fool she'd been, taking fairy tales for gospel.

She smiled, touched by his fierce loyalty. He truly liked her. Still, he was a man, and she had always gotten along well with the masculine gender. Until Dr. Prescott Parrish, that is; the two of them struck sparks, metal against metal. If that was "getting along," that excitement, that quivering rush in the pit of her stomach, it was damn scary. "There is a perception that goes with working in a saloon, Trey. You know that. It's all right for you—it just makes you a bit of a rogue, but for me it's a very different matter. I sing in barrooms. I sell whiskey to people who would probably be better off without it." *I was misled by a man I trusted, even looked up to, and my own father turned me out of his house.* She sighed. "It's just assumed that I do other things, too."

Trey spat a curse. "If anybody dares to say that, I'll flatten their nose with the back of a shovel," he said. He sounded sincere.

Savannah laughed, though in truth she felt more like weeping, because of what she remembered, and because what she wanted to be was such a far cry from what she was. "That would change nothing at all," she pointed out. "Come along, Trey—I've got to get back to the station. There'll be talk about you and me soon enough as it is, without our dallying in the dark to lend credence to the gossip."

Trey was scowling, but he started walking again, toward the golden squares of light that were the windows of Springwater station. "You suppose Jacob'll be able to talk that sorry-looking doc into staying on?" he asked, when they were almost to the porch.

Savannah felt the strangest urge to defend Parrish, to say that he was really quite presentable, now that he'd had a bath and a good night's sleep, but she stopped herself. It wasn't her task in life to smooth that scoundrel's way; she had both hands full just looking after her own affairs and, truth to tell, she wasn't exactly assuring herself an honored place in history.

"He'll stay on awhile," she answered, as they gained the base of the station house steps. "He lost his horse at faro, back in Choteau, and this morning Jacob checkered him out of his money and a stage-coach ticket."

"We could use a doctor around here," Trey allowed. Savannah wondered if he was imagining Rachel, months from then, laboring to bear his child, but of course she wouldn't have asked for anything. She and Trey were close friends, but not *that* close.

"He conducted himself well enough yesterday, when Miranda gave birth," she said. "He was sober at the time, but who knows how long that will last?" In her mind, she saw the doctor at the Hell-bent Saloon, consuming whiskey like he was feeding a fire in his belly. Or dousing one in his soul.

Trey's face was craggy with shadows in the rising light of his lantern. "He didn't take so much as a swal-low when he came into the Brimstone today. Just sat there, staring at the wall like he could see through it to some other place. I tried to strike up a conversation, but he didn't have much to say. Just his name, as I recall."

Savannah mounted the first step. Through the station's thick log walls, she could hear Miranda's baby crying. The sound was lusty and somehow heartening, for all that it was an ordinary thing. "You can go back home now, Trey. I believe I'd like to stay out here for a few minutes and gather in my thoughts."

"You're all right, aren't you?" Trey sounded genuinely worried, in the way a protective elder brother might have been. "It can take a lot out of a person, that stage trip from Choteau. Why, when Rachel came, the coach nearly turned over in Willow Creek, and I had to go out and fetch her ashore on horseback."

Savannah smiled again, clasping a lodge pole hitching rail in her hands and looking up at the black sky, where a few faint stars winked and twinkled. The wind was rising, promising a storm; the portent of lightning was a silent reverberation in the hot air. "I'm just fine, Trey. Go home to your wife." She'd thanked them both for a pleasant evening, and so did not press the matter of her gratitude. "I'll see you tomorrow morning."

Trey hesitated a moment, then glanced toward the saloon, no doubt thinking of Rachel, awaiting him in their rustic rooms upstairs. It was enough, evidently, to propel him toward home. "Good night," he said, as he moved away, the lantern light swinging easily at his side.

"So that's your partner," said Prescott Parrish, from the darkness behind her.

Savannah was so startled that she nearly swallowed her tongue. She turned, one hand to her breast in an unconscious attempt to slow her heartbeat down to a reasonable pace, to see him materialize out of the gloom like some sort of specter. "I despise a sneak, Dr. Parrish," she snapped, when fury and fear made way for speech. "How dare you lurk in the shadows and eavesdrop on a private conversation?" *How dare you have such a frightening effect on me?*

He chuckled and had the out-and-out temerity to stand right beside her, there on the McCaffreys' porch, one shoulder braced against a supporting pole. "I wasn't lurking," he said. "I came around the corner from the barn and heard you discussing me. Naturally, the topic was of interest."

Savannah blushed to remember the nature of that conversation, and most of the steam went out of her. "All the same, announcing yourself would have been the gentlemanly thing to do."

His teeth flashed white in the darkness. She could see him now, in the light coming from the window behind them, if only as a shadow towering over her. "Ah, but there you have it, Miss Rigbey. I am not a gentleman, and therefore cannot be expected to behave as one."

Savannah stood her ground. "On the contrary," she said, "you were *born* a gentleman. And if you do not behave as such, it is not for want of training. I think you choose to be obnoxious. You're angry and you mean to make the world suffer for all your petty grievances."

He leaned in very close, and she smelled soap and clean water on his skin, but no hint of whiskey, stale or otherwise. "I do not recall asking for your opinion," he said pointedly. "But since you gave it so readily, I will reciprocate with my own. You, Miss Rigbey, are no lady. Since I am no gentleman, we ought to suit each other just fine."

They just stood there, the two of them, for the longest time. The air seemed awash with liquid lightning, and Savannah's heart was beating so fast that she feared it would race right out of her throat and leave her behind.

He reached up, touched her mouth with the tip of an idle index finger. "What's happening here?" he murmured, and he might have been talking to himself, the mountains, or the moon as much as to Savannah, given his distracted tone.

His touch seemed to sear her, through and through. She didn't have an answer, and so didn't offer one. Nor did she move away, flee into the station as a decent woman would have done.

At last, and very slowly, like a man making his way through a dream, he took Savannah's shoulders in his hands, pulled her close, and lowered his mouth to hers for a long, softly tempestuous kiss.

She supposed she should have struggled—kicked—slapped—something. But she didn't. She just stood there, letting him kiss her, kissing him back, and enjoying the whole experience. When it was over, and he fairly tore his lips from hers, she might actually have swooned if he hadn't still been holding on to her shoulders. She had reveled in the exchange, indeed, she wanted more, but she would have died before admitting as much. In point of fact, all she could do was stare up at him, astounded.

His dark eyes glittered in the thin light. Somewhere in the distance, thunder boomed, and the horizon seemed to tilt at a wild angle as lightning flashed. If she hadn't known better, Savannah would have sworn she'd just kissed the devil himself.

He smiled at her, almost insolently, then turned and walked off into the night, whistling under his breath.

Savannah took a few moments to breathe deeply, in the hope of calming her heart and letting the blush in her cheeks fade a little, then went inside the station. Jacob and June-bug were seated in their rocking chairs, facing the evening fire, June-bug holding the newborn baby gently in her arms.

"There you are," she said, in a quiet voice that held music even when she wasn't singing. "Did Trey walk you home?"

Savannah summoned up a smile as she set down the now-empty basket and removed her shawl. Inside, she was trembling, and she could still feel Parrish's mouth on hers, at once conquering and surrendering. Forceful, yet totally unlike the way Burke had kissed her. "Yes, he did. Rachel is a lovely woman, and quite a good cook."

June-bug nodded and crooned something to the

sleeping infant. "She's made all the difference in the world to Trey, and to Emma, too. I suppose she's all excited about that new house of hers."

Jacob ruminated on his wife's remark for a few moments, then joined in the conversation. "I didn't figure they'd get it here before spring. Maybe they oughtn't to get their hopes up, Rachel and Trey."

"Nonsense," June-bug said, in a tone of mild reproach. "Seattle isn't that far. Those freight wagons will be here any day now. Just you wait and see."

Jacob's response was typically good-natured and dry as sun-bleached bones. "I hope you're right, Miss June-bug," he said. "I surely do."

Thunder sounded again, closer now, and June-bug raised worried eyes to the ceiling. "You ought to fetch the doc inside, Jacob. He's liable to catch his death, sleepin' out yonder in the barn on a night like this."

Jacob might have smiled; it would have been hard to tell, even in good light. "Never you mind," he said. "Never you mind. Young Dr. Parrish is right where he ought to be."

CHAPTER

4

IT WAS STILL EARLY—the air was chilly as the inside of a spring-house in January and the sky was pearl-gray, shot with a watery apricot, above the lacework tangle of evergreens and deciduous trees rimming the horizon. There was a carpet of pine needles and last year's leaves on the ground. Jacob, riding beside Pres's borrowed mare on a fractious old mule he called Nero, pointed out a faint curl of smoke higher up in the foothills, amidst the gray-white trunks of birches and alders.

"That would be Granny's place, there yonder," he said. "Leastways we know she's up and around and has her cookin' fire built."

Pres rubbed the back of his neck and refrained from comment.

"There's one thing I ought to warn you about, before we get there," Jacob allowed, after chewing on the thought for a while.

"What would that be?" Pres asked, with deliberate

mildness. His patience was short, maybe because laying off whiskey had left his insides raw and empty, with no more substance than a rotted log eaten through by bugs. Maybe because he was being haunted by thoughts of Savannah Rigbey, sure as Hamlet was haunted by his father's ghost. His temples seemed to be trying to reach across his brain and fuse themselves into a single throbbing pulse, and his stomach had shriveled to a dry shell. Had there been anything in it, he'd have long since heaved up the lot.

"Granny's likely to shoot at us," Jacob replied, with no more inflection than if he'd been saying she enjoyed chasing fireflies with a fruit jar in one hand. "Her eyesight ain't too good, and until she recognizes me and old Nero here, she's liable to be unfriendly."

Pres gave a short bark of a laugh, a sound utterly without humor. "Wonderful."

"No cause to worry," Jacob assured him. "She won't aim to kill."

Sure enough, in the next second, a shotgun blast rent the sky, sending birds flapping and squawking from the trees and small animals skittering through the underbrush.

"You jest hold it right there!" warned a thin, wavery voice.

Jacob and Pres didn't have to draw up on the reins—Jacob had to fight Nero to keep him from wheeling around and laying tracks back to Springwater, and the mare did a little sideways dance that might have been amusing, if it hadn't been for that crazy old woman up ahead, wielding a gun.

"Now, Granny," Jacob yelled good-naturedly, "put that thing aside. It's me, Jacob McCaffrey. I've brought a doctor to have a look at your rheumatiz!"

A brief silence followed, then Granny's brittle old voice crackled through the morning chill, spreading itself in a gradually widening web of sound like a hairline fracture in an egg shell. "What sort of doctor?"

Jacob gave Pres a sidelong look, as though assessing him so as to give an honest answer. "The real kind, I reckon, with proper schoolin' and plenty of practice behind him." He waited a heartbeat or two, letting his words sink in. Then he spurred the mule forward. "Now, Granny," he called out, "we're comin'. You put a nick in my hide and you'll have Miss June-bug to deal with, so you just leave off shootin' right now."

Pres was fascinated by the spectacle of a scrawny little woman wielding a gun that was bigger than she was. He wanted, for some ridiculous reason, to laugh out loud.

When it was plain that no more potshots were forthcoming, he persuaded the little mare to follow Jacob's mule, along a narrower, upward-curving path, through clouds of rich green leaves and the clean, Christmas-scent of fir trees.

The old woman stood on the sagging porch of her shack, even smaller than she'd appeared from a distance, a wizened, toothless little creature in a poke bonnet and a dress made of mismatched flour sacks stitched none-too-neatly together. On her tiny left foot she wore a black, lace-up boot, on her right, a slipper of some sort.

Pres met her gaze and held it.

"Granny, this here is Prescott Parrish," Jacob announced. "He's a doctor, like I said. We mean to keep him around Springwater as long as we can."

Granny looked Pres over and apparently found him wanting, judging by the little *harumph* sound she made. He hid a grin and inclined his head slightly.

"Morning, Mrs. Johnson," he said, in respectful tones.

She squinted at him, as though trying to discern his innermost motives, though it was more likely that she simply needed spectacles. "You a Yankee?" she demanded, bristling with suspicion.

Pres heaved a sigh. "No, ma'am. I'm not a Confederate, either. Just a plain American, I guess."

She hobbled forward a few steps, peering from beneath the wide brim of her bonnet. "I ain't never been seen to by no doctor," she said. "Never had the need. But I reckon if Jacob McCaffrey will keep company with you, you're probably a decent feller."

Pres's natural bent toward the practice of medicine had edged aside his own discomforts; he dismounted, tethered the mare to a sapling that grew beside an old, rusted water pump, and untied his bag, having lashed it to the saddle horn before setting out from Springwater. He stood before Granny, looking up because she was on the step and he was still on the ground, and addressed her bluntly, as he did all his patients. "Have you got the rheumatism all through your system, or just in that foot?" He nodded to indicate her slippered foot.

"My whole right side pains me some," Granny admitted, though grudgingly. "It's a sight worse from my hip on down, though."

Pres nodded again. "Well, let's have a look," he said.

Granny's dried-apple face showed alarm. "You mean, you want to see my bare hide?"

He swallowed a chuckle. "Your virtue is safe with me, Mrs. Johnson. I'm a doctor."

Granny squinted at Jacob, still towering against the lightening sky on the back of that mule. He looked, to Pres, like an Old Testament prophet, a solemn herald of wrath and destruction. "You'll come a-runnin' if I holler for you?" the old lady asked.

To his credit, Jacob cracked a smile. He swung down off the mule's back and tethered both his mount and Pres's to a hitching rail that didn't look strong enough to restrain a spindly-legged calf. "Yup," Jacob said.

Granny pondered. "Well," she said, at long last, "all right, then. You come on in, Doc, and I'll hitch up my skirts."

Pres tossed a wry glance to Jacob over one shoulder, and followed Granny into her cabin. The inside was typical of such places, he supposed, and certainly better than he was used to after four years of improvised military hospitals, set up in everything from open fields to musty tents and appropriated horse barns. There was no bed, just a straw pallet on the floor, with one quilt for a cover, and that so worn that it was colorless, and the stuffing showed through. The woodstove was hardly bigger than a milk bucket, giving off only a promise of heat. Pres caught the unmistakable smell of a chamber pot too long unemptied, underlaid with the musty odor peculiar to elderly recluses like Granny.

"When was the last time you had something to eat?" he asked, in a deliberately gruff tone that implied she might have feasted on any number of delicacies, had she but chosen to do so. In actual fact, he didn't feel sorry for her, except when it came to the pain of her rheumatism. She seemed happy enough to him, otherwise.

"I been eatin' right along," Granny said, none too graciously. "Miss June-bug McCaffrey was up here recentlike, and she brought me some victuals and made me take them. I just used up the last of 'em this mornin'."

"You like living out here, all by yourself?" Pres said, in what was for him a companionable tone of voice. He heard Jacob out on the porch, caught the tantalizing scent of pipe smoke.

Granny seemed to relax a little. "This here's my home. Ain't lived nowhere else in all the time since I got hitched. I ain't goin' to town, so don't you start in on me about it."

He grinned. "Yes, ma'am," he said. Then he set his medical kit on an upended crate, weathered to gray, and snapped the catch. Something of his father always rose to meet him when he opened it, a scent maybe, too subtle to discern consciously, or the ghost of a faded memory.

"Jacob!" Granny whooped, all of the sudden.

The old man opened the door, though slowly. He and Pres exchanged glances. "What?"

Granny made a shooing motion with one hand. "You can go on," she said. "I've taken a likin' to the doc here. I reckon he's all right."

Jacob's eyes smiled, if his mouth didn't. He nodded. "I'll go and catch one of those chickens out there," he said, pausing on the threshold. "I could put the bird on to stew before the doc and me head back down to Springwater."

"Don't you go slaughterin' one of my layin' hens by mistake, Jacob McCaffrey," Granny warned, peering at her old friend. "You chase down that old red one with the missin' wing."

Pres wanted to laugh, not from derision, not from irony, but for the joy of it, for all the reasons he *used* to laugh, before the titans of the North and the South had driven their children into bloody conflict, leaving him and others like him to attend to the horrific consequences. The memories would always be with him, he knew that; he had absorbed and assimilated them into his very being, like food he'd eaten and air he'd breathed. But, oddly, they seemed more deeply buried in those mundane moments, far less immediate than usual. Maybe it had begun, this deep-seated and mysterious change in him, when he'd delivered Miranda Leebrook's baby, though it more likely had to do with Savannah, and the kiss they'd shared.

"Lie down on that pallet over there," he told Granny quietly, "and let's see that hip of yours."

Jacob pursed his mouth, but his Indian-dark eyes were sparkling as he retreated to assassinate an unsuspecting chicken, closing the door behind him.

Granny gave Pres one more looking-over, then made that *harumph* sound again and hobbled over to the pallet. She lay down on her left side, facing the wall, and hiked up her skirts.

Pres had expected inflammation, but he was unprepared for the degree of swelling he actually found. Granny Johnson weighed about as much as a tobacco pouch full of dried bird bones, and her crepe-paper skin looked fragile enough to crumble into dust at a touch, but the flesh covering her hip and the length of her thigh was distended, hard and hot. The pain, he thought, swallowing a low whistle of exclamation, must have been excruciating.

He yearned, in those moments, for proper supplies—opiates, camphor, and the like, but he was down to a quarter bottle of laudanum and a few tinctures and powders. His equipment consisted of the most basic tools of the trade: scalpels, various needles and catgut for sutures, a stethoscope, a mallet for testing reflexes. A saw. God help him, always and forever, a saw.

"Well?" Granny demanded, fractious again. He didn't blame her, there being no kind of grace in her position. "You through lookin' yet? It ain't like I don't feel the breeze."

Pres smiled and replaced the time-grayed petticoat and tattered skirts as gently as he could. "You have a washtub around this place, Mrs. Johnson?" he asked, when she rolled over and sat up, her bright chicken eyes narrowed. "Something you could bathe in?"

"You remarkin' upon somethin' personal?" she wanted to know.

"I wouldn't think of it," Pres disavowed, though, of course, he'd been doing precisely that all along. More than Granny's temperament had gone sour; she probably hadn't taken a bar of soap to that leathery hide of hers since before Lincoln left Springfield. "Hot water might ease you a little, let you rest."

"Corn whiskey'll do the same," Granny responded, sitting up and settling her skirts modestly around her. "Don't need no fancy Yankee-fied doctor telling me how to look after myself, neither." She paused, peering at him speculatively. " 'Less, of course, you happen to have some corn whiskey in that bag of your'n."

Pres had dealt with much more obdurate types than Granny, and he wasn't afraid to let her know it. Unruffled, he looked her straight in the eye and said, "No whiskey. Furthermore, if I have to haul you down to Springwater and dunk you in hot water myself, I'll do it."

Granny glared at him for a long time before finally settling her feathers. "All right, then," she said. "But if I die of the pneumonia, my passin'll be on your conscience."

Savannah wore the garnet gown with the black lace, that first day as mistress of the Brimstone Saloon, just to get it over with. She painted her face and piled all her hair on top of her head in a saucy tumble of curls, and pulled on fishnet stockings and high-heeled slippers for effect.

The first person she met, leaving her room, was June-bug, who couldn't quite hide her misgivings. Miranda, a surprisingly resilient soul, had already emerged from her confinement, and was sitting at one of the trestle tables, puzzling over an open book.

"Joseph and all his brothers!" June-bug exclaimed softly, upon seeing Savannah, one hand splayed over the bosom of her own modest, everyday dress. It was a brown and white calico print with touches of blue that accented the color of her eyes. "You don't even look like the same *person* as before."

Miranda looked up, then down again, quickly. It was plain enough, though, that she was as startled as June-bug had been.

Savannah could have told her friend—at least, she *hoped* Mrs. McCaffrey was still her friend—that indeed she was looking upon someone quite different from the Savannah she was just beginning to know. It seemed futile to explain that this was merely a costume she wore, for a role she played, in order to earn a living. She could have solved the problem by marrying—she'd had more offers than she could count over the years—but for her, entering into matrimony with a man she didn't love would have been a very real sort of whoring. Besides that, even though she mostly knew better, she was still afraid.

When Savannah didn't speak, couldn't speak, June-bug peered into her face, squinting a little. "You all right?" she asked. "You look as if your knees might be saggin' just a little."

Savannah swallowed. "There are reasons for who—what I am," she finally said, in misery.

June-bug laid a hand on her shoulder, left all but bare by the dress. "I reckon that's true of all of us," she said. "For better and for worse."

Already, the sounds of horses could be heard in the road out front, underlaid by the more distant bawling of cattle. That meant thirsty cowboys, willing to pay for a song or two as well as copious amounts of whiskey. Trey had warned her that large and small herds would be driven through town deep into the fall, there being a plentitude of water at the springs.

Savannah wanted to stay, wanted to pour it all out to June-bug, how Burke had said he loved her, when all the while he was lying, and the law was after him. How her father had blamed her, not Burke, and refused to speak to her until the day he died, and how the grief of it all had killed her grandmother. In the end, though, she couldn't risk it.

"You don't have to do this," June-bug said. "Trey's been runnin' that place right along, and he can go on doin' it." Miranda had closed her book and was no longer even pretending not to listen.

Savannah sighed, then shook her head. "I've got to do my part," she said, as much to herself as to June-bug. "Half the business is mine, after all."

June-bug had taken both Savannah's hands in her own, and she held on to them for a moment longer, dropping them only after a final, fierce squeeze.

"Them cowboys, they might not understand about you being a lady," she said softly.

Savannah could have kissed the woman, just for assuming the best the way she had. For believing. "I've dealt with many a cowboy and lived to tell the tale," she answered, with a slight smile. "Most of them are just harmless kids, you know, trying to figure out how to be men." She didn't add that she was carrying the derringer in the pocket hidden among the folds of her dress. She had never shot another human being, man nor boy, and she prayed that the necessity would not arise, but she was ready nonetheless.

"And some are no better'n outlaws," June-bug added. "I've seen bitter, hard-eyed men ridin' with these herds since me and Jacob have been out here. The war done somethin' to their souls, made killin' an everyday matter."

There was nothing Savannah could say to that, for she knew it was true. It would be a hundred years at least, she reckoned, before the scars of the great conflict were properly healed. Maybe longer.

"I've got to go," she said, and turned from June-bug, with a nod to Miranda, turned from quiet pleasures, household tasks like sweeping and cooking and putting food by for winter. From tea-drinking and quilt-stitching and gentle talk. There were tears in her eyes as she set her face for the Brimstone Saloon. Trey was across the road from the station, shovel in hand, digging the foundation for his and Rachel's mail-order house, but Savannah pretended not to see him and went on.

She entered the saloon—*her* saloon—by the front doors, and was greeted by a nod from the bartender and the interested leers of a dozen pimply-faced boys, hardly old enough to wear long pants, let alone drink rotgut whiskey, chew tobacco, and gamble away their paltry wages.

One of them made an audacious whooping sound upon seeing Savannah walk in, and then added a suggestive comment; she sought, found, and advanced upon the culprit with such pride and purpose that he backed up hard against the bar and went right on trying to retreat. His compatriots chuckled among themselves. Color climbed the cowboy's grimy face, and his eyes glittered, as though with fever. His Adam's apple bobbed up to his tonsils and back down again. Savannah felt the weight of the silk-swathed derringer against her hip, but she knew she would not be required to use it. The kid wasn't mean, merely ill mannered, and if she was going to start shooting people for that, she'd soon run out of customers.

"What's your name?" she demanded, hands on her hips.

"J-Jimmy," said the boy. "Jimmy Franks."

"Well, Jimmy Franks," Savannah went on, "it seems to me that your manners leave something to be desired. You'd best address me respectfully from now on, if you don't want me to toss you head first into the horse trough."

The others laughed and, after a nervous interval, during which his face got even redder than before, so did Jimmy. "Yes, ma'am," he said, and doffed his filthy, weather-beaten hat to her.

Savannah winked at the bartender. "Give this man a drink," she said. "On me." With that, she went to the piano, raised the lid, and sat down on the rickety stool with a flounce of her red-ruffled skirts. After flexing her fingers briefly, she began to play a sprightly tune, and then to sing, and soon all the cowboys were singing with her.

When they reluctantly took their leave, sometime in the early afternoon, they were promptly replaced by the men they had relieved. The herd was a constant presence, a low rumble filling the sky with dirt.

Trey came to look in on Savannah just as the changing of the guard was taking place, bringing a sandwich wrapped in a cloth napkin, compliments of June-bug. "Looks like a lively crew," he said, assessing the dirty, travel-worn revelers.

Savannah, seated at the only empty table, with Trey across from her, delicately unwrapped the sandwich. Egg salad, with onions and plenty of butter. She nodded in agreement to Trey's statement and bit in appreciatively. She had not realized, until the food arrived, that she was ravenous.

"You have any trouble with them?" Trey prompted, meaning the cowboys, of course.

Savannah chewed, swallowed, and dabbed at her mouth with the napkin before shaking her head. "They're just a bunch of overgrown boys," she said. "Nobody here I can't handle."

Trey's expression was solemn. "Rachel doesn't

think you ought to be left here alone," he said. "I'll come and take over for you in an hour or so, after I've had time to wash up and rest awhile."

Savannah was touched by his concern, and especially by Rachel's, yearning for respectable woman friends as she did, but she was more than equal to a room full of saddle-sore cowboys, rowdy or not, and by her accounting, Trey deserved some time off from the Brimstone. "You just stay away," she ordered good-naturedly, "and give me a chance to get the feel of this place. I sunk a fair bit of money into it, after all, and I'll do my part to run it, with no special favors asked."

Trey's forehead crumpled in a dusty frown. "You sure as hell are a stubborn woman," he said, with a marked lack of admiration.

Savannah laughed. "You've known me for five years, Trey. Are you just now figuring that out? You go ahead and spend the evening with your bride; I can look after our investment just fine on my own."

Trey still seemed doubtful, but he knew a losing battle when he saw one. Usually. "I'll be right upstairs. You need me, you just whack on the ceiling with a cue stick, and I'll come right down."

Savannah smiled at the image. "If you say so," she agreed.

"Sing another song, Miss Savannah," one of the cowboys urged, from the bar, where the whiskey was flowing freely. "Somethin' melancholy."

Savannah rolled her eyes at Trey, but she'd finished as much as she could of the sandwich by that time, and she got up and sashayed over to the piano. It was a part of her performance, that swinging and swishing of silk, and it raised an appreciative cheer from the customers, just like always.

She was midway through her song, a maudlin piece about a silver-haired mother watching the road for her "loving boy Billy," never to return from the war, when Dr. Parrish came in. He seemed to set the very air to churning, just that easy.

The sleeves of his borrowed butternut shirt were rolled up, revealing powerful forearms, and his dark hair was rumpled and, at the same time, sleek, like the wing feathers of some predatory bird. Seeing Savannah in her red dress, face paint, and tousled hairdo, he narrowed his eyes.

Savannah had long since come to terms with the facts of who she was and what she did to earn a livelihood, for the most part anyway, but seeing herself reflected in Parrish's handsome face stung, and that in itself was enough to make her angry.

She played harder and sang louder, pretending to ignore the doctor, but instead watching him out of the corner of one eye. They might have been alone in that saloon, the two of them, for all the attention he paid to the bartender or the flock of hooting cowboys washing trail dust from their throats. He didn't go near the bar but instead came straight toward the piano.

Savannah braced herself, more than ready for a fight, but he stopped short of her and sat down at the nearest table, tumbling a drover into the sawdust when he appropriated a chair. The cowboy scowled, then went off to find another place to sit.

Savannah's voice trembled a little, but her audience didn't seem to care. They cheered uproariously when she launched into an encore. She wanted to look away from Parrish's face, wanted to in the worst way, but he seemed to be holding her gaze by means of some fierce magic, and she could not break the spell. Her own voice faded from her ears, as did all the other sounds of that noisy, smoke-hazed place, and she knew she was still singing only because she could feel the sound resonate in her vocal chords.

When the song ended at last, the cowboys bellowed for more, but Savannah couldn't oblige. She remained a captive, could not turn her eyes from Parrish's face.

After a lot of shouting and toasting, the customers gave up trying to persuade her, at least for a little while, and turned back to their drinking in earnest. The doctor did not move, let alone go to the bar and order a drink, as Savannah would have expected him to do.

When the spell slackened, she managed to rise and make her way through the sawdust to where he sat. He was alone by then; the men who had shared his table were engrossed in a game of faro being played in a far corner of the room.

"Pour you a drink?" Savannah inquired, though she knew he didn't have the money to pay. He'd lost every cent remaining to him playing checkers with Jacob McCaffrey.

He shook his head. "Sit down," he said, just as if he had the right to make demands like that. His voice was quiet, though, as if he was making an effort to be polite.

Savannah sat. She told herself it was because the day had been a long one and she was feeling tired, though the truth was, something about this man's presence electrified her as surely as if she'd laid both hands to a lightning bolt. She could barely breathe. "How was Granny Johnson?" she asked, because she needed to say something. The silence might have stretched on forever if she hadn't, with Parrish just sitting there, staring at her.

He ignored the question. "You oughtn't to be seen in public in such a getup," he said. "I have half a mind to wash that stuff off your face myself."

Heat stung Savannah's throat and forehead, made a hot ache beneath her cheekbones. She was hurt and embarrassed, but he didn't need to know that. She wasn't about to let on that his opinion mattered in the least. "You might just as well try to take soap and water to a singed wildcat," she answered mildly. "You'll come away with half again as many scratches if you try it with me."

He sighed, thrust one graceful, long-fingered hand through his hair. She noticed, oddly, that it trembled only slightly. He was well and truly sober, though for how long was anybody's guess. "You're not a whore," he said. "Are you?"

Had it not been for her pride, that question, coming from him, would have caused Savannah to lay her head down on the gouged top of that saloon table and weep. Still, she held on. Spoke moderately. "I most certainly am not."

He looked her over as though she were one of the curious and thus fascinating specimens he'd surely studied in his medical school laboratory. "Then why in hell do you dress and act like one?" He sounded honestly confused, which only went to show that he was lacking in manners as well as tact.

She drew a measured breath and let it out slowly. It would do no good to fling herself upon him, screeching and scratching, even though that was precisely what she wanted to do, all of the sudden. She had to live at Springwater, after all, and a tale like that was sure to spread from one crew of drovers to another until it reached the Mexican border, by which time it would have grown to epic proportions. "If you don't like the way I'm dressed, *Doctor*, I invite you to get out of my saloon. I've got songs to sing and whiskey to sell. Unless you're buying, I have nothing more to say to you."

He leaned toward her, his dark eyes snapping. "Well, I've got a few things to say to you," he countered. "You don't belong in this place, and you damn well know it."

She bent toward him, and the red feather skewering the pile of curls on top of her head slipped a little, falling between them. She swiped it aside with an angry gesture, and was even angrier when she spotted a smile hiding at the back of his eyes.

"That's where you're wrong, Dr. Parrish—I do

belong here. I own half interest in this place. I've been working in saloons since I was sixteen years old. And I see no need to account to you or anyone else for the choices I've made."

He reached up, plucked the feather out of her hair, examined it as though he expected to see something crawling amidst the downy fluff, and laid it aside on the table. "Sell your share of the business to Hargreaves," he said, as confidently as if he had the right to dictate such things. "You could probably live indefinitely on the proceeds, if you were careful."

Savannah could feel a tiny muscle twitching under her right eye. "And do what?" she hissed. She'd go crazy, just sitting around some parlor, waiting to get old and die.

"Something worthwhile," Parrish answered, undaunted. His tone was mild. Reasonable. Damnably certain. "Like nursing. You handled yourself fairly well with the Leebrook girl. You might even have a talent in that direction."

Nursing? Who would accept care from her, a saloon woman and supposed prostitute? No one, that's who. "Thank you," she said evenly, "for the benefit of your wisdom."

He grinned and raised an invisible glass in an impudent toast. "At your service," he said.

Chapter

5

THE ENCOUNTER at the Brimstone Saloon set the tone for other meetings, in the days and nights to follow, or so it seemed to Savannah. A sort of prickly tolerance arose between her and the doctor, both of them going on about their business, each giving the other as wide a berth as possible. It wasn't always easy, this last, given the crowded state of the Springwater station, and the fact that both of them were staying there.

Savannah had been "in town," as Jacob and Junebug McCaffrey so optimistically said, for nearly a month when Rachel and Trey's mail-order house arrived from Seattle, over a period of three sultry midsummer days, via a variety of freight wagons. Each new arrival was an occasion of much excitement and speculation, and on the fourth day, as if by magic, people began arriving from far-flung farms and ranches, the men armed with tools and opinions, no doubt, the women with preserves and quilt pieces to be shared or exchanged.

Savannah watched the gathering of friendly females from a distance, and with no little envy, learning from Emma that this one was Evangeline
Wainwright, wife of Scully, a prosperous rancher, that
one was Mrs. Bellweather, mother of Kathleen, who
attended school at Springwater, and there was
Granny Johnson, who was looking sprightly despite
her ailment. June-bug had visited the old woman
often over the past few weeks, Savannah knew, and so
had Dr. Parrish.

Not, of course, that Savannah had been paying
overmuch attention to what Dr. Parrish did. She
couldn't help noticing, though, that he didn't drink
or gamble when he came to the Brimstone Saloon,
though he often took a chair at this table or that, listening earnestly to the tales of drovers, peddlers, and
just-plain drifters passing through. More than once,
she saw him mount one of Jacob's horses and set out
with harried, grim-faced riders, sent by some trail boss
to fetch him. Cowboys being cowboys, the doctor was
in high demand for setting broken bones, treating
snakebite, and digging out the odd bullet. He continued to pass his nights in the McCaffrey hayloft, insofar as Savannah knew, and took his meals with good
appetite, according to June-bug's unbidden reports.

Now, with the sparse though enthusiastic populace
of the region clustered in the high grass next to Trey
and Rachel's home site, he materialized again, pushing up his sleeves with the rest of them.

Now, the steady *thwack-thwack* of hammers rang up
and down the rutted road, punctuated by the back-

and-forth rasp of saws. Looking on from the front window of the deserted Brimstone Saloon—even the clientele had gone to help raise the walls of the Hargreaves house—Savannah knew a piercing sense of separation and loneliness.

"You ought to go down to the station and join in," Emma said, looking up at her. The child wasn't supposed to be in the saloon, per Rachel's explicit orders, but she must have had the run of it before her father's marriage the year before, because she knew every inch of the place—where everything was kept, what brands of whiskey were to be had, the rules of every game of chance.

Savannah gave a slight snort and looked down at her bright green silk dress with its resplendence of feathers, bangles, ribbons, and beads. She looked like a tropical bird, or a piece of tasteless furniture run amok. "I don't think I'd fit in very well," she said, in a deliberately pleasant voice, because she liked Emma and already feared that her ungracious response might have offended the child. "Do you?"

Emma shrugged. Her eyes were thoughtful as she turned her gaze to the window again, and the scene beyond, and it came to Savannah that the girl, being half Lakota Sioux, surely knew all about being a misfit. "Pa says everybody who comes out here to the back of beyond has at least one secret, or something that makes them different anyway. That gives us things to learn about each other."

Savannah smiled, albeit a bit sadly. She'd been shunned enough times in her life to know those

Springwater women, with their noisy, chasing children, their calico dresses, and baskets full of homey food, would never welcome her into their midst. Miranda, on the other hand, was already one of them, despite her own fall from grace. She'd been helping June-bug cut and assemble quilt pieces for weeks, and it was no secret that she'd developed an eye for Landry Kildare, a handsome rancher with two hellion sons.

"You go ahead," Savannah said to Emma, very gently. "I have things to do here."

Emma took in the empty room. Even the bartender had gone to join in the work party. "What?" she asked reasonably, looking around, as though expecting some task with Savannah's name on it to step up and present itself.

Savannah sighed, laid a hand on Emma's shoulder. "When you're older, you'll understand," she said.

Emma's gaze was narrowed with an intensity of thought. "I think I understand right now," she said. "You've already made up your mind that those women won't like you. You aren't even going to try to be their friend, I'll bet, just because you're scared."

Savannah wondered when this kid had turned into an old woman.

"I'm not scared," she lied.

Emma did not look convinced, to say the least. In fact, she all but rolled her eyes. "You'll be missed, you know," she informed Savannah, shaking a verbal finger under her nose. "Miss June-bug will see you're not there, or Rachel will, and they'll come after you, one or the other of them. Maybe both. Mrs. Wainwright, too, probably. She's real sociable."

Savannah was still dealing with Emma's insights, and the prospect of being sought out and dragged into the center of the festivities was more troubling than being deliberately excluded. Emma was, after all, a bright, damnably observant child, and she didn't miss the fact that Savannah was flustered.

"You're scared," the girl accused baldly, and for the second time.

Savannah's heart did a half-turn, then tightened. She swallowed. No sense in lying; this child would see through any attempt at subterfuge. "Scared isn't exactly the word."

"Oh, yes it is," Emma replied. In that instant, she looked more like her father, who could be downright implacable when the spirit moved him, than ever.

"I agree," put in a masculine voice, from just inside the swinging doors. Prescott Parrish, of course; the man was a plague, or so she constantly told herself. She would have done anything to be able to change the way she reacted to his presence, but she'd long since learned that there was no changing it. Every time he came into a room, especially unexpectedly, her heart started thrumming, and pretty soon all her pulses were beating like drums. "You're a coward, Miss Rigbey," he observed. "You'd tuck your fancy feathers and crawl under the floorboards if you could."

Savannah's gaze shot to the doctor's face. Who did he think he was, coming into her place of business, saying things like that? Making things tighten and melt inside her? "How kind of you to come all this way," she said sweetly, "just to share your opinion."

Emma looked from one adult to the other and, being no fool, made a hasty excuse, turned tail, and fled.

Parrish favored Savannah with one of his lopsided, lord-of-the-manor grins. He looked good, damn him, brown from the sun, his formerly gaunt frame filled out from June-bug's fine cooking. His eyes strayed along the length of her before coming back to lock with her blue ones; the impact was equivalent to a pair of railroad cars coupling on a spur. "I wish I could take the credit," he said. "For affronting you with my opinion, I mean." He shrugged, and his mouth took on a mock-rueful shape. "As it happens, though, I'm merely an emissary for Mrs. McCaffrey. Your absence from the festivities has been noted and commented upon. A decree has gone out, from June-bug if not Caesar Augustus, that you are to present yourself at the station forthwith, there to sew, cook, or just gossip with the other females of the community. It looks as though this house-building party might go on for days."

Savannah felt such a yearning that she feared it showed in her eyes; her pride, usually a fortress in which she could take refuge, teetered around her, providing only the most tenuous shelter. "You ought to know, if June-bug doesn't, why I have to stay away."

Parrish raised an eyebrow. His arms remained folded, and after letting her squirm for a few moments, he repeated his earlier accusation. "Coward," he said.

Savannah realized that she'd clenched her hands

into fists, fists full of green beaded silk, and forced her fingers to go slack. "Look at me," she responded, with a note of desperation in her voice. "In case you haven't noticed, I'm not wearing calico."

He ran his eyes over her again. "Oh, I've noticed," he said dryly. "God help me, I *have* noticed."

"Tell June-bug that I'm—I'm busy."

"She's not stupid, Savannah. She'll just come down here after you herself, even if it means endangering her immortal soul by setting foot inside a den of iniquity like the Brimstone Saloon."

Savannah feared that he was right. She looked out the window again, too miserable even to clasp at the last tattered shreds of her dignity. She'd faced outlaws in her time, as well as drunken, marauding cowboys and miners and Pony Express men too long on the trail. None of them had unnerved her the way those ordinary women did, in their blessedly plain dresses. Only when the doctor took a gentle hold on her arm and turned her to face him did she realize she was gnawing on her lower lip.

Parrish laid a hand to her cheek, passed the pad of his thumb lightly over her mouth, as if to smooth away the evidence of her distress. She should have pulled away from him right then, she knew that, but she didn't. There were so many things she should have done, and hadn't.

"Under all that rouge and kohl and rice powder," he said quietly, "you are more than passably pretty. Even if you were ugly as dried mud, you'd still have as much right to participate as any of the others."

Savannah's heart did something acrobatic, something she hoped to high heaven hadn't shown in her face. "I believe there is a compliment hidden away in that insult," she said, and could not help the shaky smile that came to her mouth.

He laughed, but he did not lower his hand. "Tact has never been my strong suit," he said. "Come on, Savannah. Join the party, or June-bug, for one, won't get a moment's joy out of it, for fretting about you. I suppose you've noticed that social events are not exactly thick on the ground here at Springwater."

She let out a long, despairing sigh. "How can I go in these clothes?"

"I'll head back to the station and fetch whatever you need. You have a few——" he chose the word carefully, "*proper* things. I've seen you wear them. I assume whatever underthings you have on will suffice?" From the look in his eyes, she guessed that he was thinking she must not be wearing any, given the revealing nature of her dance-hall getup. The hell of it was, he was right, though she sure wasn't about to say so.

Savannah knew she was beaten; June-bug, kind hearted to a fault, would indeed come looking for any lost sheep, and if she still refused to attend the festivities, her friend was sure to fret over the fact, thereby missing out on all the fun herself. "The blue skirt, then. And the white shirtwaist. They're on pegs, in my room."

Parrish executed an abbreviated salute. "Back in a trice," he said, and was gone. Savannah watched, through the window, as he strode off down the road again, strong arms swinging at his sides. It seemed that he'd made a place for himself at Springwater, for all his faults and foibles, and she envied him that. She also missed the feel of his hand resting against her cheek, missed the stroke of his thumb and the warm pressure of those nimble surgeon's fingers, though she would have been even less willing to admit to it than to confess that she coveted his ease of belonging.

As promised, he returned in good time, with her clothes draped over one arm. She did wish he had come by the back way, instead of striding straight down the middle of the road, for all and sundry to see.

"Don't forget to wash your face," he said, in a confidential whisper, plainly drawn toward the buzzing hive of builders at Trey and Rachel's place.

Savannah was almost grateful for that remark, even though it shot through her, stinging like turpentine poured over a fresh cut. She'd best get her schoolgirl feelings toward this man under control. He clearly looked down on her; hadn't he criticized her clothing and her face paint and her occupation time and time again?

"Thank you," she said briskly, almost snatching her good skirt and shirtwaist from his arms.

He gave her high marks for courage, but then he'd known that about her almost from the first. Even back in Choteau, when he'd watched her working the crowd that frequented the Hell-bent Saloon, he'd noticed how she always kept her backbone straight and her chin up, how she looked people straight in the eye and gave as good as she got in just about every kind of situation.

He would have given a great deal himself, just then, to watch her with the women parlaying around June-bug McCaffrey's long tables. He had no doubt that she could hold her own, and it had surprised him to discover that she didn't share the same confidence. She really was scared, pretty as she looked in her prim little skirt and blouse, with that fine face of hers scrubbed with such vigor that he could see the glow even from a distance. She'd taken her hair down— the thought of that tightened something in his groin—brushed out countless loopy curls, and rearranged the coppery tresses into a loose bun just above her nape.

A good-natured punch in the arm jolted Pres out of his musings; he turned his head and saw Trey Hargreaves standing beside him, grinning with all the pride of a homeowner. "Jacob and me, we've been talking," Hargreaves said. "Looks like there's going to be a fair amount of lumber left over, after we're through here. There's some from when they built the station, too. We—I'm speaking for the town now— we'd like to put up a little place for you, over there behind the Brimstone. Nothing fancy, of course. Just a couple of rooms and a place where you could attend to folks when they have need of a doctor."

Pres was taken aback by the magnitude of the offer. He hadn't considered settling at Springwater, or anywhere else for that matter. He'd gotten stranded there, that was all, and that wasn't the same thing as deciding. "You'd do that?" he asked, amazed.

Trey grinned. "Hell, yes. You'll never get rich, mind. There isn't a lot of cash money around here, and I don't imagine there'll ever be, unless somebody strikes gold. But we need a doctor, if we're going to make this a place where folks will want to settle down, and all of us pretty much agree that you'd do."

Pres shoved a hand through his hair, somewhat at a loss. He'd been living in the McCaffreys' hayloft—not a cold or uncomfortable place, though certainly a humble one—and he supposed he'd probably worked off the cost of his room and board. Summer wouldn't last forever, however, and even though he'd earned the price of a stagecoach ticket several times over, putting splints and bandages on hapless cowpunchers, most of his patients had paid him in venison, dried beans, fresh eggs, or stewing chickens. He'd kept the money for much-needed supplies, and given the food to June-bug; she and Jacob had a veritable army to feed, what with all those kids, the studious, blossoming Miranda and her baby, himself, and Savannah.

"I guess I don't have anything better to do," he said, at some length.

Trey laughed and slapped him on the shoulder. "Glad to hear it," he said, and then lowered his voice by several notches to confide, "I think my Rachel might be in the family way. She's peevish of late, and queasy in the mornings. I'd sure feel a lot better knowing you were going to be around to catch the baby."

It was a common phrase, "catch the baby," but it

always struck Pres as humorous, raising a mental image of an infant shooting through the air like a cannonball, with the attending physician scrambling, arms outspread. He indicated the assemblage of house parts and eager if inept carpenters with a nod of his head. "Looks like you and the missus will have a roof, walls, and floors before a week's out," he said. His mind had returned to Savannah by then; he imagined her living in the soon-to-be vacant rooms over the Brimstone and felt a sense of indignation rise within him like steam.

"Looks like it," Trey agreed. His gaze was at once proud and fond as he glanced toward the walls of the station, behind which the women were huddled, busy as a flock of hens pecking up corn kernels. "Rachel will be glad to see the last of that saloon, and we'll have Emma with us again, too." He paused and shook his head. "I'm in debt up to my ears, though, and that's a fact," he added ruefully.

"I guess Savannah—Miss Rigbey—will go to live in the rooms you and Rachel have been using," Pres said. He imagined amorous cowboys sneaking up the stairs of a night, stray bullets rising through the floor. His belly ground painfully, and his fists clenched and unclenched at his sides, with no conscious instructions from his mind.

Trey's expression was serious all of the sudden, and a little too astute for Pres's comfort. "She's not a whore, you know," he said. "I've been Savannah's friend for a long time now—five years or so. Except for my Rachel, there's no finer woman in the world."

Pres ran his hand over his jaw; his beard was coming in, but then, it was always coming in. He ought to just give up and let it grow, that being the fashion, but he didn't like the feel of hair on his face; it was unhygienic and, furthermore, it itched. "You don't need to explain Miss Rigbey to me," he said, with an implied shrug.

Trey offered no trace of a smile now; his eyes were slightly narrowed, and everything about him testified that he was in earnest. "Don't I?" he asked. "I've seen you watching her, Doc. And since you don't come to the Brimstone to drink or play cards, I figure Savannah must be the reason you spend so much time there."

Pres folded his arms. "Are you about to warn me off, after that friendly speech about how the 'town' needs a doctor and I'll do as well as the next sawbones to wander down the trail?"

"No," Trey said, still solemn. "I can see that there's something between the two of you, everybody can—except for you and her, maybe. What I'm telling you is this: Savannah's a friend of mine. One of the best I've ever had. I'm prepared to like you—fact is, I already do—but if you treat my partner as anything short of a lady, I'll leave you with some marks to show for your mistake."

Pres had never run from a fight in his life—unless, of course, you counted the ones he might have had with himself—and he wasn't about to start then. Still, he had wondered about Savannah, through many a long night.

"What happened to her?" he asked.

Trey raised his hat and thrust a hand through his hair. "I'm not sure. Something pretty bad, I reckon. She's got no family that I know of, and before she came here, I'm pretty sure I was the only friend she had. If you want to know what makes Savannah who she is, Doc, you ought to ask her." The hint of a grin might have been lurking at the back of his mercury-colored eyes; Pres couldn't be sure.

"She's as likely to spit in my eye as answer," he said.

Trey laughed. "You're right about that," he agreed, as Jacob approached.

He still looked surprised that the house had arrived, since he'd oft predicted that it wouldn't get there before spring. He kept glancing back and shaking his head.

"I'll be derned," he said, for the hundredth time.

Pres slapped him on the back. "Life is full of surprises," he said, and then wondered if he wasn't addressing himself as well as Jacob.

Jacob McCaffrey was nothing if not a good sport. Voice booming, brooding eyes full of good-natured understanding, he demanded, "You two mean to stand around here jawin' and leave the rest of us to do the real work?"

Trey and Pres exchanged another look, then went their separate ways, Trey to help assemble the roof, Pres to unload lumber and kegs of nails alongside Landry Kildare.

They all looked up when Savannah entered the public room of the station, as though sensing that there was an imposter in their midst. June-bug beamed at her, and Rachel's expression was friendly, too, but the others were watchful, assessing the new-comer and being none too subtle in the process. Had they been discussing her before her arrival? Just the thought made Savannah want to run until her knees gave out—to hell with Dr. Parrish and his chiding and his challenges.

Rachel brought an attractive, fair-haired woman over to her, almost shyly. "Savannah," she said, "this is my dearest friend in all the world, Evangeline Wainwright. We knew each other in Pennsylvania. Evangeline, Savannah Rigbey. She's an—investor."

Without hesitation, Evangeline put out a strong, slender hand. "I'm very pleased to meet you," she said, in a clear voice. She was smiling warmly, and her eyes were full of light. "Will you be settling here at Spring-water?"

Savannah stammered something, though her mind was whirling at such a pace that she didn't know what. An *investor?*, she thought. What could have prompted Rachel to assign her such a title? Everyone would know—must already know—that she owned half interest in the Brimstone Saloon, that she worked there, sang there, sold whiskey there. But then, those things probably couldn't even be *men-tioned* in polite company. "Yes," she answered belated-ly. Weakly. "I'm staying."

"Come and sit down," Rachel said, pulling her toward the tables, where the women had laid out a series of colorful quilt pieces, apparently working out a pattern. "June-bug's made tea, and there's coffee, too, if you'd rather have that. What do you think of the wedding ring?"

"Wedding ring?" Savannah echoed stupidly. She might have been wearing regular clothes, but she felt as if she were still in silk and feathers. The paint, washed off because it was only sensible and certainly not because Dr. Parrish had suggested that she do so, left a sort of physical echo on her face.

Evangeline laughed, but pleasantly, the way she probably laughed with Rachel and the others. Savannah was heartily confused, having been scorned so many times in the past, by just such women as these.

"It's the name of a quilt pattern," Evangeline said. "See?" She pointed out the interlocking circles of colored fabric worked into the squares.

Savannah's hand trembled slightly, but she couldn't stop herself from reaching out, touching the cloth. She'd always dreamed of owning such a quilt; to her, the colorful patterns symbolized normalcy. "How beautiful," she said, and blinked rapidly, fearing she would disgrace herself and weep for all she had missed.

After working up her nerve, she looked from one face to another, and it seemed to her that the women were not so wary, nor so severe, as when she'd first come in. Those she didn't know were still a little distant, though. "Did you all contribute?"

One woman—Savannah would later know her as Mrs. Bellweather—spared a nod. Miranda, seated at the far end of the table with a pile of bright scraps before her, was watching Savannah with an expression of eager encouragement in her eyes, like someone trying to persuade a baby to take its first faltering steps.

"It's for the next Springwater bride," Evangeline said, eyes bright. "We made one for Rachel already—Jacob's ladder, it's called—and mine is a log cabin pattern. June-bug and Sue stitched that one up, over a snowy winter."

Savannah looked about. Her throat felt tight. "Someone is about to be married?"

Rachel laughed. "No one in particular. We're all sewing our bits and pieces of calico together, though, and matching them up when we meet. When there's a wedding, we'll be ready."

Savannah was charmed and a little bemused. She sat down, at only a slight distance from the others, on one of the long benches, and June-bug set a steaming cup of tea in front of her, already laced with milk and sugar, just the way she liked it. "She'll be a lucky bride, whoever she is," Savannah said, perhaps a bit wistfully.

"I hope it's someone for Landry," said another woman, the wife of a farmer. "Poor man. All alone, with those demon boys of his to raise. Mark my words, one of these nights, they'll burn the house down, with him right inside."

Miranda, who had been sewing industriously again, seemed to catch on Kildare's name like a fish on a hook. "How does it happen that he's got no wife?" she asked shyly. "Somebody as fine to look at as he is, I mean."

The others giggled, though not unkindly, but Miranda went brick-red all the same. Savannah felt sorry for her, though she hadn't been able to help smiling a little herself. Just for a very few moments, she forgot that she could never truly be a member of this little group; she was, after all, a dance-hall woman and assumed prostitute. If it hadn't been for June-bug and perhaps Rachel, the others probably wouldn't have spoken to her at all.

"Well," insisted Evangeline, seated across from Savannah, beside her good friend Rachel, and stitching away, "he *is* handsome. Landry, I mean."

"Had him a wife once," said another woman, after everyone had clucked over Evangeline's daring remark. "The cholera took her. Pretty thing, delicate-like, with quiet ways."

Miranda twisted her hands, her face a study in sympathy for all the Kildares. "It's a terrible thing, the cholera," she said. "We saw plenty of it on the way out here from St. Louis." She paused. "How long ago was that? When Mrs. Kildare passed over, I mean?"

"Must have been quite a while back," June-bug put in. "It was before Jacob and I came to run the station. He already had that place of his when we got here."

"He was one of the first to settle around here," affirmed Mrs. Bellweather, who looked worn-down to Savannah, as though she'd known too much hardship, too much work and sorrow for one body to sort through. "Came to this country about the same time as Big John Keating and Scully Wainwright." She paused and tightened her narrow little mouth. "She's buried right there, too. They say he used to sleep beside that grave, till the weather got too cold."

Rachel and Evangeline exchanged glances and stitched a little faster.

"What was her name?" Miranda dared to ask. Her voice was hardly more than a whisper, and her fingers were knotted together, white at the knuckles, her quilt square forgotten on the table before her.

"Caroline," the woman answered, after a few moments of consideration. "Why do you ask?"

Miranda flushed and swallowed.

June-bug laid an affectionate hand to the girl's shoulder. "She's just curious, that's all," she said, with a broad smile, neatly dismissing the subject. "Nothin' wrong with that."

The sewing continued, and so did the talk, the pouring and sipping of tea, the merry laughter. Savannah was glad she'd locked up the saloon and ventured into this circle of women; maybe they hadn't exactly enfolded her, but they hadn't shut her out, either. She was a part of the group, if only at the fringes, and she relished the novelty of that, pretending to herself, just for that long, hot afternoon, that she was an ordinary wife, with a house to keep, and a husband to feed and humor and plague about flower seeds and glass windows and what to make for supper.

The preparation of the evening meal was a spectacular enterprise, with tasks for everyone to perform, all of them orchestrated by June-bug, and Savannah was included without hesitation. Although she knew little or nothing about cooking, she did remember how to peel potatoes, so June-bug assigned her that job.

Now and then, one or another of the men straggled in, looking for coffee and a temporary place out of the sun, but they soon became uncomfortable in the presence of so many women and departed again. Until Dr. Parrish came in, that is. He stood quietly on the hearth, leaning at his ease against the mantelpiece, cup in hand. His ebony eyes sought Savannah, found her, held her captive, by means of some strange and elemental magic. She did not look at him directly— refused to do so—but she was aware of his observance all the same, conscious of him in every cell of her body and every wisp of her soul.

She was annoyed to find herself in such a state, again. She wanted to run, from him, from the calm embrace of Springwater itself, to get up from that table, throw her few belongings into a satchel, and dash off into the night, without even bothering to choose a direction first. She could not, would not ever be vulnerable again; the one time she had let down her guard, she'd all but ruined her life.

Unconsciously, she raised a hand to her mouth in abject panic, realized what she'd revealed only when it was too late. When he'd seen, of course, and understood. The expression in his eyes said he understood only too well.

She managed a smile as she stood, on unsteady legs, the room seeming, for the merest fraction of a moment, to sway and dip around her. It was ridiculous to react in such a fashion. Downright silly. She was not a schoolgirl, for heaven's sake, not some witless virgin, far from home, but an accomplished business woman, a person of substance and common sense. She should know better, be able to control her responses, even to quell them entirely, when that would be suitable.

"Good night," she said, to the general assembly, and turned, very nearly stumbling over her own feet, to make a beeline for the door.

Outside, on the step, she drew in great, gulping draughts of fresh evening air, hugging herself with both arms against the chill. Across the road, the men were still working, their shirts soaked through with sweat. The framework of Trey and Rachel's house was already outlined against the dusky sky, where the first stars were just beginning to pop out.

"Are you all right?"

She should have been prepared for him to follow her, should have expected it, but she hadn't. "No," she said, without turning to look at him. "No," she repeated.

He came to stand beside her, his upper arm brushing, just barely, against her shoulder, sending a shock of sensation bolting through her. "Perhaps you should go in and lie down." He looked and sounded genuinely concerned.

She shook her head. "I'll be fine in a minute or two." She pressed the fingertips of her right hand to her temple. "They spoke to me. They're planning a quilt, to present to the next bride. They don't even know who it will be—" She was rambling, prattling, could not seem to stop herself, or even slow her tongue.

Suddenly, he took hold of her, turned her to face him, and lowered his mouth to hers. The kiss was fiery, consuming, and desperate, and might have led to all manner of troubles, had it not raised a rousing cheer from the other side of the road.

CHAPTER

6

THOUGH THERE WAS still a lot of finishing work to do on the Hargreaves house, outside as well as in, the place was habitable after only a week of concentrated community effort. There was a working wood furnace to provide heat when the fierce Montana winters came, and glass in the windows. The fancy plumbing and other luxuries would take longer to install, and the pre-cut wooden floors were bare of varnish, let alone rugs. The fireplace in the front parlor consisted of a pile of rocks gathered from the countryside and a few bags of dry mortar, but the small family did not seem to mind the prospect of rough accommodations. With appropriate ceremony, Trey, Rachel, and the child Emma took up residence, hurrahed by their friends and presented with gifts—food, mostly, every sort of preserved vegetable, fruit, and meat, but fire-wood, too, and what spare linens could be ferreted from trunks and bureaus. Jacob McCaffrey was already building a cradle out in the barn behind the station; Pres was the only one who knew, that being unavoidable since he was still sleeping in the hayloft then.

It made an ache in him, the sight of that cradle; for the first time in years, he wanted children of his own. And he wanted them by Savannah. Exasperating as she was, even impossible at times, she'd taken up residence in all his senses at once, infused his mind and his spirit with her own, until he couldn't tell one from the other. Was this love?

God in heaven, he hoped not.

In the meantime, the promised house/surgery was well under way, utilizing the modest surplus of supplies remaining after the Hargreaves place had been pieced together, like the parts of a giant puzzle, though most of the work was being done by Trey, Jacob, and Pres himself, with an occasional helping hand from Landry. The others had had to leave for home, since all of them had farms and ranches to run; most left reluctantly in the charge of son, brother, or hired hand.

Savannah had not yet moved in above the saloon—June-bug was vociferously opposed to that, bless her—and besides, she didn't appear to own a stick of furniture, so she remained at the station, in the little room behind the kitchen stove.

As the days began to grow shorter, ever so slowly, and colder as well, Pres wished he could share it with her. Thoughts of Savannah and babies and patchwork quilts disturbed his sleep and distracted him during his waking hours.

Finally, the last week in August, when a series of heavy rains came, turning the fields to a dense mud the locals called "gumbo"—Jacob allowed as how it wasn't uncommon for the weather to turn suddenlike and counted them all blessed of the Lord—Pres was able to move into his own humble dwelling. He soon found that the place was only a little warmer than the McCaffrey barn had been, but at least there was a rusty old stove, scavenged from an abandoned homestead a few miles from town. He had a bed, hastily nailed together by Jacob, with rope to support the mattress June-bug and Miranda stitched together from flour sacks and last year's corn husks, and a table, fashioned from one of the crates in which the Hargreaves' mail-order mansion had arrived. His chairs were of similar construction, and the floor was so poorly planed that he didn't dare set his feet down in the morning without pulling on his boots first. Come winter, there would probably be a layer of frost to greet him as well.

In spite of all these shortcomings, Pres was happier than he had been in a long time. There was no lack of patients from the first day, and every passing stagecoach brought more of the supplies and medicines he'd sent to Choteau for. He took his meals at the station, having no pots, dishes, or skill for cooking, though of course his reasons had more to do with Savannah than with June-bug McCaffrey's victuals. Now that he was practicing medicine again, he simply didn't have the leisure to pass long hours at the Brimstone, pretending not to watch her.

It was ill advised, he knew, this fascination with a woman who obviously mistrusted him. Ever since that night when she'd taken her rightful place among the ladies of Springwater, and he'd been brash enough to kiss her in front of half the population on the front step shortly afterward, she'd been keeping a careful distance. Not that he'd apologize or anything, given that he'd meant to do it, all right, and wouldn't do differently even if he could go back to that night and take another run at the whole encounter.

He was considering the matter of Savannah Rigbey, between advising June-bug McCaffrey on her arthritis and an aging cowboy on his dyspepsia, when all of the sudden the surgery door blew open and Savannah herself swept in with a rainy wind, wrapped in a brown velvet cloak with a graceful hood. Great droplets of water clung to her lashes and her clothes, but her eyes were fiery enough to dry up a lake.

"Shut the door," Pres said reasonably.

"Dr. Parrish—"

"Prescott," he corrected her, lifting his donated coffeepot from the top of the little stove and giving it a shake to see if anything remained of the batch he'd made at breakfast. "Pres, if you want to be friendly. Tell me, where does it hurt?"

She slammed the door. "I *don't* want to be friendly, as it happens," she snapped, "and nothing hurts."

He enjoyed watching her temper flare almost as much as kissing her. "Then to what do I owe the honor of this visit?"

"I think it would be better for everyone if you just

left town," she announced. She'd folded her arms, and under the hem of her dress he saw that one small foot was tapping soundlessly against the splintery floor, though whether from nerves or temper, he couldn't tell. "Move on, I mean. From Springwater."

The surgery, like the sleeping quarters to the rear, was scantly furnished. "Sit down," he said, indicating one of the packing-crate chairs with a cordial nod. Then he lifted the dented pot. "Coffee?"

She sat, but not graciously. Nor did she take off her cloak. Under the table, he suspected, that same foot was still tapping. She was acting as though she were angry, but her eyes conveyed something else—a sort of despairing confusion. "Did you hear what I said?"

He grinned, pouring a dose of what could only be described as axle grease for himself. "Oh, yes," he said. "My hearing is fairly good, actually, despite three and a half years of almost constant canon fire. Why do you want me to leave?"

She looked very uncomfortable and a little peevish. Barely eleven A.M., by his father's pocket watch, and already the day was shaping up to be a memorable one. "Because—" she hesitated, visibly searching for words. She had not thought this visit through beforehand, it would seem, but instead come on impulse. "Because you kissed me. Twice."

He kept his distance, lest he scare her away. "Is there an ordinance against that?" he asked, very cheerfully. He was rewarded by the apricot blush that rose in her cheeks. God in heaven, but she was breathtaking. Body, mind, spirit, he loved—yes, loved—everything about her.

Savannah laid both hands on the tabletop, palms down, with a little slapping sound. She took several slow, deep breaths, and closed her eyes for a moment, in an admirable bid for control. "I would leave myself," she said moderately, and at some length, "but I've tied up every penny I have in that dratted saloon."

"Maybe Trey Hargreaves would be willing to buy you out. If you really want to move on, I mean." It was a bluff; the last thing he wanted was for her to go anywhere. She was, of course, the reason he'd stayed on at Springwater in the first place, though he'd be a pure fool to say as much, under the circumstances.

She leaned forward a little way, providing a tantalizing glimpse of cleavage despite her heavy cloak, and gave him that look he'd seen her use to intimidate obnoxious cowboys. It wasn't going to work with him.

"It would be much easier," she said reasonably, "if *you* were the one to leave."

"Why is that?"

"Because there's nothing holding you here, really. Except for this—this shack."

"And my patients," he added. He was doing his best not to smile, since he figured that might prompt her to get up and walk out, but it wasn't easy. Even— maybe *especially*—in a state of agitation, she was a pleasure to watch and a balm to his jaded spirit. "Mustn't forget them. And you still haven't answered my question, Miss Rigbey. Not really."

She looked at him in stubborn silence, though she knew damn well what he meant.

All right, he'd give in. "Why do you want me to leave? Besides as a punishment for daring to kiss you, I mean?"

She bit down hard on that luscious lower lip of hers. He wanted to nibble at it, along with a few other sensitive parts of her anatomy. Her eyes got very wide and darkened a little, and that delectable peachy color pulsed beneath her cheekbones again. "You're going to make me say it, aren't you?"

"Yes," he said bluntly. He allowed himself just the suggestion of a grin and waited, arms folded again, coffee mug forgotten on the nearby windowsill.

"I can't think. I can't sleep." Her color heightened still further, and she seemed to have trouble meeting his eyes. There was a note of desperation in her voice. "I can't afford to fall—to feel—"

He crossed to her then, dragged up the other chair to sit facing her, and leaned in a little, his nose an inch from hers. "To fall where, Miss Rigbey? And feel what?"

To his utter surprise, and his chagrin, sudden tears welled in her eyes. She raised her chin a notch, just the same. "I was in love once, or I thought so, anyway," she said, and if she'd refused to look at him before, now she wouldn't look away. "His name was Burke—I knew him, growing up. He was already wild, even as a boy, but after we ran off, well, he—he—"

He tightened his grip on her hands, spoke quietly. "What, Savannah?"

"We were about to get married." Her smile was wobbly and fragile. "The fact is, we were standing before the justice of the peace. A U.S. Marshal interrupted the ceremony to arrest Burke. Turned out, he'd been involved in some robberies. They took him away, then and there, and later on, he was convicted and sent to prison."

Pres ached for her, for the woman before him, and for the young girl she had been. "What did you do?"

She looked at him with round, fearful eyes, as though expecting judgment. "I went home," she said. "Papa called me a whore and told me never to come back." He ached to pull her into his arms, hold her close, but it wasn't time for offering comfort, not yet. She wasn't finished. "I didn't know any other way to earn a living than singing in a saloon. Nobody was going to take me on to watch their children or clean their house, not with the scandal I'd raised. Why, it was even in the newspapers, how I'd eloped with a thief—how Burke was arrested right in the middle of our wedding."

Pres opened his mouth, closed it again. He rasped an exclamation.

Her gaze remained direct, though her pain was as intense as any he'd seen on the battlefields of Pennsylvania, Virginia, Tennessee, and too many other places. He wanted to take her by the shoulders, but she still seemed delicate as glass, ready to shatter at the gentlest touch. "I was only sixteen. I couldn't go to Burke, and there was no one else. So I went to work to support myself."

"There's no shame in that, Savannah. You made a mistake. Welcome to the human race."

She looked at him with mild surprise. Nevertheless, I've had to live with the consequences. My life was changed forever. And my grandmother died because of what happened."

He frowned. "How do you figure that? Grandmothers die, Savannah."

"She was heartbroken after Papa sent me away. She went into a decline. Papa made sure I heard about it, and when I tried to go to her funeral, he had me barred from the church."

Pres wanted to overturn tables and fling things in every direction, a feeling he'd had many times during the war, though he had never indulged himself and didn't intend to begin now. "Your father was wrong, Savannah. And you're wrong, too, if you blame yourself. What you did wasn't evil, or malicious. It was natural for a young girl, believing herself to be in love. Does it make sense to spend the rest of your life under your father's wrongheaded judgment?"

She blinked, obviously jarred by the question, and said nothing.

"Savannah," he persisted, but gently. If she fled him now, he knew, she would never come back.

She ran her tongue over her lips; it was merely a nervous reaction, nothing more, and yet it set his groin to aching. "I was an ordinary girl," she said, "with a good singing voice, a head for numbers, and a whole passel of dreams I was sure would come true. I had a grandmother and a father who loved me—

once—and friends. Lots and lots of friends. I wanted to have children, six of them, and head up the church choir. I wanted to cook and go to quilting bees, like Gran did—"

He waited, even when her voice fell away.

"Two months after my grandmother died, Papa passed away, too. Up until then, I could pretend that things might be all right again, that he might forgive me. Once he was gone, though, I had to accept the fact that I was probably going to spend the rest of my life in saloons. In some ways, that was the worst moment of all."

"It must have been a lot like my first shift in a field hospital. Nothing I learned in medical college prepared me for what I found in that place."

A long silence fell between them, oddly comfortable, given the situation and the topic of conversation.

"Was it very terrible?" She barely breathed the words.

"Beyond that," he answered, and sighed, letting her hands go, resting his palms on his knees. They were still facing each other, still very close. "I don't suppose I'll ever completely leave it behind. But I'm trying, Savannah. That's the point. You've got to do the same. We need to shake off these demons of ours, both of us."

He saw a protest forming on her mouth, in her eyes, but in the end she did not offer it. "I'm not sure I can do it," she whispered. It was a momentous admission for her; he could see that.

He had never wanted to kiss her as much as he did in that moment, and that was saying something, considering how much time he'd spent lying in Jacob McCaffrey's hayloft, staring up at the log beams and aching to do just that and a whole lot more. He restrained himself, and what he said astonished him as much as it did Savannah. "Marry me."

She stared at him, and her mouth dropped open—he put one hand under her chin and lifted, closing her jaw. "You're not serious," she said, in the next moment.

"I think I am," he said. He'd given the idea a lot of consideration, all the while trying to fool himself into believing that it was only idle speculation. Now, it seemed as if he'd glanced inside himself one day, while passing by, and found another person there, someone better than he'd been until he came to Springwater, someone capable of loving and believing and hoping that the future could be better than the past.

"But why?"

He wasn't ready to tell her how he felt. He was still explaining it to himself. "Because you need a husband and I need a wife. Plenty of people have gotten married for less practical reasons."

"You're insane!" She flushed yet again, and her hands rose to her hips, though she looked more broken than angry. "We're not in love—"

"Be sensible, Savannah," he counseled, as if he was being sensible himself. "You're not happy running the Brimstone Saloon and wearing those silly dresses—

admit that to yourself, if not to me. You were a great help when Miranda's baby came—calm and competent. You'd make a fine nurse and a very good doctor's wife."

"You'd marry someone who's spent most of her life singing to drunken cowboys?"

"Yes," he answered. Savannah was levelheaded, for the most part, and she had an unruffled, caring way about her. He'd liked the way she'd spoken soothingly to Miranda, during the height of the girl's labor, the way she'd held the baby almost reverently, not caring that the squirming, squalling little creature hadn't been washed or wrapped. She could be firm, too, obviously, when the situation called for it.

She got up, and for a moment he feared she meant to leave, but instead she began to pace, like a lawyer formulating an impassioned appeal to put before a waiting jury. "Where would I sleep?" she asked.

The question caught him so off guard that he nearly swallowed his tongue. "With me," he replied, at some length, and in a voice he nearly didn't recognize.

She stopped, and her eyes were wide again. "You mean—?"

"That's exactly what I mean," he clarified. "A wife is a wife. I expect mine to share my bed." No sense having any misunderstandings on that score.

"I am not a whore, Dr. Parrish. I don't sell myself for money, and I won't take a wedding ring for payment either."

He wanted to shake her. Why couldn't she let herself be happy? But he knew, of course. She was afraid of being hurt, not just physically, but emotionally, too. "I didn't say you were. I said if you marry me, you'll have to lie beside me every night. That's what wives do, among other things." He stood, went to face her, laid his hands gently on her cheeks. "I swear to God, Savannah, I'm not like him. I won't let you down."

She seemed to want to fly off in every direction, and she was trembling, but he could tell that she was entertaining the prospect of marrying him, that she really did want to wear calico and have babies and be called "Mrs." Somebody. Mrs. Parrish, he thought, would do nicely.

"Nobody within fifty miles will be surprised," he said, in case it made a difference. He forgave himself this inanity on grounds of being in shock.

"What is that supposed to mean?"

"Remember how the men cheered when I kissed you, Savannah?" he countered. He dropped his hands from her face, took a light, supportive hold on her upper arms. "Everyone knows we want each other. Everyone but you and, all right, me too, until very recently."

She looked him over, rather like a farmer's wife inspecting a rooster at the fair, prior to purchase. "Suppose you take to drinking again?"

He raised one hand, as if in an oath. "I won't," he argued, but calmly, placing just the merest emphasis on the second word. "I didn't drink before I went into the Army, or during my term of service. It started afterward, Savannah, when I had to stand still long enough for all of it to catch up with me."

She bit her lower lip again and furrowed her brow, afraid to believe in happy endings. He didn't blame her. "Suppose I came to care for you very deeply, and you never returned the sentiment? Suppose you took a mistress—"

"The best kind of love isn't spontaneous, Savannah," he said, wondering where the declaration had come from even as he uttered it. "It grows, over time, because two people live and work together. Because they share a life."

She folded her arms. She was weakening, he could tell. "And the mistress?"

"I wouldn't have the time, let alone the inclination. You have my permission to shoot me if I ever break our vows."

"Don't worry," she said decisively, "I would. With or without your permission."

He grinned. "Then it's settled. When's the wedding?"

She gulped. "It isn't settled. Not at all."

He kissed her then, tenderly at first, teasing her lips apart, then with a passion that, like Paul's experience on the road to Damascus, might just leave him blind for three days. Or so it seemed at the time.

Savannah gasped when he finally withdrew, but she didn't pull out of his arms; indeed, she leaned against him, breathing deeply, letting her forehead rest against his shoulder. "I wouldn't be the sort of wife who takes orders," she warned, after a few moments. "I won't carry your slippers, like a pet spaniel, and if women *ever* get the vote, I'll cast my ballot for whatever candidate I choose. I won't necessarily hold the same opinions as you do. And if I sell my share of the Brimstone to Trey, it might be a very long time before I see a penny of the money. When I do, I intend to bank it in Great Falls or Denver or even San Francisco, under my name and my name alone."

He laughed. "Fine," he said. "I don't mind supporting you. Just be forewarned—country doctors don't make much money, so we won't be living in grand style."

Her eyes were alight with the desire to trust him, to step out of the fortress she'd erected around herself. "I need time to think," she said.

He was jubilant that she hadn't turned him down out of hand. "Do all the thinking you want," he said, but he kissed her again and, again, she didn't resist.

Marriage. To Prescott Parrish.

Was she mad?

The wind was liquid as Savannah walked back toward Springwater station, through a spattering downpour, but she barely noticed. Her senses were a-riot, and it was all Pres's fault for kissing her. For talking about—about the things he'd talked about.

She couldn't actually *marry* the man, of course. Oh, she felt passion for him, even longing. And she'd lived in the world too long not to know that what he'd said about love was true—it didn't always strike unexpectedly, as it had with Rachel and Trey, or the Wainwrights. More often, especially between men and women settling out west, where the work was uncommonly hard and there were so many ways to die or be grievously injured, good marriages began as partnerships.

Across the road from the station, lights glowed in the windows of the Hargreaves' splendid five-room house. Smoke curled from the chimney over the kitchen cookstove, and as Savannah stood there, in the gathering rainstorm, she wondered if Trey and Rachel really knew how lucky they were.

It was then that she decided, or at least, she would always remember it that way. She would accept Pres's proposal, and take her chances. Maybe someday, she might even be able to admit that she loved him, that she had from the night he'd delivered Miranda's baby. In the very instant he'd handed her that squalling, messy newborn child, she'd felt a telling shift, deep in her soul. She simply hadn't recognized that fierce and sudden yearning for what it was—how could she have, when she'd never experienced anything like it before?

Perhaps, in time, Pres would come to love her in return.

She went inside the station, found the main room empty, which was both a relief and a disappointment. She wanted to tell June-bug her news, and yet she wasn't quite ready to share it. She hadn't gotten used to the idea herself, after all, and she would be awhile working it through.

It was only when she reached her snug little hideaway behind the cookstove and took off her cloak that she looked down at the scarlet taffeta dress she was wearing and recalled that she'd been headed for the Brimstone when she left the station. In fact, she'd only stopped to call on Dr. Parrish—Pres—on a crazy impulse. He'd kissed her, asked for her hand in marriage, and all the while she'd been wearing the clothes he hated and the "face paint" he'd taken exception to on several occasions.

A door closed in the distance, and she heard Junebug's voice. "Savannah? Darlin', are you sick?" The other woman appeared in the entryway to Savannah's room, wearing a lightweight bonnet and a woolen cloak. Her brow was crumpled in a worried expression. "Weren't you headed to the Brimstone?"

Savannah had no explanation to offer, even to herself, but in that moment, she burst into tears and sat down hard on the edge of her bed. June-bug discarded her bonnet and cloak, cluck-clucking all the while, and came to perch beside her and drape a sympathetic arm around her wobbling shoulders. "Well, sweetheart, what on *earth*?"

"I can't do it anymore!" she wailed.

"Do what?" June-bug asked, reasonably enough.

"Put on these dreadful clothes and all this kohl and rouge and spend all my time in that saloon!" Savannah sobbed.

"There, now," June-bug said, rocking her a little. "There, now." She didn't offer a solution or any sort of advice, and Savannah loved her for those attributes, among many others. "I'll make us some tea. You wash your face and put on another dress. Jacob can step across the way and tell Trey you won't be working tonight."

Savannah had been on her own for a long time, and it was bliss to be mothered for a little while, to be cosseted and comforted and soothed. "Th-that would be n-nice," she snuffled, making a brave effort to collect herself.

June-bug patted Savannah's back before rising to her feet. "Everybody needs a good cry once in a while," she said. "You just carry on all you want."

Savannah couldn't help a small burst of laughter at the advice. "I feel like a perfect fool," she said. "What good does crying do?"

"Why, tears are like medicine," June-bug said, sounding surprised by the question. "They heal all manner of ills and soften up some of our sorrows, too."

Savannah took a pressed handkerchief from the drawer of her bedside table and delicately blew her nose. "My grandmother used to say things like that."

June-bug, poised on the threshold, smiled. "I reckon I would have liked her a lot, your grandmother. Now, you wash your face. You got all them colors to runnin'."

She laughed again, this time with spirit, and when June-bug left the room, she got up, poured water from the pitcher into the washbasin, both items being kept on a scarred table under a high window, and scrubbed her face with one of the few luxuries she allowed herself—fine-milled French soap. Then, when the last streaks of red and blue and black were gone, she let down her hair and brushed it until it crackled. The dress was the last to go—she slipped the garment down over her hips and kicked it over into a corner of the room in a symbolic act. When she joined June-bug for tea, ten minutes later, with her hair in a loose bun at the back of her head, she was wearing a blue bombazine dress, and Jacob had been despatched to deliver the message to Trey.

Her partner came across the road right away, looking worried. "Are you sick?" he asked, in much the same tone as June-bug had done earlier.

Savannah, seated in a rocking chair near the fire, teacup in hand, shook her head in response, unable, for the moment, to explain. June-bug went to look in on Miranda and the baby, still referred to as "little Isaiah-or-Ezekiel," and Jacob herded Toby and Christabel outside to help him with the chores.

Trey drew up the other rocking chair. "What is it, then?"

"I'm going to be married," she said, without planning to. "I don't want to be a saloon-keeper anymore."

From anyone else, she might have expected anger, but Trey was her friend, closer than a brother. She saw immediately that he understood, maybe because he was so happy with Rachel. "Doc Parrish?"

She nodded. So Pres had been right, then. Everyone knew.

Trey beamed. "That's wonderful."

"But our partnership, yours and mine, I mean—"

He was thoughtful. "I can buy you out, if you're willing to wait a spell for the money. A *long* spell, I reckon. If that won't do, we could bring somebody in from Choteau or Great Falls to take your place. Pay them a salary."

Suddenly, Savannah was filled with panic. Suppose she hated being a doctor's wife? Suppose she hated being *Prescott Parrish's* wife? If she sold her share of the saloon to Trey or anyone else, she would have nowhere to turn, nowhere to take refuge.

But that was silly. She could take care of herself, whether penniless or with a fat bank account tucked away in Denver or San Francisco. She had already established that much; she had nothing more to prove, either to herself or to the world in general. Marrying Pres was something she would do simply because it was what she *wanted* to do.

"Savannah?" Trey prompted, and she realized she'd let his suggestion about bringing in someone else to take her place at the saloon go unanswered.

"No," she said firmly, after another moment or two of hard thought. "A marriage can't work, if you've got one foot in the agreement and one foot out, ready to spring for parts unknown. I'll sell, Trey. I know you're a fair man—I wouldn't have dealt with you in the first place if I thought otherwise—so you make me an offer and come up with some terms, and we'll settle the whole thing, once and for all. I don't care how long it takes you to pay me."

Trey's silver eyes were alight, and it gave Savannah something of a pang to realize that he'd probably wanted to own the Brimstone outright for a long time. "I'll have to speak with Rachel, of course," he said, with barely controlled eagerness. "But I think we can consider the sale already made."

Savannah leaned over and kissed her old friend lightly on the forehead. "Thank you, Trey," she told him softly.

No looking back now, she added to herself. It was time to leave all the old demons behind, just as Pres had said, and keep company with angels instead.

CHAPTER 7

THE WEDDING WAS a quiet one, held before the hearth at Springwater station, three days after Pres's unorthodox proposal. Jacob McCaffrey officiated, Trey and Rachel were witnesses, and the children, Emma, Toby, and Christabel, served as eager guests, along with June-bug and the pensive Miranda. Savannah felt wildly dizzy the whole time the brief but binding ceremony was going on, like someone trying to walk blindfolded over uneven ground. By the time it had ended, and Pres had kissed her exuberantly to seal the bargain, she was seeing everything through a haze, and all the ordinary sounds of the room, the station itself, and even the surrounding wilderness were underlaid with a peculiar thrumming buzz.

Pres, ever the doctor, ate cake and accepted congratulations with that strange, blunt grace that, Savannah was learning, was a hallmark of his personality, but his attention had been caught by young Christabel's twisted foot.

"I'd like to have a closer look at that," he confided, with a thoughtful frown creasing his forehead.

Though Savannah was certainly not without sympathy for the shy, crippled child, her mind was fixed on other matters entirely, just then. She was *married*. Someday, with luck and good behavior, she might even be respectable.

And in a very short while, she would be alone with her husband. Sharing the double bed borrowed from Miranda's room at the station; Trey, Jacob, and Pres had dismantled the thing that morning, and carried it over to Pres's "house." Miranda and little Isaiah-or-Ezekiel would move into Savannah's old nook, behind the cookstove. Already, dusk was gathering at the windows, and a light rain had begun to fall, pattering on the roof and against the windows like sweet, rhythmic music. Savannah, who had known the intimate attentions of a man, however unwillingly, who had spent years in the saloon business, was so deliciously nervous that she might have been the most uninitiated of brides.

"Was Christabel born with that bad foot?" Pres asked of Jacob, who was standing nearby, tall and imposing in his dark "preachin' suit." "Or was there an accident?"

"Born with it, I reckon," Jacob said, in his quiet, rumbling way.

June-bug poked Pres in the ribs. He looked wonderfully handsome in the clothes she'd provided, no doubt belonging to one or the other of the lost twins. "Never mind that," she said. "Christabel's foot will keep; she's lived with it this long. This is your *wedding* day, Doc."

A broad grin broke over Pres's handsome face. "Yes," he said, with a sidelong glance at Savannah, who blushed in spite of her best resolve to be circumspect. "It is indeed. I think perhaps it's time for the bride and me to say our farewells, for the night, at least."

Savannah, standing there in her best dress, an ivory silk from her saloon-girl days, hastily altered with bits and pieces from other frocks, judiciously assembled—Savannah, who did not have a retiring bone in her body, lowered her eyes and could not bring herself to raise them again.

She was therefore caught completely by surprise when Pres suddenly swept her up into his arms, right there in the main room of the Springwater station. Everyone applauded merrily, and someone opened the door. A moist breeze rushed in and made the rainy-day fire dance in the grate.

"Put me down," Savannah whispered, though half heartedly, her face buried in Pres's neck.

"Oh, I will," he promised softly, for her ears only. "As soon as we get to our bed." And so it was that he carried her down the middle of the Springwater road, through a misty benediction of rainfall, the skirts of her improvised wedding dress tumbling down over his legs as well as hers. Indeed, he carried her around the back of the Brimstone Saloon and, finally, into the little house/office that would be their home.

The place was chilly, but Savannah didn't feel the

low temperature. She was warmed by an inner fire, being held like that, and in such close proximity to Pres's—her *husband's*—strong chest, wrapped in his arms. He didn't set her down to open their front door, but bent awkwardly, and kicked it closed with the heel of one boot once they'd crossed the threshold. Without so much as pausing, he made for the single room that would be their living quarters for the foreseeable future.

Finally, as promised, he dropped her playfully onto the bed, where she landed in a heap of silk and ruffles and lace, a make-do bride in a make-do wedding dress. His expression was somber as he looked down at her.

"You'll never regret taking me for a husband, Savannah Parrish," he said, and his voice sounded gruff.

Her throat tightened with some emotion it seemed better not to name. "I know that," she replied, and somehow, she *did* know. For all his arrogance, for all his terse tongue and errant past, Pres was a good man, the one the Fates had chosen for her, and presented as a gift. She wanted to say she loved him then, that she'd fallen for him on that first night in Springwater, but she couldn't risk being rebuffed.

He began by undoing his borrowed string tie, loosened his collar, tossed aside his coat. Savannah watched, as if entranced; it was like the beginning of a dance, this encounter between them, this first sweet, fiery union. She had expected to feel fear; instead, she felt excitement and anticipation. She'd been a girl when Burke entered her life and turned it upside down, but she was a woman now, and she wasn't afraid to trust her assessment of this man she'd married. She could believe in him.

Pres unbuttoned his cuffs, rolled his sleeves loosely, midway up his forearms. His manner was cool, but his eyes were hot as branding irons. Where Burke had been a mere boy, and a selfish one, at that, Pres was a man, in every sense of the word, and the very grace of his movements bespoke tenderness, power, and skill.

"You're sure?" he prompted quietly. "We can still go back and have Jacob tear up the papers, but once we've been—" he actually stumbled, just there, and reddened a little, "once we've been intimate, Mrs. Parrish, it's for life."

It was a gallant offer; he was giving her the chance to change her mind, with no apparent repercussions. She shook her head, began to unbutton the bodice of her dress.

He sat down on the edge of the mattress and, very gently, put her hands aside to take up the task himself. She trembled, sitting there, feeling every pass of his fingers, no matter how light, watching the subtle changes in his face as he unveiled her that first time. It was all so new, so fresh, so poignant.

Her breasts were bared; their tips tightened in response to the coolness of the air and, conversely, to the heat of Pres's gaze. He weighed her tenderly in the palms of his hands, chafed the already-taut nipples with the pads of his thumbs. "Lovely," he breathed. A slight, sleepy smile crooked his mouth at one corner and twinkled in his eyes. "Oh, Savannah, you do make me believe in good things again. A Grecian statue awash in moonlight couldn't be more beautiful than you are."

She was stricken with a sort of quiet joy; such words, coming from this man who was usually straightforward to the point of poor manners, were beyond precious. Tears prickled her eyes. "You've got poetry in you, Dr. Parrish," she whispered, and shivered with pleasure because he was still plying her, still preparing her for the inevitable conquest. "I would never have guessed."

The smile crooked again. "I'm full of surprises," he said, and then he bent his head and began kissing and nibbling his way down her neck, across the length of her collarbone and, finally, along the rounded swell of her upper breast. When he boldly took her nipple, she gasped; the sensation was like waltzing amid flames of pleasure.

Gently, he pressed her back onto the pillows, and somehow managed to divest her of most of her clothes while still feasting at first on one nipple, then the other. Savannah, stripped of all but her garters, stockings, and velvet slippers, moaned and arched her back.

"Ummm," Pres murmured. "Be patient, Mrs. Parrish. These things should take time."

"I don't *want* it to take time," Savannah gasped. "I want you now."

He chuckled. The windows were fogged, and the soft rain whispered over their heads. "So that's the way of it, is it? For shame." He moved down her rib cage to kiss a light circle around her navel; his breath radiated through her like sunlight on a hot day. She was perspiring when he finally sat up, and very short of breath. Everything inside her seemed knotted into a single straining ache. "Where is your patience? Where is your virtue?" he teased.

"To hell with my virtue," Savannah whimpered and, locking her hands behind his neck, she drew him down for her kiss. "To hell with yours, for that matter," she added, barely able to speak, when it was over.

The tide had turned, to her delight; she could see that Pres was losing control, that the kiss had robbed him of that damnable cool efficiency of his. He groaned, muttered an imprecation and got rid of his own clothes so quickly that some magician might have cast a spell to melt them away.

Savannah was still wearing her stockings and garters, though she had managed to kick off the slippers. Pres lay between her legs—he seemed bigger, heavier, and harder, now that he was naked—and drew up her knees with his hands, to make her more accessible.

"Savannah—?"

She laid an index finger to his lips. "Yes, Pres," she said, answering the incomplete question. "Oh, God, yes."

He hesitated only a moment, then arranged himself and entered her in one forceful thrust of his hips. Pleasure surged into her with him, interwoven with a brief, fierce pain, pleasure so intense that it forced out all other sensation, and Savannah cried out in jubilation and despair, surrender and challenge.

He withdrew, delved again, and the sensation was even keener that time, for both of them. His face was set for a grim and primitive struggle, as old as mankind, his powerful arms held the upper part of his body suspended above Savannah's breasts and belly, above her heart.

"Let go, Pres," she pleaded. "Please, please—let go—"

It was all unleashed then, all the loneliness, all the yearning, all the sorrow and pain that belonged to both of them. The joy came too, at long, long last, even more fierce than the storm of emotions that had cleared the way for it. They moved together with a force made of desperation, a holy, healing thing created out of both their minds, both their bodies, both their spirits.

Release overtook them simultaneously, and only after they had exhausted themselves to achieve it; Savannah was consumed by hers, calling out his name as a series of sharp tremors shook her, from the inside out. When she could breathe and see again, she looked up into Pres's face, watched as he moved in the last throes of his own climax.

Finally, he fell beside her, gasping, their bodies still joined. Savannah stroked his damp hair, let her fingers delve deep into it. "I love you," she said; the confession had simply escaped her, unplanned.

He lifted his head, searched her eyes. "You do?"

She waited a moment, her teeth buried in her

lower lip, then nodded. No sense in denying it now. She'd told the truth, to herself and to him, but she wished she hadn't. Very possibly, she'd spoiled everything.

He kissed her lightly, tenderly, on the mouth. "I've never been in love before," he said, at long last. "Oh, there have been women, of course. Plenty of them. But nobody I cared about, until you. Even so, I feel something for you, Savannah, something deep, something that will last. Maybe it's love, I don't know. But whatever it is, it's good."

She blinked away tears, happy ones. "That's enough for now, isn't it?"

He chuckled and ran a lazy hand up her belly to cup her left breast and play with the peak. "I guess that depends on whether you're talking about the feeling, or all the things I want to do to you in and out of this bed."

Savannah slipped her arms around his neck. "Why, Doctor. I do believe you're something of a rascal."

"As far as you're concerned," he said, hardening within her, exciting her anew, seeking the same breast with his mouth, now that his hand had mapped the way, "I'm the devil. And this time, wife, we're taking it slowly. After all, we've got all night."

Soon, she was writhing and pleading and bucking beneath his fingers and his lips again, but he took her at his leisure, and he was a long, long time at it.

They were entwined, both of them deeply asleep, when, sometime in the depths of the night, a loud pounding sound awakened them.

"Doc!" Trey shouted, from the other side of the door. "Doc, wake up! Quick!" More hammering. "Damn it, *wake up!*"

"I'm on my way!" Pres yelled back, already out of bed and scrambling into his clothes, from the sounds of it, without benefit of a lamp. He'd probably had a lot of practice, Savannah concluded, in sleepy shock, getting dressed in the dark, rushing to answer some urgent summons. "Hold your horses!"

Savannah sat up, blinking, and moved across the mattress to reach for matches and fumble with the globe on the lantern. By that time, Pres was already in the front room, technically his office, opening the door. His tones were low, even, calming. Trey, for his part, sounded frantic. Although she strained to hear what was happening, she couldn't quite make out the words.

She arose—she was a doctor's wife now, after all, even if she'd only been one for a few hours—and hastily donned a practical calico dress. She was still wearing her garters and stockings, she noticed, with a slight blush, and quickly found her slippers, one on one side of the room, one on the other.

Pres had shrugged into his coat and grabbed his battered medical bag by the time Savannah joined him and Trey in the front room. "What is it?" she asked, thinking Rachel must be ill, or Emma. Trey's face was the color of dried clay.

"It's Jacob." Pres flung the words to her, over one shoulder, as he went out. "From the symptoms, it sounds as if his heart might be failing."

With that shattering news, he was gone, Trey following close behind him.

Savannah gripped the back of one of the packing-crate chairs, stunned. Jacob? He'd always seemed impervious, and though she'd only known him and June-bug for a short time, both of them meant a great deal to her. They were more than friends, they were family, almost like parents. She yanked her cloak down from its peg by the wall and dashed into the night after her husband.

She didn't call out to him to wait; she knew he couldn't match his pace to hers, and wouldn't, not in an emergency. He was a shadow up ahead, sprinting through the darkness toward the station, Trey right beside him. The Hargreaves' house, too, was spilling light from every shiny new window.

"No," Savannah prayed, in an anxious murmur, as she ran after the two men, noticing only when she slipped and nearly fell that it was still raining, that the ground was blanketed in mud. "Please, God. Don't take Jacob. June-bug needs him—we all need him—please—"

June-bug was up, of course, when Savannah burst into the station, silver-threaded brown hair trailing down her back. She looked like a young girl in her white flannel nightdress and wrapper, but every year of her life showed in her deep blue eyes. Seeing Savannah, she held out both arms, asking for comfort and, at the same time, offering it.

Savannah embraced her hard. "How is he?" she asked, a moment later.

"I don't know," June-bug said distractedly. She started to walk toward the back, where she and Jacob slept, then stopped and took a few steps in the direction of the stove.

"Sit down," Savannah said gently. "I'll make you some tea."

June-bug took a seat in one of the rocking chairs facing the hearth—the very place where Savannah and Pres had been married such a short time before—and stared blindly into the fire. "What would I do, without my Jacob?" she whispered.

Savannah was making the tea when she became aware of young Toby; he was crouched in the space between the stove and the pantry wall, his knees drawn up to his chest, his head down. He was the personification of despair, and when he looked up at Savannah, her heart turned over.

"He's strong," she said. It was all she had to offer at the moment, all he would accept from her, she expected. Otherwise, she might have taken him into her arms right then, like any frightened child in need of comforting.

Toby simply nodded and rested his head on his knees again.

Savannah brewed tea, poured it, brought a cup to June-bug, and a cup for herself. Neither of them touched the concoction; sometimes it was the ritual that was needed, rather than the tea itself, and that was one of those occasions.

The chair squeaked as June-bug rocked slowly back and forth, still gazing into the fire. "We was getting ready for bed," she said, lapsing deeper into the hill-country vernacular of her youth than usual, no doubt because of her distress. "Jacob jest put a hand to his chest and said, 'Why, June-bug, I don't believe I feel the way I ought.' That was all. He turned real white and laid down on the bed and shut his eyes to sleep, but I could see he was in terrible pain. Jest terrible. And it got worse and worse, until finally I woke up Toby and sent him to fetch Trey." She looked at Savannah, blinked quickly and swallowed. "I reckon I forgot we have a doctor at Springwater now, I was so wrought up."

Savannah reached across to pat June-bug's arm. "Do you want to go in and sit with him?"

"He told me I'd be in the way, that I should give the doc room enough to get close and take a look at him." June-bug's eyes were suddenly brilliant with tears, and she laid a hand to her bosom, fingers splayed, as though willing her heart to beat for Jacob, as well as for her. "I'll tell you what I think—I think Jacob don't want me lookin' on when he dies. Old fool. He's got a vain streak in him, you know, even if he does have a way with the Word of God."

Savannah wanted to weep along with her friend, but this wasn't the time. Pres was in the McCaffreys' room with Jacob, doing everything he could, and she had a great deal of confidence in his abilities as a physician. Everyone at Springwater did, for he'd proven himself, treating his cowboy patients and dealing amiably with crotchety old settlers like Granny Johnson. For now, Savannah thought it wiser to keep her own emotions in check, insofar as possible, and provide support for June-bug.

"If anybody can save him, Pres can," she said softly.

June-bug nodded. "Doc and the Lord. That's who we've got to count on now. Doc and the Lord and Jacob himself, of course."

It seemed as if hours had passed before Pres finally came out of the sickroom, Trey still trailing him like a worried shadow, but it was probably not more than thirty minutes or so. He pulled his stethoscope from his neck and tossed it into his bag, and his eyes were bleak as his gaze strayed first to Savannah, as if seeking courage, then moved on to June-bug.

"He's alive," he said. "But it's bad. Even if he lasts the night and gets through the next few days, he's got a long road ahead of him."

Savannah wanted to go to her husband, put her arms around him, share her strength as he had shared his, but at this point it wouldn't be a favor. She stood beside June-bug's chair, with a hand on her friend's shoulder, and regarded him in silence.

Pres sighed and rubbed the back of his neck with one hand. "You'd best get some rest," he said to June-bug. "There's no point in exhausting yourself."

June-bug squared her shoulders and raised her chin. "Women have been sittin' up, keepin' vigils, for longer than God's Aunt Bessie can remember. I didn't get to watch over my boys before they was taken, but I will surely sit beside my husband and hold his hand."

A lump formed in Savannah's throat; she swallowed hard and reminded herself not to cry for Jacob, for June-bug, for their lost sons, and for the grieving families of all the other sons and brothers and fathers who would never come marching home, even though the war was long ended.

"I need to stay here for the rest of the night, Savannah," Pres said. "Trey will walk you back home."

She shook her head and spoke at last. "I'm not leaving," she said. "I'm a doctor's wife, remember?"

The shadow of a smile touched his mouth, that mouth that had wreaked such havoc with her senses only a few hours before, in their bed. She wanted Pres, suddenly, not in the passionate, playful way of the wedding night just past, but in a primal manner that had more to do with the affirmation of life itself. She knew he felt the same way, that when they were alone again, however long the interim might be, they would make love in a ferocious, elemental celebration of heartbeats and sunrises, wildflowers and the smells of baking bread and hot coffee, and a multitude of other blessings, small and large.

June-bug rose a little shakily from her chair; Savannah was ready to catch her if need be, but Jacob's wife was the most stalwart of women, despite her diminutive size, and she would not fall. "I've got to go to him," she said.

Savannah merely nodded.

"The children—they'll be frightened," June-bug fretted, raising a slightly tremulous hand to her mouth. "Poor little Toby, why he thinks the sun surely rises and sets in Jacob McCaffrey."

"I'll look after both of them," Savannah said quietly. "You just concentrate on Jacob and yourself."

June-bug nodded, and her eyes glittered with fresh tears. "Thank you," she said, and then she turned and went in to sit with her husband.

Pres's look held admiration. "Yes," he affirmed, to Savannah, before following June-bug into the corridor at the back. "Thank you."

Trey lingered, looking torn, as well as exhausted and worried.

"Go home, Trey," Savannah said. "Rachel and Emma are probably waiting for word, and there's nothing more you can do here."

"You'll send someone, if we're needed?"

"Yes," she promised. "I'll come myself."

That satisfied Trey, evidently, for he left, and after a few minutes, Savannah went to the window and saw the lights in the mail-order house go out one by one.

After a little interval spent gathering her thoughts, she turned and walked briskly over to the stove. The boy was still sitting where she'd last seen him, huddled against the wall, the picture of abject misery.

"Toby," she said firmly.

He looked up at her, blue eyes filled with injury and defiance. He would grow to be a handsome man, she thought, of the rakish variety. He did not speak.

"How old are you?"

"Eleven," he answered, after a long time. He was small for his age; no doubt that was one of the many reasons why he behaved like such a cocky little rooster when he felt threatened.

"Not so very old, then," she said. "Come out of there." She extended a hand and waited.

Amazingly, he took the offered hand and rose, mostly under his own power, but with a little tug from Savannah. In a very matter-of-fact way, she led the child to the hearth, sat down in June-bug's rocking chair, and took him onto her lap. He tried briefly to pull away, then sagged against her in relieved defeat, and she held him, careful to avoid making him feel restricted.

"You love Jacob very much, don't you?" she said, into his fair, straight hair.

He nodded, his head propped beneath her chin. She felt the wetness of tears through the bodice of her dress, but of course did not mention them.

"So do I. So does Dr. Parrish. He'll do everything he can to help Jacob get well, Toby. I can promise you that much, at least."

The boy snuffled, relaxed a little more. And after that, no more words were needed. Savannah simply rocked, and Toby nestled against her until, at last, he slept.

Jacob survived that night, and the days and nights to come, as well. By the time the leaves began to change colors, he was up and about, with the use of a cane. He could not do his former heavy work, and he was pale and gaunt; it seemed to Savannah and to everyone else at Springwater, that something vital had gone out of him. He rarely preached of a Sunday morning, or even spoke of the Lord, fondly or otherwise. He even left off working on the beautiful cradle he'd been crafting for the Hargreaves baby, Rachel's pregnancy being an acknowledged fact, now that Pres had properly examined her.

Savannah feared that Jacob was about the business of dying; he was simply taking his time with it. It was plain that he'd given up the struggle.

She felt guilty for the wild, private happiness she and Pres had found together. They made love every chance they got, often enough that it didn't matter how inadequate their little rusted stove was because they didn't need it to keep them warm. Pres treated a lot of patients—they seemed to come from nowhere—in off the surrounding ranges, down out of the foothills, from passing wagon trains, from line shacks and farms and ranches, far and wide. Savannah helped him, learned to sterilize wounds and even stitch them closed, and how to set broken limbs, too. Mostly, though, she just kept the sick and injured distracted while Pres did whatever mending that happened to be needed.

Autumn was on the horizon, and still Jacob's spirits did not rise. Savannah knew Pres thought about the other man often, as she did as well, at a loss for how to help him. She didn't need to be told that her husband had seen such cases before, and that he was very troubled.

The women of the community made no effort to hide the fact that they were curious about Savannah, apparently wondering if she went around Springwater and her husband's office wearing feathers, face paint, and beads.

The last week of September brought a string of summery, blue-skied days. A celebration was planned, partly in the hope of raising Jacob's spirits. That Sunday, after Landry Kildare had delivered a layman's sermon, the men carried tables out of the station and set it in the withering grass under Junebug's carefully nurtured trees; food was produced and eaten. Tales of bitter cold winters were told, perhaps as a hex against the trials of the one to come, of sick children and animals, and suffering Indians passing through. Then the men went off to play a game of horseshoes.

Evangeline Wainwright, eyes sparkling, produced a sewing box from the back of the family wagon, and the others did the same. Savannah, having nothing to fetch, stayed behind, as unsure of herself as ever.

The food and dishes were cleared away, and then the mysterious boxes and bags were opened, to reveal quilt blocks in every imaginable shade—blue and yellow, green and red, purple and brown. All were carefully stitched into the wedding ring pattern.

"Are we agreed, ladies?" Evangeline asked, of the assembly.

Rachel, already big with the forthcoming baby, was the first to nod in accord. She too had produced quilt blocks, having sent Emma across the way to fetch them. The others looked at each other, faces full of silent questions, but then they all nodded, too, and even smiled. Within moments, the tabletop was covered in colorful pieces of fabric.

"The quilt is for you, Savannah," Evangeline said softly.

Savannah put a hand to her heart, overwhelmed. She had been wishing she had needlework to contribute, thinking that might make them more likely to accept her. "For me?" she echoed, sure there must be some mistake. "A stranger?"

"Most of us were strangers, one time or another," said Mrs. Bellweather. "Out here, we all need each other."

Rachel beamed, fairly bouncing with friendly excitement. "We said we'd piece a quilt for the next Springwater bride, remember? Back when the house was raised? You're that bride, Savannah."

Savannah blinked rapidly, but it didn't do any good. Tears spilled down her cheeks anyway, and she smiled through them, as brightly, June-bug would later say, as the sun shining through clouds. She'd been the one to erect barriers between herself and the others, she realized, just as Emma had once said. She had been so afraid of being rejected that she'd never given Rachel and the others a real chance.

"I don't know how to thank you," she whispered.

Evangeline laughed. "I'll tell you how," she said. "Sit down and help us finish this up. We'll plan a quilt for the *next* bride as we work."

It felt so very good, just to take a place among them, to belong, to be a part of their plans, privy to their secrets, their hopes, their dreams and sorrows.

She fit in nicely between Rachel and Sue Bell-weather.

"I say we do a crazy quilt this time," Sue said. "We'll just put the pieces together any old which way and see what happens."

There was a brief conference, and everyone agreed. A crazy quilt it would be.

Savannah dried her cheeks with the back of one hand, trying to be subtle about it, and reached for a square of bright pink and white gingham. Never having participated in a quilting bee before, she was relieved that there wouldn't be a complicated pattern to follow.

Evangeline was looking down the length of the table at Miranda, who carried her baby boy in a sling, close against her bosom, head down, snipping shyly at a piece of worn green velvet, shaping it into a triangle.

"Maybe you'll be the next bride, Miranda," Evangeline said gently.

"None too soon, either," remarked Sue Bell-weather, only half under her breath.

"Oh, hush yourself," June-bug scolded. She was subdued, because of Jacob's illness, but she was enjoying her friends' company all the same. "Everything in this world happens when it ought to, and that's a fact."

Savannah thought of the wedding ring quilt that would soon grace the bed she and Pres shared, and felt a rush of joy so sweet and poignant that it hurt her heart. Then she took in the dear faces around that table, awash in firelight, and rejoiced that, at long, long last, she was home.

Miranda

For Gina Centrello
Grazie

CHAPTER

1

Fall 1875

"I'VE GOT TWO KIDS to tend to, and hogs to butcher," Landry announced forthrightly, that crisp, early October morning, in the dining room of the Springwater station. "Potatoes and turnips to dig, too, and fields to plow under. The fact is, I need a wife in the worst way." He paused, hat in hand, colored up a little, and cleared his throat. "So I've come to ask if— well, if you'd marry me."

It wasn't the most romantic proposal, Miranda Leebrook reflected, but she'd wanted Landry Kildare for a husband from the moment she clapped eyes on him a couple of months back, while the Hargreaves house was being raised, and she wasn't about to refuse his offer. Besides, she and little Isaiah-or-Ezekiel couldn't expect to stay on with the McCaffreys forever. Heaven knew the baby's real father didn't want either of them, and Pa and his woman, Lorelei, were long gone.

Landry was a handsome man, with his mischievous

hazel eyes and wavy brown hair, and Miranda enjoyed looking at him on any account. Now, gazing into that earnest face, Miranda tried without success to think up a bright and witty remark, something Rachel might say, or Savannah.

Landry glanced around—June-bug and Jacob McCaffrey were pointedly absent—and cleared his throat again. "Of course I won't expect you to—well, what I mean is, you'll have a while to get used to things." A hot rush of crimson washed up his neck to pulse in his lower jaw. "Having a husband and the like." His expression, normally boyish and winsome, proceeded from bleak panic to pure desperation. "What I'm trying to say is, you'll have your own room and all the privacy you want. Until—until you're ready—"

She couldn't resist touching him any longer, and laid the tip of an index finger to his mouth. His lips felt warm and supple, and an odd little jolt of pleasure rocketed through her hand and up her arm to burst, a faint, delicious ache, in a soft fold of her heart. "Jacob and Miss June-bug warrant that you're a good man," she said quietly. "That's all the say-so I need. I'll have you for a husband, Mr. Kildare, if you truly want me for a wife."

He swallowed visibly. "I want you, all right," he said. He averted his gaze, then made himself meet her eyes again. "I guess every woman likes to hear pretty words at a time like this. The plain truth is, I don't have any to say. I loved my wife, Caroline, and I never got over losing her. I don't reckon I'll ever feel just that way about anybody again. But I'll be good to you, Miranda, and I'll raise your little one like he was my own. I'm not a rich man, but I can provide for the both of you, and I'll never bring shame on you, nor lay a hand to either one of you in anger."

She wished he could have claimed to love her, for she surely cherished deep if undefined feelings toward him, but at the same time she knew it was better that he hadn't. He'd have been lying, and she would have known it full well, and never given weight to another word he said from that moment until the day one of them died. Young as she was, barely eighteen, Miranda understood that no alliance could stand, let alone thrive, without trust.

"I guess we should get on with it, then," she said, and blushed herself. She was painfully certain that neither Rachel nor Savannah would ever say anything so stupid when their whole future hung in the balance, and with it, that of their child.

"I'll speak to Jacob," Landry said, with a slight, nervous nod. "About saying the words over us and all, I mean. You might want to get your things ready while I'm about that."

She replied with a nod of her own. She had very few belongings—just four dresses, two made by the industrious June-bug, and two donated by Savannah Parrish, the Doc's wife. There was a stack of flour-sack diapers and some little clothes for the baby, too, and a reading primer Rachel Hargreaves had given her. Rachel was a schoolmarm, despite her marriage and prominent pregnancy, and she'd been helping Miranda with her reading now and again. She could make out the words all right, it wasn't that, but the task was difficult.

Perhaps twenty minutes had passed when Jacob hobbled in, supported by his cane. He was tall, but his big frame had wasted. The light had gone out of his eyes since his heart had nearly given out on him, and he didn't hold forth of a Sunday morning as often as before, but the nearest justice of the peace was in Choteau, and he was the only real preacher for miles around.

June-bug hastily summoned Savannah for a second witness, and when she'd arrived, beaming with delight at the prospect of a wedding so soon after her own, Miranda and Landry took their awkward places before Jacob, both of them listening earnestly to every word he said and responding whenever he asked them to speak.

And so Miranda Leebrook was married, and became Miranda Kildare, all in the course of an October morning. She wore her best dress, a blue calico, and the cornbread June-bug had baked for the midday meal served as wedding cake.

There was no party, no dancing, like when the Doc and Savannah got hitched, but Miranda didn't care about any of that. She and little Isaiah-or-Ezekiel were part of a family now; they had a home to go to, and folks to call their own, and a lifetime of unsullied days, just waiting to dawn.

Her heart sang when Landry helped her into the seat of his well-used buckboard, then stepped aside so

June-bug could hand up the baby, solid and heavy in his bundle of blankets. Then Landry was beside her in the wagon, his right thigh touching hers, his strong callused hands taking up the reins. He released the brake lever with a practiced motion of his left leg, and they were on their way.

He raised his hat to the small assembly of well-wishers in front of the stagecoach station, still without smiling that famous smile that had made Miranda's insides quiver, and urged the team of two mules to a faster pace with a raspy sound from his throat and a slap of the reins.

He did not look at Miranda, but kept his thoughtful gaze fixed on the track ahead. The far edges of the clearing where the town of Springwater was slowly taking shape were a fringe of gold and crimson, rust and dark green. The sky was a pristine, chilly blue, dabbed with white, and there was a quiet, thrilling sense of new beginnings, it seemed to her, woven in the air itself and into the bright, eager glow of the sun. She held her small son closer against her bosom as he began to fidget, and sat proudly beside her husband.

Her husband. Miranda let her thoughts wander back to the day the Doc and Savannah were married. There had been a party then, and dancing to the tunes of a fiddle, and she'd been Landry's partner in a reel. When that spin around the floor of the Springwater station's main room had ended, Miranda was a different woman, totally changed. She'd loved the smell of Landry Kildare from then on, loved the sight of him, and the sound of his voice.

Now, officially his wife, Miranda wanted to laugh aloud with joy, but she knew that would startle the baby and Landry, too, and maybe even the mules, so she held her exuberance inside, contained it, like a deep breath, drawn against a plunge underwater. In her mind, she rehearsed the life that lay ahead—Landry's boys would come to love her like a second mother, she'd see to that. She'd stitch curtains for every window in the house, and keep the place so clean that folks were sure to remark upon it for miles around. She wasn't the best cook—her fare tended to be plain and a little on the heavy side—but she'd learned a few things helping Miss June-bug in the Springwater station kitchen, and she'd manage just fine. With practice, she expected she'd be able to make biscuits as feathery as anybody's.

Yes, she assured herself, she would make it all work. Landry Kildare would never be sorry he'd taken her for a wife. Maybe one day, he might even come to love her, if she worked at things hard enough. It made her heart pound a little, just to imagine him looking at her the way Trey looked at Rachel, for example, or the way Doc looked at Savannah.

The ride to his home—glory of glories, it was hers now, too, and the baby's—was short by comparison to the distance to say, the Wainwright place, or Choteau. Or Ohio, for that matter.

The thought of Ohio, and the home place where her ma was buried, took a little of the shine off that magical day, bringing the farm to mind as it did and, with it, her lost mother. Miranda set the memories firmly aside. No sense looking back, longing for places and people she would never see again. No, sir. Miranda Leebrook Kildare meant to fix her gaze straight ahead, from that moment on.

Miranda was a pretty little thing, Landry thought guiltily, as the team covered the last couple of miles, the buckboard rattling along over a rocky, rutted track. Eighteen, no more than that, and here he was, thirty-five, come next June. Nearly twice her age.

He ground his back teeth. It wasn't like he was betraying Caroline; she'd been gone a long time, and he'd been lonely enough to howl ever since. He'd never stopped loving her, not for a moment, but he'd taken something of a shine to Rachel Hargreaves, when she'd come to teach at Springwater the year before. She'd been Rachel English then, spirited as a filly raised on the open range, but book-smart, too, and pretty. Alas, she'd married Trey Hargreaves, then half owner of the Brimstone Saloon, and never thought of Landry as anything more than a friend.

Just as well, he supposed, given the fact that Trey and Rachel clearly loved each other as deeply as he and Caroline ever had. Landry couldn't have offered Rachel that kind of sentiment, much as he admired her, so she was better off with the man she'd chosen.

Landry sighed to himself, and prodded the mules to travel a little faster. Maybe he'd lost his mind, waking up that morning with the intention of getting married before the day was out, but here he was, with a bride in tow, and sunset still a good four hours off.

Oh, he'd been mulling the idea over for a long while, of course. Ever since Rachel English's arrival at Springwater, anyway. Maybe before that, if he wanted to be honest with himself.

Well, in any case, the deed was done. He and Miranda were hitched, right and proper, and even though they could probably get an annulment, given that the marriage hadn't been consummated, Landry had no intention of seeking one. He'd thought the whole thing through, the way he did every new undertaking, looking at all the fors and againsts; he'd made his decision and he would abide by it.

He set his jaw.

"Mr. Kildare?"

At first, he didn't know who she was talking to; proof enough of his state of mind, he thought ruefully, given the fact that he was the only one there, besides the baby and a pair of jackasses. "You can call me Landry," he said, and for the first time since he'd opened his eyes before dawn and set his mind on getting married, he smiled. "My boys are Marcus, he's eleven, and Jamie, he's nine. I don't mind telling you, they're a handful."

Just for a moment, a shadow of uncertainty moved in her eyes. She'd met his sons, of course, Springwater being a small place. Heard tales about them, no doubt. Hell, they'd all be lucky if she didn't take to her heels before supper was set out. "How do they feel about having me and little Isaiah-or-Ezekiel around?"

Landry ran the tip of his tongue along the inside of his lower lip. "I didn't mention that I was planning to get married today," he said. "I had enough to do, just getting those little heathens off to school."

She stared at him, held her baby a little closer. "You haven't told them?"

He started to pat her knee with his free hand, then thought better of the gesture. Better not to touch her, lest he start getting ideas he didn't have any right to entertain. "Don't go fretting yourself about my boys," he said. "They'll be glad enough to eat somebody's cooking besides mine."

Miranda didn't look all that reassured. He'd have sworn she gulped, as a matter of fact, and he fully expected her to say she'd heard his boys were monsters, which, regretfully, they were. Had been, ever since their mother died. Instead, she asked, "What made you pick me? For a bride, I mean?"

They rounded the last bend, and the ranch house and barn were visible up ahead; Landry felt the same brief, skittering sensation of pride he always did when he first got a look at the place, whether he'd been away an hour or a week. All the same, he fixed his full attention on Miranda's troubled face.

"Well," he said, a forthright nature being his private curse, "you were the only unmarried woman around here."

A difficult silence settled over them, broken only by the jingle of harness fittings and the *cloppity-clop* sound of hooves.

She drew the baby close again, murmured something to him, even though he hadn't stirred or made a sound. While she spoke, her gaze was on the house, the barn and corral, the trees, though it seemed to Landry that she might have been looking past those things to some other place, some other time. "I reckon that makes about as much sense as anything," she said, in a small voice. It made him hurt, the way she straightened her spine and raised her chin. "You probably could have sent away for a wife, but that would have taken some considerable time."

He felt a stab of pity for her, but he understood pride, having an overabundance of it himself, and so did not let the emotion show. They were nearly at the gate now; he drew up on the reins, set the brake lever, and moved to jump down and raise the wooden latch. Something he'd heard in her voice, however, kept him from leaving the buckboard seat.

"You truly don't mind? About the baby, I mean?"

He had, of course, given the child a great deal of thought, and long since decided that the sins of the father—or the mother—should not be visited on the son. "You're my wife now," he said quietly, "and I expect you to be faithful to me. But whatever happened before today is your own business. We'll go on from here."

She gave him a shaky smile that stirred something awake inside him, something that had been asleep for a long time. "You're not like most men, Landry Kildare," she said. There was a glint of shy admiration in her eyes.

He grinned that time, more because he had no answer to offer than because he was amused, and got down to let the team through. When the mules and wagon were inside the fence, he closed the gate again and climbed up beside Miranda once more, to take up the reins.

"I'll put the buckboard away," he said, "and turn the mules out to graze awhile, before I start on that field. You and the baby go on inside and make yourselves at home. I'll come in after a bit to see that you've settled in and all."

She nodded, somewhat primly he thought, and looked down at the top of the infant's head, which was hidden by the blankets. He wondered if the kid could breathe freely, swaddled up that way, but couldn't quite bring himself to ask. He brought the wagon to a halt and helped Miranda down, lifting her by the waist.

She was light, but sturdy, and strong as an otter pup. She held on to that baby like she thought he was going to snatch the little mite out of her arms and throw him down the well. When she was standing on her own two feet, he wrenched off his hat and held it out, stiff-armed as a scarecrow.

"There's the house," he said, like she couldn't see it, standing right there where he'd left it. "You can go on in."

Another woman might have laughed, or at least smiled, at his discomfiture, which must have been as obvious as that cabin or the mountains or the sky over their heads, but she didn't. She just stood there, with the last-gasp-of-summer breeze dancing through tendrils of her chestnut hair, some of which had come down from its pins during the ride out from

Springwater, her eyes dark as bruises and so full of naked yearning that it nearly killed Landry just to look at her.

He averted his eyes for a moment, out of plain decency. "I'll be in after a while," he said. Then he took hold of the harness, near the lead mule's jawbone, and started off toward the barnyard. The team followed, the buckboard bouncing along behind them, flimsy without the weight of its passengers.

Miranda stood in the doorway of the Kildare house, struck by the neatness of the place. It didn't seem like a household of men, with its polished floors and sootless stone fireplace. There were curtains at the windows, crisp and new enough that they hadn't faded, and the rag rugs made splashes of color here and there, just inside the threshold, under her own feet, in front of the hearth, over by the big wood cookstove. There was a bright red-and-white checked cloth on the table, and somebody had picked a handful of dandelion ghosts and the very last of the wild tiger lilies and set them on a windowsill in a fruit jar bouquet.

It was as though the lost Caroline Kildare had just left the room, moments before; Miranda could almost catch the scent of her perfume in the air, delicate and simple, but perfume nonetheless.

She sighed and closed the door gently behind her, unwrapping her sleeping child from his many blankets. She was a bit overprotective of little Isaiah-or-Ezekiel, but it wasn't something she could help. The world was a dangerous and unpredictable place, and she'd seen countless babies die since the time she'd begun to take notice of such matters. It was important to keep him warm.

The baby began to fuss a little, weary of being held and jostled. He probably needed his diaper changed, and some nourishment as well; she remembered that her belongings were still in the buckboard and set her shoulders. Mr. Kildare—Landry—would bring everything along when he came back to the house.

Patting her son's sturdy little back, for he was starting to carry on in earnest now, Miranda went in search of whatever loft, lean-to, or nook was meant to serve as her private retreat. The first room she entered was plainly Landry's; his bed, covered by a truly magnificent quilt, was large and hand-carved, with images of horses and eagles in the headboard, his boots were lined up under a window, his spare clothes hung neatly on pegs along the shady wall.

Miranda felt a stirring she understood all too well, and slipped out.

The next room, which was as untidy as Landry's was neat, clearly belonged to the boys. There were two beds, both unmade, and little shirts and trousers spread from one end of the floor to the other.

She closed the door and proceeded to the last door. Inside, she found a slanted ceiling, a plain, narrow bed, and a comfortable chair with a stitchery basket sitting beside it on the floor. This, no doubt, had been Caroline's refuge, a place to rock her babies, to sew, to dream and think. Miranda felt an uncharitable—and uncharacteristic—pang of envy toward this unknown woman. Even though she'd been gone for several years—June-bug had said her grave was in a copse of trees nearby—Mrs. Landry Kildare was still a presence in that house.

Resigned, Miranda laid her now-squalling baby on the bed and searched until she found some old pieces of cloth in one of the bureau drawers—big squares of blue calico, probably intended for a quilt top. Having no other choice at hand, she put one to practical use, and she was sitting in the ornate rocking chair, one breast bared to nurse her baby, when she heard the cabin door open and close in the distance.

Before she could consider the immodesty of her situation any further, Landry was standing in the doorway. His stance was easy, relaxed, yet his hands looked hard where they gripped the wooden framework on either side of him, and his gaze lingered a moment too long on her breast before shooting up to her face.

"I brought your things in from the wagon," he said, awkwardly, and after a long time had passed.

Miranda was embarrassed, for all that it was an ordinary thing to breast-feed a baby, and the suckling sound seemed to echo off the cabin walls. She wanted to cover her burning face, not to mention her naked bosom, but the only way she could have done that without disturbing the baby would be to pull her skirts up over her head, which was, of course, no sort of solution. Still, she knew her discomfiture showed, knew by the heat in her flesh and the anxious leap in the pit of her stomach. "Thank you," she said.

He stared at her for a few moments longer, looking hard at her face, and then thrust himself forward and into the room with a small action of his powerful arms. Going to the bureau, he rooted around and found a lacy crocheted blanket, infant-size, which he draped over her and the baby with a motion so gentle that it tugged at a tiny muscle in the back of Miranda's throat. His was a simple, earthy sort of tenderness, nothing she ought to take meaning from, she knew, and yet she set store by it, even prized it. That particular brand of kindness had been sorely lacking in her experience.

She thought Landry would leave then, but instead he sat down on the edge of that narrow bed, the springs creaking beneath him. He looked around the small room as though he hadn't been inside it in years, and maybe he hadn't, though it showed the same degree of neatness as most of the house did. "Caroline used to sew in here," he said, with a sigh that conveyed humor, rather than sorrow, and was somehow, therefore, all the more poignant. "She said it made her feel like she was living in a mansion, having a whole room to herself when she wanted some peace and quiet."

Miranda smiled because he was smiling, but deep down, and for a reason she could not put a name to, she would rather have wept. "I reckon I would have liked her a lot," she said, and it was true, for all that she wished, in that moment, that the other woman had never existed. That, somehow, she could have managed to be first in someone's life, rather than a mere afterthought, a person who barely sufficed, except as a substitute.

He expelled his breath in a combination laugh and chuckle, a sound, Miranda would soon realize, that was uniquely his, like so many other qualities she saw in him.

"Speak up if you need anything," he said, and hoisted himself to his feet. Sure enough, the old satchel Miss June-bug had given her the loan of was sitting just inside the doorway, with the bundle of diapers and blankets and little baby clothes packed away inside. "I'll get you some water for washing up, if you'd like."

She nodded, biting her lower lip. She was absurdly grateful, maybe because no man had ever treated her with such courtesy, not even the one who'd persuaded her to lie down beside him, to surrender her innocence, and then left her, pregnant with his child. Tears sprang to her eyes; she nodded once more and turned her head, hoping Landry wouldn't see, wouldn't question her.

He did both. He caught her chin in his gentle, callused grip, and raised her face, looked full on at her sorrow and didn't flinch. "You'll have no call to fear me," he said. "I promise you that."

"I ain't—*I'm not* afraid of you," she sniffled, patting the baby as he let go of her nipple under the faintly musty infant's blanket and fell headlong into a sated, milky sleep. "I just—well—a lot's changed for me just since I got out of bed this morning. I don't rightly know what to make of it all."

He drew back, and she was sorry for that; she experienced the withdrawal of his hand as a tearing-away. "You've got plenty of time to sort things through," he said quietly, and though his expression was serious, there was a certain tender mischief dancing in his eyes. "I'll get that water for you," he reiterated, and then he was gone.

Miranda fastened her bodice and laid little Isaiah-or-Ezekiel on the bed, with a pillow propped on either side to keep him from rolling off onto the floor. He slept contentedly, his long pale lashes lying like gilded fans on his cheeks. Just looking at him made her feel better.

She was taken by surprise when Landry appeared with a basin in one hand and a bucket in the other, and started a little. He was looking at her in that strange, thoughtful way again, as though he'd never seen a woman with a baby before. Or, she reflected, a moment later, as if he hadn't seen one in a very long while.

"Thank you," she said, pretending she was Rachel Hargreaves. She did that sometimes when she was scared, or overwhelmed, which was a good bit of the time. Made believe she was somebody else, most often Rachel or Savannah. It was a childish game, she knew, and by rights she ought to give it up, but she hadn't quite been able to let it go.

Landry set the basin on the bureau top, the bucket on the floor beside it. Inside the basin, he'd set a bar of soap and a square of clean cloth.

"I'd best get back to work," he said, in that same

hoarse voice he'd used to ask for her hand in marriage earlier that day. "The boys will be home from school long about four—you tell 'em I'll tan their hides if they don't put that room of theirs to rights. I'll carry my dinner out to the fields and come in for supper by sundown."

Miranda could only nod yet again. She'd contrive to have something ready for him to eat even if she died in the effort, she promised herself. She wasn't so sure of her ability to deal with Marcus and Jamie, though. They were a pair of red-haired terrors, those boys, and even pretending to be Rachel probably wouldn't be enough to buffalo them into minding her. Then again, if she didn't get the upper hand right away, they'd surely make her life a pure and certain misery.

"I'll be looking for you to come in after the work is done," Miranda said, belatedly realizing that Landry was waiting for an answer to his statement, or at least an acknowledgment.

"You'll find canned goods and the like in the pantry," he said, as if reluctant to go, "and milk and butter out in the springhouse. We've got chickens and a cow, and once I get the butchering done, there'll be ham, too. I could show you—"

Miranda squared her shoulders. She couldn't have him thinking he'd tied himself to somebody helpless. "I reckon I can manage," she said.

He nodded, made a parting gesture with the hand that still held his hat, and went out. Miranda immediately washed her face and hands, tidied up her hair, and then rummaged through the bureau again, until she found a pretty gingham apron to tie around her waist.

She was peeling plump, smooth-skinned potatoes when the boys burst into the house, moving fit to out-run their own skins. Seeing Miranda working by the stove, they stared at her with round blue eyes, and it seemed their freckles might just leap right off their faces.

"By gum, it's true," marveled the taller of the two. That would be Jamie, Miranda knew. Although he was younger than his brother, he was the bigger one.

"Pa took himself a wife, just like Toby said!" Marcus added.

Miranda couldn't tell whether her new stepsons were delighted or outraged, and she pretended not to care one way or the other. "I imagine you're hungry," she said. "Learning taxes a body. You'll find some molasses cookies there in the pantry."

She'd used June-bug's recipe to bake those cookies, stirring in a generous portion of bravado. The boys' response to the offering was important to her, but she didn't dare let them know. Rachel wouldn't show her hand like that so early in the game, and neither would Savannah.

They rushed the pantry, those boys, like soldiers taking an enemy fort by storm, and came out with cookies in either hand.

"Where's Pa?" demanded Marcus.

"Why did he pick you?" Jamie added, face squenched with confusion.

Miranda held her ground, didn't let on for a moment that she was nervous. "Your pa is where he usually is, at this time of the day—working. He said you're to clean up your room or he'll tan your hides for sure. And I reckon he picked me because he thought I'd do as well as anybody else."

The boys just stared at her for what seemed like a long while; they were handsome lads, she thought, with a sort of pride. They'd grow up to be fine men, if she had anything to say about it. Oh, yes, she thought, with new resolve, if she could give Landry nothing else, she would give him a mother for his sons.

Jamie looked her up and down. "You ain't hardly any older than Marcus here," he said.

"I'm eighteen," Miranda said. "And I've got a baby."

"You weren't married when you got him, neither," observed Marcus.

"I know," Miranda answered reasonably. Calmly. But inside, she felt like a deer on ice.

"You're supposed to be married if you mean to have babies," Marcus informed her.

Jamie assessed her again, thoughtfully, this time, and quite without rancor. "Are you and Pa going to make any? Babies, I mean?"

She swallowed. "I reckon," she allowed.

"Well," Jamie retorted, "if you do, see that you just have boys. The last thing we need around here is a passel of squalling *girls*."

Miranda smiled. She hadn't had time to think

about bearing Landry's child, not since marrying him anyway, but now that it was in her mind, she found she liked the idea. "I think it would be nice to have a girl. Somebody to keep me company." She had no more than drawn her next breath after saying those words when Landry filled the gaping space in the doorway.

It was plain from the expression on his face that he'd heard what she said, and he had thoughts of his own about making babies.

CHAPTER

2

LANDRY WATCHED, intrigued, as his new bride, seated across the supper table from him, dished up a plate of cornbread and beans for him, then one for each of the boys, before serving herself. Her thick brown hair was pinned up at her nape in a lopsided, wifely do, with a few tendrils straggling down here and there around her cheeks and temples and one side of her neck. Her good skin seemed to glow in the light from the lamps and the fireplace, and her dark blue eyes were bright. She seemed surprisingly happy to Landry, given the fact that she'd married a virtual stranger just that morning.

The baby, little Isaiah-or-Ezekiel, whom Landry already thought of as "Little One-or-the-other," cooed cheerfully nearby, cosseted in Caroline's wicker laundry basket. Landry felt a muscle tighten in his jaw. Caroline's house, Caroline's pots and pans, Caroline's children, Caroline's husband. How long would it be, he wondered, before he got used to seeing this strange and lovely woman-child filling places that rightfully belonged to his first and only love?

As if she felt his gaze, Miranda glanced at him and flushed in the lamplight. She looked as innocent as an angel, sitting there, hair and skin and eyes all shining, but she wasn't any such thing, he reminded himself sternly. She was a fallen woman, and that was one of the reasons he'd decided to marry her. There would be no danger of his caring too much for somebody he couldn't respect. No threat to Caroline's memory.

"Is everything all right?" Miranda asked, her brow puckering a little, but prettily. Damn, but he hadn't realized she was so fetching—had he?

The boys were eating, mannerly as a couple of Jesuits fresh from some Eastern seminary. He wondered what *that* was about, even as he swallowed hard, feeling oddly guilty, and rummaged through his mind for an answer to her perfectly ordinary, perfectly simple question.

"Fine," he said, at some length. Now *there*, he chided himself, was an intelligent reply. Maybe he was never going to love this young woman, but if she was going to live with him for the next however-many years, she'd be likely to expect more in the way of conversation. Women were that way—even Caroline, sanctified by his memory into something resembling a saint, had wanted to talk from the moment he stepped over the threshold after a day's work, straight on through supper and half the night, if he let her. It was as if they stored up their words all day, these females, and then unleashed them in a frightening torrent at the first sight of a man.

Marcus leaped into the breach just then, bless his skinned knees and mismatched socks. "We ought to call that baby something in particular," he said, gazing thoughtfully toward the gurgling infant waving both hands and both feet in the depths of the washbasket. "What's he need with two names, anyhow?"

"Let's call him Rover," Jamie suggested.

Landry sucked in a snicker at that, and saw Miranda schooling a smile of her own. She even managed to look like she was considering the idea carefully before reluctantly ruling it out with a shake of her head. "He has a name. Isaiah—" she paused and frowned. "Or Ezekiel."

"Rover's a dog's name, stupid," Marcus informed his brother. Though he was the elder of the pair, he was usually a beat behind Jamie. It worried Landry a little sometimes. "He ain't a dog."

"Isn't," Landry corrected his son automatically. He'd picked the habit up from Caroline and never gotten away from it, even after her passing. If she'd wanted one thing in the world, Caroline had, it was for those rapscallion boys of theirs to grow up into decent, hardworking, mannerly men. As far as Landry could see, there wasn't a whole lot of progress being made toward that end.

"How about George?" Jamie suggested. They were studying history in school, Landry knew, and the boy was probably thinking of the country's first president.

Miranda smiled at Landry, with her eyes, and continued to eat, without comment. She took small, delicate bites, despite the obvious fact that she'd been raised rough-and-tumble, and something about the way she moved, the way she held her head and shoulders, stirred him on a deep and very private level. He didn't want to let her or any other woman into that place inside him, where he'd set up a shrine to Caroline.

"*George*," scoffed Marcus.

"Enough," Landry interjected quietly. "It's Miranda's place to decide on the baby's name, not yours."

"Where's that baby's pa, anyway?" Jamie asked bluntly.

Miranda stiffened, but only for a fraction of a second. Not surprisingly, she'd had a good deal of practice where that inquiry was concerned. "I don't rightly know," she said. "Somewhere between St. Louis and Laramie, I reckon." For an instant there was a bruised expression in those near-purple eyes of hers that nearly closed off Landry's throat.

That was why it took him a moment too long to intercede. "Jamie," he said, "there are certain things you just don't say to people. One more step in that direction, and you'll leave the table."

Jamie flushed with righteous indignation, but he backed down. Landry, for all that he'd set his son straight on the issue, wondered himself about the man who had charmed Miranda into a mistake that might well have ruined her life, and wondered mightily. Maybe at some point, when she'd had time to settle into the household, he'd just haul off and ask her. In private, of course.

After that, Miranda seemed to lose her appetite. She left the table and scraped the remains of her supper into the scrap bucket by the stove, a wooden one reserved for slopping the hogs. Her shoulders were especially straight, almost to the point of rigidity, and Landry thought he heard her sniffle once or twice. The baby, as if sensing his mother's discomfort, began to fret and fuss.

"Sit down a spell, Miranda," Landry told his bride evenly, but in a tone meant to convey that he was giving an order, not making a request. "The boys will do up the dishes."

Amid wails of protest from Jamie and Marcus, Miranda stood stock still, plate still in hand, staring at Landry as if he'd told her to build a room onto the house before morning. He knew all too little about her, but it wasn't hard to deduce that she was used to doing all the "women's work" that needed to be done.

The baby began to holler, tiny fists knotted, feet pummeling the air. He had gumption, that kid, Landry thought, with a peculiar sort of pride. He hadn't fathered Little One-or-the-other, but he was already getting attached. He liked kids, especially the really small ones that didn't give you much guff.

Biting her lip, Miranda finally nodded in acquiescence, put aside the plate, and crossed the plank floor to lift her child from his basket and prop him against one shoulder, murmuring and patting his back. He was hungry, Little One-or-the-other, and Miranda was already headed toward the privacy of the spare room, in order to nurse him.

The thought of that tightened Landry's groin; in order to distract himself, he fixed his attention on his squabbling sons. "Get on with it," he said, nodding toward the metal sink.

Grumbling, the boys cleared the table, scraped their plates, and began scooping hot water out of the stove reservoir to fill the sink. Landry got his cherry-wood pipe from the mantel, along with a match and a pouch of his best tobacco. He was no longer a widower, but somebody's husband, he reflected, marveling at the changes one decision, one day, could make in a man's life.

Outside, he filled the pipe, struck a match off the heavy door frame, and tried his level best to concentrate on smoking.

Jehosaphat. He was married.

There was a woman living under his roof now, a stepmother for his boys, a companion, of sorts, for him. He couldn't help thinking of her, there in the spare room, with one well-shaped breast bared to suckle the baby, and stopped trying to deny that he wanted a wedding night, wanted Miranda. He'd have done better, he reprimanded himself, to find himself an ugly woman. What had possessed him to choose one who was young and pretty and, well, plainly receptive to the intimate attentions of a man?

He made himself remember Caroline. She hadn't cared much for the private aspects of marriage, he had to admit, though she'd accommodated him willingly enough whenever he turned to her in the night.

Irritated, for a reason he couldn't precisely define, he thrust himself away from the support pole he'd been leaning against and strode off into the darkness. He'd make a pilgrimage to Caroline's grave, sit there awhile in the dry autumn grass, and go through his memories of her one by one, feeling the shape and weight of each, like a man fingering holy beads.

He hadn't consciously planned to pass the spare room window, but he did, and he glanced in, too. Miranda was there, all right, seated in the soft glow of a single lamp, unaware of him, looking down at her suckling baby with an expression of such tender devotion that Landry's eyes burned a little. He blinked and looked away.

"Damn," he muttered. The night seemed almost solid after that; it settled over him like a dark blanket. He went on toward Caroline's final resting place, crossing the creek at a narrow place and heading for the copse of birches, alders, and cottonwoods that surrounded the fine wood cross he'd carved for her, working on it throughout that first long, impossible winter after her passing.

"I got married today," he said, as soon as he got near enough. The fall wind was chilly; he felt it through his shirt. "I know you'll understand, if there's a way you can hear me." He thrust one hand through his hair; he'd forgotten his hat, in his haste to get out of the house and away from his new bride. "I don't love her, Caroline. Hell, I don't hardly know her. But the boys have been running wild ever since you left us and I—well, sometimes I get so lonesome, I fear to die of it."

There was no answer, of course; just the whisper of the wind in the tree branches, the rustling of leaves as small woodland creatures went about their business, and the steady murmur of the creek. It usually made Landry feel better, at least marginally, if he came out here and told Caroline what was on his heart, but somehow tonight was different. He was more aware than ever that Caroline had long since gone on to some other, ostensibly better place, and left him behind.

He crouched beside the creek, tapped out his pipe on a smooth, damp stone. He'd made a mistake in taking a new wife, he thought now, with rueful certainty. That was the reason he'd lost the precious sense of reaching out to Caroline, finding her there in the mystery just beyond what he could see or hear or touch.

He sighed, raised himself to his full height again, and tucked the pipe into his shirt pocket, alongside the tobacco pouch. "I don't reckon I'll be spending as much time here, after this," he said quietly, though whether he was addressing himself, God, or the surrounding countryside, he didn't know. The sense of loss was profound, aching in every part of him, settling into the very marrow of his bones.

He went to the barn, even though he'd already done all the evening chores, to check on the livestock. He was a prosperous man, thanks to years of single-minded hard work and prudence, and he'd doubled the size of his holdings a year before by buying up Trey Hargreaves's homestead. He had healthy sons, friends aplenty, a good house, land and livestock, cash money stashed in the safe at the Springwater station and in a lard can hidden beneath a floorboard in the toolshed. Everything that was supposed to make him happy—except for a woman he truly loved.

Oh, Miranda would sit next to him when Jacob McCaffrey preached of a Sunday, she'd probably even share his bed if he asked it of her. But it wouldn't be the same. He was, he reasoned, as lonely as he'd ever been—maybe more so, because he didn't even have the consolation of bedding this wife he'd taken on what seemed a foolish impulse.

Presently, resigned, he returned to the house.

The boys had finished washing the dishes, in their haphazard way, and were seated at the table again, bent over their slates. Miranda, holding the baby on one well-rounded hip, was supervising.

"Is that the right way to spell 'legislature'?" Jamie asked, holding up his slate for her to see.

Her gaze had connected with Landry's as soon as he stepped through the doorway, then skittered away. Now, she bit her lower lip and narrowed her eyes. There was a slight flush on her cheekbones.

"I don't reckon I know," she said, at some length, with a note of soft misery in her voice.

Landry shut and latched the door, crossed to the table, looked over his son's shoulder at the word scrawled across the small chalkboard. "Try again," he advised, and glanced up at Miranda.

She turned away quickly, busied herself tucking the baby back into Caroline's basket. Her embarrassment was almost palpable, all the same, and Landry felt a stab of something resembling pity. He wondered if she could read at all, or if she simply had difficulty deciphering long words. One thing was certain: it would only make matters worse if he asked her about it in front of the boys.

In good time, and under violent protest, Jamie and Marcus washed their faces and their teeth at the washstand by the fireplace, then took themselves off to bed. Landry watched them go with a feeling of fond good humor, standing with one elbow braced against the mantelpiece, his pipe and tobacco in the opposite hand.

"You aren't going to smoke, are you?" Miranda asked. He saw it then, the first spark of challenge he'd ever glimpsed in her. She *did* have a certain spirit, he thought, and was pleased.

Still, the inquiry itself surprised him. In the first place, he hadn't expected her to speak up so firmly, she'd seemed so shy around him. In the second, this was his house and he'd smoke if he damned well wanted to. It was just that he didn't happen to want to, that was all—he'd only taken the pipe and tobacco from his shirt pocket so he could put them in the cigar box on the shelf over the hearth, where they belonged.

Landry put the items away with pointed motions,

and the lid of the cigar box closed with a little *slap*. "Are you against tobacco?" he asked, in a tone just this side of annoyance.

She glanced at the baby, now sleeping soundly in his improvised bed. "It makes the air bad," she said nervously, but with conviction. "I don't much cotton to drinking, either. You don't take liquor, do you?"

Landry rarely indulged—he simply didn't like the taste of wine or whiskey—but it was the principle of the thing. "I do my smoking outside," he allowed quietly, evenly, not wanting the boys to overhear, "and I'm not fond of spirits in general, but I'm the head of this household and I wear the pants. I'll thank you to remember that, Mrs. Kildare."

She looked surprised that he'd called her that; he was a little off-balance himself. *Caroline* was "Mrs. Kildare," he thought. Miranda was merely, well, Miranda. She started to say something, then knotted her hands in the apron she'd probably appropriated from the bureau in the spare room and held her tongue.

He looked her up and down, assessingly, without desire or any other emotion. He told himself that what he felt was cool detachment and wondered at one and the same time when he'd come to find lying so easy. "Do you know how to sew?" he asked, after clearing his throat once. It was a rare woman who wasn't handy with a needle and thread, in Landry's experience, but Miranda was not the usual sort of female.

She swallowed. "I can mend," she said, sounding a mite defensive. "I can darn socks, too. I can do the wash and use a flat-iron and make soap. I can hoe and weed and slop pigs and chase down lost cows—"

He almost chuckled at her earnest expression, but stopped himself just in time. God knew, he was no hand with the ladies, having married Caroline right out of school, after living on the next farm from her father's place virtually all his life, but he knew better than to laugh at a woman. That was straight-out asking for trouble, even when you didn't mean anything by it.

"What I meant was, you'll be wanting some dresses and the like." He was afraid he might have reddened a little, just to touch on the subject of the fripperies women wore beneath their everyday clothes. Caroline had liked to wear lace, and ribbon, too, though they were hard to come by, so far from a big city. "I reckoned you could make them."

She looked almost wretched. "Well, I ain't—I'm not very good at such. I could manage dresses and petticoats, I figure, but drawers and camisoles take a fine hand—"

Now it was Landry who swallowed. Drawers and camisoles? Dear God. "Maybe June-bug McCaffrey would be willing to teach you," he said, and the words came out sounding like bits of rusted metal run through a grinder. "I should have the hogs butchered and strung up in the smokehouse in a week or ten days. We'll take the stage into Choteau and get whatever you want."

Her eyes widened. "You mean, you're going to *buy* things? Brand new?"

He smiled. "That's what I mean, all right. You'll be
wanting yard goods—something heavy to make a
cloak, too. It gets right cold around here, long about
the end of October." He paused thoughtfully, glad of
a mental errand to take his mind off things he
oughtn't to think about. "Those shoes won't last
another season," he decided aloud, looking at her
feet. It should be safe, looking at her feet, since he
couldn't see her ankles or anything. "We'll get you
some sturdy boots for when the snows come, and a
pair of high-buttons to wear to church."

That fetching color bloomed on her cheeks again,
turning them pink as wild sweetbriar blossoms. "I can
make do with what I've got," she said. "I been doin'
that for as long as I can remember."

He wanted, not so suddenly, to touch her, even if it
was only to cup that proud little chin of hers in one
hand, but he didn't dare. He was on the verge of
sweeping her up in his arms and carrying her off to his
bed as it was, and he had given his word that she'd
have ample time to get used to living in a new place,
with new people all around her. He was not a man to
go back on his promises.

"I don't plan to buy out the stores, Miranda," he
pointed out, with a gentleness he hadn't known was
in him. No, he'd wanted to present himself as matter-
of-fact, even stern. Head of the household, wearing
the pants, making the decisions, etc. "We'll just get a
few things. Maybe some knickers for little—" he'd
been about to say One-or-the-other, but he caught
himself just in time, "for the baby, there."

She blinked, pressed one splay-fingered hand to her bosom, and sank into a chair at the table, as though overcome. "Well, don't that beat everything!" she murmured.

"*Doesn't,*" Landry corrected, and started into his nightly routine of lowering the door latch, shuttering the windows, turning down the damper in the stove, banking the fire. When he thought to look toward her chair again, Miranda was gone.

She sat on the edge of the narrow bed, both hands pressed to her cheeks, which were as hot as if she'd taken a fever, and tried to stop her mind from spinning. She'd carried the baby's basket-bed along with her when she left the main room, and little Isaiah-or-Ezekiel was sleeping as peacefully as if his mother's life, and therefore his own, hadn't been turned upside down and shaken loose, just since the sun rose that morning.

Miranda had kept house for her father following her mother's passing, and she'd waited on him afterwards, too. Not once had he ever offered so much as a ribbon for her hair—even though she'd once prayed for a strand of blue grosgrain for a solid six months—let alone suggested going into a real store and laying down cash money for woman things. Miranda had been clothing herself in hand-me-downs and cast-offs for as long as she could remember—even when her ma was living, and sewing when she could, there usually hadn't been money for yard goods. The garments Mrs. McCaffrey and Rachel and Savannah had given her since her arrival in Springwater showed barely any wear. She was grateful for them, and hadn't imagined having anything better. Anything made just for her.

The concept was almost frightening, and she rocked slightly back and forth, trying to calm herself and gather in her scattered thoughts. It was bad enough that Landry was so handsome, that just looking at him always left an aching thumbprint on her heart. If he was going to be generous on top of it all, well, she didn't for sure know what she'd do. Did he expect something from her, besides the things he'd outlined when he'd proposed to her back at Springwater? Would he come to the spare room in the night, to lie with her, or look for her to come to him?

She recollected how it was before, giving herself to a man, lying in the tall grass, with the stars scattered all across the sky like a spill of crystal beads and the breeze washing over her bare flesh, cool and smelling of prairie wildflowers . . .

Miranda closed her eyes tight and hugged herself harder, but it didn't help. She remembered being taken, remembered it all too clearly. It hadn't been pleasant, the way Evangeline and Rachel and Savannah all hinted that such things were supposed to be, not at all. She'd merely endured, and listened to him whisper pretty words that she'd guessed, even then, were lies. Still, to someone as starved for affection as Miranda had been, lies notwithstanding, the trade was worthwhile.

Landry, now, he made her feel entirely different about the whole subject. Ever since she'd first

glimpsed him, not long after her arrival at Springwater, in fact, she'd dreamed about lying down with
him. Hadn't been able to *help* imagining what it
would be like if it were Landry who unbuttoned her
dress, loosed the ribbons of her camisole, bared her
breasts, lifted her skirts—

She moaned aloud. *Stop*, she commanded herself.
Stop thinking about that, stop thinking about him!

It did no good at all, giving herself such an order.
Her mind, her body, even her soul, were full to bursting of Landry Kildare.

A rap at her door startled her so badly that she
actually gasped aloud. "Y-yes?" she called, when she'd
reined in her runaway breath.

Landry's voice came through the door, pitched low,
but with no effort at persuasion. "I forgot to ask if you
needed to go outside. If you're afraid, I'll walk with
you."

Miranda closed her eyes again, tighter than ever,
and realized that her bladder was painfully full. "No,
thanks," she chimed, in what she hoped was a cheerful and offhand tone. She'd die of mortification, sitting there in the privy, relieving herself, with Landry
standing guard right outside the door. "I'll just take a
lamp."

He hesitated, then bid her good-night. She heard
him walking away. When the sound of his door closing reached her ears, she jumped up, grabbed the
kerosene lantern on her bedside table, and hurried
through the house. She was back in the darkened
main room of the cabin, washing her hands and face

at the basin, before she realized that Landry was in the room, still fully clothed except for his boots and seated in a chair before the hearth.

She started again. "I didn't see you," she said.

He didn't answer for a long while, but simply stared into the embers in the grate. "Five years," he mused aloud, without so much as glancing her way. "This March, it'll be five years since Caroline died."

Miranda didn't bear any ill feelings toward the dead woman; in fact, she felt a certain odd kinship with her. It was indeed a tragedy for a young wife and mother to pass over before her time the way Caroline had. Still, Miranda was glad to be the one to take her place—after a fashion.

Without thinking it through first, she moved to stand behind Landry's chair and laid a hand lightly on his shoulder. He jerked, as though she'd touched his flesh with a flat-iron fresh off a hot stove, and just when she was afraid he would thrust her arm aside, he reached up instead, and laid his own hand over hers.

"Who was he?" he asked. His voice was quiet, and there was no rancor in his tone. None of the judgment and contempt that had been forthcoming from so many other people before she got to Springwater.

He was asking about the baby's father, of course, and she supposed he had a right to know, being her legal husband and all. She removed her hand from under his and came around to face him, seating herself on the apple box he used for a footstool. She stared into the fire awhile, arms wrapped around her knees.

"We came west with a wagon train. Tom was the scout—he knew the terrain and Indian habits and the like from being a sergeant in the cavalry. He told me he loved me, and that we'd be married as soon as we got as far as Laramie, and I believed him. We made a baby."

"Does he know? About his son, I mean?" Landry's voice revealed no emotion at all, and she didn't dare look at his face just then. She doubted she could have read his expression if she had, since she'd turned down the lantern when she came in from the privy, and it was dark in the room, except for the faint glow of the dying fire.

She thought a long time, debating whether or not she ought to answer, then gave a brisk, reluctant nod. "He said I must have been with somebody else, because he and his wife had tried to have children for the better part of ten years and never had any luck. That was the first time I knew he *had* a wife." She paused, blinked hard, and swallowed. After all that time, she still felt the sting of Tom's rebuff. "She had a millinery shop in Laramie," she added, for no particular reason. "It was all her own, too. Her name was Katherine."

"You met her?" Just the faintest trace of surprise in his voice, but still no verdict on her morals, one way or the other.

"I didn't actually meet her, to shake hands and the like. I was in our wagon, holding the reins while Pa was in the livery stable, trying to swap our oxen for a couple of horses, and I saw her then. She came run-

ning out of that shop when Tom rode in behind the
last of the wagons, and her face was shining fit to
shame the moon. When he caught sight of her, he
broke into a smile and hauled her right up onto the
horse with him, kissed her right there in front of the
whole town."

"I'm sorry," Landry said, in his own good time.

Miranda sighed. She didn't regret bringing little
Isaiah-or-Ezekiel into the world. Never that. All the
same, she wished she hadn't made a fool of herself,
not to mention an adulteress. "So am I," she replied
softly, still watching the bright orange coals in the
fireplace. "So am I."

CHAPTER

3

FIRST THING the next morning, Landry commenced to slaughtering and butchering the hogs. Miranda reckoned she'd be called upon to help him, and she dreaded that wholeheartedly, being that bloodshed—animal *or* human—always made her swoony, but he left the house at sunup, having made his own breakfast without so much as a rap on her door to awaken her.

She'd nursed the baby hastily, sleepily, then washed and dressed and poured herself a cup of Landry's coffee by the time the boys straggled out of their room, still in long johns, looking rumpled and none-too-amiable. They had obviously forgotten their new stepmother; when they caught sight of her, they high-tailed it back where they'd come from. When they returned, wearing pants and shirts, if not shoes, Miranda was already frying eggs and salt pork to feed them.

They ate a pile of food between them, and seemed glad enough to go off to school. The alternative would have been to help their father with the pigs, so they probably considered themselves lucky. Miranda's own pa would have made her stay home and work right alongside him.

She dallied as long as she could, cleaning up the breakfast dishes, sweeping the floor and the hearth, making up her and the boys' beds. She couldn't quite bring herself to step over the threshold of Landry's room again, but she figured he'd probably already tidied the place anyway. He was that sort of man, and Miranda couldn't rightly recall ever knowing another one quite like him.

Even Jacob McCaffrey, a man she looked up to and had come to love like a father, didn't cook for himself, sweep floors, or spread up the beds. He expected Junebug to do that kind of work, and she did, without seeming to mind. Mrs. McCaffrey had been known to aid her husband by pitching hay, too, as well as milking cows and even shoeing horses, and nobody, most especially Miranda, thought it unusual. It was just the way of things.

Now, standing inside the solid, tidy house to which she'd come as a bride less than twenty-four hours before, Miranda braced herself to be summoned to the hog pen. When considerable time had passed, with no word from Landry, she made a sling to carry little Isaiah-or-Ezekiel against her chest and set out, ready to work.

The hog pen, boasting six sows and a boar just the night before, was empty, and there was no sound of pigs squealing, no sign of the spilled blood and gore typical of such an enterprise. In fact, the whole place seemed eerily quiet.

"Landry?" she called out, in a tentative voice, raised only high enough to carry.

He appeared in the doorway of the smokehouse, crimson from the middle of his chest to his feet. He did not look pleased at the interruption, though he was, as usual, mannerly. "What is it?"

Miranda swayed as the crisp fall breeze brought the coppery scent of blood to her nostrils, mingled with the pleasant scents of dried leaves and wood smoke. "I was just—just wondering if you wanted me to—to help—"

Landry looked at her curiously. "Are you all right?"

She was, in fact, woozy. Only the fact that her baby would fall with her if she went down kept her on her feet. "I don't much like—b-blood."

His expression was eloquently ironic. "It's not my favorite part of raising pigs," he agreed, in dry tones. "You go ahead in the house and find Caroline's—find the big kettle, the one we use for laundry and making soap and the like. Carry it outside, fill it with water, and build a fire under it. You can boil up a couple of the heads while I finish hanging these critters up to cure."

Miranda gulped and turned blindly away. She was infinitely relieved to be spared the slaughtering and butchering, and she didn't let herself think as far as "boiling up a couple of the heads." She'd get through this challenge hand-over-hand, she told herself, a moment at a time if necessary.

The kettle Landry had mentioned turned out to be more of a cauldron, made of solid iron, and after several attempts at lifting the thing, she finally turned it onto its side and rolled it across the floor and over the threshold, into the front yard. She built the fire, as instructed, after fetching kindling and wood from the appropriate shed, and began lugging water from the outside pump to fill it. On about the fourth trip, with the weight of a bucket pulling either shoulder halfway out of its socket, she began to wish she'd built the fire closer to the well.

She'd just gotten the kettle to a nice rolling boil, and she was damp with sweat from hairline to toenail with the effort, when Landry appeared, carrying something big and bloody in both arms. He flung it into the pot with a resounding splash, and headed back toward the smokehouse with no more than a nod to Miranda.

She used an old broom handle to stir the grisly contents of the kettle, and kept herself half turned away. All the same, she saw Landry approaching with another horrendous burden out of the corner of her eye, winced when she heard a second splash.

"Miranda."

She couldn't look at him, didn't dare. "W-what?"

"You don't have to stand here the whole time those heads are boiling down, chilling yourself and that baby to the bone. Just come out and make sure the fire's going once in a while. Maybe pour on some more water."

She stiffened her backbone and nodded, careful to

keep her chin high. Fact was, she wanted to break down and weep with gratitude and relief. "You'll be coming in for dinner after a spell?" she asked, with a spindly effort at good cheer.

"Not like this," Landry said. "I'll strip off these duds down by the creek when I'm finished and sluice myself off as well as I can. You might bring out a plate around noon, though. Just set it on that crate outside the smokehouse door. Bring me some fresh clothes, too, while you're at it."

Miranda's face was hot as the bottom of that iron cauldron, and the heat had nothing whatsoever to do with the crackling fire or the steam off the boiling water. Her mind had gotten snagged on the image of Landry taking off his clothes by the creek, and she'd barely heard anything he said after that. Maybe her pa had been right, she thought, thoroughly chagrined. Maybe she *was* just plain no good, through and through.

She nodded rapidly, dropped the stirring stick, and hurried into the cabin. The baby was hungry again, and fussy, so she fed him, changed his diaper, and laid him down in the basket to sleep. After that, she washed her hands and face and tried to neaten her sagging, steam-dampened hair a little.

Soon, she was making biscuits, the way June-bug McCaffrey had showed her back at Springwater and sorting through the pantry for canned meat and vegetables. She made a stew from a mixture of preserved venison, carrots from a sealed jar, and onions, chopped real fine.

Within an hour, the house smelled of home cooking, though she could still catch the underlying scent of boiled hog-head, wafting up from her dress and permeating her hair. She went outside periodically, to add wood to the fire and water to the cauldron, all without once looking into the brew, and when the sun reached the middle of the sky, she figured it was time to carry a meal to Landry.

The idea of it filled her with pleasure. She washed again, spruced her hair again, and then squared her shoulders and marched right into Landry's bedroom to fetch the fresh clothes he'd requested earlier.

The window was open, lace curtain fluttering in the breeze, and the bed, to her surprise, was unmade. Even from the doorway, Miranda could catch the clean, sun-dried laundry scent of Landry, clinging to the sheets and floating through the air itself. She found the clothes, trousers and a clean shirt, stockings and another pair of boots, a lightweight set of long underwear, stacked all of them into a neat pile, and started out of the room. She intended to come back later and smooth out the bed.

As she was turning away, however, she saw the small, ornate picture frame propped on the night table, alongside a lamp and a book resting open on its spine. Knowing all the while that she shouldn't pry, she moved toward the item that had drawn her attention, picked it up in one slightly tremulous hand.

It was a photographic likeness, oval in shape and faded with the passage of time, showing Landry and Caroline Kildare on what was presumably their wedding day. She stood behind his chair, a slender, fair-haired woman, with finely made features and the hint of a smile in her eyes, one hand resting on her husband's shoulder. Landry, seated and sober, as was the fashion, looked as though he was barely suppressing an exuberant shout, maybe of joy, maybe of triumph.

Miranda felt a distinct pang, looking at the two of them, so happy, neither suspecting how short their time together would turn out to be. She set the picture down, after a few moments, and turned away from it, mentally as well as physically, by sheer force of will. As she left Landry's bedroom, carrying his clean clothes, she was wondering where Jamie and Marcus had gotten their bright red hair. Certainly not from their father or from the blond Caroline.

She couldn't help thinking about Caroline as she made the first trip to the door of the smokehouse, where she set a full plate on the upturned wooden box, covered with a pie tin. It was gone, moments later, when she returned with the stack of clothing. She hesitated a moment, there on the other side of the high threshold from her new husband, but in the end she could not make herself step inside. She doubted, in fact, that she would be able to eat pork ever again.

After going back to the cabin once more, to make sure the baby was safe, and still sleeping soundly, she went out to add wood to the fire in the dooryard, and water to the kettle. Then, with her mind still on Caroline, she made for the copse of trees on the far side of the creek, where she knew the other woman was buried.

The grave was some distance from the stream, but she found it unerringly. It was marked by the most beautifully carved wooden cross she had ever seen—mahogany, unless she was mistaken. Where had Landry gotten mahogany, there in the wilds of Montana, where the trees were mostly pine and Douglas fir, cottonwood and cedar and birch?

He'd carved Caroline's full name into the marker, and surrounded it with delicately wrought flowers and vines. There were even birds, perched here and there among the foliage, and Miranda touched it with a feeling of wonder. It was, this sad creation, certainly among the most beautiful things she had ever seen, whether in nature or man-made.

"I love him," Miranda whispered, surprising herself with the revelation. It seemed to strike her at the very moment she said it; she had fallen in love with this man who, even in a few short days' time, had made her feel special, needed. For the very first time. "I think I have since the first time I saw him, at Springwater."

She bit down on her lower lip. "You needn't worry, though, because he still cares for you. I reckon he always will." She sighed. "I've got to get back now. The baby might wake up, or that dratted pot could boil over, and I'd best be thinking about supper, too. I just wanted to—well, I don't rightly know what I wanted to do. Just say a how-do-you-do, I guess."

She stood up straight, lifting her eyes as a breeze blew through the leaves of the trees surrounding Caroline's grave, set them raining down, rustling and bright, in a shower of red and gold, crimson and rust. She was not a fanciful person, and she didn't for a moment think of that occurrence as any sort of blessing, but she felt a certain peace where Caroline was concerned all the same.

The wind picked up as she made her way back to the cabin, and when she got to the yard, she was alarmed to find that the bonfire under the kettle had started to spread into the tall, dry grass and was quickly approaching the house. Miranda had seen the prairies blazing on the journey west, and she felt a rush of fear surge through her like venom from the bite of a giant snake.

Dashing into the house, she snatched up the first blanket she came to and rushed out to battle the fire.

"Landry!" she shrieked, her eyes watering from the smoke by then, her breath coming in coughs and gasps that left her throat raw.

She was barely aware of the approaching riders, or even of Landry, until someone threw her onto the ground and rolled her through the dirt. Only then did she realize that the flames had caught on the hem of her dress.

"Get inside and make sure the baby's all right!" Landry yelled, rising and pulling her up with him in almost the same motion. She could see that part of the fire had reached the door before it had been snuffed out by her efforts. "Then start pumping water!"

She nodded, fairly choking by then, and rushed in to see that little Isaiah-or-Ezekiel was safe. Indeed, he was cooing and trying to catch his own kicking feet with his fat little hands.

Breathlessly thankful, Miranda murmured a prayer of gratitude, snatched up the water buckets next to the stove, and raced outside again. Landry and the two men helping him—through the smoke Miranda recognized Trey Hargreaves and Doc Parrish—had nearly contained the blaze. When at last the fire was subdued, Landry was so covered in soot that you couldn't even tell he'd been butchering all day.

Grinning, Trey dragged a blackened sleeve across a forehead that nearly matched it. "Next time I come to call," he said, directing his words at Landry, "I'd appreciate it if you'd just offer me coffee and water for my horse."

"Amen," agreed the Doc, just catching his breath. He looked more like a chimney sweep just then than the town doctor. He wasn't much of a talker, Doc Parrish, but he knew his business and he was well-liked at Springwater.

"I'll make the coffee," Miranda said, still hoarse from the smoke, and went inside.

When she came out again, with the handles of three mugs hooked over two fingers of one hand and the coffeepot in the other, the men were seated side by side on the edge of the horse trough, talking seriously. Miranda wasn't an eavesdropper, but when she heard Jacob McCaffrey's name, she stopped to listen and made no effort to hide the fact.

Landry met her gaze, and raised his brimming cup in a gesture that plainly said, "Thank you."

"I was just telling Landry that Mike Houghton's back," Trey said. "Now that the boy's big enough to work for a living, he's come to claim him."

Miranda nearly dropped the coffeepot and splashed her ruined skirts with the grounds. "Toby? But Jacob and June-bug are his family—"

"Be that as it may," the Doc said grimly, "Mike's come to claim him."

Miranda couldn't move for several long moments, she was so stricken by this news. Toby, found by Rachel Hargreaves in an abandoned camp up in the timber about eighteen months before, when she'd first come to Springwater to teach school, had been taken in by the McCaffreys. Jacob, especially, adored the boy, and he was still on the mend from a bad spell with his heart right after the Doc and Savannah got married. He and June-bug had already lost two sons in the war; it might destroy them to give up Toby as well, when they'd come to think of him as their own, and to love him so dearly. Parting would be even worse for young Toby, who had never known a real family before.

"No," she whispered.

"There's nothing anybody can do," the Doc said, to nobody in particular. He was staring off into space. "Toby's still too young to decide for himself, and Houghton is his legal father."

Miranda was full of sorrow and fury. "He's no kind of a father!" she spouted. "What kind of man goes off and leaves his own boy to starve in the woods?"

"Miranda," Landry said firmly, but gently, too.

"I've got to go to town," she replied, reaching back, automatically, to untie her apron.

But Landry shook his head. "There'll be preaching on Sunday, like as not. We'll speak to the McCaffreys then."

"But—"

"Miranda."

She went into the house, turning furiously on one heel, but she wasn't happy about it. Landry Kildare had his share of gall talking to her like that, when he wasn't even a real husband. She was slamming kettles onto the stove and filling them with water from the reservoir when she heard the visitors riding away, heard Landry push open the door and step into the house.

"The boys are staying in town tonight," Landry said. "Toby's their friend."

She didn't turn around, but just went on banging things around. Little Isaiah-or-Ezekiel, far from being frightened, seemed to love the clatter and clang, for he was gurgling away in his basket, happy as a pig in muck.

She stopped. It was a poor choice of images, a pig.

"Miranda, look at me." His voice was quiet, and contained no kind of threat, but she didn't like to disobey him when he spoke to her like that.

She looked. He was black from the fire, and his clothes, first bloodied and now burned and soot-covered, would probably never come clean. "What?"

"There's no point in our going to town ahead of time and adding to the fuss. Jacob and June-bug know we'll come if they need us, and we'll see them day after tomorrow, at the preaching."

It had become rare for Jacob to offer a sermon, though he did on occasion. Landry often took his place, or Tom Bellweather. Since Rachel and Trey Hargreaves' baby had been born, a little boy called Henry, even the keeper of the Brimstone Saloon had been known to get up, on occasion, and hold forth on the sayings of the Good Book.

Tears sprang, unbidden, to her eyes. She dashed at her cheeks with the back of one hand. "I didn't mean for the grass to take fire," she said, because she had to say something to fill the silence, and that was the first thing that came to her mind.

"It wasn't your fault," Landry answered, winding a sooty finger in a loose tendril of her hair. "I'd best go and see to the chores. I'll be in after I've cleaned up."

"I'll go ahead and start supper, then," Miranda said, with a sniffle. She was heartbroken for the McCaffreys and for Toby, that hadn't changed, but Landry was right. It would do no good to go rushing off to town and intrude on a private grief.

On another level, she marveled that he wasn't blaming her for the fire. Her father would have berated her in a loud voice, maybe even beaten her. After all, they might have lost the house, the barn, everything, because of her carelessness and inexperience, but it seemed Landry had already dismissed the whole matter from his mind.

Landry had merely nodded, acknowledging her statement, and left her to her cooking. Only then did she have time to examine the riot of feelings he'd roused in her, just by touching her hair and speaking gently.

When he returned, nearly an hour later, by the loud old clock on one end of the mantel, Miranda had a meal ready to set out, and she nearly dropped the pot of chicken and dumplings at the sight of him. He was merely *clean*, she supposed, with his hair washed and combed through with his fingers, and his clothes all tidy, smelling the way he was supposed to smell, and yet the mere sight of him fairly stopped her heart from beating. If he smiled, she didn't know what she'd do.

He went right ahead and smiled. "Smells good," he said.

Miranda was so dazed that it took her an unlikely amount of time to reason out that he was talking about supper. She nodded, probably looking down-right foolish, and set the pot down on the table with a thump. "You start right in. I just want to see if the baby's asleep."

"I'll wait for you," he said, mannerly as a prince in a storybook, standing there behind his chair.

It was useless to protest, Miranda figured, for the man was as stubborn as could be, though she had to admit he was fair-minded. She looked in on little Isaiah-or-Ezekiel, snoozing away in his basket in her bedroom, and returned to the main room.

Landry was still waiting, and patiently. Only when she sat down did he take his chair. As he had done the night before, he led a short, plain prayer of thanks for the food, and then the meal began.

Miranda wondered what was on his mind. He was always gentlemanly, for a man who didn't put on a coat and collar except on Sundays, but he hadn't waited for her to sit down before starting in on last night's supper. She looked at him curiously, figuring that she probably never would understand him, even if she lived to be as old as Granny Johnson, up there on the mountainside.

"I'll be another few days getting those hogs cut up and hung," he said.

Miranda's stomach rolled. She took a sip from her water cup in hopes of settling herself down a little. "What about them—those heads, out there in the cauldron?" she said, in a nigh-unto-normal tone of voice.

Landry was chewing a mouthful of chicken and dumplings. "I reckon you'll be able to put the first batch of meat up in jars tomorrow," he said happily, when he'd swallowed. "I'll make head cheese from the others."

Miranda pushed back her chair, preparatory to rushing for the door. She was no sissy. She'd chopped the heads off chickens before, cleaned and plucked them, too. She'd skinned rabbits for stew and even boiled up a prairie dog once, on the trail from St. Louis, when game had been scarce, but she wasn't going to eat anything that had been scooped out of some critter's skull and that was the end of it.

Landry's eyes were dancing. "It's tasty stuff," he teased.

Much as she cared for him, she could have murdered him just then. He looked as mischievous as one of his boys, sitting there, with one side of his mouth twitching that way, all but wriggling his eyebrows. "I'd rather starve."

"Then I guess you've never been hungry," he answered, and went on eating.

Miranda was finished, but she didn't leave the table. She just sat there, with her hands folded in her lap, waiting. Waiting—for what, she did not know. The place was quiet without the boys, and the very air itself seemed to hum around her ears. The day had been a long and difficult one, and she was tired, but if anything troubled her, it was the vibrant yet ordinary *happiness* of just being there, with Landry.

He tilted his head to one side, taking in the ruined skirts of her dress. "You'll have to cut that up for rags, it looks like," he commented. Apparently, he was in a mood to talk.

The thought horrified Miranda, even though she knew he was right, and very little of the gown would be salvageable. It was the prettiest of her hand-me-downs, having belonged to Rachel Hargreaves, a bright yellow fabric with eyelet at the neckline and mother-of-pearl buttons. She looked down at it sadly and then gave a brief, reluctant nod of agreement.

He looked sympathetic and, at the same time, he seemed a little amused. No doubt, she looked a sight, in her scorched and sooty clothes. The merriment in his eyes made him seem like a scamp, hardly older than his sons. "Don't fret," he said. "We'll get you something twice as pretty when we go to

Choteau." He frowned thoughtfully, while spearing
yet another dumpling from the kettle in the center
of the table. It amazed Miranda how much the man
could eat, and still be made of nothing but muscle
and bone. "You'd look real nice in scarlet, I think, or
dark blue."

The thought of traveling to Choteau cheered Miranda not a little, but she managed to keep her
expression prim and matronly, lest he think she was
too eager, or even extravagant. "I don't think proper
ladies wear scarlet," she said.

That time, he did laugh, and she was wounded.
Didn't he think she was a proper lady? She pushed
back her chair and would have fled if he hadn't
reached out and caught hold of her wrist when she
started past him, on the way to her room.

"Miranda," he said and, just like that, with a simple tug, he pulled her down onto his lap. "I'm sorry,"
he said. His breath was warm on her face.

She was disturbed by the other complex sensations
their proximity wrought in her, too, and none of it
helped her mood. "Yes," she hissed, and she could feel
her ears throbbing, which meant they were probably
red as a rooster's comb, "I made a mistake. I trusted a
man I shouldn't have trusted. But that doesn't mean
I'm not a decent woman, Landry Kildare!"

He was still smiling, damn him, but the light in his
eyes was tender. He laid the tip of one index finger
against her mouth to silence her. "Hush," he said. "I
laughed because, all of the sudden, I had a picture of
you in my mind, stirring that pot out in the dooryard

today, twisted halfway to Texas to keep from looking in and seeing hog eyeballs looking back at you."

His thighs were hard as tamarack, and so was his chest. His arms, though loosely clasped, nonetheless encircled her. She could barely think. "Maybe you should let me up," she said lamely.

He sighed. "I know for sure that I should," he agreed, "but damn if I can make myself do it. We'll take the stage to Choteau in a week, Miranda. We can stay in a hotel and take all our meals in restaurants, just like we were on a honeymoon. Do you think you'll be ready by then—to share my bed, I mean?"

She wanted to say she was ready *now*, but that would only have made him think twice about counting her a lady. Miranda knew almost nothing about the relations between a husband and wife, despite the fact that she'd already borne a child, but she understood that it wasn't proper to be too eager, even when the man was your honest-to-God, by-the-Good-Book husband. "I—I guess," she answered miserably. "As long as you don't smell like pigs."

He laughed again, actually threw back his head and shouted with it, but that time, she didn't take offense. Heaven only knew how long he would have held her there, perched on his lap and feeling all her vital organs melt, one by one, into a hot puddle deep inside her, if little Isaiah-or-Ezekiel hadn't let out a wail when he did.

Landry put his hands on Miranda's waist and lifted her to her feet, and she made for the bedroom, lickety-split. When she returned, after nursing the baby and holding him until he went back to sleep, she was surprised to find Landry at the sink, drying the last of the supper dishes.

She had never seen a man do that, and the sight made her mouth fall open. She closed it right away, but not quickly enough to keep Landry from seeing how startled she was.

He chuckled and shook his head. "There's plenty of hot water in the reservoir," he said. "If you'd like to take a bath, I mean."

Miranda swallowed. Either he was insulting her again, or he was trying to drive her crazy. It was hard to tell which one. She might have broke right down and cried with confusion, if she hadn't had just a shred of pride left. "Kind of you to offer," she said, though she didn't know whether that was the truth or not.

"I'll carry the tub into the spare room for you," he said, "or you can bathe out here, in front of the fire."

"Where will you be all this time?" she wanted to know. She might have been a lot of things, but immodest wasn't one of them.

His face cracked into a grin, but he made a credible effort at looking serious. "In my room," he said. "I like to read a little while before I turn down the lights."

Miranda closed her eyes for an instant. She could imagine him in that room, in that big, Landry-scented bed, only too well. And after the trip to Choteau, she'd be sharing it with him, unless he found her wanting in some way. "All right, then," she said, agreeing to the bath and a whole lot more, if you wanted to know the plain truth.

Fortunately, Landry didn't pursue the matter. He just brought the tub in from one of the sheds, set it in front of the hearth, and began filling it with water. It was still steaming when he set out a towel and a bar of soap and left her to herself. She was out of her clothes and into that bath quicker than quick, and sunk right down to her chin. It was blissful, and she let out a long breath in sheer appreciation, but soon enough she got bored, idling in the middle of what served as a parlor, wearing nothing but soap suds and a washtub, and finished up her bath. Climbing out, she wrapped herself in Landry's towel—she hadn't thought to fetch a nightgown—and tiptoed toward her room.

As she passed, the line of light underneath his door faded to darkness.

CHAPTER

4

NEEDLESS TO SAY, Miranda was surprised to run into the big boar the next morning, when she carried out a bucketful of scraps to feed the yearling pigs. She'd thought he was in the jars and crocks she'd been sealing with hot wax since just after breakfast or, at the very least, hanging in the smokehouse along with several of his lady friends.

Instead, he was on the loose, facing Miranda on the path, snorting ominously and pawing at the ground with one front hoof, just like a bull. In fact, he looked big as a bull to Miranda at that moment. He was as dangerous as he was ugly, a quarter ton of sorry pork, with a mean spirit and a made-up mind.

Shakily, Miranda tossed the scraps to the ground, pail and all. There were barely four feet between her and the boar by then, and though he snuffled the offering of stale bread, potato peelings, eggshells, coffee grounds, and the like, it didn't hold his interest long. He raised that massive head again right away and fixed his little eyes on her.

"L-Landry," she called, in an almost musical tone, as though being real polite would somehow keep the pig from charging and tearing her apart with razor-sharp teeth.

"Don't move," Landry advised, from a few feet behind her. She was so relieved at his presence that she nearly fainted dead away, but in the next instant, the boar charged, with a horrifying, squeal-like bellow. The whole universe seemed to slow down; Miranda heard a rifle being cocked, then the loud report of a gunshot. The beast fell, inches shy of where she stood, its head a bloody pulp, already drawing flies.

Miranda got messages from a hundred parts of herself, body and soul, and all in the space of a heartbeat. Someone cowering in a rear corner of her brain was screaming in shrill terror, and it was only by the grace of God and good muscle tone that she held on to the contents of her bladder. Her stomach bounced between her throat and her hip bones, unsure where to settle.

She stood frozen for what seemed a long time, trying to put herself back together. She watched like a detached spectator as Landry passed her, laid his rifle on the ground, and crouched down to inspect the dead boar. She began to weep, but silently, for she couldn't seem to force out a sound—not a sob, a shriek, or even a hiccough.

Landry rose to his full height again, rifle in hand

once more, shaking his head and looking sadly down at the animal who had just attacked his wife. "That," he said, "was a perfectly good hog."

The words loosed Miranda's locked knees, and she turned, one hand pressed to her mouth, and fled into the cabin. All the rest of the day, while she preserved what seemed like an endless supply of pig meat, following the instructions in an old cookery book that had, of course, belonged to Caroline, she relived the whole episode, from the first fearsome comprehension that the boar meant to rip her apart where she stood, to the gunshot, to Landry's words.

That was a perfectly good hog.

Landry gazed ruefully down at the dead boar and wondered how the hell the miserable critter had gotten out of the holding pen. He'd planned to keep the animal for a long while, and use him for breeding, but now he wasn't good for a whole lot more than ham and bacon. God knew, there'd be no head cheese from this one.

He sighed. He still had yearlings, and a couple of them were boars. There were three young sows, too, which meant he'd have another crop of piglets in the spring. No sense in stewing over what couldn't be helped; he was still in the hog business, after all.

He glanced toward the house, where Miranda had fled just moments before. Only then did he allow himself to think of what could have happened to her, what *would* have happened, if he hadn't seen her trying to face down that evil-natured pig. His stomach pitched, and he thought for a moment that he'd be sick, right there in the barnyard. However long he lived, he didn't reckon he'd ever forget looking down the barrel of that rifle, so scared that his heart was jammed into his throat fit to cut off his wind, and pulling the trigger.

He thought about going into the house and trying to soothe Miranda, maybe even taking her into his arms, the way he would have done with Caroline, but he felt strangely tongue-tied, and he had more than a day's work yet to do and a lot less time to do it. Besides, he smelled like pig.

With another sigh, he made for the barn, left the rifle leaning against an outside wall, and went in to hitch up Nicodemus, the strongest of his two plow horses. Then, using about equal portions of muscle and sweat, he and the horse dragged the boar behind one of the sheds, where Landry, cursing every now and again, skinned the hog, and cleaned it.

He worked through the afternoon and well into the evening; only when he saw lamplight coming from the cabin windows did he realize it was dark. Resigned, exasperated, and hurting in every joint and sinew, he went down to the creek with a bar of soap and the clean clothes Miranda had at some point left for him by the smokehouse door, and gave himself a scrubbing in water cold enough to set his teeth to chattering.

When he got inside the house, every inch of him covered in goosebumps, hungry as a bear in April, there was no sign of supper, and Miranda was seated at the table, bent over what looked like a reading primer. Little One-or-the-other was in the basket, waving and kicking and making baby sounds for all he was worth.

Miranda had been so engrossed in the shabby little book that Landry's entrance must have startled her, for she jumped half out of her skin when he shut the door. Then, almost guiltily, she slammed the volume shut and put it on her lap. Her cheeks were glowing with either embarrassment or indignation, maybe even both, and her eyes had a snap in them.

Landry felt a muscle bunch in his jaw. He'd be damned if he understood women—he'd saved that milk-and-honey hide of hers, and killed the best pig he'd ever owned in the process, and despite all that, she was in a pet. He lowered the door latch with a *thump* meant to show that he wasn't going to put up with any nonsense.

"I'm hungry," he said, hanging up his hat. "What's for supper?"

Her gaze cut toward the warming oven above the stove. "Pig," she said.

He wanted to laugh, all of the sudden, but he couldn't figure why. He went to the stove, opened the door on the warming oven, and peered in to see a plate heaped with shredded pork, boiled to a thought-provoking shade of gray. Quick as that, his mirth dissipated. He was so irritated that he forgot to use a pot holder when he reached in to retrieve the plate and burned his fingers good.

He was cursing under his breath as he wadded up a

flour-sack dish towel, got the plate out, and dumped everything on it into the scrap bucket. Then he went to the pantry to fetch some hard, dry bread and a hunk of even drier, harder cheese to appease his growling stomach.

Miranda narrowed her eyes at him, but she didn't say a single, solitary word. She just sat there, hiding that reading primer, or whatever it was, and glaring at him, like she was glad—*glad* he'd burned himself and was now reduced to eating victuals better suited to a flock of chickens than a full-grown man who'd just put in sixteen hours of dirty, back-breaking work.

He slapped the bleak meal he'd scrounged from the pantry onto a blue spatterware plate, carried it to the table, and set it down with a crash before dropping into his chair. He had been unjustly used and he wanted her to know it.

She didn't back down an inch.

The standoff continued until Landry had choked down enough food to ease his stomach pangs; after that, he couldn't force another bite past his lips. "What's in the book?" he snapped, because something had to be said or he was going to go crazy, and everything else he could think of was downright inflammatory.

She blushed; even in the dim light, he could see that. Her jaw jutted out slightly, though just for a moment, then she lowered her eyes and her shoulders went slack. He'd won, after a fashion, but he didn't feel especially good about it. He didn't even feel vindicated.

"You've got to promise not to make fun of me if I tell," she said, after a long time. He nodded his agreement, then she laid the book on the table between them, still avoiding his gaze.

It was a tattered, falling-apart copy of McGuffy's Reader, which didn't surprise him, of course, because he'd thought he recognized it. They were both silent. Miranda chewed on her lower lip, and Landry simply waited. He wished that he hadn't challenged her, but there was no going back now.

"I can read," she protested. "Don't you go thinking I can't."

He simply watched her. There were a lot of people who struggled with the printed word; it came as no particular surprise that she might be one of them.

"It's just that it's—hard for me." Her eyes filled with tears of humiliation and of desperate dignity. "I'm bound to get real good at it, though," she added, with determination.

He reached across the table, laid a hand over hers. "I'm sorry, Miranda," he said.

She sniffled and jerked her hand back. "Don't you dare feel pity for me, Landry Kildare!" she cried, and the baby, alarmed, began to fuss.

Perhaps from old habit, Landry got to the basket before she did, picked up the infant, and held him the same way he'd held Jamie and Marcus, when they were little. "I didn't say I felt sorry for you," he told Miranda, patting the baby's small, heaving back with one hand. "All I meant was, I wanted things to be all right between us again. That's all."

She deflated a little, and there was something of softness, something of incredulity in her eyes as she watched him with her son. What was it, he wondered, that made women believe they were the only ones capable of holding a baby? It wasn't like the little critters weighed anything at all.

Miranda lifted the corner of her apron and dried her eyes with it. She was just standing there, sniffling and looking mournful, and for once, it seemed she had nothing to say.

"Miranda, in the name of God, what is it?" Landry asked tightly. The baby fretted; he bounced him a little. Settled him right down.

For a moment there, it looked like she was going to come straight out and tell him, but in the end, she just walked over, took the baby from him, and disappeared into her bedroom. She came back only to fetch the basket, by which time Landry was back in the pantry, searching for something else to eat.

Despite his exhaustion, he read far into the night, unable to settle his mind, and five minutes after he'd turned down the wick on his bedside lamp, Miranda started screaming fit to start up the resurrection of the saints ahead of schedule. By the time Landry pounded through her door, wearing nothing but his long johns, the baby was howling too.

Frankly, Landry had expected a band of renegade Indians or a bobcat, at the very least, but all he found was Miranda sitting up in bed, sucking in air in great, panicked gasps, and the baby yelling in sympathy.

He jiggled the basket, somewhat hurriedly, on his

way to Miranda. "There now, little fella," he said, wishing the kid had a manageable name, "it'll be all right." He had barely sat down on the edge of the spare room bed—he hadn't realized it was so narrow and so hard—when Miranda flung both arms around his neck and clung to him like a swimmer about to go under. He hesitated only a fraction of a moment before enfolding her in a cautious embrace of his own.

"That pig," she sputtered into the curve between his neck and shoulder, "that awful pig was after me—"

"Shhh," he said, and brushed his lips across her temple. It wasn't really a kiss, he told himself. "It was just a dream. Nothing's going to hurt you." He was struck by the emphasis he'd put on that assurance—the desire to protect Miranda from anything and anyone meaning her harm was almost overwhelming. Even there, in what had always been Caroline's sanctuary, he found he couldn't quite remember his first wife's face. Her image was fading from his mind, like thin ink on an old letter.

It shamed him, this forgetting of a woman he'd sworn to remember unto death and beyond, and yet he couldn't seem to put Miranda from him. She was so warm, so soft, so sweet. And she was weeping into his shoulder.

"Shhh," he said again, and smoothed her tangle of silky hair with one hand. The baby, at least, was settling down a little, just hiccoughing now and again.

"B-because of me," Miranda wailed, "a pig is d-dead!"

Landry might have smiled, under other circumstances, but this, of course, was not the time. Besides, he was too stricken by the discovery that he couldn't call Caroline to mind the way he always had before. He held Miranda away so he could look into her face. It was awash in moonlight and tears, and unbelievably beautiful.

"Hush," he said, with a sort of tender sternness. "There'll be other boars."

She snuffled, her small shoulders moving in the effort to calm herself. Her eyes sought Landry in the gloom, still opaque with fear and bright as buttons. "I-I was so scared," she confessed, and he knew she wasn't talking about the dream, now, but about the actual confrontation with that devil's whelp of a hog. "I've heard so many stories—"

Landry kissed her forehead; he wasn't sure why. It was a light kiss, a kiss in passing, but it left him troubled all the same, first because he did it in the place that had been Caroline's refuge, and second because it only left him wanting more. So much more.

"You've got to let that go," he counseled, and he wondered if he was talking to himself in some ways as well as to Miranda. "There's nothing to be gained by going over what happened today, either waking or sleeping. The important thing is, you're alive." Dear God, wasn't she, though? Holding her like that made Landry feel things he didn't remember feeling before, ever. Not even with Caroline, who was the only other woman he'd ever been intimate with.

"He'll come back—he'll be right there in my head, soon as I close my eyes—"

"No," Landry said. "I won't let that happen." With that, he lay down beside her on that skinny bed, he in his underwear, she in her nightdress, and kept his arms wrapped around her. "Go to sleep now, Miranda," he said, though he didn't figure he'd close his own eyes all night. "We'll have to be up early to get the chores done before it's time to leave for the preaching."

She allowed him to hold her, even settled comfortably into his arms. It was torture for him, though; he was as engorged as a stallion mounting a mare, but with no honorable way to relieve the agony. He wondered what she'd do if he made love to her, slowly and tenderly, but he made no move to find out. He'd given his word, after all, and he meant to keep it, whatever the cost to his own sanity.

Miranda awakened just before dawn and saw Landry through her lashes, sitting on the edge of the bed with his head in his hands. It was a moment or two before she remembered her nightmare, and how he had come to her, and held her, and lay down beside her just so she'd feel safe. She'd known he wanted her; she'd felt that, what with the two of them lying so close together and all, and she would not have refused him. All the same, he hadn't made her his real wife, perhaps because this room was a reminder of Caroline.

She put a hand out, touched his warm, solid back. He was wearing long johns, and he managed to make even those look good. "It's all right," she said, very softly. She didn't know what made her choose those particular words; maybe it was just that he'd used them to reassure her the night before, after that terrible dream.

He didn't answer, not directly, at any rate. From his words, you'd have thought she hadn't said anything at all. "I'll get the stove going," he said. "You stay in bed a little while."

She didn't want to let him go. "Landry," she said softly.

The muscles in his back hardened beneath her hand. Maybe he thought she was about to try and seduce him, and had set himself to resist. "In a quarter of an hour or so, you might get up and start breakfast. I'll see to the chores and get the buckboard ready for the drive to Springwater."

They were going to the preaching, she recalled, with a little swell of joy. She had forgotten that. She bit her lower lip to keep from leaning forward and kissing the curve of his shoulder. "Landry," she repeated, with a sort of gentle insistence.

He turned his head, at long last, and looked down into her eyes.

She cupped his cheek with her hand, felt the rough stubble of a new beard, the strong bones of his face. "Thank you."

He looked puzzled.

"For shooting a perfectly good hog yesterday, to save me. For coming in here when I had a nightmare, and for staying so I could sleep without being afraid. The McCaffreys have been good to me and little

Isaiah-or-Ezekiel, and so have the other folks at Springwater, but nobody's ever, well, looked after me the way you do."

"Miranda?" There was a light in his eyes again, and the faintest hint of a smile twitched at the corner of his mouth.

"What?"

"Give that baby one name or the other. Sometime soon, he's going to start wondering who the heck he is."

She smiled, and it was hard not to put her arms around him again, and kiss him on that square chin of his, or that wonderful mouth. "I reckon you're right," she said. "I had a mind to get him named proper by now, but more's happened to me in the last few days than in my whole life put together, it seems like. I haven't had time to think which I ought to call him."

He touched the tip of her nose with a work-callused index finger, and she thought, out of the blue, of that carving he'd made for Caroline's grave. It turned the moment sober again, the remembrance of that exquisite marker. It was a monument to an even more exquisite love, Miranda knew, and if she wanted to get her heart broken right in two, all she needed to do was forget that.

Landry had been about to say something, but now he frowned slightly. "What are you thinking?"

She couldn't tell him, not then. Nor did she want him to leave her just yet, even though she had more of a sense than ever that she had no right to this man.

He still belonged to Caroline, a loving and faithful husband in death as well as life.

"I'd like you to help me," she said. "Think up a proper name for the baby, I mean. What would you call him if he was yours?"

"He is mine," Landry said, flooding her heart with light just like that. "I reckon of the two names—both of them are good, right out of the Old Testament and all—I favor Isaiah. I like the sound of it, and Isaiah is the book I like best."

Miranda felt a mixture of sadness and joy—it was, for those few moments, as though she and Landry truly had conceived this baby together. As though Landry were her own, and not Caroline's. "All right, then," she agreed, "it's Isaiah, then."

He smiled. "Isaiah it is," he said. Then he stood to leave the room. "I'd better get to those chores of mine."

"I'll have breakfast made when you come in," she said. It felt good, having someone to say simple, homey things like that to, Caroline or no Caroline.

"You'll need to gather the eggs first," he told her. "I'll milk the cow."

She nodded, and then he was gone. She heard him enter his room, leave it again after a few minutes, heard the stove lids clattering as he built up the fire.

Miranda fed Isaiah—it sounded big on such a little baby, that lofty name, but she knew her son would grow into it in time—bathed and changed him, and carried him with her in the improvised sling while she fetched the eggs. She was at the stove, fixing bacon, of course, and eggs, when Landry came in, wearing his work clothes and carrying a bucket of fresh milk.

He set the bucket on the small worktable next to the stove, and Miranda was painfully aware of him, even though she tried not to let it show. Every time he got close to her, it seemed, she started melting inside, like a honeycomb abandoned to the summer sun.

"You might want to put that boy on cow's milk pretty soon," he said.

Miranda felt a blush climb her neck, and she was glad to have the bacon and eggs to fool around with. She didn't have to ask why Landry had suggested weaning the baby, because she knew it was one of two reasons: either he didn't want to take an infant along to Choteau on their honeymoon trip, or he wanted her breasts for purposes of his own. Both ideas filled her with heat.

"Miranda?"

She had to answer, had to say something. "Breakfast is ready," she told him, and filled a plate for him from the pans on the stove. She herself had no appetite, though she might be ready to eat after the preaching. She'd pack a basket for picnicking under the trees next to the Springwater station, just the way the other wives did.

He wasn't going to be put off that easily. "Miranda," he said again, and more firmly this time.

She met his gaze. She loved that baby, loved him more than her life, but nursing him was hard, when she had so many other things to do, and there could be no arguing that he was a sturdy little mite, off to a real good start in life. And, even though it would be a wrench to leave Isaiah behind with June-bug or maybe Rachel or Savannah for a few days, she wanted that time with Landry more than a mortal being had the right to want anything. "He'll need a bottle," she said.

Landry grinned. "That's easy," he replied. He disappeared into the pantry and, after the sound of much rummaging, came out with a baby bottle in each hand. "They just need washing up. Jamie and Marcus used them when they were little."

Miranda nodded and flushed again. "Sit down and eat your breakfast, Landry Kildare," she said, feeling like a real wife, "before it gets cold."

He sat. "Aren't you going to eat?"

She shook her head. "I'm not ready to face pig meat just yet," she admitted frankly.

Landry chuckled. "Well, you'd better learn to like it, Mrs. Kildare, because you've married a hog farmer."

"You've got horses, and a few cattle, too," Miranda argued, but good-naturedly, pouring coffee for herself. "I'd rather think of you as a rancher."

He gestured toward her unoccupied place at the table, just as good-naturedly. "Get yourself a plate," he persisted. "I won't have the town of Springwater saying Landry Kildare has a puny wife."

She still wasn't hungry, but she managed to put away half an egg and some toasted bread, just because she was so pleased at Landry's teasing attentions. Why, he talked to her the same way Trey talked to

Rachel, and the Doc talked to Savannah. If only he could really make room for her, in that stubborn, loyal heart of his, alongside the hollow place Caroline had left behind.

The dooryard of the Springwater station seemed crowded with buggies and wagons, tethered mules, and horses. Some of the men, Tom Bellweather, Trey Hargreaves, and the Doc, were out front, under the front slant of the roof, handsome in their best clothes. Their expressions were serious, though, and Miranda knew they were talking about Mike Houghton's return, and the effect his claim on Toby might have on the McCaffreys.

Miranda was more than anxious to speak with Jacob and June-bug, and see with her own eyes that they were holding up under the strain, but she had Isaiah in her arms and thus waited until Landry had braked the buckboard, secured the reins, and then jumped down and came around the side to help her to the ground.

While Landry tarried outside with the other men, Miranda hurried inside. As was usual for a Sunday morning, the tables had been moved to one side of the large main room of the station, thus making room for the benches to be lined up before the hearth, pew-style. Jacob usually stood in front of the fireplace when he was preaching, a habit he'd acquired, he was fond of saying, over the course of a dozen harsh territorial winters.

There was no sign of him now, although June-bug

was standing over by the stove, stirring something, and Rachel and Savannah were close by, doing little keep-busy tasks so they'd have an excuse to hover. Miranda wanted to be a member of that group as much as she wanted anything except Landry's love, but this was no time to be thinking about what she wanted, so she put it out of her mind.

Seeing her and the baby June-bug came forward and gently tucked back the blanket. "Would you look at him?" she said, smiling a wan ghost of a smile. "I swear he's grown just since you and Landry got hitched the other day."

Savannah stepped forward. "Could I hold him, Miranda?" she asked softly.

It was no secret how much the Parrishes wanted a baby, and everybody knew they hadn't gotten one started yet, too. That was the way of a small place like Springwater; there weren't many secrets. Miranda smiled and handed Isaiah over to the other woman. Then she put her arms around June-bug and hugged her tight.

June-bug, usually so spry and energetic, felt fragile in her arms, as though something had broken down inside her and she just couldn't get it mended. She clung to Miranda for a long moment, then thrust herself away, with a sniffle and an attempt at a laugh. "Here I am, on the Lord's day, actin' like I don't have a whit of faith," she said.

Rachel, still plump from the birth of her own baby, was peering into the basket where her little Henry slept, looking like an angel. She fussed with the blankets. "Where is Jacob?" she asked of June-bug, in a tone so careful that Miranda knew she'd been waiting for a good time to put forward the question.

"He took a walk down to the springs, him and Toby both," June-bug answered, and that faraway, misty look was back in her eyes. It crushed Miranda's heart to see this woman who had been so kind to her feeling so unhappy, and being so brave in the face of it. The McCaffreys had suffered enough, by her reckoning, losing not one but both their own boys on the same battlefield. "Toby's been talkin' about runnin' away, lightin' out for Mexico or some such nonsense. Jacob's tryin' to make him see reason and stay with his daddy, if that's what it comes down to, but that boy is hard-headed and he's got ideas of his own."

Toby was indeed hard-headed, but he was a good boy, and he'd make a fine man one day, thanks to the McCaffreys. Provided Mike Houghton didn't turn him into a robber or a drunk, anyhow. He ran with bad companions, Houghton did; everybody knew that.

"He'll be all right," Rachel said, with spirit, but she looked worried all the same. She too had a special interest in Toby, having found him in the woods the way she had and brought him home to Springwater, where she'd been his teacher up until baby Henry came into the world. "He's one of us. He belongs here."

At that, all the women looked at each other, as if seeking assurance that what Rachel said was true. All of them except Savannah, that is, who was gazing down at little Isaiah with her heart shining in her eyes.

CHAPTER

5

MIRANDA'S FIRST SIGHT of Jacob, when he entered the station with a red-eyed, rebellious-looking Toby in tow, left her heart as crackly as an old china plate. He was painfully thin and seemed no more substantial than if he'd had hay for stuffing, like some wind-whipped scarecrow, instead of muscle and bone and vitals. His dark eyes, always so solemn and so kindly, seemed to have sunk deep into his head. Only the determined set of his jaw gave cause for hope—the fight had not gone out of him entirely, then. She was relieved to know that much.

"Hello, Toby," Miranda said quietly, and crossed the room to lay a hand on the boy's thin shoulder. During her time at Springwater station, she'd come to know Toby and to respect him for his diligence and his loyalty to the McCaffreys. He'd be a big man one day, but at twelve, nearly thirteen, he was still more sapling than tree.

His blue eyes locked with Miranda's, full of angry

misery, and in that moment she wanted to crush him to her and hold him tightly until Mike Houghton gave up and went away. That would have done no good, of course, even if Toby would have stood still for it. "I don't want to go," he said.

Miranda pressed her lips together and looked up at Jacob. His face echoed the sorrow she'd seen in Toby's. Again, it came to her that this trial might be the one that finally broke an otherwise unbreakable man.

"Where is Mr. Houghton now?" she asked of Jacob, her hand still resting on Toby's shoulder. He would tolerate little in the way of coddling, she knew, but he permitted her that much.

Jacob's voice was a hollow boom, but there was some of the old thunder in it, faint as it was, like the rumble of a storm a-borning on the far horizon. "He's camped outside of town. Said he'd be by for the preachin' this mornin'."

Miranda's hackles rose at that; there was a thing or two she wanted to say to Toby's so-called father, but she knew it would be a waste of breath. Some people were just so mean and greedy that nothing would shame them into behaving like they should. She'd had a father like that herself; only reason he'd kept her around after her ma died was so he'd have somebody to do the cooking and the wash. The sad truth was, Houghton was sure to tire of Toby at some point and turn him out, just as her pa had done, only he'd likely do it someplace far from Springwater and the McCaffreys. With all these thoughts showing plain in her eyes, she was sure, as she ruffled the boy's fair hair, that she felt him tremble under her hand.

Folks began to arrive in earnest after that, and soon everyone had taken their places on the benches facing the hearth in the main room of the station. Jacob, unable to preach for some time, stood shaky but proud before his small congregation, and offered up a ringing prayer to get things started. The day being warm and fair for October, the door stood open, and when Mike Houghton stepped over the threshold, he seemed to bring a spine-stinging winter wind right along with him.

Everyone turned in mid-hymn, having sensed his presence, and one by one the various voices fell away, until there was nothing left of sound but for the slow, insolent clapping of Houghton's beefy hands.

He was a brute, brawny as a stagecoach mule, fairly filling that doorway, and Miranda suspected folks would hardly have been more taken aback to see the devil himself standing there. He wore a dirty leather vest over a colorless shirt, threadbare trousers with that, and scuffed boots, run down at the heel and in sore need of mending. His hat looked like he'd left it in the road for a month or two.

"Come in," Jacob greeted him, as he would have done any other man, "and join us in worshiping the Lord."

Houghton ambled inside, without bothering to remove his hat, and out of the corner of her eye, Miranda saw Landry's jawline tighten as he watched the other man's entrance. For all that her husband was in most respects a stranger to her, she knew this was not a good sign.

"Polecat!" somebody cried out, and Miranda realized it was Granny Johnson who'd spoken up. She might have smiled if the situation hadn't been so delicate. The old woman was likely to say whatever came to her mind, and wouldn't spare the horses. Saint Paul himself probably couldn't have talked her into taking back what she'd said, so no one made the effort.

"Now, that ain't no kind of Christian welcome," Mike Houghton said, taking off his hat at last, revealing a head of thinning, oily hair and a freckled pate. Clutching the hat to his chest in a mocking show of respect for everyone present, he took in the assemblage arrayed on either side of the narrow aisle between the rows of benches.

Miranda sought Toby with her eyes—he'd been seated next to June-bug the last time she'd seen him, with Marcus and Jamie at his other side, looking as fiercely defiant as their young friend—but there was no sign of him now. Her stepsons, she noted, with a sense of slow but heightening alarm, were gone, too. Another sidelong glance at her husband revealed that he'd noticed the absence as well, whether or not he'd felt called upon to comment.

Jacob, meanwhile, left his post in front of the fireplace and came forward to meet Houghton. "Sit down, brother, and join us in raising our prayers and songs of praise. Your business here will wait."

"I came to get my boy." Houghton looked around,

as though Jacob hadn't spoken at all. "Where's he got to?" He returned his gaze to the man before him. "If you've hid him someplace, Preacher, you'd best tell me where, so I don't have to do anything to upset these good folks."

At this, moving almost as one, Landry, Tom Bell-weather, Trey Hargreaves, Scully Wainwright, and Doc Parrish all left their various places in the congregation, found their way to the front of the room, and aligned themselves behind Jacob. Although she feared violence—she'd never seen anything good come of it, not one time—Miranda was prouder than ever, in that moment, that Landry was her husband. Even if he was so in the legal respect only.

Houghton paused and rubbed his chin with one hand, assuming an injured expression, as though he'd come in expecting hospitality and been ill-used instead. "I just want my boy," he said. He sounded pitiful that time, and if she hadn't known the true facts, Miranda might actually have felt sorry for him.

Jacob searched the room with genuine concern, clearly looking for Toby, and June-bug, hands clenched tightly in her lap, turned from her customary seat on the bench up front and did the same. A murmur arose from the congregation as other people began to realize that young Houghton really *had* vanished, and only the five men aligned behind Jacob remained as they were, watchful and ready to fight, be it the Sabbath Day or not.

"He was here when I started the prayer," Jacob said quietly. He met Houghton's gaze and did not flinch or look away. "We'll find him soon as the service is over."

For a long time, he and Houghton just stood there, staring at each other, like an archangel and a demon come face-to-face over the same broken and straying soul, both of them set to lay claim. Then, remarkably, Toby's long-absent father sat himself down, right up front. Sue Bellweather moved over to make room for him, but stiffly. The brim of her Sunday bonnet hid her face, but Miranda didn't need to see to know the other woman's countenance was not one of welcome.

The hymn went unsung, and Jacob started right in on the preaching, but folks were mostly interested in what Mike Houghton might do, so nobody paid much attention. Landry and the others remained where they were, throughout the whole remainder of the sermon—a well-planned and pointed message about the love between Abraham and Isaac.

Miranda kept looking for her mischievous stepsons, but they were just as gone as Toby, and she knew, as Landry surely did, that Jamie and Marcus had spirited the Houghton boy away. Heaven only knew where they might have hidden him; they were as footloose as prairie savages, those boys—when they weren't in church, at school, or directly under Landry's eye—and they knew the terrain for literally miles around. They could probably hide out until the first snow, maybe longer, and stay unfound as long as they considered necessary.

At one and the same time, Miranda feared for their safety and wished them Godspeed. They might be going about it all wrong, but their motives couldn't be faulted—they were trying to protect their friend. Watching Landry's stiff face, she wondered what he was thinking, if indeed he might not know precisely where his sons—and Toby—had gone.

"I'll have the law down on the whole lot of you," Houghton threatened, rising to his feet. He was sweating under the arms and blotted his beaded forehead on the sleeve of his shirt. He swayed, stabbing a fat index finger in Jacob's direction, and Miranda realized he was drunk. "I want my boy, and I want him now. You bring him on out here, Preacher, or you'll be sorry."

Jacob hardly seemed intimidated, though he was a much older man than Houghton, and at a physical disadvantage, too, despite his own significant size, because of his recent illness. His gaunt face was flushed, and his eyes seemed to blaze with righteous fury, and it seemed to Miranda that he stood taller in those moments than he had in a long while. "Sit yourself down, brother," he told Houghton, and when he seemed a bit unsteady on his feet, and Trey and Landry stepped forward to grasp his elbows in an offer of support, he shrugged them off. "I believe we ought to sing another hymn before we leave off worshipin'."

Houghton hesitated, cast an assessing glance around the room, perhaps to see if he had any supporters in the crowd, and then, amazingly, sank back to his bench.

Miranda thought she'd never heard a congregation sing with such spirit before, but then, she'd had few enough opportunities to attend church in the years since her mother's passing. Her father was not a religious man.

Finally, however, the service was truly over, and the women of the community gathered around June-bug, patting and smiling and embracing Mrs. McCaffrey and then one another, as women will do in times of difficulty. They included Miranda in their circle as though she had always been one of them, and that warmed her through and through. Rachel even went so far as to remark that marriage seemed to agree with Miranda, as well as with Landry, and June-bug, though fitful and distracted, allowed as how she had not seen Landry look so hearty in all the time she'd known him.

Mike Houghton, meanwhile, had been shepherded outside by the men, and although the occasional raised voice pierced the chinked log walls of the station, Jacob's and Houghton's being the most easily recognized, the brawl Miranda had half-expected did not come.

In time, Landry came in to collect her and baby Isaiah. After taking the infant from the large basket he'd shared with Rachel and Trey's Henry, Miranda kissed June-bug on the cheek and made her promise that she'd send word if she had a need of company. Only when she was seated in the wagon beside Landry, and well away from the church, did Miranda speak of the three missing boys.

"Do you know where they are?" she asked.

Landry considered. "They could be any one of a thousand places," he said, with a sigh. "I've let them run wild since Caroline passed on, and this is what comes of it."

On impulse, Miranda linked her arm loosely through his. True, he had spoken of Caroline, but that was to be expected, given that he'd been married to the woman and fathered two children by her. There was a tense moment, but Landry did not pull away. "But Toby is with them?" Miranda asked.

"I'm sure of it," Landry said, with a crisp nod. "I suppose they figure if they just stay gone long enough, Houghton will give up and move on."

"Will he?"

Landry heaved a sigh, then shook his head. "I don't reckon so," he said. "He's got some use in mind for the boy—probably to keep track of the horses while he and his friends hold up banks and stagecoaches."

Miranda shivered, held her baby son close against her chest, even though he was well protected from the cold, being bundled in a woolen blanket Landry had searched out before they left the ranch for the preaching. "Toby could be shot," she protested, "or arrested and hanged."

"Houghton figures he's expendable, I expect."

"Ex—?"

Landry's mouth crooked upwards at one side, but his eyes were kind. "Expendable. Something—or somebody—a person can get by without."

Miranda ran her teeth over her lower lip once, weighing the word and its definition. "My pa felt the same way about me," she said. *And so does my husband,* she added to herself. There was no bid for sympathy in her tone when she spoke aloud; what she meant was, she understood some of what Toby must feel. "What was your family like, Landry? The home-folks, I mean?"

He grinned at some private memory, urged the team to a slightly faster pace. The hills made a spectacle of brilliant color in the distance, and the air was sharp with the approach of winter. "My pa was a good man," Landry replied. "He had a fair-sized farm, back in Missouri. Caroline's family leased the land next to ours. I had two younger sisters and an older brother—my brother, Jack, died in the war, and one of my sisters, Mary Elizabeth, passed on, too, of a fever. My other sister, Polly, is a schoolmarm, like Rachel was."

There were more questions Miranda wanted to ask, flocks of them, but she didn't want to pry. "Your mother?"

"She died when I was little. Pa remarried her first cousin, Ruth. She had Mary Elizabeth and Polly. She still lives on the home place, though Pa died five years ago, around the time we lost Caroline."

Miranda held her tongue. There was ever so much she wanted to know about Caroline, but she wasn't going to ask. She *wasn't*.

He didn't volunteer anything more, either. Naturally, his mind was on the whereabouts of his sons, and young Toby, of course. "I'll see you and the baby home safe," he said, "and go out looking for those three little hooligans. I just hope I find them before they get themselves caught in an early snowstorm or come across some slat-ribbed cougar."

She hadn't allowed herself to think as far as wild animals and uncertain weather, not to mention the many other dangers the wilderness had to offer. Now, she cast a nervous glance at the sky. It was still a heart-piercing blue, that sky, with no clouds in sight, but Miranda had been in the west long enough to know that a blizzard could come up within a matter of hours, especially in Montana Territory.

Soon, they reached the cabin, and Landry lifted Miranda and the baby down from the wagon and watched them go inside before taking up the reins again and driving the team on toward the barn.

The inside of the house seemed unusually cold, and Miranda made haste to lay Isaiah in his basket, still wrapped in the blanket, so she could build up the fires, first in the stove, then on the hearth. When the place was reasonably warm, she unswaddled the baby and set about the wifely pursuits of lighting lamps and then peeling potatoes and onions to fry for an early supper. Landry meant to go out and search for his boys, but she intended to see that he ate first.

She brewed coffee—an extravagance, since the stuff was usually reserved for breakfast or for entertaining guests—and was adding fresh eggs to the sizzling skillet when Landry finally came in. He looked strained, and his ears and hands were red from the cold.

"I might be away overnight," he warned, taking off his coat and setting the rifle he'd carried to town earlier, beneath the seat of the buckboard, in its rack near the door. He accepted the mug of coffee she'd poured for him with a grateful nod and took a sip right away. His hazel eyes searched her face. "You'll be all right here by yourself?"

She had been alone for much of her life, even when she was in a room full of people, but the idea of Landry being away for a whole night seemed like an almost unbearable ordeal. She couldn't and wouldn't let that response show, of course; he had enough on his mind, with three young boys missing. "I'll be fine. Wash up and stand by the fire for a while, Landry. I'll have your supper ready in just a few minutes."

He nodded again and did as she asked, and when the mixture of potatoes, onions, and eggs was cooked, she served him a plate at the table and sat down to join him. Although it was only midafternoon by then, the days were getting shorter as October progressed toward November, and the first purple-gray shadows of nightfall were already darkening the windows. Now and then, he glanced uneasily toward the now nearly opaque squares of thick glass, no doubt growing more worried with every passing moment.

Miranda figured he was thinking what it would mean to lose Jamie and Marcus, the way he had lost their mother, and just then she could have shaken those boys for frightening him that way. On the other hand, though, she understood why they had done what they had.

"Don't be hard on them," she said quietly. "They're doing the only thing they know to do to help their friend."

Landry's jaw hardened. "Running away from trouble never solved anything. No, ma'am. When I catch up to those little outlaws, they'll be lucky if I don't tan all three of them on the spot."

She felt her eyes widen. "You wouldn't really lay a hand on them—?"

He huffed out a breath, smiled a sad and rueful smile, and shook his head. "No, but it comforts me some to think of it."

She laughed, though she was as frightened for those three rascally boys as he was. The wind was rising, beginning to howl around the corners of the house, and the fire danced and flickered in the hearth.

Landry finished his food and went to pull on his heavy coat, take down the rifle again, and gather spare ammunition. He went into his room and came out with a bedroll. She stood near the door when he was ready to leave, not quite daring to embrace him as she wanted to do, and whispered, "You'll be careful?"

He took part of a step toward her, or perhaps she just imagined that part. He was looking at her, though, as he raised the wooden latch. "I will. You look out for little Isaiah there, and see you that you don't open that door to anybody you don't know. You'll find a forty-four caliber pistol in the strongbox on the high shelf in that wardrobe in my room. Use it if you see the need."

She swallowed. So far, she'd contrived to avoid laying hand to a firearm, and she did not want to start then. "Do you think—?" She couldn't quite bring herself to finish, to ask if Landry expected Mike Houghton to turn up there, looking for Toby.

"There's no telling," Landry answered, when the silence lengthened. "I'll be home as soon as I can. You'll see to the animals if I'm not back by morning?"

She didn't even want to think of Landry not returning before the sun rose, though she knew he probably wouldn't. She simply nodded.

He hesitated—for a moment she thought he would kiss her good-bye, as any husband might do—but in the end he merely told her to fasten the latch behind him and went out, closing the door smartly behind him. Miranda stood there for several long moments, eyes closed, both palms pressed to the rough wooden panel.

Keep him safe, she prayed.

The wind rose still further, as if in answer, and nearly blew out the fire. Miranda bolted the door and turned away.

It made sense to look in at Springwater, to make sure the boys hadn't found their way back there, once the wind came up and the temperature began to drop. Landry rode past the lively Brimstone Saloon, his collar drawn up around his ears and his hat drawn low over his face, making for the station.

Jacob greeted him at the door, and the expression on his weathered face made it clear that he'd been cherishing the same vain hope Landry had—that the boys had given up on their flight and come home. Both men were disappointed.

"No word of them, then?" Jacob asked, stepping back and nodding Landry into the warmth of the Springwater station.

"I was hoping to find them here," Landry admitted. He wouldn't stay long, but neither could he stand on the threshold on a cold night, forcing a friend to hold the door open to an autumn wind. "What about Houghton?"

"He seems content to drink up Trey's liquor over at the Brimstone," Jacob said grimly. "I guess Trey's trying to keep him in sight as long as he can."

Landry nodded. At least he didn't have to worry that Houghton would head out to the ranch and give Miranda any trouble—not yet. He was surprised to realize how much that calmed him, given the fact that his sons were almost certainly in danger, along with young Toby. "I mean to go out looking for them," he told Jacob. "They know this country almost as well as any Blackfoot or Sioux would, though. It won't be easy finding them if they want to stay hidden."

Jacob was reaching for his round black hat and heavy dark coat, both of which hung on sturdy pegs next to the door. "I'll ride along, if you don't mind." He broke loose with something that might have been either a smile or a grimace. "Fact is, I intend to ride along whether you object or not."

Landry knew better than to argue. Jacob was in no condition to go tearing off into the night looking for a trio of wily boys, but he probably knew that without being told. Not that telling him would have done any good.

June-bug appeared from the rear corridor, hands bunched into fists in her apron pockets. "You have a care, Jacob McCaffrey," she said. "I can't spare you, and that's a fact."

The big man crossed the room, kissed his wife's upturned face. "I'll be fine," he assured her. "And if I have my way, so will those boys." He stroked her cheek with a gentle pass of knuckles as gnarled as the roots of an old tree. "You tend to the prayin'. Don't you give the Lord a moment's peace until we've got young Toby and the Kildare boys back home safe, you hear?"

She smiled, her eyes overly bright. "Yes, Jacob," she said. "I hear."

The night outside was bitter cold, and the wind was sharp as the prongs of a new pitchfork, but Jacob had his big mule saddled in the time it took to whistle twice and spit, and Landry welcomed his presence, even if he wasn't one to say much of anything. Thus the two men rode in easy silence, each one keeping his own counsel.

Miranda stayed busy for a while, feeding and bathing the baby, rocking him to sleep, clearing up the dishes, and banking the fire. After she'd bedded Isaiah down in his basket, she tried to settle at the table, with the reading primer Rachel had given her to study on, but she couldn't concentrate and that made it hard to pin the words down to where they made sense.

She rose and went to the window, once, twice, a

third time. She hoped to see her stepsons, and poor Toby, and of course Landry. Without Jamie and Marcus, without her husband, that modest house seemed huge and very empty.

Eventually, she gave up and went to bed, but she heard every coyote, every change in the wind, every creak of the house's heavy wooden walls and tightly laid floors. After several hours of tossing and turning, Miranda got up and, carrying Isaiah and his basket, took herself off to Landry's room. She had no right to be there, wife or none, but her longing for him was an ache, soul-deep, and she could no longer ignore it. Boldly, she set Isaiah down close at hand, then threw back the covers and climbed right into Landry's bed.

The sheets smelled deliciously of him, a unique combination of fresh grass and sun-dried linens and hard-working man, and it was a comfort to lie where he had lain, to rest her head on his pillow. She would make the bed up in the morning, she promised herself, as she finally began the long, slow tumble toward the solace of sleep, and he would never know she'd been there.

"Pa! Over here, Pa—come quick!"

The voice was Jamie's, and the panicked sound of it wrenched Landry's breathing to a painful stop in his throat. Still, he spurred his horse forward, knew the direction to take. Jacob kept pace, and it was he who called out, "We're comin', boy!"

Jamie stumbled out of the brush, teeth chattering, face bloodied and scratched. "Pa, Mr. McCaffrey—it's

Toby. He's bad hurt. We figured to hide in our cave—that one you showed us when we was huntin' bear last year—and Toby fell a long way—" When Landry leaned down to offer his younger son a hand, Jamie took it and sprang onto the horse behind him, agile as a monkey. "It's up ahead there, through that little draw. Marcus is with him. We covered him up with a blanket, but we was—were—scairt to move him."

"You did right," Landry said. They'd discuss the drawbacks of running off some other time, when all three boys were safe.

Jacob was the first to reach the place where the boy lay, and he was off the mule and crouched on the ground next to him before Landry had even dismounted. A kerosene lantern, no doubt purloined from the barn at home, glowed next to the prone figure of Toby and the kneeling one of Landry's elder son.

"Tell me where it hurts, boy," Jacob said, and Landry felt a sweep of relief. Until then, he hadn't known whether or not the lad was conscious. "We're here now, Landry and me, and we're going to take you back home. Doc Parrish will fix you up neat and tidy."

Drawing near, Landry saw that Toby had a broken leg. Marcus, white with fear for his friend, looked up at his father with a plea in his eyes.

Landry simply held out his arm, and as quick as that, he had a son on either side, clinging to him as if to keep from toppling over the edge of a cliff.

"We didn't figure on Toby getting hurt, Pa," Marcus said.

Landry squeezed his son's thin but widening shoulders. They'd be men all too soon, his boys. They were growing up fast. "I know you didn't," he said. He addressed his next words to Jacob, who was running practiced hands over Toby's ribs, checking for more injuries. Until Pres Parrish came to Springwater, Jacob had been the closest thing to a doctor they had. "Is it all right to move him?"

Jacob didn't look up. He was gazing down into Toby's dirt-smudged, bruised face. "I reckon so," he answered, "but it's going to hurt some. You understand that, don't you, boy?"

Toby nodded. Then Jacob lifted him off the ground in both arms, blanket and all, and his face reflected the child's agony when Toby cried out from the pain. "Hand him up to me," Jacob said, offering the boy to Landry, who held him while his friend mounted and then bent to recover his burden.

"Fetch that lantern," Landry said to Marcus, when his sons' spotted pony ambled out of the bushes, dragging its reins, "and we'll follow Jacob into Springwater."

Marcus nodded, picked up the light, and scrambled onto the pony's back.

"You gonna whip us when we get home, Pa?" Jamie asked. For once, he seemed younger than Marcus, which he was.

"I ought to," Landry replied. He was worried about Toby still, and about Jacob as well, but at the same time he was as thankful for finding his boys safe as he had ever been for anything.

"Will you?" Marcus wanted to know. He'd brought the pony alongside Landry's gelding.

"I've never done it before," he said, after keeping a judicious silence for a while. "I don't reckon I'll start now. But don't go thinking you won't be punished for this, because you will. That was a damn fool thing you did."

Jacob and Toby and the mule were ahead, riding through the thin moonlight toward the warmth and safety of Springwater, and Landry saw no reason to keep pace. He reckoned, though, that he'd never forget the look of Jacob McCaffrey when he'd lifted that boy up into his arms and gathered him close against his broad chest.

He was worth ten of Mike Houghton, if you asked Landry Kildare.

CHAPTER

6

IT TOOK MIRANDA a long, sleep-fuddled moment to
realize that the man looming at the foot of the bed
wasn't Landry, and when she did, the awareness
brought her breathing to a hard stop and nearly did
the same to her heart. She suppressed an urge to raise
herself onto her elbows and peer through the thick
darkness; better to pretend she was still asleep. Recalling the .44 Landry had told her about before he
left the house, she wished she'd taken the time to get
the pistol down and set it within reach on the bedside
table.

"Where's your man?" Mike Houghton demanded.
He knew, then, that she was awake; she'd most likely
gasped aloud when she saw him.

"How did you get in here?" Miranda countered.
She'd latched the door and checked all the windows
before retiring, and she would have heard any
attempt at breaking in.

Houghton chuckled. He was a huge, featureless

shadow in the gloom, but Miranda could see his bulky outline clearly enough, and catch the brew of sour smells coming off his skin and clothes. "Came up through the root cellar," he said, with a degree of pride. "Now, like I asked you before, where's that man of yours?"

Miranda wet her lips with the tip of her tongue, stalling. She was in powerful trouble, she knew that, but it was little Isaiah she was afraid for; all her instincts were geared toward protecting him. "He went out looking for his sons," she said finally, when she was afraid the intruder might finally round the end of the bed and come at her. "I reckon he'll be back any time now."

Houghton heaved a sigh. He'd obviously thought Miranda and Landry were hiding Toby themselves, had him secreted away in the cabin someplace. Probably, he'd already searched every nook and cranny.

Miranda wondered when she'd gotten to be such a heavy sleeper; the slightest peep from Isaiah invariably awakened her instantly. Houghton was a big man, and not particularly graceful, so he'd surely made some noise. She guessed she'd been extra tired from the strain of the past few days.

"I'm getting real weary of dealing with you people," Toby's so-called father said, with another sigh, this one sounding long-suffering and much put-upon. "I reckon I'll just have myself a seat at your table and wait for your husband to get home. You get up and make me something to eat. I'm starving."

Miranda was at once relieved that Houghton

didn't mean to force himself on her, at least not right away, and very frightened of the reception Landry would get when he returned, unsuspecting, almost certainly bringing the boys with him. Eager to get the unwanted visitor as far away from her baby as she could, Miranda spoke firmly. "You go on out and sit down at the table. I'll be right out to build up the fire."

Houghton started toward the gaping doorway— thanks to Landry's thoroughness, the hinges hadn't even squeaked when he entered—then paused and turned back to face Miranda. She saw him extend one beefy arm and shake a finger at her, even though she couldn't make out his features in the dark. "Don't you try nothin', either," he warned. "You come through this here door with, say, a gun in your hand, I'm going to be ready for you, and that man of yours will meet with a sorry mess when he comes in."

Miranda felt a chill hand-spring down her spine. She knew he meant what he said; she'd have to find another opportunity to fetch that .44 down from the wardrobe shelf, and she'd have to do it soon, if she wanted to get the better of Mike Houghton. Landry had said it was in a strongbox; did that mean it was locked? Surely, with young boys in the house, and both of them reckless little rascals, it must be. Where, then, was the key? "I just want to wrap up in something warm. There's a bite in the air."

She heard a pistol cock, saw a flash of moonlight on the barrel, icy cold and blue-black. "I don't want no foolishness," Houghton growled.

She nodded, unable, for the moment, to speak. He must have seen, because he grunted and turned to lumber out of the room.

Miranda paused to draw a deep breath in an effort to calm her racing thoughts and figure out what to do. In the end, there was nothing much she *could* do, besides put on a wrapper, fix Houghton a meal, and hope to God that Landry wouldn't stumble in and get himself shot to death, right in front of her and his boys.

Help me, she prayed, and hurried down the way to her own room to fetch a wrapper she'd seen folded in one of the bureau drawers. The garment had been Caroline's, of course, and Landry probably wouldn't appreciate her wearing it, but for now there was no choice. If he didn't understand, well, she reckoned that was his problem.

When she reached the cabin's main room, Houghton had made himself at home, lighting the lamps, settling in Landry's chair at the table, bold as brass. He was smoking Landry's pipe, too.

Miranda calculated her chances of braining him with the fireplace poker before he managed to pick up the big hog-leg of a gun he'd laid beside the kerosene lantern in the center of the table and decided they were unfavorable.

She went to the stove instead, made a lot of clatter opening doors, stirring embers, stuffing in kindling and chunks of wood. Only when she had a good snapping fire going did she turn to look at Mike Houghton. He ran his gaze over her in a way that made her skin shrink back and quaver against her bones.

"You said you were hungry," she reminded him, pretending to a bravery she didn't really feel. Landry was sure to show up soon, and there was the baby to think about, and the boys. What was she going to do? "What do you want?" she demanded.

He ran his eyes over her once more, eyes that put her in mind of that old boar hog Landry had shot just the day before yesterday. They had the same black-hearted glint in them, the same evil intentions. "Now that, little lady, just depends on how long that man of yours stays gone. I've got business with him, right enough, but I think maybe I might have some with you, too." He paused, chewing on the stem of Landry's pipe, filling the air with tobacco smoke and the general stench of his own person. "For now, some hot-cakes would do. Bacon, too, if you can scrounge some up, and five or six eggs."

Miranda nodded, hands on her hips. "You'll have your bacon and hotcakes and all. Then you better just ride out, because if my husband finds you here, he's likely to kill you deader than the Confederacy. You may not have noticed, Mr. Houghton," she put just the slightest emphasis on the Mr., "but you aren't welcome at Springwater. Toby is one of us now, and you ought to leave him right where he's been since you left him."

"I listened to the preacher's sermon this morning," Houghton said. "I don't need one from you, too. Just make me them eggs and a stack of hotcakes about that high." He indicated a sizable height between his two hands. "A pound or two of pork, too. And some coffee. I've had me a mite too much whiskey in there at the Brimstone Saloon. Hell of a thing if I was to pass out."

That, Miranda thought, was too much to hope for. She went to the pantry, returned with the flour and other ingredients she needed. While in the pantry, she nearly tripped over the rag rug on the floor, and hastily smoothed it with one foot. Then she eyed the butcher knives, aligned in a neat row in a handmade rack, as was typical of Landry, but she ruled out the idea of using one against Houghton almost as soon as it came to her mind. He'd shoot her dead before she took the first swipe at that filthy hide of his.

She stirred the hotcake batter with unusual vigor, her mind going as fast as the spoon in her hand, but achieving a whole lot less.

"What I don't see," Houghton confided to her stiff back, sounding genuinely puzzled, "is why you folks around here think so highly of that boy of mine. He's just like his mother—and she was no better than she should be. A whore, down New Orleans way. He ever tell you that? He's got her looks and her crafty mind. Can't trust him any further than you can throw a mule."

Miranda straightened her already-straight spine and turned to glare at the man, the bowl of batter clasped in both arms and propped against her middle. "Why do you insist on taking him away, if you feel that way about him? He's been happy here. The

McCaffreys love him like their own. He goes to school and to church. What could you possibly want with one skinny little boy, when it's plain you don't give a hoot or a holler what happens to him and probably never have?" She wasn't just talking to Mike Houghton, she realized. She was talking to her own father, who had been equally worthless, and absent even when he was in the same room with her.

"We—I need him to help me with some honest work," Houghton all but whined. "He might be just a boy, but he can earn a man's wages."

Miranda set the big iron skillet on the stove with a bang and lobbed in some lard from the grease jar Landry kept on top of the warming oven on the stove. "You and I both know he can't do any such thing," she snapped. "You want to make him into an outlaw and a saddle-tramp, that's all."

For a moment, she thought she might have gone a step too far. Houghton's whiskey-reddened face grew even more flushed, and his boarlike eyes narrowed until they were almost gone. "It ain't none of your concern *what* I make out of that boy, now is it? He's mine, and I can do with him what I want."

"For God's sake," Miranda spat, furious beyond all good sense, "he's not a mule or a half-starved dog, he's a boy, a human being with a heart and a soul and a mind, same as everybody else. He belongs to himself and the good Lord, and besides that, you gave up any claim a long time ago when you left him alone in the woods to fend for himself!"

Somewhat to Miranda's surprise, Houghton didn't

pick up the pistol and shoot her. He seemed taken aback by her accusation, if only briefly, even anxious to prove himself without guilt. "I meant to get back afore I did," he said. "I ran into some trouble, that's all."

The sun was beginning to lighten the gloom at the windows. Landry would be home soon. *Come quickly*, she pleaded silently. *Stay away*. "What sort of trouble?" she asked, without sympathy. "Jail, maybe?"

Houghton looked pained and not a little insulted. "You ain't very respectful, you know that? I've got half a mind to backhand you, teach you a lesson."

"You lay a hand on me, and I'll kill you," Miranda said. She didn't know where the words had come from, they just tumbled out of her mouth all on their own, but they were gospel-true, each one.

Houghton laughed. "You? You ain't hardly bigger than that boy of mine." His expression turned to a speculative leer. "But you are a pretty thing, I vow. Right sweet-smellin'. Warm, too, I reckon, and soft in all the right places."

Just the thought of Houghton laying hands on her made bile rush into the back of Miranda's throat, but she wasn't going to let him know she was scared if she could keep from it. "Here," she said, and served him a plate of food with a slam of the plate against the tabletop. "Eat and get out."

She watched his face while he weighed the urgings of a naturally mean spirit against what was probably an insatiable appetite for food. In the end, to Miranda's well-hidden relief, he chose the victuals. While

Houghton ate, Miranda listened for Landry's horse and hoped to high heaven she wouldn't wind up a widow before she ever got a chance to be a real wife.

Upon reaching Springwater, Landry hurried to fetch Doc Parrish while Jacob took Toby into the station, with some help from Jamie and Marcus. When Landry returned with Pres, they found the boy lying on one of the tables in the main room. June-bug was doing her best to comfort Toby, but it was plain that he was suffering. Little wonder; part of the big bone in the youngster's thigh was protruding right through the torn fabric of his pants.

Landry looked away, and swallowed hard once before looking back.

"Everybody out of the way," Doc Parrish said, practically as soon as he'd cleared the threshold. Most likely, Landry reflected, nobody had ever accused the man of mincing words.

Jamie and Marcus were already huddled in a corner, the freckles standing out on their pasty white faces. Landry reckoned he ought to haul them both to the nearest woodshed and raise a few blisters on their backsides—that was what his own pa would have done—but he couldn't bring himself to do it. It just didn't seem right to him, beating on another human being, especially ones you loved.

Jacob and June-bug weren't about to leave the boy, no matter what the Doc said, and the expressions on their faces made it plain. However, they did make way for him.

Pres's voice was remarkably calm as he bent over Toby to examine what had to be the worst break Landry had ever seen. No doubt the Doc had seen worse, though, given that he'd served as a field surgeon in the war. "Looks like you fell off a mountain," he said cheerfully.

The boy's face was pale as death and popping sweat, but he worked up a crooked grin all the same. "Yes, sir," he said. "I reckon I dropped twenty or thirty feet afore I hit the ground."

Pres put the ends of his stethoscope into his ears and listened thoughtfully to Toby's heart. "Well, that was a damn fool thing to do," said the Doc. "Now you and I and especially the McCaffreys here are in for a long night." He let the stethoscope dangle from his neck and popped open his beat-up doctor bag. "You're in shock," he continued, still speaking to Toby, although he raised his eyes and met first Jacob's gaze and then June-bug's, over the boy's head. He looked down at Toby again. "That's why I can't use ether or chloroform to put you to sleep. I'm going to give you a dose of laudanum, though, and that'll take the edge off. Once I've wrestled that leg bone of yours back where it belongs—and that's going to hurt like hell, Toby, and there's no point in telling you otherwise— I'll sew you up and put on a splint. Long about that time, you ought to be able to swallow some more medicine and have a good, long rest. Fair enough?"

Young Toby clenched his jaw against pain that was already pretty fierce—had to be right up against the edge of unbearable, in fact—and nodded his head.

"Fair enough," he agreed staunchly. It made Landry's heart ache, seeing such a little kid suffer like that, no matter that he'd brought the whole thing on himself, with some help from Jamie and Marcus.

"We're thankful to you," Jacob said to Landry. He was still standing at the end of the table where Toby lay, one of the child's hands pressed between his own. "You'd best be getting those boys of yours home now. Your bride will be watching the road."

His bride.

Miranda hadn't been far from the forefront of Landry's mind the whole of the night, for all that had happened. He longed to see with his own eyes that she was all right, to simply be under the same roof with her again. He wondered if the strange mingling of tenderness and almost ferocious desire she stirred in him—he was ready to admit to such feelings, at least in the privacy of his own mind—was the beginning of love. He just didn't know, since he'd never felt exactly this way before, even with Caroline. By comparison, though, his feelings for Miranda were richer, deeper, and more powerful, the emotions a man held for a woman. Knowing Caroline from his boyhood, he'd loved her as a youth loves his sweetheart, with a certain shallow innocence.

"You're sure we won't be needed," Landry said. The question came out sounding like a statement instead. He was too worn-out to go putting a lot of inflection in his words.

A corner of Jacob's mouth lifted slightly in what might have been an inclination toward a smile. "You came in mighty handy tonight, my friend, but I believe it's Doc here we need now. You go on home. We know where to send if there's call to do it."

Landry nodded a farewell at Jacob, then at June-bug. The Doc was occupied, as he should have been, with Toby's leg, having already dragged off his coat and pushed up his sleeves. Savannah joined them, began heating water on the stove without even being asked. When Landry turned to summon his sons, they were already on their feet and wearing their jackets.

"You want us to stay, Toby?" Jamie asked, peering at his friend but carefully avoiding looking at his injured leg. Landry couldn't really blame his son; it was a nasty sight, all that torn flesh and splintered bone. It was sure to take the Doc a long while to put it all back together the way the Lord had it in the first place.

"You go on," Toby answered. "I'll look for you tomorrow, though."

"We'll be here," Marcus assured him, from Jamie's side. Then he glanced up at Landry. "If our pa will let us leave the ranch, anyhow."

Landry didn't make it easy on them. "Fetch the horses," he said.

Three-quarters of an hour later, the ranch house was in sight, and Landry felt some surprise to see that the windows were alight. Granted, it was nearly sunup, but in his brief experience, Miranda wasn't an early riser. He was usually up, with the coffee brewing, before she stirred from the spare room.

"Pa," Jamie hissed. He was riding behind Marcus

now, on the pony. "Look there, behind Ma's oak trees."

Landry felt his heart flatten out and roll right up into the back of his throat. Sure enough, there in the midst of the trees Caroline had raised from acorns gathered back home in Missouri before they headed west, was an unfamiliar horse, still saddled and grazing. Mike Houghton's horse, he'd be willing to bet; he didn't recognize it as belonging to any of the men around Springwater.

"You suppose he done hurt her, Pa?" Jamie asked. He sounded plaintive.

"Stay here," Landry said, drawing his rifle from the scabbard affixed to his saddle and swinging down off the gelding's back. How the hell had Houghton gotten in, he wondered, as he ran over the situation mentally. He'd bolted the windows himself, and he'd heard the bolt fall into place behind him a few seconds after he'd closed the door to go looking for the boys.

"Pa," Marcus insisted. "He's mean. Toby swears he killed his ma, made her drink poison. He might shoot you."

"Do as I told you," Landry whispered. "Stay put and don't make any noise." Just then, one of the horses neighed, and he could only hope Houghton would think it was his own.

"But, Pa—how you gonna get in there?" Jamie asked. He was beside Landry, that fast, and had caught hold of his sleeve. "He might hurt Miranda— or you—or the baby. You've got to sneak up on him."

"How the devil am I going to do that?" Landry snapped. He was asking himself and God that question, more than the boy.

"Through the root cellar," Jamie said. He gulped and glanced at Marcus once; obviously, he'd just betrayed a closely guarded secret.

"I sealed the doors to that root cellar a long time ago," he said, growing impatient now, anxious to see that Miranda and little Isaiah were safe. He wouldn't be able to breathe right until he knew they hadn't been harmed.

Jamie swallowed again. "Me and Marcus fixed them so we could go in and out that way, without you knowing. I reckon that's how Houghton got into the house, too."

Landry swore under his breath and started to the other side of the cabin in a half crouch. Entering through the old cellar, he could come up into the pantry through a trap door. Soon as he got under the house, he could hear Houghton's voice overhead.

"That was a mighty fine breakfast, missus," he was saying. "Now you come on over here and sit down on my lap."

Landry set his jaw and concentrated on lifting the trap door quietly enough to keep from attracting Houghton's attention and thus getting his head blown off. This was no time to make a mistake.

"No," he heard Miranda say firmly. "I made you the food you wanted. Now you just get out of here before my husband comes home and shoots you for a scoundrel."

Landry eased the door up, reached through and laid his rifle soundlessly on the pantry floor, then climbed up after it.

"You ain't gonna make me turn mean, are you, little lady?" Houghton drawled. "I'd hate to make my point by going in that bedroom, fetching that baby of yours, and—"

"You touch my child," Miranda broke in, "you just lay one of your filthy paws on him, and I'll see you spend a good long time dyin'."

Houghton laughed, and his voice took on an oily, cajoling note. Landry's hands flexed spasmodically around the rifle; he'd never wanted to shoot anybody down in cold blood before that moment, but he was ready to kill this sorry excuse for a man without waiting for another heartbeat to pass. For Miranda's sake, and the baby's, he made himself wait, slipped to the doorway of the pantry.

There was a lantern burning on the worktable beside the stove, and Landry cast a glance over the floor to make sure he wasn't throwing a shadow. He saw Miranda's reflection in the glass of the window across the room, and Houghton's, along with the faintest suggestion of his own, and held his breath.

Miranda was standing only a few feet from Houghton's chair, and she was directly in the line of fire between the center of that bastard's heart and Landry's rifle. He willed his wife to step aside, willed it so hard that for a moment he was afraid he'd actually spoken aloud.

A horse nickered outside.

"What's that?" Houghton asked. He was quick, that one.

Miranda's arms were folded. "I reckon it was a horse," she said, and if she was afraid, there was nothing in her voice to indicate as much. "My husband's back, I guess. You'd better start saying your prayers."

Under any other circumstances, her audacity would have made Landry smile. As it was, he was too worried about keeping her alive to be amused. He knew he cared for her, that was plain by the way his gut was wound up around itself, but they'd sort that out later, when he'd dealt with Houghton.

Houghton went toward the window, taking the pistol with him. That must have been when he saw Landry's almost transparent image in the glass.

He whirled and in an instant the air was singing with bullets, Landry's, and Houghton's as well. Landry heard Miranda scream, heard the baby wailing in fright somewhere nearby, watched as the other man dropped to the floor, bleeding from the shoulder.

Landry was wounded himself; he wasn't sure where, though he'd bet on his ribs being cracked, and didn't give a damn. He crossed to Houghton and kicked the handgun out of his reach.

Miranda stood staring at him, both hands pressed to her mouth, her eyes big as pie tins. "You're shot," she sobbed. "Oh, Landry, you've been shot—"

"Hush," he said, as Jamie and Marcus poured into the room from the pantry, having entered, as Landry had, through the root cellar. Marcus picked up Houghton's gun and held it on him. He was face-down on the floor, bleeding copiously, moaning and just beginning to pull himself up toward consciousness.

Miranda flung herself at Landry then, hurtled right into his arms, like a little cannonball, and he held her, even though it hurt. Held her tight. *Thank you,* he said to God, in the silence of his heart.

"Did he hurt you?" Landry asked, with the next breath. "Or the baby?"

She shook her head, her beautiful violet eyes brimming with tears. Landry would never forget the way she'd held up tonight; she had more courage than a lot of the men he'd known in his life. "But you're *shot,*" she sniffled insistently. Poor little Isaiah was still howling.

"What should we do, Pa?" Marcus asked.

He didn't so much as glance in the boy's direction. "One of you tie up that polecat, hand and foot. Make sure he can't get loose. The other, head for Springwater and bring back Trey Hargreaves."

Just that morning, before church—Lord, it seemed like a lifetime ago—Landry and the other men had made an agreement that Trey would serve as a sort of unofficial lawman, just until they managed to rope in a real one. He'd been chosen because he had steady hands and a mean streak, as well as a storeroom with no windows and a door three inches thick.

"Let me look at you," Miranda said, stepping back at last, pulling Landry's shirt out of his trousers, clawing at the buttons. "Look at all this blood—"

The room swam around him, seemed to undulate, like a heat mirage in the field. He caught both his wife's frantic hands in his, stayed her from undressing him right there. "Miranda," he said.

She swallowed convulsively and stared up at him, speechless. He felt her shivering. "Wh-what?" she asked, after a long time.

"Go get that baby before he brings the roof down with his hollering," Landry said. Then he let go of her, sat down in his chair at the table, and did his level best not to pass out from the pain.

CHAPTER

7

By THE TIME Trey came to fetch Mike Houghton, bringing an exhausted Doc Parrish with him, the sun was high and Miranda had already cleaned Landry's side wound and bound his ribs up good and tight with an old sheet torn into strips. He was asleep in his own bed.

The Doc came in and examined him, first thing, while Miranda hovered nearby, twisting her hands. Landry awakened and grinned wanly.

"Hello, Pres. How's Toby?"

Doc smiled. "He'll be fine in six weeks or so. Young bones heal quickly." He cast a reassuring, sidelong glance at Miranda, and that eased her mind. "Near as I can tell, this bride of yours did a good job fixing you up. That's a flesh wound you've got there. Your ribs are a little the worse for wear, though. You'll have to take it easy for a while. No heavy work."

Landry tried to sit up in protest. "I've got a field to plow under—"

"I guess it'll just have to wait," the Doc said, in dismissive tones. "Now I'd better go out there and have a look at that fellow your boys have got hog-tied on the floor." With that, he went out.

Landry looked pale, lying there against his pillows, but handsome, with his rumpled brown hair, new beard, and soft, expressive eyes. While she was undressing him, her thoughts had been anything but romantic, but now that the danger was past, well, it made her warm inside to remember. He extended one hand to her.

"Come here," he said.

She went to him, sat down carefully on the side of the bed. All of the sudden, her throat was so tight and dry that she couldn't speak, didn't even dare to try.

"Looks like we might have to put off that honeymoon in Choteau for a while," he said gently, "but we'll go, Miranda. I promise you that. Before winter sets in."

She had to blink back tears; she loved him so much, and she'd come so close to losing him. The slightest turn of Houghton's wrist, just a hair's breadth to the left, and that bullet would have gone straight into Landry's heart instead of creasing his ribs. She and all three of her boys would have been alone.

"I love you," she blurted out. She shouldn't have said it aloud, she supposed, but she hadn't been able to help it any more than she could help drawing her next breath.

He was still holding her hand, and he raised it to his mouth, ran her knuckles lightly across his lips. His eyes were warm, with a tender look in them that affected her just the way a summer sky did, when it was a mite too blue to be borne. "I love you, too," he said quietly. "I knew that when I saw Houghton's horse tied up out there last night and realized that I might lose you. We can build on what we feel, Miranda, if you're willing to give me, oh, say, fifty years of your life." He grinned impishly. "Starting right now."

Having said that, he drew her down and kissed her soundly, for the first time, right on the mouth. It made Miranda feel as though she'd just sat herself down on a shaft of lightning, spearing upwards through her vitals and exploding in the center of her soul like fireworks.

She was gasping when he released her, and surely flushed, too, since her blood felt hot. "My goodness," she said. Tom had never kissed her like that; she'd remember if he had. Not that she could rightly recall what he'd looked like, let alone how it was when he touched her. He might have been somebody she'd heard about in a story, for all the substance of his memory.

Landry laughed, but his expression was ever-so-tender. He traced the outline of Miranda's jaw with the tip of one index finger. "You move your things in here when you get a chance, Mrs. Kildare. You'll be sleeping with me tonight, and every night after this."

Miranda felt a swell of joy and anticipation. She didn't figure Landry could manage much in the way of lovemaking, laid up like that, but just lying beside him, like a real wife, would be pure bliss to her. She nodded shyly.

Landry reached past her, to the bedside table, and when he drew back his hand, she saw that he was holding the wedding picture he'd taken with Caroline, so long before. He seemed to be bidding the image a silent farewell, then he held it out to Miranda. "The boys will want this one day. Will you put it aside for them?"

Again, Miranda couldn't speak. She nodded, trying not to cry.

Landry cupped her chin in one hand and ran the callused pad of his thumb across her mouth, setting her insides on fire all over again. His grin was both rascally and gentle. "Don't," he chided softly. "I'll never give you reason to weep. You have my word on that."

She leaned forward, let her forehead rest against his chest. It was a while before she could bring herself under control. "I'll do you proud, Landry. I promise I will."

He touched her lips again, made her want him, and desperately, as easily as that. "You already have," he said.

"I can't read too well," she confessed. She didn't want to mislead him, make him think she was smarter than she was.

"I'll help you," he said.

That was when Miranda knew for sure that everything was going to be all right, that, together, she and Landry would build a love with walls as thick and sturdy as any castle in faraway England. It might take time, it might take effort, but it would rise against the sky to stand forever, providing shelter and solace to them and to all their children, born and unborn.

When Mike Houghton had been locked up in Trey's storeroom for a solid ten days, the U.S. Marshal came out from Choteau to collect him. He'd been implicated in half a dozen holdups, Houghton had, and the lawman said it was likely he'd be in jail for a long stretch. Long enough, it was safe to assume, for Toby to grow up and become his own man.

In the meantime, of course, he would remain with the McCaffreys. Somewhere along the line, he'd taken to calling Jacob "Pa," and June-bug "Mama." Nobody corrected him, and Jacob was like a new man, gaining weight, preaching a rousing sermon that first Sunday after the marshal took Mike Houghton away.

Winter was coming, and the snows would be upon them soon, but the people of Springwater were in high spirits, almost giddy with relief. Whatever affected one of their number, for good or for ill, affected all of them, in one way or another. They were a unit, a family, and growing fast.

Miranda stood with her husband that blustery day, Landry using a cane but already much recovered. The preaching was over, and they were waiting for the stagecoach. Its approach was clearly audible in the near distance, even over the excited talk of the folks gathered to bid Mr. and Mrs. Kildare Godspeed on their honeymoon trip to Choteau. Miranda, clad almost entirely in borrowed clothes, was so excited she could barely keep from dancing for joy. She had never in her life made any kind of journey just for the sake of pleasure.

Savannah, eyes bright with happiness at the prospect, was to keep Isaiah, who had taken well to the bottle, and Marcus and Jamie, somewhat subdued—Miranda was sure it was only temporary—since their latest brush with disaster, would stay right there at Springwater station, with Jacob and June-bug. Landry had promised them a memorable hiding if they got into any kind of trouble while he and Miranda were away, and since he'd laid one hand on a Bible when he said it, everybody knew he'd keep his word, even though he was not a man to administer harsh punishment.

Finally, the stage came, and it was empty, except for Guffy O'Hagan, the driver. He was a big man, with hair the color of ground ginger and eyes as brown and gentle as a deer's. Even though he actually lived in Choteau, everybody at Springwater considered him one of them.

"Well, then," Guffy boomed, remaining high up in the box, reins in hand, as Landry helped Miranda into the coach, as fancily as if they were two storybook people about to take an airing in a golden carriage. "So I've got me a pair of passengers after all. Thought I'd be making this run alone for sure."

Landry paused to grin up at him, then hoisted himself into the coach and sat beside Miranda, laying his cane on the opposite seat. Ever since they'd declared themselves, one to the other, Miranda had shared Landry's bed, but they hadn't done much besides some kissing and the kind of touching that made the blood sing but never quite satisfied. Now, Landry was almost well, he'd made that plain in a hundred ways, and when they'd gotten to the hotel in Choteau and locked the door of their room behind them, he meant to make love to her. For real.

The trip did not pass quickly; it was a long, rough road from Springwater to Choteau, but Landry and Miranda had a great deal to talk about. They worked out how many children they'd like to have—three more, all girls—and what they ought to plant in the field Tom Bellweather and Scully Wainwright had plowed under for him while he was laid up. There were long silences, too, times when they just looked out the windows and watched the countryside jostle by, thinking their own thoughts, and that was as comfortable as the talking.

Some men, Miranda knew, might have taken advantage of being alone with their wives in a moving stagecoach, but Landry was a gentleman. It wasn't, he told her, eyes twinkling with affection and mischief, that he didn't want to strip her to the skin and learn every part of her. He'd do that on the way back, if they had the coach to themselves again, he warned, but he wanted their first time to be a little more leisurely and a lot more comfortable. He wanted to have her on a bed, he said, and he told her in great detail what he meant to do, and even outlined how she would respond.

By the time they finally pulled into town, when it was nearly nightfall, Miranda could barely keep from squirming, she was so aroused.

The stagecoach stopped in front of the National Hotel, where a man with a young and very nervous wife was waiting to board. Miranda overheard the man telling Guffy that their name was Barnes, and they were on their way to Springwater to start up a newspaper. They had equipment and a stake to put up a building, though they meant to winter over at the coach station run by some people name of McCaffrey.

Miranda smiled to herself as her husband squired her toward the open doors of the hotel. Jacob was right; Springwater *was* growing, and a newspaper would probably draw a lot of new settlers. They would make a point when they got back home, she knew, of paying a call at the station to welcome the Barneses.

The lobby of the hotel would have been rugged by Savannah's standards, Miranda thought, and especially by Rachel's, but to her it looked like a grand palace, with its horsehair settees, potted plants, and long wooden registration desk. Blushing a little, eyes downcast—surely everyone must know that she and Landry were on their honeymoon, about to go upstairs and, well, be there. Upstairs. Alone together.

She swallowed hard. *Don't let me faint*, she prayed.

In good time, Landry had the key to their room, number forty-four, at the back, as requested in Mr. Kildare's letter, the clerk said, and Landry took Miranda by the arm and squired her toward the stairway. He must have felt just fine, because he didn't even seem to realize that he'd left his cane behind, propped against the desk where he'd signed the guest book with a flourish. *Mr. and Mrs. Landry T. Kildare, Springwater.*

The room itself was small, dominated by a large brass bed, but the spread looked clean and the sheets, white and clean, had hardly been mended. Miranda took notice of that when, as soon as a boy had brought their satchel up from downstairs and left with a nickel for his trouble, Landry immediately drew back the covers. He hadn't even taken off his hat yet.

Miranda stood stiffly in the center of the room, which still put her within her husband's easy reach, since she could almost have touched any one of the four walls from right there. Landry's eyes, usually full of lively humor, smouldered now, they seared Miranda's flesh wherever his gaze lit—at the hollow of her throat, on her mouth, on her full breasts, which were practically back to normal, since she'd stopped nursing Isaiah. Practically. They were still unusually sensitive.

Landry tossed aside his good, go-to-preaching hat, then his one and only suit coat. He was unfastening his celluloid collar, which he hated with a passion usually reserved for the territorial governor, when he finally spoke.

"Get out of those clothes, Mrs. Kildare, and let me look at you."

Miranda wanted him to look, wanted him to touch—with all her heart, she *did*—but she was nervous. What if he found her lacking in some way—in a thousand ways? She didn't know much about love-making, or about pleasing a man, for all her supposed experience. Tom hadn't expected her to do anything but lie there while he strained over her.

Trembling a little, she untied the ribbons that held her bonnet in place, and set it aside. Took off her cloak.

"Let down your hair first," Landry said hoarsely, when she moved to undo the buttons at the front of her bodice. He'd stopped undressing after removing his shirt, to reveal the bindings still tightly wrapped around his middle, and his suspenders were hanging in loops at his sides.

Miranda raised her arms, pulled the pins out of her hair, so that it tumbled, heavy and rich, around her shoulders.

Landry made a growling sound and took a step toward her, and that was far enough, because there hadn't been much space between them in the first place. He pulled her close, held her against his hard chest, and bent his head to take her mouth with his own.

Knowing there would be no stopping, that this time they would truly become one flesh, set Miranda's blood afire. She moaned as Landry deepened the kiss, at the same time finding her breasts, weighing them in his strong, working man's hands. He smelled deliciously of laundry starch, sunshine, and—even though it was early November—summer grass.

Nimbly, as though he'd practiced the motions in his mind a thousand times beforehand, he opened the front of her dress without breaking the breathless kiss, and Miranda felt a sweet, fierce catch, somewhere down deep, when he broke away to look into her eyes.

"You'll have to lie down," he said, with a slanted and roguish grin, "because I can't bend to kiss those breasts of yours, and that's something I've got to do."

She couldn't speak, just stood there while he stripped away her dress, her camisole and petticoats, leaving her in just her drawers, stockings and shoes. She'd intended to wear a corset, to trim her waist to a fashionable size, but Landry had forbidden that. She was never going to own anything with spikes in it, let alone wear it, he'd said, and that was the end of the discussion.

Now, he knelt, like the prince trying the glass slipper on Cinderella's foot, untied Miranda's laces and pulled off her shoes. Rolled her stockings down, slowly, slowly, over her thighs and knees, calves and ankles. Everywhere he touched her, with just the lightest pass of his fingers, seemed to leap with a pulse all its own.

He coaxed her to stand, in murmured words, when he'd taken away everything but her bloomers, and she felt his breath through the thin fabric and groaned when he kissed her there, in that most private place, then nipped at her lightly with his teeth.

She let her head fall back, surrendered without protest when he removed the drawers, too, and parted the nest of silk between her thighs to reveal a place even she had never touched before. When he tongued her lavishly and then took her into his mouth in one greedy suckle, she cried out in lusty, wordless welcome.

Hands splayed over her bare buttocks, Landry held her firmly, burrowed deeper, drew on her still more eagerly. She was not even trying to be quiet—it would have been a hopeless effort—and he certainly did nothing to silence her cries of steadily mounting pleasure.

Finally, finally, a fierce tremor shook her, beginning in the very core of her and spreading arms of fire in every direction. "Landry," she sobbed, her hands buried in his hair, "Landry, *Landry*—"

He eased her onto the bed with the most infinite tenderness, and rose slowly, carefully, to his feet. He was breathing hard and his gaze left a path of heat as it swept over her, once and then again, hungrily. She held her arms out to him.

He was out of his trousers and shut of his boots in a moment's time. He stretched out over her, magnificent, as hard and heavy as fallen timber, even though he was holding himself in such a way as to keep from putting all his weight on her.

Her own musky scent was on his mouth when he kissed her, and started everything all over again, from the beginning, drawing all the strings inside her up tight enough to snap again, like they'd just done. Maybe harder.

The thought of that took her breath away. She'd barely survived the last round; another climb like that, to burst against the inner sky like a Chinese rocket, might just be the end of her.

Even knowing that, she wanted him, and raised her hips in an instinctive invitation. Only then did he enter her, carefully at first, and then with a powerful thrust that sent her scrambling up one side of the sky again, and the faster he moved upon her, inside her, the higher she soared.

The silent explosion happened in a place where there was no air, no clouds or stars, either. Indeed, there was nothing to see or hear, but only to feel. She clung to Landry, lest she fall forever, and felt his cries of satisfaction as he joined her there, at the edge of heaven, just seconds after her own ascent.

When it was over, they slept, arms and legs tangled, utterly spent. When Miranda opened her eyes, it was dark, and Landry was teasing one of her bare nipples into a shape he favored.

Choteau was not a large place, but it had a dress shop, a general store, and other such attractions. It might have been London or Paris, so spectacular did it appear to Miranda, who had been raised without so much as coming within looking distance of luxury. She delighted in the colorful bolts of fabric on display in the mercantile, the ready-made yarn, the barrels and crates filled with wonderful things. The smells— leather and coffee beans, books and cheese, soap and smoke from the potbellied woodstove at the heart of the store—would live in her memory forever, and always bring her honeymoon trip to Choteau to mind.

They made a number of purchases—Landry did

not seem overly concerned by the costs, though Miranda thought five cents was a perfectly ridiculous price to pay for a twenty-pound sack of flour—including small gifts for the boys and a bolt of flannel to make diapers for Isaiah. Too, Landry bought several things in secret, and arranged to have them sent to Springwater by stage, refusing to tell what they were no matter how Miranda plagued him. He said she'd find out at Christmas.

Every morning, every afternoon, and every night, they made love, sometimes urgently, sometimes in long and drawn-out rounds, sometimes standing up, sometimes lying down.

"I never felt like this before," Miranda confided, on their third and last night in Choteau, snuggled next to Landry in their hotel bed, loose-limbed and sated with lovemaking. "All the pitching and hollering, I mean. Are we supposed to carry on like we do?"

Landry chuckled against her temple, amid the damp tendrils. He liked to let her hair down himself; it was a sure sign that he intended to make love to her, and right away. "Oh, yes," he said. "The more carrying on, the better." He kissed the side of her forehead. "I love you, Miranda," he sighed. "I never realized how lonely I was, until you came to live at my place. I thought I'd lose my mind, with you lying just down the hall, on that lumpy spare-room bed."

Miranda was as content as any mortal being had the right to be. She knew she and Landry would see their share of trouble and heartache in the years ahead, just like everybody else did over the course of a long marriage, but there would be joy, too. Laughter and mischief, plans and babies. The future stretched before her, bright as the land beyond the River Jordan, and, she sighed. "I would have taken you in," she admitted. "If you'd wanted me, I mean."

"I wanted you, Miranda," he reminded her.

"And I wanted you."

She heard a puzzled frown in his voice; it was odd, how often she heard or sensed Landry's expressions and even his thoughts. Even if she went blind the next minute, she knew she'd always be able to see him clearly in her mind's eye. "Then why didn't you let me know?"

Miranda hesitated, then took the plunge. She couldn't be holding things back from Landry if she expected their alliance to be a sound one. "I was afraid you'd think I was a loose woman. You know, since I'd had little Isaiah outside of wedlock and all."

He rolled onto his side to look into her face. "He's part of you, Isaiah is. What you did is part of you. And I *love* you, Miranda. Not just the pretty parts, like your eyes and your smile and your hair. Not just the places I like to kiss, either." She could feel his erection growing against her thigh, but most of her attention was fixed on what he was saying, on what no one had ever said to her before. "I love all the things that go together to make you who you are, good, bad, and indifferent," he finished.

She couldn't hold back the tears then. She blinked rapidly, and tried to wriggle away, in a fruitless effort to hide the fact that she was crying, but finally gave up when he wouldn't let her go, and slid her arms around his neck. "There isn't another man like you in all creation, Landry Kildare," she vowed.

"Not for you, there isn't." He grinned, showing those white teeth that she hoped her babies would have, and slid one hand down her belly to ply her shamelessly into almost instant arousal.

The sound of gunfire didn't distract them.

The sky was dark with the promise of snow, that last morning, when Landry came back to the hotel from the marshal's office down the street. Miranda was waiting in the lobby, dressed to travel and surrounded with boxes and crates containing all the wonderful things they'd bought. His expression was serious enough to worry Miranda a little.

"What is it?"

He spoke quietly, taking her arm, nodding to the boys who'd come to load their baggage into the pouchlike compartment at the rear of the stagecoach. "Some of Mike Houghton's friends tried to get him out of jail last night. The marshal and his deputies were ready for them, and Houghton was killed in the fight, along with several of the others."

Miranda felt no particular grief for Houghton's violent death—it had probably been inevitable, the way he lived—but she was sorry for the loss of a life that might have been spent in so many better ways. Experience had taught her that people didn't go bad without reason; they went wrong someplace along the way, early on usually, and just never managed to get back on the right path again. She didn't express any of her thoughts aloud, but simply nodded.

Outside, the wind was brisk, and the team of eight horses hitched to the stagecoach seemed restless, eager to run, even with a heavy burden behind them. Guffy came forward, inclined his head to Landry, took off his hat and pressed it to his chest when he turned to Miranda.

"Good to see you, Mrs. Kildare. The womenfolk up at Springwater are missing you somethin' ferocious, I hear tell." His voice took on a teasing note. "They mean to put together a quilt for you. You'll be lucky if Mrs. Doc gives back that baby, though. She's taken to him real powerful."

Miranda was eager to see and hold Isaiah, never having been away from him before. "Savannah will have a family of her own in no time," she said, and then blushed, because that was a mighty personal thing to say about a person, and to a man in the bargain.

Beside her, Landry laughed and took her elbow. "Time to board the stage for home," he said, and opened the door. He turned to Guffy, once Miranda was seated. "Any other passengers on this run?"

Guffy's voice was loud enough to echo off the mountains and roll back over them all in a wave. "No, sir. You and the missus have the coach to yourselves, all the way to Springwater."

Landry looked through the window of the coach at Miranda, wriggled his eyebrows mischievously, and grinned. "Hear that, Mrs. Kildare?" he teased. "We're traveling alone." He put just the slightest emphasis on the last word.

Miranda felt a delicious shiver move through her, and she blushed, too, but she said nothing as he climbed in and took a seat beside her, laying a proprietary hand on her knee.

The stagecoach bolted forward at a shout from Guffy, and Miranda might have tumbled to the floor if Landry hadn't caught her in the curve of his arm. Easily, he pulled her up onto his lap. By the time they were out of town, he'd arranged her astraddle of his thighs and was slowly unfastening the buttons of her dress.

"I'm going to make love to you, Mrs. Kildare," he said, matter-of-factly. "Right here, right now."

Mrs. Kildare offered no protest at all.

∽Jessica∾

Jessica

CHAPTER

∼⊙ 1 ⊙∼

Winter 1880

BEHIND HER, Alma was weeping.

Plump, glistening flakes of snow swayed like languorous dancers past the bay windows set into the rear wall of the tiny parlor, but Jessica Barnes took no note of their feathery beauty. Her attention, indeed the whole of her being, was fixed upon the new grave in the churchyard just across the way. The place where her brother, Michael, a true and devoted friend through all twenty-three years of her life, lay buried. He had died precisely one week prior to her arrival yesterday in the remote Montana Territory town of Springwater.

How he had gone on about this place in his letters: the scenery was breathtaking, he'd written; the people had gathered him and Victoria in like family; there was so much sky that you could lie on your back in the deep, sweet grass, looking up, and lose yourself in all that blue. Not that he ever had time for such things, he'd been quick to stress, always working on the next issue of the paper the way he was.

Jessica swallowed a bitter sob. They had killed him, in her opinion—the work *and* the town. He'd always been a frail man, physically at least, and as far as she was concerned, the whole enterprise—buying that ancient press, traveling across prairies, deserts, and mountains in a wagon drawn by oxen—had been plain foolhardy. He should have stayed in Missouri, put aside his pride, and worked on their uncle's newspaper, as he'd been raised to do, instead of traveling way out here and exhausting himself. But no. Instead, he'd sold what little he had and turned his back on a respectable family business. He'd bought that huge, greasy, secondhand contrivance he called a press, dismantled it, and loaded it up—along with his frightened bride, a few sacks of dried beans, and a paltry assortment of supplies—for the journey west. Jessica recalled the day of their leaving with a clarity that stung even now, nearly six years later; seventeen and strong, she had begged to accompany Michael and Victoria on the trip west. Michael had refused her gently, saying it was far too dangerous a trip for a scrap of a girl like her—she was but a year younger than Victoria—and she'd realized that she would be in the way, an unwanted encumbrance.

So it was that she had, with her uncle's hearty approval, stayed and accepted a post as companion to an elderly but spry widow, Mrs. Frederick Covington, Sr. For two years she and Mrs. Covington had trav-

eled on the European continent, and Jessica had
enjoyed the experience and learned a great deal from
her lively minded charge.

The dear old woman had passed away in her sleep
on the journey back across the Atlantic, leaving
Jessica a small, secret legacy and several pieces of jewelry, neither of which had been directly mentioned in
her will. By that time Jessica's uncle had died as well,
but there was no bequest this time—only a stack of
demands from his impatient creditors.

She had sold everything—the newspaper, her
uncle's modest house and personal belongings, even
the clock from his mantelpiece—to settle his debts,
and waited for Michael to send for her.

He didn't. The offer of a new position, in the
household of Mrs. Covington's only son, Frederick II,
and his wife, Sarah, had seemed a godsend. Appear-
ances, however, were deceiving—unhappy in his marriage, Frederick soon began pursuing Jessica.

She had managed to avoid being alone with him
for a very long time. Then one of the maids found the
jewelry his mother had given Jessica on her deathbed,
and, thinking Jessica had stolen it, turned it over to
Mr. Covington. It was exactly the blackmail he needed. After that, he'd threatened her with ruin and
scandal at best, prison at worst, if she continued to
refuse him her bed.

She'd been prepared to plead with Michael and
Victoria to take her in when, on the very day of Covington's ultimatum, her brother finally broached the
subject himself in one of his more revealing letters.

Things weren't going well, he'd written. Victoria was having a hard time with her pregnancy, and his debts were mounting. He suspected a certain lawyer, a Mr. Gage Calloway, of persuading the bank in Choteau to call in his loans. That was when she'd fled St. Louis for good and used part of the money Mrs. Covington had left her to travel west. What remained—and there was precious little—was secure in a Missouri bank.

Jessica brought her mind back to the present with a forceful tug. The injustice, the humiliation—all of it was too much to bear on top of losing Michael. She must think of it another time or, better yet, put it behind her forever.

Now, watching as the snow outlined her brother's plain wooden marker in an airy, lace-trimmed script, Jessica pressed the back of one hand to her mouth in yet another effort to contain her grief—and her fury. The world ground and clanked and clattered around her like the works of some enormous mechanism, and on the edges of her consciousness she was aware of Alma Stewart's soft voice singing a lullaby in the next room; the fretful whimpers of the two babies, left orphaned only weeks after their birth; the damnably steady, ponderous ticking of the mail-order clock on a rickety side table.

Wagons and buggies jostled by over rutted ground frozen solid beneath the snow, and both men and women called to each other in jovial, wintry voices. But beneath her feet, in the offices of the town's fledgling newspaper—the *Springwater Gazette*—the press was utterly still.

"Jessie?" Alma's gentle inquiry caused her to turn at last from considering Michael's final resting place. No one, save her brother, had ever called her Jessie, but she did not protest. Alma, too, was mourning, not only for Michael, but for his wife—her niece—Victoria. Weakened by her own illness, Victoria had perished in childbirth, barely a month before Michael's fever, born of exhaustion and despair, took his life.

Jessica turned to face the deceptively delicate-looking woman who was just entering from one of the two nooks they called bedrooms. "Yes?"

Although she had a husband waiting for her on a ranch some forty miles away, Alma had come to Springwater when Victoria was due to have the babies, just to lend a hand. She was generous and capable and understandably anxious to get back home.

"He tried," Alma said staunchly. "He tried his best to hold on, Michael did. But when Victoria died, it was like something had been torn out of him. He worked himself blind after that, down there setting and resetting type and repairing that secondhand press all day and half the night. That was what finished him, Jessie. He just used himself up." Alma paused; her chin quivered and she dabbed at red-rimmed eyes with a wadded handkerchief. "You understand, don't you—I can't raise these babies? I'm an old woman, past the age for such things, and frankly it's all I can do most days to look after what's mine to tend. I've left a good and patient man alone too long as it is."

Jessica had given little thought to children in general or to her infant nieces in particular, having been met with the news of both Victoria's and Michael's deaths directly after stepping off the stagecoach, though she had practically lived for word of them before fleeing St. Louis. Now, suddenly, she felt a fierce, almost primitive desire to protect them. They were so small, so fragile, so beautiful! Was this, then, what it felt like to be a mother, this swift and ferocious love?

They were a beacon of light, the twins were, in the otherwise impenetrable darkness of her grief, something to cherish and move toward. As dear as the Covington children—Susan and young Freddy—had been to her, and she had loved them with the whole of her heart, despite the contempt in which she held their father, this was a keener, deeper sort of caring. These babies were blood of her blood, bone of her bone, soul of her soul. They were *family*.

"It's all right, Alma," she said as tenderly as she could. She'd come west because Michael had summoned her at long last, because she'd had nowhere else to go, her reputation thoroughly spoiled, and she was set on taking hold and making a good life for herself and for the babies. "I'll provide for them."

Alma looked decidedly relieved as she groped for the back of a chair and then lowered herself shakily onto the frayed cushion of the seat. Jessica knew a moment of deep chagrin; yes, she had lost a beloved brother, and with shattering suddenness, but Alma had cherished Victoria, daughter of her long-dead and much idolized brother, Frank. Jessica knew all that from her correspondence with Michael. Alma and her husband had never had children of their own.

Settled at last, the older woman looked up at Jessica with eyes awash in tears. "You won't put those poor little darlings into a foundling home, will you?" she asked in a breathless rush. "Why, there are folks right around here who'd take them in. Good people. Gage Calloway told me just the other day—"

Gage Calloway. Now there was a name Jessica definitely remembered from her brother's letters. Mr. Calloway had wanted to be mayor of Springwater, and Michael had campaigned against him. He'd responded by using the power of his wealth to destroy her brother, however indirectly.

Jessica raised a slightly tremulous hand to call a halt to Alma's discourse. Under other circumstances she might have waxed indignant at the mere suggestion—consign *Michael's children* to an orphanage?—but she knew Alma's emotions were as brittle as her own, and therefore made a sturdy attempt to hold her annoyance in check. They were both doing the best they could under very trying conditions, and there was nothing to be gained by the exchange of harsh and hasty words.

Jessica straightened her shoulders and smoothed

her black sateen skirts, as she generally did whenever she was challenged in any way. "You may rest assured that I will raise those children with as much care and devotion as I would if they were my own." She paused, then slid her teeth over her lower lip once, in a gesture of suppressed exasperation. Her voice, when she spoke, was almost plaintive. "How could you think for one moment that I would give them up? Those little girls are the only family I have now." Michael had no doubt told Alma how his and Jessica's parents had died in a carriage accident, leaving their two small children to be raised by a bachelor uncle who took little interest in the task.

Alma would not meet Jessica's gaze—not immediately, in any case—and even though she started at the sound of footsteps on the covered stairs leading to the crude board sidewalk out front, there was an air of profound relief about her, too. She had been spared making a reply and that was probably just as well. Michael, no doubt, had described his sister as a spinster, somewhat distant, with no knowledge or particular fondness for babies. The Covington children, being older, had needed an entirely different sort of care.

Indeed, she did wonder how she was ever going to adjust to Springwater, with its one store, one church, and scattered handful of houses. Without Michael, it had little or no appeal.

Patting her fair hair to make sure none of it had escaped its pins to tumble untidily down her neck, Jessica put her private reflections aside for the moment at least, crossed the room, and opened the door. The caller, a dark-haired man of imposing height, with eyes the color of malachite, had one fist raised, poised to knock. A chill wind rushed past him to nip at Jessica's very bones, and yet the sight of him caused a warm wrench, somewhere deep inside, leaving her with a sense of having turned some mysterious spiritual corner.

Always wary of strangers and equally determined to disguise that fact, Jessica lengthened her spine and did not even attempt a smile. The man's effect upon her was, she concluded, reason to be extra cautious.

"Good day," she said politely, if not warmly, lending the greeting the tone of a question. She might as well have told him "State your business and leave."

"Miss Barnes?" His teeth were as white as any she'd ever seen, and he smelled of fresh air and snow and the distant pine trees that covered the foothills.

She tried to look pleasant, if not exactly glad to see him. These were frontier people, and it was probably considered neighborly to pay a call on any new arrival. "Yes?" she said. She did not step back or invite the visitor inside. This was, after all, a household in mourning and, therefore, seclusion.

He removed his hat, a rather dapper affair with a round brim and a band of shimmering silver conchos, holding it in both hands. His hair was thick and had a silky gloss to it, Jessica noticed, and she was amazed at herself when she felt an instinctive desire to reach up and flick a lock of it back from his forehead with the ends of her fingers. Her reaction was curious indeed, and she would have been the last person who would presume to explain it.

"My name is Gage Calloway," the man announced after clearing his throat once. Even that simple statement sounded eloquent coming from him, but of course it landed on her with all the weight of a derailed freight car. Here, then, was her brother's enemy. *Her* enemy, now that Michael was gone.

"I'm the mayor of Springwater." He paused, looking pained. "We're awfully sorry about your brother, Miss Barnes. The townsfolk, I mean. It must have been a real shock to step down from the stage and be told right off that a loved one had passed over. . . ."

Jessica's throat constricted at the memory; it was indeed fresh to the point of rawness, and her eyes stung. A sort of cold fury filled her, mingled with a deep sense of guilt because she knew she had instantly warmed to the man despite all he'd done. Had the visitor been practically anyone else, she would have invited him in, offered him tea, perhaps, and certainly a chair next to the fire. As it was, she simply could not make the necessary effort. "You will forgive us, Mr. Calloway—" she began, fully intending to send him on his way, but before she could complete the sentence, Alma interrupted.

"Why, Gage, it's dear of you to come calling," the other woman said from the doorway of the tiny kitchen, in a voice Jessica would have sworn was fluttery. "Do come in out of the wind. I've put some coffee on to brew, and you look frozen straight through."

Gage Calloway met Jessica's unyielding gaze, albeit briefly, and nodded his acceptance of Alma's invitation. The smile he gave, reserved for Alma, was dazzling. "I wouldn't mind a few minutes by the fire," he allowed. "Looks like we're in for a pretty bad winter."

Jessica was left with no viable choice but to step aside, short of spreading both arms and barring his way. Judging by the size of Mr. Calloway, the effort would have been futile as well as ludicrous; he stood over six feet tall, and his shoulders very nearly brushed the door frame. "Yes," she said in a slightly clipped tone that was more defensive than scornful, "do come in."

A smile played at the corners of Calloway's fine, supple mouth as he entered. His eyes, though solemn with sympathy at the moment, were normally more given to mischief, calculation, and merriment, Jessica ascertained, via some as-yet-unrecognized sense.

"No one makes better coffee than you do, Miss Alma," he said, though he was looking straight at Jessica all the while he spoke. "Just don't tell June-bug McCaffrey I said so. She's downright prideful about her cooking."

Alma made a sound that was part laugh, part twitter; maybe she didn't know that this man had been Michael's foe. In fact, it was obvious that she enjoyed Mr. Calloway's company, even in this time of sorrow. Probably a great many women would, Jessica thought pragmatically; she had to admit that he was a very attractive specimen, scoundrel or not. She, on the other hand, had good reason to dislike him.

His manner reminded her of her own nemesis, Frederick Covington. He'd been handsome, too. He'd had money and power, just as this man did. He'd also been a devil, and it was likely, given what Michael had said about Mr. Calloway in his editorials, that the two men were the same in that regard, as well.

When Alma went back into the kitchen, Jessica gestured stiffly toward one of the two chairs facing the inadequate brick fireplace. She had to make a home in Springwater for herself and for her nieces, and she needed the good will of the townspeople if the *Gazette* was to prosper. Therefore, she would be as civil to everyone as possible—including this man, however much it galled her.

"Sit down, Mr. Calloway," she urged, with a sort of wry resignation. He moved as gracefully as she imagined an Indian warrior might do, or a panther on the prowl. Inside, she seethed just to think of all the suffering he must have caused her poor brother.

He smiled as if they had every reason to be friends—it might have been more apt to say he grinned, for the expression was boyish—but hesitated. "After you," he said.

Jessica took the second chair, and her quiet rage was pushed aside by a fresh and sorely painful sense of sorrow. Surely Michael and Victoria had sat together on that very hearth many times, planning their happy life in Springwater. They'd dreamed of expanding the weekly newspaper to a daily, of building a spacious home and filling it with children. In more than one letter, Michael had referred to Springwater as "idyllic," though from what Jessica had seen so far, it was merely a small conglomeration of plain buildings huddled together in the midst of a fierce wilderness, like wild horses trying to find shelter from a high wind.

The babies had quieted at last, and Jessica almost regretted that, for a little fussing on their part would have given her a reason to excuse herself and leave the entertainment of this unexpected and most unwanted guest to Alma.

Once Jessica was seated, Calloway took a chair as well, and stared into the fire for a few long moments. She was just beginning to hope he did not intend to make conversation when he turned to her and said, "Your brother was a good man and an asset to the community. We all liked him, and Miss Victoria, too."

It was a bold-faced lie, of course. She'd seen Michael's editorials. This man could not have liked him.

Jessica felt tears threaten yet again—dear Lord, she was so weary of weeping, for she'd cried more in the past twenty-four hours than in all her life put together—and she did not like for Mr. Calloway, of all people, to be a witness to her weakness. She raised her chin. "Yes," she agreed. "Michael was a wonderful person, and Victoria was the heart of his life."

Alma reappeared just then, bearing a tray set with three cups and a steaming china coffeepot, and Mr. Calloway immediately got to his feet, managing to display proper deference by taking the burden from those small, blue-veined hands in one smooth motion. Jessica felt herself flush slightly—it was as though the floor had suddenly dissolved beneath her feet—and she looked away for a moment in order to recover her composure.

When she looked back, it was with narrowed eyes. Exhausted by grief and despair, coupled with the long and difficult journey out from Missouri, first by train and then by stagecoach, she felt downright peevish. She wanted to sleep for a month and cry for *another* month after that.

There was a small stir, in which Mr. Calloway found and brought over another chair, and Jessica, backbone rigid, observed the rites of hospitality out of the corner of one eye. Surely he would not stay long, she assured herself. He would take himself and the curious electricity that surrounded him *away*.

"I suppose you plan to sell the newspaper and go back home," said the mayor—that he'd triumphed in the election despite Michael's efforts to oppose him was one more reason not to like him—when what he probably regarded as a decent interval had passed. He looked down into his cup for a long moment, then raised those arresting eyes of his to lock with Jessica's. "It may be too soon to speak of such matters, ma'am—forgive me if I offend you—but I am prepared to make you a very generous offer on this place. One that should enable both you and Miss Alma to live comfortably for some time."

Jessica glanced quickly at Alma, who was watching the snow fall with a wistful expression. It probably would make sense to sell the *Gazette*, but now, in the face of an actual opportunity, she wanted to hold on to it more fiercely than ever before.

She raised her eyebrows slightly and stirred her coffee with a tinkling clatter of spoon against porcelain. "I should like," she announced, surprising even herself by the certainty in her voice, "to keep the *Gazette* for my nieces."

His expression sharpened, but it was only a moment before he had relaxed that spectacular face into a placid mask. Mr. Covington had possessed that same ability, that affinity for easy deceit. Both men were lawyers, members of a profession Jessica deemed only slightly above prostitution.

Calloway shifted in his chair, revealing only the mildest discomfort; no doubt even that was merely a pretense. Men like him spent their days and nights breaking as many commandments as possible.

He put his cup and saucer down and, with another glance at Alma, leaned forward a little way, his hands dangling between his knees, his fine round-brimmed hat resting on the floor beside his chair. Alma was still lost in her own thoughts, probably missing home and husband and thinking of household tasks that needed doing.

Jessica wondered what on earth she was going to do once Alma went back to the ranch. She'd never fed or diapered a baby in her life; indeed, until the twins were four or five, poor little things, she wouldn't have the first idea what to do with them. Only one thing was certain—she was fresh out of choices.

Calloway cleared his throat again and lowered his voice. "It has been mentioned that you, being an unmarried woman and all, might not wish to raise your brother's daughters on your own. I understand you've been serving as a governess for some time now, and that you travel a great deal in your work. Therefore—"

Jessica waited, content to watch him squirm a little and suspecting, with a sick feeling in the pit of her stomach, that she knew what he was going to say.

"I thought you might be willing to consider a formal adoption. My clients are able to offer your nieces a fine home—"

"Your clients?" She gave the words an edge. One of the babies began to cry and Alma rose, with a sigh, and toddled away to attend to the child. "Why, Mr. Calloway, you gave me the impression this was a condolence call. I suppose next you're going to tell me that Michael appointed you the executor of his will."

Jessica had been guessing, where the will was concerned, but it was plain from Mr. Calloway's expression that she'd struck her mark. The realization that Michael hadn't trusted her to serve in that capacity—indeed, that he had put more faith in his worst enemy—was devastating, but she managed to keep up her facade.

Calloway, meanwhile, had the decency to redden a

little along the base of his jaw, but there was a glint of determination in his eyes, too. "Dr. and Mrs. Parrish are good people, Miss Barnes. Upstanding citizens, well-regarded by everyone in town. They have a four-year-old daughter of their own, but Savannah—Mrs. Parrish—well, they'd like more children."

A charged silence filled the room, punctuated only by the popping and shifting of the pine logs burning in the grate. The pleasant scents of wood smoke and stout coffee filled the room, and beyond the windows the snow, so quiet and so white, seemed sadly, poignantly magical.

When she could trust herself to speak in a moderate fashion, Jessica made her reply. "I'm sure your clients are very nice people," she said in tones measured out as carefully as a length of exceedingly fine cloth. "However, I have no intention of surrendering my brother's children—my only living blood relations—to anyone, however worthy they might be. If you have completed your business, sir . . ."

A muscle tightened in Mr. Calloway's closely shaven cheek, but he was a lawyer, after all, and he smoothed his features before Jessica could even be sure that he was irritated. "I'm sorry," he said, glancing in the direction Alma had taken when she left the room. "I was given to understand—"

Only then did it occur to Jessica, in her grief-addled state, that it had not been Alma alone who had suggested this arrangement, but Michael, too. Perhaps, even on his deathbed, he had been reluctant to leave the raising of his daughters to her. That stung even more than the fact that he'd appointed a virtual stranger to see that his last wishes were carried out.

She was filled with an inestimable and echoing sadness.

Still, she decided, after a few moments of inward reeling, she must make an effort to be charitable. It *was* possible that Mr. Calloway meant well, though not very likely. "I'm sure," she said, in what was almost certainly too abrupt a manner, "that you are only trying to help." She took a thoughtful sip of her coffee, which had grown cold, and her next words were meant to come as a shock. "I'm planning to run the newspaper myself," she said. "Provided that Michael left it to me, of course." She felt safe in assuming *that*, at least, since Mr. Calloway wouldn't have offered to buy the business from her if she hadn't been the rightful owner.

He looked truly startled, and did not even bother to comment on her statement, yea or nay. "You're not returning to St. Louis?" he asked. She couldn't rightly tell whether he was pleased or disappointed by this news, but he was definitely astounded. In all likelihood, she concluded, he did not care one way or the other *what* she did—why should he?—as long as he got what he wanted. "Your brother told me—"

"I don't care what my brother told you," Jessica lied, a bit pettishly. She wanted very much to know, but she was also weary to the innermost wellsprings of her soul, too weary to pursue the matter further. "I'm staying right here. In Springwater."

She had enjoyed her work in St. Louis before the

trouble with Mr. Covington, not only because it paid unusually well, but because she was deeply fond of her two charges. In truth, however, the children were growing up fast and would soon go away to their respective boarding schools—Susan's in Switzerland, Freddy's in England—where, of course, they would not need a governess. She would have had to leave them soon anyway.

Besides, she had always wanted children of her own, and now she had them, even if they were her nieces and not her daughters. "This Dr. Parrish you referred to," she began cautiously, holding all her emotions at bay until she could sort them out, one by one, in the privacy of her own mind. "Did he look after my brother? At—at the end, I mean?"

"Yes, ma'am," Calloway said. He looked a mite grim, and had retrieved his hat from the floor to turn it slowly, round and round, between his fingers. "It isn't possible to find better medical care than you'd get right here in Springwater. Pres did everything he could to keep Michael alive, but he was real sick. The fever took him down fast."

Jessica closed her eyes against the image of Michael breathing his last, slipping away forever, but it was imprinted on her mind and she could not escape the force of it. She would gladly have died in his place but, alas, she had not been given a choice in the matter.

"I should like to speak with the doctor," she said, when she was fairly sure she would not break down and sob as she had done the whole night through. "There are questions I want to ask. About Michael's passing. And—of course—about Victoria's, too. I trust this Dr. Parrish attended her as well?"

The mayor of Springwater narrowed his eyes again, as if he were on the alert for a slur directed at the town doctor, who was obviously his friend. "Like I said, you won't find a better man anywhere than Pres is."

It was then that Alma returned. "I declare," she fretted, "that those two defenseless little darlings know they have"—she paused, perhaps for the sake of drama—"neither father nor mother to look after them." By then, Jessica was looking at the visitor, and not at Alma.

"They have me," she said pointedly. Then she rose from her chair, all dignity and bravado. She wasn't such a bargain, she reckoned, but she was a blood relation, and she loved those babies with all the scattered pieces of her heart. "We mustn't keep you, Mr. Calloway," she said. "You surely have a great many things to do."

Because Jessica stood, Mr. Calloway was, of course, forced to stand as well. She found she could not draw an accurate measure of his response merely by looking at his face, and that nettled her. He was a lawyer, she reminded herself, and that meant he had probably cultivated wily ways.

"If there's anything you need," Mr. Calloway said, and though he glanced at Jessica it did seem that his polite words were directed more toward Alma, "you just let me know. The people of Springwater look after their own."

Once again Alma was almost blushing, and Jessica

glimpsed in her the pretty and charming girl she had once been, long ago. It was Alma, in fact, who saw Mr. Calloway most graciously to the door.

His departure was audible; his boot heels made a firm, even distinctive sound on the outside stairs.

When Alma turned back to face Jessica, her color was still high, and her eyes were snapping with uncharacteristic fury. "Whatever possessed you to be so rude to such a fine man as Gage Calloway?" she demanded, with such spirit that Jessica was quite taken aback.

She ignored the question, having no good response to make, and returned to her post at the set of windows overlooking the main street.

As she watched Mr. Calloway stalk across the snowy street, his strides long and angry, she smiled. What a good thing it was, she thought, that she did not have to explain her reactions to this disturbing man, for she did not begin to understand them herself.

Clouds were moving in from the west, heavy with still more snow, and the light was fading. Quickly Jessica hurried in to fetch her warm cloak.

"You're going out?" Alma asked, clearly surprised.

"I'll be back shortly," Jessica promised, and made for the door. The wooden stairway was steep and slick, exposed as it was, and she was careful making her way down. If she fell and hurt herself, she and the babies would starve.

Looking neither to the right nor the left, lest someone catch her eye and expect to converse, Jessica rounded the side of the humble newspaper building and made for the churchyard across the way.

She had some trouble with the gate, for the metal latch had frozen in place, but soon, by sheer force of will, she had wrestled it open. The snow, ever-deepening, was heavy, and she had to push hard before she could enter.

She raised her gaze briefly to look at the church itself. A small, trim structure, painted white, it boasted its own bell tower and mullioned windows. The double doors were closed fast against the cold—not that Jessica had any desire whatsoever to set foot inside. She and God were civil to each other, but that was the extent of the matter. Michael's death had only served to widen the gulf.

Holding her cloak more tightly around her, Jessica began slogging laboriously toward the small graveyard on the left side of the building. It was guarded by towering maple trees that were bare of leaves but lined with a fine tracery of frost and snow.

Her knees were wet by the time she gained the place where Michael had been buried. The snow was shallower there, hardly covering the still-raw earth of the grave. The wooden marker looked even more forlorn up close than it had from the apartment windows.

She blinked back stinging tears and breathed slowly and deeply. She was torn between kicking at the mound in pure outrage, and throwing herself down upon it in a fit of sobbing. Neither option was acceptable.

"I'm here," she said, and sniffled. Her nose was turning red—she could feel it—and her eyes were puffy. Her whole face felt swollen, in fact. "I'm here, Michael, and I'll look after the babies and the newspaper, I promise. Somehow, we'll all get by."

There was no reply, naturally, only more snow drifting down from the charcoal sky, and a wind that prickled even through her clothes. Jessica was seized by such a sense of loneliness that she might have been the only person in the universe, lost and wandering.

"You can depend on me," she vowed, in a whisper. Then she touched the cross once, where Michael's name was carved, before turning to make her way back to the gate.

CHAPTER

2

"GIVE THE GIRL some time," June-bug McCaffrey counseled as she set the station house table for one of her legendary "plain" suppers. Her blue eyes gleamed with what struck Gage as tender amusement. "She's new in town, and she's just lost a close relation, into the bargain. 'Sides, those babies are her own kin, and it's a natural thing for her to want to raise them up herself. Poor little things. Why, I do believe I would think less of her if she'd turned her back on her own brother's children."

A bachelor used to being on his own, Gage was a competent cook, but he preferred June-bug's meals to his own concoctions and enjoyed passing an evening before the McCaffreys' fire, swapping tall tales with old Jacob. Especially a cold, snowy evening like this one. The big white house around the corner was as lonely as a tomb, and not much warmer, for all its fancy furnishings.

He'd been a fool to go to all that trouble and

expense. For one thing, it reminded him too much of the place he'd grown up in, an echoing San Francisco mansion that was either empty or full of shouting and strife, but never peaceful and certainly never warm, the way the Springwater station was. He'd left California after one last shouting match with his tyrannical old grandfather, and he was never going back—not that he'd been asked. He'd ended up in Springwater purely by accident, liked the place, and stayed.

He thrust out a sigh. "I know you're right," he said to June-bug, recalling her assertion that it was only right for Jessica Barnes to raise her own nieces, "but Pres and Savannah are going to be disappointed that they can't adopt those little girls."

"Pooh," June-bug scoffed, with a wave of one competent hand. That was about as close as she ever got to swearing, at least in Gage's hearing. She and Jacob had been running the Springwater stagecoach station for a long while before the town grew up around it, and both of them were clear thinkers who generally spoke their minds. "Savannah and Pres have little Beatrice, and they know they're blessed. Why, the Lord may yet see fit to send them a whole passel of kids anyways. They're still young."

Jacob, a powerfully built man with a head full of dark hair, only lightly threaded with silver, had been holding his peace throughout the conversation, though he had a way of listening that made it seem like he was taking the sense of the words in through his very pores. Seated by the fire, he seemed intent on his whittling, but June-bug's remark inspired him to look up. The wooden horse he was carving looked minuscule in his big, callused hands. "I reckon Miss Barnes must have chosen not to sell you the newspaper," he said. "Seems to me, that's what's got you so riled, most likely."

Gage thrust a hand through his hair, which was still damp from walking hatless through the snow. "She took a dislike to me right off," he confessed, and wondered why it bothered him so much. Miss Jessica Barnes was a skinny little bluestocking with a snippy disposition, and her opinion oughtn't to matter the way it did. "She doesn't want to run a newspaper—probably doesn't have the first idea how to go about such a thing. No sir, I'd bet my best shirt that Miss Barnes had no plans to get into the newspaper business until she found out I wanted it. *Then* she got downright contrary."

June-bug gave a sigh of mock impatience. It had been a hard day and, frankly, the delicious scent of the elk stew she'd made for supper was about all that kept Gage from heading for the Brimstone Saloon to make a meal of hard-boiled eggs and beer. There were nights, and this was one of them, when he just couldn't face going back to that house by himself, that house he had so foolishly built for a bride who chose, in the end, to remain in San Francisco and marry his half-brother, Luke.

"Horsefeathers," June-bug said, jolting him out of his sorry reverie. "Michael fully expected his sister to help him put out the *Gazette*. He told me himself that he'd asked her to stay on permanent. He hoped she might even marry up with somebody from around here."

Jacob's dark eyes seemed to sparkle, but that might have been a trick of the lantern light. "She's a fetching little thing, Miss Jessica Barnes," he allowed. For Jacob, the most taciturn of men, this was unbridled, raving praise.

June-bug put her hands on her hips and tilted her head to one side. For all her sixty-odd years, she looked as coquettish in that moment as any dewy young maiden flirting by the garden gate. "Why, Jacob McCaffrey," she accused, half laughing, "I do believe you are *smitten!*"

He laughed, a sound like two great armies waging war in the distance, all but shaking the ground and rattling the windows. "I am smitten," he admitted. "Indeed, I am. With my bride of many years." He crossed the room, took June-bug's hand, and bent his head to kiss it. "That would be you, Mrs. McCaffrey."

June-bug flushed like a schoolgirl. "Jacob McCaffrey," she said, "you stop carryin' on that-a-way."

There was a moment of perfect stillness, during which something private passed between husband and wife; some elemental, unspoken language known only to them. Love them both though he did, Gage felt a brief and acidic sting of envy, looking on. Once, fool that he was, he'd thought he had that same affinity with Liza. He'd trusted her utterly, shared the most secret, the most fragile of his dreams and, ultimately, she had betrayed him. Sided with Luke and his grandfather. No doubt, it had all been a joke to Liza, from the first, but Gage had a network of soul-scars to show for the experience, and no other kind of risk scared him the way that one did. Love, to him, was a dangerous undertaking.

But Jacob and June-bug had been married for more than forty years, and in that time they had raised and lost twin sons and faced innumerable other trials and tribulations as well. In the not too distant past, Jacob had suffered a heart condition that had nearly killed him, but they'd overcome that, too, and now the old man was as healthy as the mules that pulled coaches for the Springwater stage line. It seemed to Gage that every sorrow, every joy, had merely served to draw them closer, until their very souls were fused, one inseparable from the other.

Gage wanted what the McCaffreys had and feared with his whole heart that he would never find it. Maybe, God help him, Liza had been the only woman he would ever dare to care about, but down deep he wanted passion and fire. He wanted love.

Indeed, whatever mark he might make in the world, Gage knew he would be a failure if he did not find that one right woman. It would help like hell, he reflected grimly, if he had any idea where to look.

"Sit down and eat, both of you," June-bug commanded, breaking the spell as she reached back to untie her calico apron. "And where's Toby run off to, just when I've got supper on the table? That boy don't stay put any better'n a basket of kittens."

Toby, the McCaffreys' fifteen-year-old foster son,

was much taken with young Emma, daughter of Trey and Rachel Hargreaves, and spent most of his spare time across the road at the Hargreaves house, according to Jacob, "getting underfoot." Trey and his pretty missus didn't seem to mind, though—they nearly always had a houseful anyway, what with the two smaller children of their own and the Wainwright kids coming and going whenever they had the yen to pass some time in town.

"Toby'll be along," Jacob said. He and June-bug took their places at the table, and Gage joined them as soon as they were both seated.

Sure enough, Toby burst in while Jacob was offering the blessing, about as subtle as a snowstorm in July. The boy washed hastily and sat down next to Gage just as the resounding "amen" was raised.

"And how are Trey and Rachel keeping these days?" Jacob asked with a smile in his voice. His rugged features were as solemn as ever. "And Miss Emma, of course?"

Toby, a good-looking kid with straight blond hair and the kind of impudent manner girls always seemed to take to right off, colored a little as he took a biscuit from the platter Jacob passed his way. "They're all right," he said and, after only a moment's hesitation, helped himself to a second biscuit before handing the rest on to Gage. "I could have stayed for supper, but I told them I wouldn't miss one of Miss June-bug's meals for anything."

Gage suppressed a smile. The kid was a charmer, that was for sure.

"Did Emma wear that pretty new dress her mama and I made for her last Saturday afternoon?" June-bug asked. Her eyes were bright with affection for the boy, but he squirmed a little all the same, well aware that he was being teased, and suitably self-conscious.

"Yes, ma'am," he said, and summoned up a winning grin. "She looked mighty good, too."

"Well," said June-bug, "of course she did. As for you, Toby McCaffrey, I will expect you to be on time for supper after this just the same. It ain't good manners to make other folks wait for their victuals."

Not, Gage thought with a private smile, that they'd been going to wait.

Toby ducked his head. Abandoned by his father as a lad and found living alone in the woods by the town's first official schoolmarm, Rachel Hargreaves, he had been staying with the McCaffreys ever since. His father, a no-good specimen if Gage had ever heard tell of one, had tried once to reclaim his son, though not because of any paternal devotion. Instead, Mike Houghton had wanted someone to mind the horses while he and his gang robbed banks, stagecoaches, and telegraph offices. That had all been settled five years back, however, when Houghton had been killed prior to going to prison, and Toby had taken his foster parents' name as his own. Gage, arriving in town about six months later, had done the legal honors himself.

Now, probably to deflect the topic of conversation from his own penchant for the company of pretty Emma Hargreaves, Toby turned a grin on Gage. It wouldn't work as well on him or Jacob as it did with June-bug, but he had to give the kid credit for the attempt.

"Well," Toby demanded cheerfully, "did you sweet-talk the newspaper lady, tell her you were sorry about her brother dyin' and all?"

It was beginning to dawn on Gage that he had indeed been too hasty in approaching Miss Barnes about the newspaper. He and Michael had not been friends, precisely, but he had served as Barnes's attorney, being the only one in town. As the executor of his will, he understood the state of the family's finances only too well, and he had hoped to ease the burden by purchasing the struggling business at a fair price. Apparently, though, if Toby had heard about Gage's plans, the matter must be the subject of considerable talk around Springwater.

"I guess I could have given her a bit more time to get her bearings," he admitted. *Had* he offered Miss Barnes his condolences? He didn't rightly remember, given that she'd had an effect on him similar to being butted in the belly by a ram. He might well have committed such an oversight and, worse still, he'd offered to take her infant nieces off her hands as though they were a pair of secondhand buggy wheels. As though she were incompetent to raise them.

He groaned out loud. No wonder she hadn't taken a shine to him.

"What did I say?" Toby asked in an aggrieved manner, looking from Gage to June-bug to Jacob.

"My boy," Jacob replied sagely, "you see before

you a man who has just seen the error of his ways."
While he imparted this wisdom, he buttered another biscuit.

Jessica would not have slept at all that second night in Springwater, except that she was utterly spent. When she awoke in the chilly light of a winter morning, feeling rested, it was to a chorus of squalling babies.

After bracing herself, she got out of bed and set her bare feet on the icy floor. Jupiter and Zeus, she thought, if she was this cold, then those poor children must be nearly frozen to death.

She hurried to the large cradle, which was situated at the foot of the bed Michael and Victoria had shared in what was now her room, and peered anxiously down at the pair of squirming, shrieking bundles tucked and swaddled in their blankets.

Both infants were fair, with wide, cornflower-blue eyes. The one at the far end of the cradle was Mary Catherine, Jessica decided, which meant that the other must be Eleanor Lorraine. Or was it the other way around?

The babies began to scream in earnest, and at an ever-rising pitch. The tiny blue veins showed at their temples, and their round faces were bright red. Desperately Jessica grabbed up one furious niece in each arm and bounced them fitfully on her hips. "Hush, now," she pleaded, as though they were amenable to reason. "Hush."

Alma appeared at last in the doorway, just cinching the belt of her wrapper. "What a ruckus," she said with a pleased smile.

"What do they want?" Jessica asked reasonably.

Alma shook her head a couple of times, with an accompanying *tsk-tsk* sound, then came briskly over and commandeered one of the infants. "Why, they're hungry, the little rascals, and no doubt you could wring out their knickers like a dishrag."

Jessica only grew more unnerved. She had changed diapers before—yesterday, as a matter of fact—but she was temporarily stymied by the intricacies of feeding these small and wretchedly unhappy creatures.

"There's a bit of milk left," Alma said. "I've got it in a crock outside the kitchen window, but you can be sure it won't be enough to satisfy Mary Catherine and Eleanor. They have hearty appetites, little pioneers that they are."

Hearty lungs, too, Jessica thought, with a mixture of frustration and pride. Helplessly, she bounced the remaining twin—whoever it was—in a vain effort to lend comfort. "What are we going to do?"

"I," said Alma, "am going to put dry diapers on these babies and then give them what's left of the milk. You, meanwhile, had better get yourself dressed and see if you can't borrow a bucketful from the McCaffreys. They keep a cow, you know, since they have to feed all those people who pass through on the stage."

Jessica laid the infant on the bed—as far as she could tell, neither of the twins had taken a breath since they'd commenced to raising the roof—and groped her way somewhat awkwardly into yesterday's clothes. She had not as yet had a chance to unpack her trunks, let alone launder her well-worn travel garments. "Borrow from the McCaffreys? I was sure I saw a general store—"

Alma sniffed. "You did, but That Woman who runs the place is no better than she should be, if you know what I mean. Essie Farham says That Woman's set her cap for Essie's own husband."

Jessica sighed. She meant to reserve judgment where That Woman was concerned, since she'd almost certainly been accused of such indiscretions herself after she fled the Covington house in disgrace, and wrongfully so.

For the moment, however, it seemed easier to comply with Alma's wishes and approach the McCaffreys for help. Michael had said, many times, that God never put a kinder pair of souls on this earth than those two.

Matters at hand were far too pressing to allow for further reflection. Hastily Jessica pinned up her hair, splashed her face with water cold enough to sting, donned her blue woolen cloak, and went out, making her way cautiously down the ice-covered stairs to the sidewalk.

The snow had stopped, and the sun was shining brightly, but the wind was bitterly cold and it was hard going, trudging through the drifts that hid the road from view.

Jessica paused, looking one way and then the other. The Springwater station, if she remembered correctly, was beyond the Brimstone Saloon and the doctor's office, at the far end of the road. She had arrived there by coach—could it have been just the day before?—but so much had happened since then. She'd expected to be greeted by Michael, all too recently widowed; instead, she'd been met by one Jacob McCaffrey, who had told her quietly that her brother was gone, that they'd buried him just a week before, beside his young wife.

She supposed she'd gone into a state of shock then—she didn't remember being escorted to the humble quarters over the *Gazette*, where Alma had been doing her best to care for two orphaned infants who seemed somehow to know that they'd been left behind.

Like Michael and I, she thought, as she marched through the deep snow. She didn't often think about her childhood, but the memories had a tendency to creep in when her guard was down. She didn't remember her mother or her father—she'd been so young when they died—but on rainy days, when they were both small, Michael had told her long and complicated stories about them. Even then she'd known they were mostly made up, those tales, but they'd been a great comfort all the same.

Samuel Barnes, their uncle and guardian, had run a small newspaper, and he'd expected Michael to follow in his footsteps and take over the business when the time came. Instead, Michael had decided to head west, and a breach had opened between the two men that was never to be mended. Uncle Samuel had died of a heart ailment only a month after Michael's departure.

Jessica peered through the snowy dazzle; best she keep her mind on fetching milk for the twins. The station was in sight now, and even though the sun was shining fit to blind a person, there were still lamps glowing in some of the windows.

Jessica was careful not to glance toward the churchyard and Michael's grave. In the frigid, blue-gold light of that mid-January moment, the loss seemed even greater than the day before, when she'd stood beside his marker, the pain even more ferocious.

She lifted her chin, and each breath she drew burned her nostrils, throat, and lungs like an inhalation of dry fire. She would not give up the babies, no matter what—but perhaps she had been too quick to turn down Mr. Calloway's offer to buy the newspaper. With the proceeds of the sale, she could have set up a modest household, telling people she was a widow, and would have made a proper home for the children.

Jessica sighed. If she'd had only herself to think about, she would have gone to Denver or San Francisco and found herself another position as a companion, for she was well-qualified and had a fine letter of recommendation from the late Mrs. Covington, despite the problems with that woman's son. Finding work with infant twins in tow, however, was quite another matter.

She'd learned, to her sorrow, that people often favored gossip over truth, and even if she'd been able to find employers who would accept the babies, too, there would inevitably be speculation, whatever her story. Better just to stay in Springwater, where folks knew what had happened, and might be expected to look kindly on a young woman trying to keep what remained of her family together.

Before she'd reached the steps of the station's narrow porch, the door swung open and a smiling woman appeared in the chasm. The scents of fresh coffee, bacon, and burning firewood wafted out to beckon Jessica inside, and her stomach rumbled audibly.

"You must be June-bug," she said, attempting to respond with a smile that kept slipping off her lips.

"I am at that," June-bug replied. "And you would be Miss Jessica Barnes of St. Louis, Missouri. Come on in and set a spell. I could do with a good visit. Rachel's so busy these days, with all those young'uns, and Savannah helps her husband most days. He's the doc, you know. Miranda lives way out of town, and so does Evangeline, and I get right lonesome for female company."

Jessica longed to accept the invitation, and she was eager to hear more about each of the women Mrs. McCaffrey had mentioned, but she had her hungry nieces to think about. Indeed, she'd have little time for visiting, most likely, between them and the newspaper, before the twins grew up and got married.

"I've come to buy milk," she blurted. "The babies are screaming like banshees."

That announcement was enough to set all the wheels and cogs of Springwater station in motion. Toby and Jacob, June-bug informed her, had ridden out to meet the stagecoach, since it was overdue, and she had her hands full with the baking, but that didn't mean they couldn't help a neighbor, no sir.

Before she knew precisely what had happened, Jessica found herself leading a borrowed cow down the middle of Center Street.

Alma stood pop-eyed on the wooden sidewalk while the babies' wails of discontent spilled down the stairs like stones toppled from a bucket. "Why," she gasped, as fresh snowflakes began to fall, "it's a *cow*."

Jessica gazed forlornly back at the beast, which was now bawling as piteously as the babies. Between that and those unceasing shrieks from upstairs, Jessica was hard put to keep from dropping the lead rope and pressing both hands to her ears. Instead, she squared her shoulders and asked, "Have you any idea how to milk this creature?"

Alma's mouth twitched—she was a rancher's wife, after all—but she laid one hand to her bosom in the profoundest alarm. "My, no!" she cried, and even though Jessica knew it was a lie, there wasn't much she could do. Alma was, in fact, gazing past Jessica and the cow, toward the telegraph office across the street.

"Well," replied Jessica, after a distracted glance in that direction, in which she glimpsed a shadow at the window, "we'd best reason it out, hadn't we?" She walked around the animal's steaming, twitching bulk. "Do fetch me a bucket," she said, in a tone that sounded as decisive as it was false. "And then go inside and shut the door before those poor children catch their deaths!" She was sorry for this thoughtless reference the moment she'd uttered it; certainly, death was not a subject to be spoken of lightly.

Alma nodded resolutely, and hurried back inside. Shortly she appeared with the bucket that had contained their drinking water.

Jessica thanked her without conviction, holding the empty pail in both arms while she pondered the bovine dilemma. She heard the door close behind Alma, heard through it the continuing angry complaints of the twins. She did not notice that she had drawn an audience—early revelers from the saloon—until she'd seated herself somewhat awkwardly on the high edge of the sidewalk and set the bucket beneath the cow's swollen udder.

Tentatively she reached out, gripped a wrinkled teat, and just as quickly withdrew. This raised raucous howls of delight from the seedy spectators.

Jessica stood up, hands resting on her hips, and glowered at the men over the cow's shuddering back. "If there was a gentleman among you," she said forcefully, "he would offer to help!"

"We herd cows, ma'am," one of the wasters called back. "We don't milk 'em." Another round of merriment followed, as though the man had said something uproariously funny.

"Idiots," Jessica murmured.

It was then that the door of the telegraph office opened behind the little crowd of drovers, and Mr. Calloway pushed his way through, albeit good-naturedly. He was dressed in a most dapper fashion, considering that this was early morning in a frontier town, and he grinned at Jessica just as if they'd gotten off to an auspicious beginning. Tugging at the brim of his fancy black hat, he crossed the road to face her over the broad expanse of the McCaffrey milk cow. "Allow me, ma'am," he said, and came around to take up Jessica's former seat on the plank walkway.

"Thank you," Jessica said, though stiffly. She wasn't sure what to make of Mr. Calloway and his admittedly chivalrous gesture, not after all Michael had written about him, both in his letters and in the *Gazette*. She did not often revise her opinions once they were set, but in the case of this man it seemed an exception might be called for—however temporary it might be.

The milk began to squirt noisily into the bucket, foaming and warmly fragrant, and Jessica wanted to weep, she was so relieved. She merely sniffled, as it happened, watching the milking process carefully for future reference. The cowboys, evidently bored, mounted their horses and rode off, spoiling the pristine ribbon of snow that was Center Street.

All around, the town began to come to life—the general store was opened for business, and the bell in the tower of the little brick schoolhouse—a recent addition to the town, according to Michael's letters—began to chime. A wagon made its way past, driven by a smiling man with his collar pulled up around his neck. The woman at his side smiled, too, and waved as the rig paused. Two gangly, red-haired boys, tall as men, leaped out of the wagon bed and immediately began pelting each other with hastily constructed snowballs.

"Mornin', Gage," the man called affably, showing no apparent surprise to see his friend milking a cow in the center of town. He ignored the boys, clearly used to their rough-and-tumble ways.

"Landry," Gage called back in greeting, as the other man got down and lifted a smaller boy from the seat. Until then, the child had been hidden between the two adults. He was a chubby little bundle, with red cheeks and fair curly hair peeking out from beneath his stocking cap. "Hello, Miranda. That you, Isaiah? Lord, you've gotten so big, I hardly recognized you."

The child beamed in response to Gage's remark. Isaiah. Such a big name, Jessica thought fondly, for such a little boy.

The woman waved, but her gaze was fixed on Jessica now, betraying an intense but not unfriendly curiosity. *Miranda*. Hadn't June-bug mentioned her, just that morning, when she had gone to the station for milk?

Still broken inside over the loss of her brother, but equally determined not to make a public display of her sorrow, Jessica summoned up what she hoped was a polite expression and waggled the fingers of her right hand in reply to the other woman's greeting.

Miranda's husband hiked Isaiah up onto his sturdy shoulders with an exaggerated grunt of effort, and started toward the school, whistling happily. Miranda turned on the seat and Jessica saw that she was not only holding a blanketed bundle that must surely have contained a small child, she was hugely pregnant, as well.

Jessica felt a deep and fearfully elemental stirring inside, sudden and sharp-edged, and realized with a start that it was simple envy. Why this should be, she could not fathom—she had two infant nieces to raise, albeit without the help of a husband, and no need of more responsibility. And yet, for the first time in a long while, she let herself feel the old longing for a home, a mate, a family of her own.

Watching Mr. Covington in action had caused her to vow never to leave herself open to the sort of pain and humiliation so many women suffered at the hands of their men, but seeing such happiness as Landry and Miranda enjoyed made her want to start over, with all new thoughts and beliefs and attitudes.

"We are really sorry about Michael and Victoria," Miranda said, holding the bundle close against her and draping the edge of her cloak over it. "They were nice folks."

Jessica's gaze strayed involuntarily in the direction of the churchyard, where Michael and his pretty bride were buried, side by side, beneath rocks and dirt and drifts of glittering snow. "Thank you," she said, though she wasn't sure she'd spoken loudly enough for Miranda to hear.

Gage went on milking, humming happily to himself, his hat pushed to the back of his head. The milk made sweet steam in the cold, crisp air.

Chattering children began to converge on the

schoolhouse from every direction—the big house down the road, just across the way from the stagecoach station, the row of more modest places beyond the church, the surrounding countryside. The man Gage called Landry—whether that was his first name or his last Jessica could not guess—came out of the school without the little boy and crossed the street to slap the McCaffrey cow affectionately on one flank. Up close, Jessica could see that he was very goodlooking, with a mischievous curve to his mouth. His hazel eyes sobered, though, as he regarded her.

"That was a shame, your brother and sister-in-law passing on the way they did. We're real sorry, and if there's anything you need, you just speak up. Folks around Springwater surely do like to be helpful whenever they can."

"Thank you," Jessica murmured, head bowed.

Gage had finished his task at last; he rose and handed the bucket to Jessica. She hoped he could see her gratitude in her eyes, for she was incapable of speaking. Her losses were still so fresh that any reference to them threatened her composure. She did, however, manage a nod.

Mr. Calloway spoke with a gentleness that was quite nearly her undoing. "I'll see that Tilly here gets back to her stall down at the station. You'd best tend to those hungry babies."

Jessica nodded again and fled.

CHAPTER

3

CLASPING THE BUCKET handle with the bare and cold-stiffened fingers of both hands, Jessica turned and hurried toward the relative solace of the upstairs apartments. The babies, all cried out, had settled into sorrowful hiccups, while Alma sat in the chair by the window, rocking them both with a sort of wry desperation. "I gave them what milk there was, and they howled for more," she said.

"Here," Jessica said, indicating the heavy bucket she carried. "We can give them all they want."

When the milk had been strained through a clean dishtowel—it barely required heating, being still warm from the cow—Jessica refilled the two glass bottles and settled down to feeding Mary Catherine, while Alma did the same with little Eleanor.

Or was it the other way around? No matter. Jessica's life as a mother had well and truly begun, and while she was overwhelmed, the fact was not without its compensations. As she held that baby, a certain special warmth stole into her heart and set up residence forever; in that odd, transcendent instant, both children became her own, as surely as if she'd carried them in her womb.

She began to weep, making no sound at all, and Alma, without a word, laid little Eleanor, bottle and all, in the crook of Jessica's right arm, that she might hold them both. From that moment on, there was never any question: Jessica would do virtually anything for those babies.

Jacob extended one time- and work-gnarled hand to accept the lead rope when Gage brought home the cow. A grin flickered in the old man's dark eyes. "I hear you've taken to doin' the milkin' of a mornin', Gage," he said in his unmistakable baritone. "I reckon June-bug should've figured Miss Barnes didn't know how to manage a chore like that and sent Trey or somebody on over there. Toby and I went out to meet the stage."

Gage chuckled and rubbed his chin—his beard was coming in and he'd forgotten to shave that morning, for thinking about Jessica Barnes and what ought to be done about her. He'd watched her slowly trudging down the road toward the station, and seen her return soon after leading the cow. He'd enjoyed watching her futile efforts for a while, but in the end simple chivalry—not to mention the fact that he could hear those children hollering with hunger from all the way across the street—had forced him to go out and help. "You suppose she knows any more about running a newspaper than she does about milking a cow?"

Jacob led old Tilly into the barn, which was redolent with the singular and not unpleasant smells of animals and hay, and secured her in a stall, where grain and fresh water awaited. As usual, he took his time answering. " 'Bout as much as you do, I guess," he observed dryly, and at some length. There was just the hint of a sparkle in his eyes.

Gage took off his hat and swept one hand through his hair. No point in bragging that he'd been raised in a press room; it didn't have any bearing on the conversation anyhow. "Maybe that's so," he allowed, with a testy edge to his voice, "but there's one thing you're forgetting: she's a woman."

Jacob gave a low whistle of exclamation and ambled toward the barn door, rummaging for tobacco and a pipe as he went. June-bug did not permit the use of such inside the station, for she believed smoking to be an unhealthy and despicable habit.

"If I was you," Jacob said, taking up where the whistle had left off, "I'd be careful about sayin' things like that. We've got some spirited women in these parts—I can think of five or six that would skin you and nail up your hide just for talking that way."

Gage let the remark pass unchallenged; after all, it was true. Springwater was indeed populated by a lot of strong-minded females, and as far as he could see, Jessica Barnes would fit in just fine. He wondered what lucky and accursed man would be the one to rope her in—probably some farmer, who'd have her milking cows like an expert in no time at all.

For some reason, he found the idea distasteful. Some women weren't meant for such chores, and the prissy, stiff-necked Miss Barnes was surely one of them.

"You gonna tell her?" Jacob prodded, drawing on his pipe. A wreath of smoke rose like a halo over his head.

Gage was beginning to feel a mite short-tempered, despite the cheerful mood he'd enjoyed earlier. "Tell her what?" he shot back, though he damn well knew the answer. Michael Barnes had owed him money—a sizable amount, as it happened—and he'd put up the newspaper for collateral. Offering to buy the place was an outright act of charity, given that he could have claimed it, with the full blessing of the law, at any time. Somehow, looking in Jessica Barnes's eyes, he just hadn't been able to get the words out.

Jacob shrugged those bull-brawny shoulders of his, and snow settled like shimmering feathers on his dark hair. "It's your money," he said, and walked away toward the station house, still puffing on his pipe.

Disgruntled, Gage took himself back to his office. He shared the chilly, cramped space with C.W. Brody, the Western Union man, who lived upstairs. A widower in his late forties, C.W. was tapping industriously at the telegraph key when Gage stepped inside to hang up his hat for the second time that morning. He kept his coat on, however, and crossed the room to stuff a few chunks of wood into the potbellied stove.

Rubbing his palms together in an attempt to get his bloodstream flowing again, he took to wondering if Jessica and Miss Alma and those two little babies were warm enough.

Landry and Jacob and Trey Hargreaves had laid in a cord or two of seasoned pine and birch logs back when Barnes had taken sick, but they'd left the task of splitting and stacking for later, having plenty of work of their own to do, and had never gotten back to it.

C.W. stopped his clicking and cleared his throat. "Here I thought you was nothin' but a fancy city boy," he said with amusement. "Turns out you're a hand with a milk cow and not too proud to show it."

Gage tightened his jaw for a moment and glanced at the large wooden clock affixed to the far wall. His first clients of the day, the Parrishes, were due in fifteen minutes. After he'd seen them and broken the news about the babies and all, he'd go over and chop some of that wood piled behind the newspaper office. It wasn't that he wanted to see Miss Barnes again, he assured himself, though he had to admit just looking at her face made him feel like he was walking a tightwire a hundred feet above the ground. No, it was his civic duty to chop that wood, and that was all there was to it.

He poured a mug full of coffee from the enamel pot on the stove and took a thoughtful sip before deciding he'd let C.W.'s comment dangle long enough. "Even rich people keep cows," he allowed, a little sharply, before heading into his office and closing the door firmly behind him. The truth was, he hadn't learned how to perform that particular lowly task until he got to Springwater. While his house was being constructed—the house he seldom used, because he'd built it for a woman who was never going to show up—he'd boarded at the station, and he'd helped Jacob and Toby with the daily round of chores. It was during that time that he'd developed a lasting affection for June-bug McCaffrey and her cooking.

Savannah arrived on time, though without the doc, who was probably busy stitching some cowpuncher back together, either out on the range or over at his office. He was a respected man, Prescott Parrish; he'd earned the esteem of the whole town over and over again, most recently by operating on young Christabel Johnson's twisted foot. He'd put it straight, and now she could walk as well as anyone else, thanks to him. She'd blossomed into a lovely, if somewhat shy, young woman who hoped to teach at the Springwater School one day, after attending normal school back in Pennsylvania.

"I'm sorry," Gage said, after he'd explained to Savannah that Miss Barnes meant to raise her nieces herself, despite the obvious disadvantages—such as not being married. He hoped she had money of her own, because Michael sure as hell hadn't left her any.

Savannah took the announcement well, though a certain sadness shone in her eyes. She and the doc had prospered, due to Trey Hargreaves giving them shares in his silver mine early on, in partial payment for Savannah's half of the Brimstone Saloon. They lived across the street from Gage's empty place and had a child of their own, but they'd wanted a big family, and it was beginning to look as if that wouldn't happen.

It was an ironic situation; Pres had helped so many other people since coming to Springwater, but this was evidently beyond even him. They'd built that big white house of theirs two years back, expecting to need the room, but now there were just the three of them rattling around the place like beans in a barrel. Sometimes the Johnson girl stayed with them, to help with the little one and the washing and cooking and such, but of course that wasn't the same thing as having a houseful of kids.

"I'm not surprised," Savannah said, after pondering Jessica's decision in silence for a few moments. "I'd do the same thing in her place. I guess I was hoping she'd turn out to be another sort of woman."

Gage settled back in his creaky office chair, tenting his fingers beneath his chin. "Oh?" he prompted.

Savannah offered a shaky smile. "Victoria told me she was a spinster—a companion or a governess or something like that, that she'd traveled. That she was used to city life and to living in big houses, whether they were her own or not. It didn't sound like she was the sort to take in babies, even if they did belong to her brother."

Savannah looked so despairing just then that Gage wanted to reach across the desk and touch her hand. He didn't, though, because he knew she was fragile, and trying hard to hold up. Sympathy could only weaken her.

He spoke gruffly. "There are plenty of orphans in this world, Savannah. I could wire a friend of mine, down in San Francisco—"

She shook her head and rose hastily to her feet, her chair scraping against the plain wooden floor. "No," she said, and tried to smile again, though she couldn't seem to manage it a second time. "No," she repeated, more calmly. "Pres is right. We've got each other, and our little Beatrice. Maybe it's just plain greedy to want anything more."

With that, she took up her cloak and rushed out of the office, leaving Gage to gaze thoughtfully after her.

He was a kind man, the doctor, dark-haired and handsome, with few words to spare and a very serious countenance. Dropping his stethoscope into a battered kit bag, he studied Jessica thoughtfully, there in the tiny parlor that stood directly over the still and silent press on which Michael had so proudly printed issue after issue of the weekly *Springwater Gazette*. "Alma's homesick for her house and her husband," he said quietly. "She'll be fine."

"And the twins?" Jessica asked. Because the doctor was there making an impromptu call on Alma, who suffered occasional palpitations, Jessica had enjoined him to examine the babies, as well, just to be on the safe side. After all, both their parents had died recently, and it was her deepest fear that they too would contract whatever malady had caused Michael's death. They were a vital part of her now, like arms and legs, and she did not know what she'd do without them.

He grinned, taking Jessica by surprise, as he'd seemed so dour before. She'd supposed his reticence was partly due to the fact that he and his wife had wished to adopt the twins as their own, but now she decided it was simply his nature to be solemn. No doubt, as a doctor, he'd seen a great deal of suffering in his time, and that would cast a shadow over anyone's spirit. "They're fine," he said. "If all my patients were as lively as that pair, I'd have to go into another line of work."

Jessica found herself liking this man, and expected to like his wife, too, for all that she'd feared them a little up until now. They were an integral part of Springwater, after all, and could surely count on the support of the community, while she was new in town, a stranger to all of them. "Won't you stay for tea?" she asked. Alma was lying down, the babies were sleeping, filled once again with milk from the McCaffreys' cow, and there was nothing at hand to distract Jessica from the facts of her life—she was alone, essentially, with two infants depending on her for everything, for Alma's husband was sure to come for her soon. The future seemed bleak in that low moment, and full of struggle.

"Can't stay," the doctor said regretfully, snapping the bag shut. "I've got half a dozen more calls to make before dark."

Jessica wrung her hands. "I wanted to ask about my

brother and—and, of course, Victoria. How it was for them. . . ."

He looked at her with a directness that she appreciated. "Victoria hemorrhaged after having the babies, and try though we might, Savannah and I couldn't stop the bleeding. She lapsed into unconsciousness and was gone within four hours." He paused, then sighed. "Michael fell over in the newspaper office one afternoon, ran a high fever that night, and died the next morning. And yes, Miss Barnes—I did everything I could to save them. Everything."

She blushed. She hadn't been going to ask, but apparently the discerning Dr. Parrish had seen the question in her eyes. "It'll be a disappointment to your wife, not to be able to adopt the babies," she said, and then wondered why she'd spoken of the matter at all. The decision had been made, and would be abided by. The news didn't seem to surprise the doctor.

"Yes," he answered readily. "Savannah longs for more children, and we haven't been able to have them."

"I'm sorry."

He simply nodded. Then, with a brief word of farewell, he was gone.

Jessica stood in the center of the parlor, fighting back another swell of terrible loneliness, and it was a while before she heard the steady *thwack-thwack* coming from somewhere out back.

Moving slowly to the window, she looked down to see Gage Calloway, coatless in the thickening snow, his sleeves rolled up to reveal solid forearms, splitting firewood with powerful swings of an ax. Something about him made Jessica's heart surge up into her throat and swell there, cutting off her breath.

As if he sensed that she was there watching him, he looked up, and their eyes met. He grinned and paused long enough to wave one hand. Jessica actually felt light-headed when he did that, but she attributed the response to fatigue and grief.

With some effort, she managed to raise the sill, and leaned out through the opening. The cold bit into every pore of her body with teeth like tiny needles. "What are you doing?" she demanded. It was all bluster and bravado; she could not let herself forget that this man, though posing as her friend, had been a foe to her brother. Establishing any sort of association with him would be an outright betrayal.

"What does it look like I'm doing?" he retorted, but good-naturedly. His breath was a white cloud around his head and, dear Lord, he had finely made shoulders, narrow hips, long, muscular legs. He might have strode right down off Mt. Olympus, if it weren't for his modern clothes.

Jessica was exasperated, not only with him, but with herself. She huffed out an impatient sigh. "If you expect to ingratiate yourself to me and thus persuade me to sell the *Gazette*," she said, "you are wasting your time."

His grin faded, and he shook his head. "You are one prickly female," he said. "*Ingratiate* myself to you? Why, I'd sooner cozy up to a porcupine!"

"Why don't you?" she retorted. It was so much easier, so much safer, not to like him.

He sighed. "I'm not trying to do anything but make sure you have enough firewood to keep warm. Around Springwater, we call that being neighborly."

Stuck for an answer, Jessica drew back from the window and slammed it down hard enough to set the heavy glass to rattling. Below, Mr. Calloway went back to his wood-chopping, and it did seem to Jessica that he was wielding that ax of his with a mite more force than before.

Early the next morning the McCaffrey boy, Toby, knocked at the door with a beguiling grin and a bucket of fresh milk, strained and separated and ready to be heated for the babies' bottles. "Miss June-bug says you ought to come to the station for a visit first chance you get," he announced happily. His nose and the tops of his ears were red with cold, and his blue eyes fairly gleamed with that special exuberance that is reserved for the very young. "You're to bring the babies, too."

Jessica accepted the milk gratefully, promised to pay a call on Mrs. McCaffrey before the end of the week, and watched as Toby descended the stairs, taking two at a time. She was closing the door when Alma came out of her room; the apartment was deliciously warm, thanks to the plenitude of firewood, and the twins were still sleeping cozily in their shared cradle at the foot of Jessica's bed. There was time to warm the milk, and the soft, quiet light of the new snow trimming the windowpanes lent the place an almost festive air.

Alma went to stand before the fire, diminutive in her sturdy woolen wrapper and slippers. "My Pete will be here to fetch me soon. I reckon he's gotten word of your arrival by now."

Jessica merely nodded. She was not looking forward to caring for the babies by herself, but she would manage somehow. She was intelligent and capable, and she could learn.

"You don't seem to get on with Gage Calloway very well," Alma observed. "He's a fine man, you know."

Jessica stiffened slightly. No doubt Alma knew, as the rest of the town surely did, of the animosity between Mr. Calloway and her brother. It would not serve to point out the obvious. "He must have some fatal flaw," she remarked instead.

The other woman faced her squarely, and her expression was entirely serious. "He doesn't," she said flatly. "Comes from a fine family down in San Francisco. Folks with money and breeding. Lives in that big house across the street from Doc and Savannah's place, all by himself. People say he built it for a woman who broke his heart."

Broken heart aside—that could happen to anyone, after all—it figured that Gage came from a rich family. He was used to privilege, used to squashing people—like Michael—who got in his way. Hadn't she seen Mr. Covington and his friends do such things, over and over? Her rage was renewed, and it sustained her; in those moments it was all that kept her from sinking into a state of complete melancholy.

"And?" she prompted, knowing that Alma would go on whether she was invited to or not.

"You could do worse for yourself," Alma said bluntly. Once she finally got around to making her point, she closed right in for the kill. "Than Gage Calloway, I mean."

Jessica laid one hand to her bosom, fingers splayed. "Good heavens, Alma," she exclaimed, careful, for the babies' sakes, to keep her voice moderate. "I barely know the man." *But I know enough.* She saw by her friend's expression that she was unconvinced. "And in any case, he has not shown the first sign of wanting to court me, let alone proposed. You have taken notice of that, haven't you?"

"Bullfeathers. It's plain to see that he's taken with you. Didn't he milk the cow yesterday? Didn't he chop all that wood?"

Jessica was losing her patience. "For heaven's sake, Alma, he was merely being kind." Gage Calloway could milk cows and chop wood for a thousand years and it would never make up for what he'd done to Michael.

"Every man in this town is kind," Alma exclaimed, as the babies began, first one and then both, to lament their empty stomachs and wet diapers. "But you didn't see any of *them* over here looking for ways to be helpful, did you?"

He wants the newspaper, Jessica reminded herself, for she found that she was weakening a little under the onslaught of Alma's conviction. "Please prepare the bottles," she said as the twins raised their howling to a new pitch. "I will see to the rest."

The next hour was occupied with caring for the infants, but once they'd been burped and bathed and bundled up for another round of sleep, Jessica could no longer escape the inevitable. She put on a shawl, went downstairs, and opened the door of the newspaper office.

It was dusty inside, and bitterly cold, but the place still gave the impression that Michael had just stepped out on some brief errand. His ink-stained printer's apron hung on a peg beside the door, precisely where he'd left it. His visor lay on the desktop, along with a box of type, carefully laid out.

Jessica blinked and ran her fingertips lightly across the smooth metal letters, the last issue, surely, of the *Springwater Gazette*, as published and edited by Michael Barnes. It took a moment to make out the headline, since the type was set backwards, but when she did, she wanted to weep: CALLOWAY: THE MAN WHO WOULD BUY SPRINGWATER. She rounded the press to read the rest of the article, in which Michael maintained that citizens should not be misled by Mr. Calloway's engaging nature and seeming generosity. He was, Michael claimed, a wolf in sheep's clothing, and taking office as mayor was only the first step in a plan that would, if unchecked, take him all the way to the territorial governor's office.

Jessica frowned. Gage Calloway had political aspirations beyond Springwater. Had he tried to put

Michael out of business simply to silence him, to quell articles like this one?

She reminded herself yet again that Calloway still entertained hopes of persuading her to sell the *Gazette*, clear as she'd been in refusing. Publishing a newspaper, even in such a sparsely populated area, would give him significant influence; as a rule, people tended to believe what they read, simply because it had been set in type and printed. She must be wary, on her guard, and never let herself be taken in by his charm.

Jessica sighed. She hadn't the first glimmer of how to run that ancient press Michael had so treasured, but she had a good mind and, given time, she would figure it out. After pushing up the sleeves of her practical calico dress, she fetched some wood from the covered bin that stood out back beneath the broad eaves, and started a fire in the small stove in one corner of the room. When the frost melted from the floors and the cold receded somewhat, Jessica circled the great, cumbersome press, studying it thoughtfully.

After a while, when it seemed to her that the construction of the machine made at least a little bit of sense, she set the type box where it seemed it ought to go, inked the rollers, and turned the heavy hand crank at one side of the looming iron mechanism. The paper, housed on a great cylinder, wrinkled and then jammed the works.

Muttering, Jessica put on Michael's apron and turned the full and formidable force of her will upon the task at hand. By that time the following week, she vowed silently—and fiercely—she would put out an issue of the *Gazette*, however humble it might be.

He paused on the sidewalk, heedless of the bitter Montana wind sweeping across the range and straight down Springwater's main street, watching as Jessica labored over the recalcitrant press. She was covered in ink, smudged and splotched and shining with the stuff, and he didn't think he'd ever seen a lovelier sight in the whole of his life.

He supposed he ought to go in there and show her how to manage the simple but stubborn machine—his grandfather published one of the largest newspapers in California, after all, and he'd virtually grown up, along with his half-brother, in the midst of the enterprise, an ink monkey by association—but the plain truth was that he was scared to approach her, feeling the way he did right then. His reason, highly developed, told him she was the wrong sort of woman for him, willful and prickly; he'd fallen for that sort of woman once, and look where that had landed him. What he needed was a sweet, pliant wife, one who needed protecting.

His heart, on the other hand, had a different opinion entirely.

He stood there for a time, torn between courage and cowardice, hope and fear, and then moved on. Reason had prevailed over more tender sentiments, but he couldn't exactly have said he was relieved, and a part of him, some reckless, rebellious portion of his spirit, stayed behind, with Jessica Barnes.

* * *

It was getting dark when Jessica finally gave up her efforts to produce one coherent page of copy—for the time being, at least—and dragged herself upstairs. Alma, bless her heart, had a simple supper of eggs and toasted bread at the ready, and the babies were sleeping soundly, blissful in their innocence. It was fortunate, Jessica thought, that they couldn't know they were at the mercy of a spinster aunt with nothing to offer them save a pile of crumpled newsprint.

"Look at you," Alma said with a little laugh as she steered Jessica to the table and set a plate in front of her. "Why, a body would hardly recognize you, under all that ink!"

It required a supreme effort just to lift her fork; Jessica simply wasn't up to idle conversation.

"What you need," Alma went on cheerfully, "is a nice hot bath. Wouldn't that be a fine thing?"

Jessica wanted to weep at the mere prospect. When had she last enjoyed such a luxury? Not since she'd left the Covington mansion in St. Louis, certainly, where she'd shared a bathroom with several of the maids.

She contrived to nod once, in order to let Alma know she'd heard, then swallowed an exhausted sob along with a bite of warm, buttered bread.

Alma was bustling about with sudden and rather alarming resolve. "Nothing like a good, hot bath to restore body and soul. Yes, siree. I'd like to go back home knowing you're strong and hearty, and well able to look after these babies."

Jessica tried to protest—Alma was not young, however energetic she might be feeling at the moment, and the setting out of a tub, the fetching and heating of water, were hard and heavy tasks.

For all of that, nothing would sway Alma from her quest, and by the time Jessica had finished her supper and washed her plate, fork, and knife, the older woman had dragged a round copper tub from the pantry to the hearth in the parlor, where a lively fire blazed. After emptying the stove reservoir and the two buckets of drinking water to serve her purpose, Alma finally ran down. Jessica, somewhat revived by the meal, took over for her, carrying steaming kettles to the tub.

At last, the bath was ready. A towel had been found, and a bar of lilac-scented soap that had been Victoria's. Jessica dimmed the last lamp to a faint flicker, undressed, and stepped into the tub, lowering herself into the water with a sigh of contentment. In that lulling, suspended state, the days ahead did not seem so overwhelmingly difficult as before. She knew, in those moments and thereafter, that even if she did not succeed brilliantly, she could at least *manage*. She could and would make a good and happy life for herself and her nieces, and devil take the plain fact that she wasn't sure how to go about any of it.

She would face down Michael's enemy and prevail. Her brother would, she thought, as she drifted off into a brief, sweet sleep, have been very proud of her.

Emma Hargreaves presented herself at the door of the *Gazette*'s humble office the next day, right after school let out. She was a beautiful girl, fifteen or sixteen, Jessica supposed, and the lively agility of her mind showed in her dark eyes and in each of the myriad expressions that played upon her face.

"I've come to help you print the newspaper," the girl announced, removing her cloak and hanging it carefully beside Michael's printer's apron. Apparently, it had not crossed her mind that her offer might be refused.

Jessica saw no reason to delay the inevitable, but she took care to speak gently, for she liked Emma already and did not wish to discourage her. "I'm sorry," she said. "I'm afraid I can't afford to hire help just now."

Emma beamed, unfazed. "Oh, you needn't pay me," she said happily. "My pa has shares in a silver mine, the Jupiter and Zeus, so I don't need money. I just want to write stories and work the machine and all like that."

It took Jessica a moment to assimilate the implications of such an offer. The girl could hardly be more inept than she herself—perhaps between them, they might actually print the news, sell advertising, and get the business to turning a profit.

Emma did not wait for a reply—indeed, she was bent over, peering into the mechanism attached to the paper rollers. Jessica had still not mastered this demon's device.

"I think this is stuck, this tiny part here," the girl mused, poking a finger into the small but baffling system of gears. There was a metallic *click* and Emma straightened, smiling broadly again. "It ought to be fine now. May I work the lever?"

Jessica gestured for her to go ahead, feeling skeptical and hopeful and a little indignant, all of a piece.

There was a shrill, grinding sound, and then the roller began to turn and the page of type Michael himself had set was impressed upon a wide sheet of paper.

Jessica tore the page off and stared at it in delighted amazement. "How did you do that?"

Emma shrugged modestly. "I used to come by and watch Mr. Barnes print the paper whenever I could. He published one of my poems once—it was about a wolf."

Jessica put out an ink-stained hand. "You're hired," she said.

Later that week Alma's husband arrived, driving a buckboard, and collected her. She glowed with happiness at the prospect of going home, even as she wept to leave the babies.

"Why, they might be grown women before I see them again," she sniffled, settling into the wagon box.

"Now, Alma, don't take on," Pete scolded fondly. He was a big, rugged man, probably handsome in his youth, and he clearly loved his wife.

"I'll bring them to see you," Jessica vowed in a rash moment, having no earthly idea what such a trip might involve. "I swear I will."

Alma took her at her word and, as quickly as that, she was gone, rattling away toward home.

Unable to face being alone just then, Jessica put on her best afternoon dress, did up her hair, and proceeded to pay the promised call on June-bug McCaffrey, at the Springwater station. It was quite an enterprise, given that she was taking the twins along with her. They made two great, bulky bundles in her arms as she high-stepped her way through the hard-crusted, glittering snow.

The other woman greeted her with a cry of delight, immediately claiming one of the babies for herself. "Why, just look at this precious little smidgen!" she beamed. "And here's her sister. I declare, in twenty years' time, they'll have broken every heart in Springwater."

Warmed by June-bug's cheerful reception, Jessica smiled. Perhaps she might fit in here after all, one day. She'd just have to stay out of Gage Calloway's way as much as possible.

June-bug bustled to make beds for the babies by stuffing blankets into wooden freight boxes and gently setting the children inside. They cooed happily, as though they too felt welcome at the Springwater station.

"Sit down and I'll make you some tea," June-bug commanded, while Jessica stood awkwardly in the middle of the room, unsure of what to do next. She'd been one step above a servant for all her adult life, and she wasn't sure how to go about being entertained. "Did Alma get on toward home?"

"She's gone," Jessica said, a little forlornly, and took a seat in one of the chairs near the fireplace.

June-bug merely nodded, busy at the stove with the teakettle, and went right on chatting. "Jacob says the pond down by the spring is froze over solid. There'll be a bonfire there tomorrow night, and skating, too. I hope you'll bundle up these dear little babies and come join the fun."

Jessica did not point out that she was, for all practical intents and purposes, in mourning. Perhaps it was due, at least in part, to the fact that she knew Michael would not approve of such withdrawal. She'd known all along that he would have wanted his life to be remembered and celebrated, not the single day and hour of his death.

"I haven't any skates," she said, at a loss for other conversation.

June-bug, still busy at the stove, was undaunted. "I do believe Victoria owned a pair." Her lovely, vibrant face darkened, if only for a moment, when she looked back at Jessica over one shoulder. "Poor girl. She was never very hearty, but Lord knows, she tried."

Jessica frowned a little, puzzled. "Tried?" she echoed.

June-bug gave a weighty sigh. "To please Michael, I mean," she said, frowning reflectively. "Her heart wasn't really in it, though. Livin' way out here, I mean, amongst plain folks. Not that she was unfriendly, or high-nosed, or anything like that. She just didn't seem to like it here much."

Jessica had known her sister-in-law only slightly, prior to her marriage to Michael. She'd been bookish, sweet. Shy and delicate, too. Victoria had begged

Michael not to go west to seek his fortune, adding her voice to Uncle Samuel's, and maybe she'd been right. If they'd stayed at home in St. Louis, if Michael had joined the family business, both of them might be alive today.

If. Jessica shook herself inwardly. Fruitless speculation, that was. What was done was done—Michael and his bride were gone, forever. It was up to her to pick up the fragments and move forward into the future, however uncertain it might be. Part of doing that was joining in community activities—like the skating party.

"Was my brother happy?" she asked, as June-bug set a tray on the small, sturdy table between the two chairs facing the fire, sat down across from Jessica, and began to pour tea. "In his last days, I mean?"

June-bug reached out to pat her arm. "Why, sure he was," she replied with reassuring confidence. "Up until poor little Victoria passed on, that is. Losin' her took a lot out of him, but that's natural. He got to workin' at all hours of the day and night, but he loved those babies of his, and the newspaper, too. Oh, he had high hopes for the *Gazette*, and that's a fact."

Jessica sipped her tea and reflected silently upon her brother's lost dreams.

"You'll make a fine mother to these children, you know," June-bug said in a quiet voice, laying a hand to Jessica's shoulder. "You just wait and see."

CHAPTER

4

Poor as she and Michael had been, Victoria had indeed owned a pair of ice skates; probably she had brought them with her on the journey west to Montana Territory. Jessica found them hidden away in the bottom of a trunk, their blades dull and rusted, amongst a sad collection of small mementos—dried flowers from her wedding bouquet; a few letters, the paper thin as a spill of light on glass, tucked into yellow-edged envelopes; and various small baubles.

Just the sight of those simple, unassuming things, so obviously treasured, filled Jessica with guilt. She had grieved so much over Michael that she had almost forgotten to mourn Victoria, a young woman who would never watch her own babies grow, or hear them laugh, would never see another spring . . .

Jessica took a deep breath and guided her mind in another direction. Holding the skates close against her chest, she remembered her girlhood, when she and Michael and a crowd of friends had spent winter afternoons skating on a pond not far from their uncle's house. Those had been some of the happiest times of her life; she'd felt free while skating, exhilarated by her own smooth velocity and the brisk caress of the wind.

Soon enough, though, her thoughts turned back to Victoria, robbed of so much. *Rest easy,* she told her sister-in-law, in the silence of her heart. *I'll look after Mary Catherine and Eleanor as long as they need me. I promise you that much.*

The babies were lying on the bed behind her, cooing and kicking, content because they'd just been fed and changed. Looking at them, their lost mother's skates in her hands, Jessica felt a surge of joy so poignant that it was all she could do not to grab up her nieces and hug them with all her might.

June-bug was right; they were precious. Treasures for whom she would go anywhere, do anything.

"I love you," she said to them. And they gurgled happily in response.

The skates might have been made for Jessica, they fit so well, but she was sorely out of practice. She stood, teetering, and flung out her arms for balance, like a high-wire artist performing in a circus. She looked at the babies, who were watching her with expressions of drunken wonder, each exactly matched to the other, although the twins were not identical.

"Suppose I fall through the ice and catch pneumonia and the pair of you are all alone in the world?" she asked.

It wouldn't work as an excuse to stay home from the skating party; even if she did meet with such a dire and dramatic fate, the Parrishes would gladly take her nieces in and raise them with love.

"All right, then," she speculated. "It's sure to be too cold out there for a couple of brand-new babies such as yourselves. Suppose *you* get sick? Why, I simply couldn't bear it."

But the babies would not take ill, her logical side argued. June-bug had told her that careful provision was always made for infants and small children. They would be held and passed around, close by the fire. In the years they'd been holding these community celebrations, not one of the little mites had been lost.

Jessica teetered over and laid a hand to each of the twins' foreheads. Both were satiny cool.

It was settled, then; she'd join the rest of Springwater in heralding what was bound to be a bitterly cold night. She might even enjoy herself, if she could stop worrying long enough.

She removed her skates, put the babies back into their cradle, where they promptly fell asleep, exhausted by a morning spent socializing with June-bug McCaffrey, and made for the kitchen without bothering to put her shoes back on. There, she made a pot of tea.

The brew smelled lovely and rich, and she heated milk to flavor it. She felt afraid of what the future might hold, that was for sure, but there was a certain quiet joy within her, too. For the first time in her life, she was truly on her own. *She* would be the one to make the rules she abided by—not her uncle, not her employer, not even her brother, much as she'd loved him. No, she was going to be independent from here on, and, scary as that was, it made her want to spread her arms and laugh as she had done long, long ago, spinning on the skating pond until the world was a blur of color and shape.

Jacob himself had built the horse-drawn sleigh for just such nights as that one, and it was already full of fresh hay and crowded with laughing people when he drew the team to a halt in front of the newspaper office.

Gage jumped down from the flat bed of the sleigh and marveled at the jittery twitch in the pit of his stomach. Just the prospect of seeing Jessica Barnes again did that to him, and the hell of it was, the reality was bound to affect him even more. He just hoped she didn't slam the door in his face, that was all, with half of Springwater down on the street listening for any word that might pass between the two of them. Trey and Landry were already ribbing him about Miss Barnes anyway, and here he was, letting himself in for more grief.

He hesitated a moment at the foot of the stairs, then bounded up them and knocked hard on the door.

Jessica answered, of course, looking surprised and damnably beautiful, even in her plain brown woolen dress. If it hadn't been for the fact that she was holding a baby in each arm, he would probably have bolted, like some shy kid, rather than risk a rebuff from her, but the twins won him over. He just couldn't walk away from them.

"Put your cloak on," he said, taking both bundles from her with a grace that surprised him as much as it did her, and speaking rapidly, as if that could stop her from changing her mind, saying she wouldn't go. "It's cold out."

She stared at him. "I was planning to walk to the pond," she said.

"Walk? With two babies? Miss Barnes, it's a mile to the springs, and even though the cattle have worn paths through the snow in some places, it's still hard going."

She blinked. He knew she wanted to snatch the babies back and refuse to have anything at all to do with him——it wasn't hard to figure why, given the political differences he'd had with her brother——but he'd be damned if he'd return to that sleigh without her.

He gestured with his head, since his arms were full. "The whole town's waiting down there," he told her impatiently. "So you needn't fear for your virtue."

That brought a blush to her cheeks, a phenomenon he thoroughly and shamelessly enjoyed. She might be a prickly little bluestocking with an icicle for a heart, but she sure made a man want to warm her up and smooth her out.

"Very well," she said, putting on her cloak and snatching up a pair of well-used skates. "I guess I have no choice." She stepped out onto the stair landing, and winter stars caught in her eyes as she looked up at

Gage, her expression uncertain, rather than saucy. "I—perhaps we could be civil to each other—just for tonight?"

He wanted to laugh. She might as well have gone on to say that hostilities would resume in the morning, so he shouldn't let himself get too comfortable. "All right," he agreed, with hard-won solemnity. He turned and led the way down the stairs, kicking himself all the way for not coming up with something memorable to say. So much for his reputation as an orator.

He sat close to her aboard the sleigh, ostensibly because he still had charge of one of the babies—June-bug had immediately claimed the other—and was annoyed to find that his heart was beating against his rib cage like a fist. He felt light-headed, as if he were suspended somewhere between the earth and the sky, and he hoped to God it didn't mean what he thought it did.

The last time he'd felt this way, he'd made the mistake of a lifetime, a mistake that had cost him virtually everything he held dear. The sizable trust fund left to him by his maternal grandmother had been—and still was—paltry comfort, compared to the loss of his family, his dreams, and Liza.

Out of the corner of his eye he saw that Jessica's face was alight; she enjoyed the company of neighbors, if not his company in particular, and knew even then that she would find her heart's home in Springwater. In no time at all, she'd be somebody's wife, deeply cherished.

The idea left a sour scowl in its wake.

Jacob was at the reins, which lay easy in his big hands, and when he glanced back once, his Indian-dark eyes smiled on Gage and Jessica, taking them both in as one, even if his mouth stayed still.

By the time they arrived, both babies had been absorbed into a cluster of chattering, admiring women. Having his arms empty gave Gage the excuse he needed to catch hold of Jessica by her narrow little waist—she didn't weigh much more than a mail sack—and lift her down from the edge of the sleigh. She looked surprised, all right, but he didn't give her a chance to comment. He just took her arm and steered her toward the huge, waiting bonfire, built earlier by Toby and the Kildare boys.

All the while, he wondered what in hell he was doing. Jessica had made it plain that she didn't like him, and he was just asking for trouble by hanging around. He couldn't seem to help it, that was the discouraging thing. It seemed to him that history was repeating itself: he was falling in love with a woman who'd sooner watch him burn than spit to put the flames out.

"This here's Rachel Hargreaves," June-bug said, tugging at Jessica's cloak to get her attention. Jessica turned to see a small, dark-haired woman smiling at her. "Rachel, here's Jessica Barnes. Michael's sister."

There was a brief and respectful silence at the mention of Michael's name, but then, to Jessica's profound relief, the conversation continued.

"And this is Savannah Parrish," June-bug went on, indicating a beautiful woman with red-gold hair. A little girl stood beside her on minuscule skates, clutching her mother's skirts. The child was lovely, pretty as a porcelain doll, and dressed all in rich blue velvet.

This, then, was the woman who wanted to adopt little Mary Catherine and Eleanor. Jessica felt a pang, for it was clear that Mrs. Parrish cherished her own child, and would have been good to the twins, as well. "Hello," Savannah said.

Jessica nodded in response, captivated by the little girl, who displayed her father's dark coloring and her mother's exquisitely formed features.

"I'm four," the child announced.

Jessica smiled. "My goodness," she marveled.

"And I can count."

Savannah bent and kissed her daughter's dark head through her hood of white fur. "Hush, now, Beatrice," she said softly.

Other introductions were made after that, but Jessica soon lost track of who was who. There were so many faces to remember, so many names. And besides, she was almighty nervous, with Mr. Calloway staying so close by the way he was. She was conscious of him in every snippet and fragment of her being.

It was indeed a relief when they finally reached the pond, where the skating party was to take place. A gangly blond boy was already there, sweeping snow off the ice with a straw broom. The light of the fire, some fifty feet away, danced orange over the snow, and wood smoke rolled toward the dark, star-speckled sky, filling the air with a pleasant scent.

Later, Jessica could only account for that night by believing that a passing angel had cast a spell over her. She might have stepped outside the ordinary world for a little while, leaving her sorrows, her doubts, her struggles all behind.

When she sat down on a log to pull on her skates, Gage appeared and knelt before her in the snow. She knew she should refuse to let him unlace her shoes, run his hands lightly over her ankles, but she couldn't. She was in the grip of some foolish, wonderful magic, and because she was certain it would be brief, she meant to enjoy it.

They skated together, arm in arm, and Jessica even laughed. She felt a part of things—part of Springwater, part of the world and the universe. Part of a couple, however silly that idea would turn out to be, in the harsh light of a winter morning. For that night, she could pretend to be Cinderella on the arm of her prince.

Later, he brought her hot cider, and they engaged in a friendly snowball fight. There was more laughter all around, and Jessica's heart, held to the ground for so long, soared against a dark sky shimmering with stars.

Finally, in the shadow of a tree, one of the few that grew below the foothills, Gage kissed her. She thought she ought to struggle, for the sake of principle, but the plain fact was, she didn't want to. She allowed the kiss, even responded to it, and when it was over, she felt as though east and west, north and south had gotten all mixed up, out of their right places.

She took a handful of snow from a low branch and tossed it playfully into Gage's face.

He laughed, his arms still resting lightly around her waist. "What makes you such an ornery female?"

"I am *not* an ornery female."

He chuckled. "I see. What are you, then?"

She was stumped for an answer, at least for the moment. The fresh, chilly air—at least, she told herself it was that—made her breathless, and she was feeling slightly intoxicated, the way she had one Christmas Eve, on shipboard, when old Mrs. Covington had persuaded her to have a glass of wine with dinner.

She was starting to remember things, though— that this man had ordered Michael's loans called in. That he wanted the newspaper for himself, was probably only trying to sweet-talk her into selling it. The spell was fading, and she felt an inestimable sorrow, quite different from the loss of her brother and sister-in-law, sweep over her as she stepped back.

"It won't work, Mr. Calloway," she said.

He knew what she was talking about; she could see that in his face. But of course, being a lawyer, and practiced in the various ways and means of turning others to his way of thinking, he tried to keep up the pretense. "Why do you have to be so suspicious?"

"You destroyed my brother. You persuaded the bank in Choteau to call in his loans. He died because of you and others like you."

Gage stared at her. Apparently he'd thought she hadn't known, and his denial came too late. "I was Michael's friend, whether he knew it or not. One of the best he ever had."

Jessica squared her shoulders and hiked up her chin. The man was stark raving mad; surely he'd seen Michael's editorials. Surely they had exchanged heated words, Gage and her brother.

Well, now the brief idyll was over. It was time she and the babies went home, where they belonged.

CHAPTER

～ 5 ～

JESSICA WAS UP even before the twins the following morning, and after feeding and dressing the pair, she wrapped each one in a wooly blanket and then carried them downstairs, one and then the other, to the newspaper office. They rested comfortably in their separate and well-padded apple crates, which Jessica had scrounged from the shed out back specifically for that purpose. It wouldn't be easy, raising two babies and running the *Gazette* at the same time, but then, she'd never expected anything to be easy. Nor had she been disappointed, at least in that respect.

The office was so cold that a layer of hoary frost covered the floor, and the woodstove was stubborn that morning, filling the whole lower floor with smoke and setting the twins to coughing and wheezing. Half panicked, Jessica threw open the door to the street and tried to shoo the smoke outside by flapping her printer's apron.

Gage Calloway burst in, followed immediately by a

woman Jessica had met briefly at the skating party the night before. Her name was Cornucopia, and it suited her well, for she was lushly made, with her shapely figure and dark red hair, the sort men generally took to right away. She ran the general store and, despite Alma's low opinion, seemed to Jessica to be a nice person.

"Good Lord," Gage demanded, "is the place on fire?"

The babies started to wail, and Cornucopia crooned to them, making her way past Gage and Jessica. "I'll take the little darlings over to the store," she said. "They'll be perfectly safe there."

Jessica was grateful for Cornucopia's offer, but she had her hands on her hips as she looked up into Gage's face. It shamed her now, to remember that she'd let him kiss her the night before. Conversely, she wished he'd kissed her again, which only went to show that he was a bad moral influence.

"I do not need your help, Mr. Calloway," she said, suppressing a violent spasm of coughing. Cornucopia went by with one of the babies wailing in its crate, with a murmured promise to return for the other twin in a minute. "Something is wrong with the damper, that's all."

Despite her subtle effort to block his way, he went around her and bent to pick up the other apple crate and, thus, the baby inside. The little traitor immediately stopped crying.

"There, now," he said.

"Put that baby down," Jessica commanded.

Fortunately, Cornucopia returned just then and claimed little Eleanor. "I'll bring them back soon as you've got the place aired out a little," she said, and made a hasty retreat.

Gage looked at Jessica squarely. The air was clearing a little, but it still stung her nose and eyeballs. "I'm not your enemy," he said. "I wasn't your brother's enemy, either. Michael's mind took a strange turn when Victoria died—he thought everyone was against him."

Jessica was mobilized by the mention of Michael. She marched over to the worktable and grasped the page of newsprint her brother had set before his death. She stabbed at the headline with one finger, the one warning that Gage Calloway was out to buy his way straight into the territorial governor's office. "How, then, do you explain this?"

"Ah," he said. "The gospel according to St. Michael."

"Don't you dare impugn my brother's honesty!"

"Your brother was crazy with grief over his wife when he wrote those words. He was about to lose the newspaper—" His voice broke off, and she saw regret in his face.

"Because of you. Because you made the bank in Choteau call in his loans!" Tears scalded her eyes; she told herself it was because of the smoke, and not because she cared for a man and it was hopeless.

He grasped her shoulders. "Listen to me, Jessie," he said. "Michael and I had our differences, there's no denying that. But I sure as hell didn't have anything to do with the bank calling in his note. The fact is, it's in my safe right now."

She felt as though the floor had opened up, as though she were dangling over a dark precipice and would surely fall if Gage merely flexed his fingers. "*What?*"

He let her go, and she didn't fall. She just stood there, stricken to the soul. He thrust a hand through his hair and heaved a great sigh, while the cold Montana wind swept in and chilled them both.

"I hold the note on the newspaper, Jessie," he said at long last. "Legally, it's mine. Morally—well, that's another question."

This time, her knees did give out. She groped for a chair and sank into it, just in time. Gage closed the door and crossed the room to adjust the stove damper.

He owned the *Gazette.* God in heaven, she had nothing, except for a few hundred dollars tucked away in a St. Louis bank account. Once that small legacy was gone, she and the babies would be destitute.

"Why didn't you tell me? Why did you let me think—?"

"You had just lost your brother. You were in no condition to hear news like that."

"But you were going to buy something that was already yours. Or were you offering me charity, Mr. Calloway?"

He drew up another chair, with a scraping sound, and sat astride of it, facing her, his arms resting on the high back. His eyes, far from pitying, were snapping with annoyance. "You've got the same kind of stiff-necked pride your brother had," he said evenly. "He couldn't accept help, either. I was his friend, and I believed in him." He paused, sighed. "Michael wanted to be a part of Springwater, but at the same time he held himself apart, just like you're trying to do."

While what he was saying had a certain ring of truth, it was entirely beside the point, as far as Jessica was concerned. "I do not need your charity."

"Oh, no? Where do you intend to go?"

She was stymied, but only briefly. "I can find work someplace."

"With two babies tagging along? I doubt it."

"What do you propose?"

"That you get married."

"Oh, that's a wonderful solution," Jessica raged. "To whom?"

"To me."

She couldn't believe it—couldn't believe, either, the fiery sensation the suggestion sparked in the deepest regions of her femininity. "You . . . are . . . amazing. Stubborn. *Insane.*" And, for all of it, so damnably appealing.

His face did not soften. She was seeing another side of him now, the ruthless, unbending side that Michael had probably known all too well. "What other choice do you have?"

He'd probably said those same words to her brother. God, what fury he stirred in her—how he intrigued and confused her! And oh how desperately she wished things could be different between them.

"Very well," she heard herself say, from somewhere in that storm of conflicting emotions. "I'll marry you—I have no real choice, do I? But I promise you, Mr. Calloway, that I shall make your life utterly miserable!"

He laughed—actually laughed. "Fair enough," he said. "The nights will compensate more than adequately, I'm sure."

Her mouth fell open. He reached out and closed it by pressing one finger under her chin.

"You expect me to . . . to share your bed?"

"As my wife? Most certainly."

"Then I won't marry you. I'll—I'll—"

"What?" he taunted, but not unkindly. He sounded genuinely curious, damn his hide. "What will you do?"

She bit her lower lip. As an unmarried woman—and a poor one at that—with no family to turn to, her options were severely limited. Furthermore, she had no other offers in hand, and none on the horizon, either. The men of Springwater, it seemed to her, were all married. Even Mr. Brody was courting a woman in Seattle, by telegram, according to Alma.

"I don't love you," she said. Unfortunately, she wasn't at all sure that was true, but she wasn't about to leave herself open to still more trouble by saying so.

He arched an eyebrow. "I don't love you, either."

"Wouldn't it be better if we—if I went on living here, while you lived in your house—just until we get to know each other a little better?"

He immediately shook his head. "I've sold the

house," he said. "Some woman back East bought it. She's on her way here right now." He lifted his gaze briefly to the ceiling. "Looks as though we'll have to share the upstairs, just till we've got a place of our own."

She was, for a long moment, tongue-tied. He'd made a case, all right, one she was finding it hard to argue with. Aside from throwing herself and the babies on the mercy of the McCaffreys or one of the other families in Springwater—and she was far too proud to do that—she had no respectable alternatives. She'd heard of women in just such a position becoming prostitutes, and it seemed to her that if she was going to sell herself, she might as well confine her favors to one man. He was not entirely unattractive, after all.

"All right," she said, looking down at her knotted hands. *Forgive me, Michael*, she whispered in her heart. "When?"

He considered the question for a damnably long time. "No hurry," he concluded finally, and got up from his chair. "I'll let you know."

I'll let you know. He meant to leave her wondering, the black-hearted rascal! He probably *enjoyed* seeing her wriggle on the head of a pin.

"You could do worse," Cornucopia said, echoing Alma's sentiments, when Jessica went to collect the babies an hour later. The story of Gage's "proposal," which she'd meant to keep to herself, burst out of her the moment she stepped into the general store.

Despite what Alma had said about Cornucopia keeping company with other women's husbands, Jessica liked her. "Heavens to Betsy, if Gage Calloway asked *me* to marry him, I'd be cooking his breakfast and pressing his shirts before you could say 'Here comes the bride.'"

Jessica was completely confused. "You knew, I suppose, about the feud between Mr. Calloway and my brother?"

"I wouldn't call it a feud," Cornucopia said, smiling fondly as one of the babies—Mary Catherine, as it happened—grasped her finger in a fat little baby hand. "Folks can disagree about most everything, it seems to me, and still treat each other decent." She met Jessica's eye across the counter, on which the babies reigned in their apple-crate cradles. "Sit down a spell, there by the stove. It's a cold day, bound to get colder, and you're frazzled. What you need is some hot tea and a little woman talk."

Jessica was too grateful to refuse, even though her pride dictated that she should be able to make her own way without leaning on others for support. She sat down, and enjoyed the delicious warmth emanating from the stove.

"I suppose that old lady told you I'm a man-chaser," Cornucopia said forthrightly, when she returned from what Jessica presumed were the living quarters behind the store, carrying two cups of steaming tea.

Jessica was startled out of her own self-absorption. "Well—"

Cornucopia gave Jessica one of the cups, sat down

in the other chair, and waved a hand as if to fan away a bad smell. "Fact is, there was this rancher, over Choteau way. I went to work cooking for him, and we got friendly over the course of a long winter. Trouble was, he didn't mention that he had a wife back East until she showed up one day. What a tongue that woman had! Like to strip the hide off both of us. I lit out right away, I can tell you that, but not before I made that old man give me the wherewithal to start up this store." She sighed and slurped up a mouthful of tea, then swallowed. "Turns out, the missus was a friend of Alma's. Alma never had no use for me from the first."

Astounded, Jessica stared at the other woman. "My goodness," she exclaimed, at long last, as the story unfolded in her mind's eye. She was a while digesting all the images, but when she had, she steered the conversation back onto its original path: the rift between Michael and Gage Calloway. "Why did you say you wouldn't call the animosity between my brother and Mr. Calloway a feud?"

Cornucopia shrugged her ample shoulders. She was truly voluptuous, with large breasts, perfect, glowing skin, and bright green eyes. "There toward the end, you couldn't put a lot of store by the things Michael said. Not that he was lying, mind you. But he was plum beside himself from the time Victoria died."

"He loved her very much."

Cornucopia sighed and nodded. "Yes, he did. But they weren't up to life out here, neither one of them. Some folks just aren't cut out for pioneering."

Privately, Jessica agreed, but out of respect for Michael's memory and all the dreams that had died with him, she didn't say so out loud. "What about Mr. Calloway? What would bring a man like him to a place like Springwater? He doesn't seem to be the pioneer sort, either."

Cornucopia weighed the question for a long time before answering. "From what I gather, he had some family problems back in San Francisco. That's where he hails from, you know. San Francisco. Anyways, he had some sort of falling out with the home-folks and I guess Springwater must have seemed like the other end of the earth to somebody like him. Far as I can tell, he's been happy here." A wistful look came into Cornucopia's eyes, and she fell silent for a few moments. "Lonely, though. Anybody could see that."

Jessica wondered if Cornucopia cared for Gage herself, wondered if he'd ever sought solace in the room or rooms behind the store. She discovered that she hoped not—and fervently—though it shouldn't have mattered.

Cornucopia must have read her mind, for she smiled sadly and said, "Don't you worry, Miss Barnes. I never managed to turn Gage's head even one time, though God knows, I tried. Until you came along, he was so full of whoever it was he left behind that he wouldn't have noticed if I'd stripped off all my clothes and ridden a stagecoach mule down the middle of the street at high noon."

In spite of everything, Jessica couldn't help laughing at the picture that came to her mind. At the same time, she wondered—as if she had any reason at all to care—precisely who Gage had left behind in San Francisco. He'd built that grand house across from the Parrishes' place for her, whoever she was. He probably loved her still.

Jessica put the thought out of her mind, for the moment at least. She had problems enough as it was.

She was alone in the newspaper office half an hour later, having given in to Cornucopia's pleas that she leave the babies at the store, where it was warm, when Gage appeared.

She held her breath, half afraid he'd come to drag her before a preacher, and half afraid that he hadn't. "I brought you some news," he said. "It came in over the wire just a few minutes ago. There's a train missing—one that passes within twenty miles of here. It should have come into Missoula yesterday afternoon, but there's been no sign of it."

Jessica was horrified. All thought of her own predicaments left her mind. "Have they sent a search party?"

Gage nodded, but his eyes were grim. "No luck. A few of us are going out to ride alongside the track for a ways, just in case."

Jessica glanced at the gaping door, aware for the first time that she was freezing. Hastily, she crossed the room and pushed it shut. The snow, so pretty before, was now coming down in small, slushy flakes, and she could barely see past the windows. "Isn't that dangerous? Going out in this weather, I mean? Cornucopia told me there might be a blizzard coming."

Gage shook his head. "What weather?" he countered good-naturedly. "Miss Barnes, that's just an ordinary winter day out there. When we get hit by a genuine blizzard, there'll be no question in anybody's mind what to call it."

Michael had described some of those storms in his letters, telling how men and cattle froze to death on the range, how whole families smothered in cabins buried past their chimneys in snow. She moved a little closer to the stove and made a concerted effort not to think about such calamities—which worked about as well as it ever did.

"Thank you," she said. "For the news, I mean. I'd appreciate any more details you might hear."

He nodded, already on his way to the door. He stopped, one bare hand on the knob. "Miss Barnes?"

"Yes?"

"Try not to burn down the newspaper office while we're gone. If one building goes up, we could lose the whole town, and then we'd all be in as much trouble as those poor souls aboard that missing train." With that, he was gone, giving Jessica no chance to respond. Which, she supposed, was just as well. If it hadn't been for the danger both to the men in the search party and the travelers on the lost train, she would have been relieved. He'd apparently forgotten, for the time being at least, that they were supposed to be getting married.

It was a mercy, that's what it was. So why didn't she feel relieved?

If Mr. Calloway's visit had served no other purpose,

it had at least given her something constructive to do. After washing up, Jessica put on her warm cloak and ventured out into the blustery chill. The air was so dry and cold, so crisp that it stung her face, the insides of her nostrils, and even her lungs, and the snow was starting to come down in angry swirls.

A flock of mounted men were milling about down by the Springwater station, and even though they were all wearing long, heavy coats, hats, and mufflers, Jessica spotted Gage right away. He seemed to stand out from the others, as though he'd taken on some extra dimension.

She bent her head against the bitter wind and pushed on until she reached the telegraph office. She would speak directly with the operator concerning the missing train; perhaps she didn't have a lot of experience at running a newspaper, but she knew better than to print pure hearsay.

The telegraph man was a pleasant sort, with ears almost as long as his head and spectacles perched on the tip of his narrow nose. His hair, such as it was, stood up in tufts of salt-and-pepper, and he was quick to smile and tug at the brim of his visor when Jessica came in.

"C.W. Brody," he said by way of introduction. "And you must be Michael's sister."

"Miss Jessica Barnes," she confirmed, politely, but in a businesslike manner. If she was going to be taken seriously as a journalist—however short her career might be—she must behave like a professional. "I've come to ask about the train."

"Oh, we don't expect to have one runnin' through here much before the turn of the century," Mr. Brody said. "Not straight through Springwater, anyways. There's some that pass by at a distance." He took in her wind-reddened face. "Come and sit down over here by the stove. You look like one of your arms might fall off and clatter around on the floor."

Jessica was disconcerted by that remark, but she recovered right away. Little wonder that she looked cold; she *was* cold. She took a seat within the shimmering haze of heat that surrounded the stove and slipped her cloak back off her shoulders. Then she took a pencil and a pad of paper from her reticule.

"I could brew up some coffee," Mr. Brody suggested. He really was quite dear, and obviously glad of company. No doubt his job was dull most of the time, and lonely into the bargain.

"You wouldn't happen to have tea, would you?" Jessica inquired. She knew that Mr. Calloway shared the building; her gaze had already strayed at least once to the frosted glass door with his name penned across it in gold script.

"I could borrow some from Cornucopia, over at the general store."

She had already imposed on Cornucopia enough as it was, by leaving the babies in her care. "Oh, no," she said hastily, "please. That would be too much trouble."

Mr. Brody, it turned out, was in possession of a great deal more information regarding the vanished passenger train than Jessica would have guessed. He spent a full half-hour giving her the details, right down to the names of the travelers thought to be aboard. One of them, a Miss Olivia Wilcott Darling, who had begun her journey in Chicago, was believed to be headed for Springwater. Mr. Brody lowered his voice and inclined his head slightly toward Jessica when he got to that part. "Gage done sold her his house."

Jessica took thorough notes, but her thoughts were with the men who had ridden out to participate in the search. Or, at least, with *one* of them.

When her professional interview with Mr. Brody ended, she ventured a private inquiry, having guessed that the harmless little man was something of a gossip. "Do you happen to know the precise amount of my late brother's debt to Mr. Calloway?"

Mr. Brody looked stunned, then reluctant. "Why do you ask?"

"I have my reasons," she replied.

He flushed, started to speak, then closed his mouth. Finally he said, "Three hundred and forty-two dollars."

Three hundred and forty-two dollars. Almost the entire amount of Jessica's legacy from Mrs. Covington. But if she had that money in hand, she could pay Mr. Calloway back and throw his marriage proposal in his face right along with it. Furthermore, the newspaper would be hers.

"I should like to send a wire," she said.

*   *   *

The train was half buried under an avalanche of snow when they found it, and the daylight, such as it was, was nearly gone. The horses were completely spent. While Pres and Trey scrambled into the one visible passenger car, which lay on its side in a drift, all of its windows broken out, Jacob, Gage, and Landry set themselves to gathering wood and getting a fire going. If there was anybody left alive inside, they'd be cold as well as hurt—maybe badly.

Gage and Landry were making a sort of lean-to out of fallen branches when they heard a shout echo from within the train. Both of them dropped what they were doing and hurried toward the overturned car, though it was hard, slow going. The wind was rising, and Gage could feel it biting right through his clothes.

Trey scrambled up out of the car through one of the windows, and crouched beside the opening. Just as Gage and Landry reached the scene, Pres handed up a small, inert body from inside—a little boy, Gage realized, no more than four or five years old. Trey took the child gently and passed him down to Landry, who immediately started back toward the lean-to and the fire.

"Here's another one," Trey said, and produced a second boy, this one around seven, and at least half conscious. One of his legs was twisted at an alarming angle, and his short pants and patched jacket were soaked with blood. Soon, Gage too was on his way toward the improvised camp, the lad moaning in his arms.

There was one last passenger—a tall, slender woman of the sort men usually described as handsome. She looked essentially unhurt, though rumpled, shaken up and very, very cold. When Trey lifted her carefully up through the broken train window, she batted at him with her handbag and told him to watch where he put his hands. Five minutes later, the wind was howling like a thousand wolves serenading a full moon, and the bonfire provided scant protection.

"What happened?" Pres asked the woman. He had climbed out of the train and was next to the fire with the rest of them, kneeling beside the boy with the broken leg. He had already set the bone, and now he was applying a splint. The other boy was awake now, but he was pale as death, and his eyes seemed to fill his whole head.

The woman blinked, and Gage realized she was trying to keep from crying. He couldn't say he'd have blamed her if she *had* broken down, after an experience like that. "The train was moving very slowly— mounting a grade, I think. Then we heard a dreadful roaring sound, and—and we were all thrown this way and that—" She paused and put both hands over her face.

Without speaking, Landry pulled a pewter flask from inside his coat and held it out to her. She hesitated for a few moments, then accepted the offering, unscrewed the lid, and poured a good guzzle straight down her throat. Her eyes didn't even water, which was something to behold, because she sure didn't look like the type who could swallow homemade whiskey without so much as a sputter.

"The engineer and the conductor—?" she began. "Are they—?"

"Dead," Pres said. Sometimes he was about as tactful as a sledgehammer. "You and these boys are the only survivors, I'm afraid. Did you have family on the train?"

She shook her head distractedly, then put a hand to her mouth, scrambled to her feet, and rounded the tree to retch into the snow.

"Couldn't you have broken the news over the space of, say, a paragraph?" Trey demanded of Pres in an irritated hiss.

Pres didn't miss a beat. "What would be the point of that? A fact is a fact. Everybody else on that train was either killed outright or died of exposure."

The smaller boy began to sob. He had a scrap of paper pinned to his coat with the number 18 scrawled on it, along with a name. Gage squinted. "Here now, Tommy," he said. "Everything's going to be all right. You'll see."

"Stop that cryin'," instructed the older boy, through teeth clenched against the pain in his injured leg. "We're alive, ain't we? That makes us lucky, the way I figure things."

Tommy sniffled, making a valiant effort to pull himself together. "But I'm cold, Ben, and I'm hungry, and now we ain't going to be 'dopted."

Gage understood then. The boys were probably brothers, though not necessarily, who'd been sent west to find homes for themselves. A fair number of these "orphan train" kids ended up working like mules, but a lot of them were taken in by good people and raised as blood kin, too.

The woman returned, looking as ghastly as she surely felt. "We aren't going to spend the *night* out here, are we?" she asked, dabbing at her slender throat with a wadded handkerchief.

Pres gave her a downright unfriendly look, probably worried that she'd raise a fuss and scare those kids even worse. "If we try to go back tonight," he said, "we'll freeze to death."

That was Pres. He knew how to embroider a phrase, all right.

Tommy had moved closer to his brother. "Does that hurt?" he asked, indicating the splint.

Ben took a swat at him but, fortunately, missed. "What do you think?" he snapped.

Gage sighed and leaned back against the trunk of a cottonwood. It was going to be a long night.

"Where did you boys come from?" Pres asked, as he finished up with Ben's leg and then patted him on the shoulder, his way of telling the child he'd been brave.

"Boston," Ben answered. "We was supposed to get adopted." His expression was fierce, even in the firelight. The kid had pride—and plenty of it—though little else, probably. "Tommy's my brother, and we mean to stay together, no matter what. We got to find somebody who wants both of us."

Pres seemed to be in a reflective mood, there for a

moment, and he even went so far as to look toward Springwater, which was a good fifteen or twenty miles off. "I think I might know somebody who does," he answered.

Landry elbowed Gage, and out of the corner of his eye, Gage saw that his friend was grinning.

CHAPTER

～ 6 ～

BY THE TIME Gage and the others got back to Springwater, at around noon the next day, roughly half the party was wishing they'd left Miss Olivia Wilcott Darling behind to freeze to death. The other half just hoped she'd hate the place and move on before the first thaw.

With some help from Landry, Pres took the two little boys, Tommy and Ben, to his house. That left Miss Darling to deal with. It was ironic as hell, in Gage's considered opinion, her having a name like that, and more ironic still that she'd turned out to be the very woman who'd bought his house, sight unseen. She meant to stay at the Springwater station until she'd rested up enough to take possession of the place, which she intended to turn into a rooming house——so it fell to Trey to get her to June-bug before somebody lost their head and strangled her.

Gage was numb with cold and too tired to think. If

he'd been a drinking man, he would have taken a shot of whiskey; as it was, he was considering taking up the habit. He left his worn-out horse tethered to the hitching rail out in front of the telegraph office and went inside, intending to stand by the stove for a while before moving on to his cubbyhole in the back and collapsing onto the too-short horsehair settee he usually reserved for clients with a tendency to overstay their welcome. He didn't expect to wake up for the better part of a week.

Nor did he expect to encounter Miss Jessica Barnes—his intended, he recalled with some surprise—when he stepped over the threshold. He already thought of her as "Jessie," though he was prudent about using the nickname, her being somewhat of a prickly type.

She was standing at the telegraph counter with a message in both hands, and it looked as though she might tear the thing right in two, she was holding it so tightly.

"Bad news?" he asked. Seeing her was better than whiskey.

She looked up at him, blinked—evidently she'd been so absorbed that she hadn't heard the door open—and shoved the telegram into the pocket of her cloak. "Nothing that need concern you," she said, for all the world as if she hadn't agreed to be his wife just the day before. "Did you find the train?"

He thrust out a long sigh, hung up his hat, and shrugged out of his sodden coat. There was no sign of C.W., which was just as well, because he wasn't up to being questioned by him, too. "We found it. Most everybody was killed outright."

Jessica went pale, and for a moment he thought he ought to reach out and steady her, but she rallied quickly. "Most everybody?" she asked.

"A woman survived, and two little boys. Twenty others weren't so lucky."

She looked past him, through the heavy glass in the door. "You just left them all out there?"

He gave her a level look before moving around her, drawn to the welcoming warmth of the stove. "No. A couple of railroad agents showed up around dawn, with a hired posse. They're taking the bodies to Missoula."

She swallowed. "That's dreadful. So many people, gone."

At least she wasn't scribbling down details, like a lot of reporters might have done. He nodded, and for the first time the true extent of the tragedy came home to him—maybe he'd been holding it at bay all this time. Now, suddenly, he felt like breaking things. Raging against the impervious forces of life and death, and no matter that it would be futile. He might feel better for doing it.

Jessica ran the tip of her tongue over her lips—it was an innocent gesture, he was sure—but it set something rusty grinding into motion within him, something long-still and silent. Until he'd caught sight of her for the first time, anyway.

"I spoke with Mr. Brody yesterday," she said.

"I wish I could have been here," he replied.

She gave him a look fit to strip paint but, perhaps out of respect for the recently dead, she did not lose her temper. He was disappointed, given that it would have been a pleasant distraction to watch. She was a passionate woman, though she did not seem to realize it. Yet.

"He told me how much Michael owed you."

Gage couldn't work up anything more than mild irritation; he was just too damn tired. Maybe when he'd rested up, he would get C.W. by his skinny, wattled neck and squeeze till he turned blue, but appealing as the prospect was, it would have to wait. It was all he could do not to keep from stretching out on the floor, right there by the stove, and going to sleep. "Did he, now?" he asked. He had hoped Jessica would drop the subject but, of course, she didn't.

"I've wired St. Louis for my personal funds. They are sending the money to a bank in Choteau. All I have to do is pick it up."

"In case you haven't noticed, Miss Barnes, there is a blizzard brewing out there." He thrust a hand through his hair. Maybe he'd have that whiskey after all. "Besides that, it's too late. The documents have already been transferred." He was being ornery and he knew it, but he was too exhausted to mind his manners.

She went paler still. "If you have any decency in you, Mr. Calloway, you will accept full payment and surrender control of the *Gazette* immediately. I, after all, am the rightful owner."

"*I* am the rightful owner," he pointed out.

She looked, for a moment, as though she would haul off and slap him. "Are you going to insist that we go through with this farce of a marriage?"

He smiled. "A deal's a deal," he reminded her.

She turned on one heel and stormed out.

He should have gone after her, should have apologized, should have said of course he'd give back the newspaper and let her out of their agreement, but he simply didn't have the stamina. It would all have to wait.

He slept for two solid days.

The weather was clear the morning he came around, and cold as a coal-digger's ass, but everybody knew there was more snow coming. You could smell it, feel it in the air.

C.W. greeted him somewhat sheepishly when Gage came out of the office in search of hot coffee. "Good to see you up and around, Gage," he said, and looked away quickly.

Gage went to the stove, poured a mug full of sludge from the coffeepot, and took a bracing sip. It was so rank he almost spit it out, but his early training in the social graces wouldn't allow him to do so. "You've got a big mouth, C.W.," he said.

C.W.'s ears turned red. "I don't know what you're talking about."

"Like hell you don't," Gage replied, flinging the miserable coffee into the fire, where it sizzled and hissed. "You told Jessica Barnes how much her brother owed me."

C.W. swallowed.

"Didn't you?" Gage persisted.

The other man gulped, then nodded. "It was out of my mouth before I knew it, Gage. She just looked at me with those eyes of hers and I turned right into an idiot." Settled at his table, C.W. began tapping out a message. "I don't suppose it'll help much, but I'm sorry."

Gage shoved a hand through his hair. He needed a bath, a shave, fresh clothes, and a heaping plate of June-bug McCaffrey's cooking, in that order. He'd do his thinking afterward.

Half an hour later, he was sitting in the McCaffreys' tin washtub, scrubbed clean, and the smell of good Southern food filled the air. Once he'd eaten, he'd go to Jessica and tell her he hadn't meant what he said about forcing her to marry him. Indeed, he might even tell her that he thought about her a lot and that he had strong feelings for her, and those were facts he'd only recently admitted to himself.

Jessica came out of the bank in Choteau, her life savings tucked carefully into her handbag, and looked right and left. Just down the street, the Springwater stage was waiting. She didn't recognize the driver, but no matter. She had the money to pay Gage, and she needed to get back to the babies and the *Gazette* as soon as possible. She had a complete issue typeset and ready to print, and as soon as she'd fetched the twins back from the general store, where Cornucopia was looking after them, she meant to go to press.

She glanced up at the sky. It was a clear, icy blue,

but there were gray clouds gathering on the horizon. Just looking at them made her shiver.

She went to the coach, where the driver was already loading her battered satchel into the boot. "Ma'am," he said, and touched the brim of his hat. "You travelin' out Springwater way?"

"Yes," she nodded, politely, but distantly. "Will the coach be leaving on time?"

"Yes, ma'am," he said, and tugged at his hat again. "I'm Jack Arthur, and I'll be filling in for Guffy today. He's down with a touch of the ague." Turning his head, he assessed the sky, just as Jessica had done moments before. "We've got a storm comin' in, ma'am," he said, when he met her gaze again. "I don't know as you oughtn't to stay right here in Choteau. It might be rough going out there."

Jessica felt a shiver climb her spine, but she shook her head. She had two children waiting for her, and a newspaper to run. Besides that, she couldn't afford to spend another night at the roominghouse, let alone several. Paying back Gage Calloway was going to take most of the money she had. "I'd rather go home," she said.

Arthur nodded. "Yes, ma'am," he said and, with one more wary glance at the sky, helped her aboard the coach. Soon they were traveling toward Springwater, moving at a brisk pace, and if the inside of the stage was a little cold, well, Jessica wasn't about to complain. She just pulled her cloak around her a little more tightly and sat back on the hard, uncomfortable seat, resigned to a long, difficult trip.

During the ride she thought of the train wreck. It seemed as vivid in her mind as if she'd actually witnessed it, complete with all its horrors. She'd written a long and thoughtful article before leaving Springwater, having gotten by wire from the railroad's head office in Missoula a list of those killed, and the story, along with a few minor items of strictly local interest, would make up her first issue of the *Gazette*.

In point of fact, next week's issue was already taking shape in her mind. She would print the first installment of the serial Emma Hargreaves was writing under a pen name, along with notice of the quilting bee in the home of Mrs. Trey Hargreaves the last week of the month, and June-bug McCaffrey's recipe for sweet potato pie. In a town like Springwater, you had to make do with whatever news you could scrape up.

Jessica felt a wrench when she thought of the babies. They'd looked like little golden-haired cherubs, lying there in their padded apple boxes on the counter at the general store, their lashes brushing their round little cheeks. At some point, she had come to love them fiercely, and she knew it was forever. Raising them would not be easy, but then, worthwhile pursuits seldom were.

Why, the mere thought of those children renewed her determination to overcome every obstacle, every setback, every heartbreak. She *would* build a life, for the babies and for herself. One thing was for sure: she didn't need Gage Calloway.

So why, she wondered, did this triumph lose a little of its glow when her mind turned, inevitably, to him? It was almost as if she were *disappointed*, which was plain silly.

Back at the Springwater station, June-bug McCaffrey had bid her farewell with a worried look and a hug. "I'm not sure it's a good idea for you to take to the road when the weather's like this," the older woman had fretted. "Why, yesterday when Guffy came through, it took us an hour just to thaw him out!"

Jessica wanted to pour her heart out to June-bug, tell her all her most secret hopes and dreams. Maybe she'd be able to make sense out of the tangle of feelings that had their beginning in Gage Calloway.

A frigid wind rattled the blind covering the stagecoach window, and Jessica moved it aside to peer out. Snow was coming down so hard that she could barely see, and she wondered, with sudden and piercing fear, how the driver could keep the rig on the road in such weather.

For the first time, she wished she hadn't been the only passenger traveling to Springwater that day. She would have taken some consolation from having another soul to talk with.

The disaster struck suddenly, as disasters generally do—before Jessica even had time to wonder what was happening, she'd been flung against the far wall of the stage, and with enough force to leave her dazed and aching all over. The wind was howling so loudly that she couldn't hear the horses or the driver. Snow blew through the broken door of the stage, stinging like a shower of sparks, and she realized with a sick feeling that the rig was half overturned. Struggling to the door and peering out, she caught a glimpse of one spinning wheel before the storm swallowed up even that.

She shrank, shivering, back into the questionable shelter of the coach.

Perhaps it was minutes later, perhaps it was hours, but the driver appeared in the chasm, his face bloodied, his hat gone. "I'll try to make it to the station and fetch back some help," he shouted. "You'd best stay here!"

Jessica wanted to go with him, wanted more than anything in the world not to be left in that bleak place, but she could see the sense in his argument, even then. The coach provided at least some shelter, inadequate though it was, and venturing out into that storm, even on horseback, was a monumental risk.

"What about the mules?" she hollered back.

"I let 'em go, except for old Squirrely, him bein' the best of the lot!" yelled the driver. "Leastways they've got half a chance that way, sorry critters that they are. You stay right here, now! You go wanderin' off somewheres, and you'll be a goner for sure!"

Jessica nodded, too cold and too shaken to carry on such a demanding conversation, and settled back to wait.

"She'll stay in Choteau," Jacob said quietly, aligning the checker pieces for another game while Gage paced the length of the hearth, about as agitated as he'd ever been over anything. "Miss Barnes might be headstrong, but she ain't stupid."

Gage went to the nearest window and glared out, watching as the snowflakes came down thicker and faster. Fifteen inches had fallen since morning, by his measurements. "No," he agreed. "She isn't stupid. But she'll try to come back because of the babies and that damned newspaper. Damn it, if Guffy decides to make today's run, she'll be aboard the stage for sure!"

"Maybe Guffy will stay in town," Jacob reflected, but he was beginning to sound uncertain.

"In the five years I've lived in this town," Gage argued, "I've never known that Irishman to miss a day's work. I'm telling you, Jacob, the two of them are going to freeze to death out there somewhere, right along with eight of your mules."

Jacob sighed, lifted the checkerboard off the table, and let the pieces slide back into their box. "And you figure the smart thing to do would be to ride out there and freeze to death with them."

Gage started pacing again. "I'll go crazy if I don't make sure she's—they're all right."

Jacob replied with one of those rare smiles of his. "So you've finally found her, have you? I don't mind sayin', it's about time. June-bug and I, we were beginnin' to despair of you."

"What the devil are you talking about?" Gage demanded, even though he knew. God help him, he knew.

"You're in love with the gal," Jacob said. "Soon as I heard you'd milked a cow for her, right in front of God and everybody, I suspected as much."

Gage muttered a swear word. The hell of it was,

Jacob was right. He just hadn't been ready to admit it aloud until now.

"Isn't this what you've been wantin'? Somebody to care about? Somebody to go home to of a night?"

Gage's mind had left Springwater ahead of him, and taken his heart right along with it, and he was scrabbling to catch up. "I don't have time to talk about this," he said, heading for the door. "I've got to find her."

He slammed out the door and strode through the dense snowfall toward the barn. Then he remembered his coat, and went back to fetch it.

"Don't you say one damn word," he warned when Jacob shook his head.

Fifteen minutes later, he set out to find the Springwater stage. His horse was opposed to the idea, and they had hard words before the matter was settled to Gage's satisfaction.

A few times, he wasn't sure of his direction, and after an hour he was wearing a bandanna over his face like a bandit, in hopes that he wouldn't lose his nose to frostbite. As he rode, he wondered how it was possible for a man to come to care so deeply for a woman that he'd risk his life for her—not to mention a perfectly good horse—in just a couple of days' time. After wrestling with the question for a while longer, he decided it didn't matter how it happened, or why. It was so, and that was that, and he'd just have to figure a way to deal with the situation.

He doubted that Miss Barnes even *liked* him, though he'd felt a charge pass between them on more than one occasion, and he knew she'd felt it too; even so, she probably would have died before she confessed to bearing him any tender sentiments.

He could no longer tell whether it was night or day when at long last he came upon the stagecoach, a mile this side of Willow Creek and lying on its side. Somebody had unhitched the mules, and they'd headed for the timber, but there was no sign of either O'Hagan or Miss Jessica Barnes.

For the first time since he was eight years old and standing at the foot of his mother's deathbed, Gage Calloway uttered a prayer. He didn't figure even God could hear it, though, the way the wind was screaming, driving snow into his flesh like little spikes. Half blinded, he urged the balking horse forward. The new snow was soft, but the layer beneath was sharp enough to cut flesh.

Then he saw her. She looked out the stage window, her face like a flicker of light in the white gloom, and called out to him. Fearing that he was seeing her ghost, he spurred the anxious horse in a vain effort to get it to move faster.

Finally, after a long struggle with the forces of an angry wind, he reached the side of the coach, bent, and pulled the door open. Jessica crawled and scrambled up to him, flinging her arms around his neck. She was soaked to the skin.

"Where's Guffy?" he yelled, in an effort to be heard over the storm.

"Guffy stayed in town—the other driver went for help—"

Gage turned the horse back toward the station, and they were halfway up a high drift when the animal slipped, shrieking in terror, and flung them both off, one in one direction, one in the other.

Unhurt, the horse scrabbled the rest of the way up the slope and ran, reins dangling, making damn good time considering that the snow was knee-deep by then. Gage made a mental note to enter that gelding in a race, should he live to round it up again.

He hurried back down the bank and hauled Jessica out of the snow with one powerful wrench of his arm. If she'd been in danger before, she was far beyond that point now, soaked to the skin as she was, and covered in snow. He had to find shelter within a matter of minutes, or she would die for certain.

He lifted her into his arms and followed his instincts through the trees, for he was too cold by then to think. He had one aim and one aim only: to keep her alive. If he failed, his own life wouldn't be worth a damn.

He fell to his knees, once, twice, a third time. And each time, he got up again, impelled by a force no preacher had ever told him about. His chest burned, his arms and legs were numb, but she was there, huddled against his chest, and he could feel the beat of her heart. It was enough to keep them both going.

"Don't you dare die, do you hear me?" Gage gasped, close to her ear.

He was all but walking on his knees when the corner of the mine shack came into view, and at first he thought his eyes were fooling him. He'd read about things like this happening to people lost in storms—sometimes they saw visions and thought they were safe, only to succumb a few paces further on.

The door gave when he put his shoulder to it, and he heard the creak of ancient hinges, even over the incessant shrieking of the wind. The whole place swayed when he carried Jessica over the threshold and, for a moment, he just stood there, braced to take the weight of the roof, along with about two feet of accumulated snow and ice.

The walls held, by some miracle. Slowly, awkwardly as a man moving through some thick substance, Gage laid Jessica down on the board floor and forced the door closed. There was next to no light in the place, but once his eyes adjusted, he could see that the structure was about eight by eight.

Lying at his feet, Jessica groaned, and his mind, befuddled by the cold, sent a sluggish message to his hands and legs. After searching the cabin, he found nothing at all to wrap her in, though there were a few twigs and floorboards that could be used to get a fire going. Hastily, he flung his hat aside, then peeled off his coat and started to put it around Jessica.

Another communication sank in. She couldn't stay in these wet clothes.

He stripped her, something he'd imagined doing once or twice, but in his imagination the circumstances had been different. Her bare skin was blue-white, and he bound her up in the coat, then set himself to rubbing her hands and feet, trying to get the circulation going again.

She whimpered. "That . . . hurts."

"Good," he said. "You're alive."

"Where . . . ?"

"Never mind where we are. Hell, I don't even know. Right now, Jessie, I want you to think about those babies, and how much they need you. I want you to think about the newspaper, and—and—" He'd been about to say *me*.

Her eyelashes fluttered against her blue-and-red blotched cheeks. Good God, even frozen half to death, she was beautiful. "And—what?"

"Never mind."

She opened her eyes and looked right through to his soul, or so it seemed to him then, in those frantic moments. "You . . . came looking for me. In this storm."

"Damn good thing, too," he said, shivering now as his flesh began to thaw. In many ways, that was the most miserable part, the painful process of getting warm again. "You'd be dead if it wasn't for me."

Unbelievably, she smiled. "Why? Why would you take such a chance?"

"Why the devil do you think?" he snapped. His teeth were chattering by then, and he was in no mood to chat. "Because I love you, that's why!"

She stared at him. "You do?"

"I said it once, woman. I'm not going to say it again. Not here, not now!"

She laughed, actually *laughed*, with both of them

right there on the verge of their just rewards. "You have to be the stubbornest man in the world," she said. Then, with a smile on her lips, she closed her eyes and drifted off someplace just beyond Gage's reach.

CHAPTER

7

SHE DREAMED they were back out in the storm. She had never been so cold; her clothes clung to her, sodden with melted snow, and she had long since lost all sensation in her limbs. She knew Gage, who was carrying her close against his chest, believed her to be unconscious, but she could not summon the stamina to let him know she was awake.

In those agonizing minutes, when she knew that she was close—so very close—to death, she wanted to live with a passion more ferocious than any she had ever felt before. She wanted to live for the twins, for this impossible man who would not let her die, for herself. For the first time ever, she was centered squarely within herself, sure of who she was and whom she might become, given the chance.

She had the strength for only a scrap of a prayer, but it shone from the innermost regions of her heart like a beacon, and she was sure God and all his angels could see it. *Please* . . .

She closed her eyes then, and found that she was lying in a dark place. She was warm, though, and she could have sworn that Gage had his arms around her, that he was holding her close against him, as if he feared to let her go.

The cold jabbed Gage awake like a sharp stick; he sat up, careful not to disturb Jessie, and looked around. That old shack seemed flimsy enough to fall over at any second, but it was one hell of a lot better than nothing.

The fire was nearly out; he'd have to get dressed and find more wood. Drawing in a hissing breath, he left the cocoon he'd shared with Jessie and dragged on his pants and shirt, then his boots. The wind was still screaming fit to deafen anybody, but Jessie didn't so much as stir.

Suddenly fearful, he crouched and laid the backs of his fingers to the pulse at the base of her throat. A long sigh escaped him. Her heartbeat was strong and steady. For the moment, nothing else mattered much.

Once again he assessed their surroundings. It was almost as cold inside as out, and the place smelled of mice and other such critters, but there were walls and a roof, and a rusty little woodstove stood in one corner, draped in shadows and cobwebs. He'd started a fire in it—how long ago?—before lying down with Jessie.

Moving as quickly as his still-stiff limbs would allow, Gage scrounged in the darkness for whatever scraps of firewood he might be able to find. In the end, he broke up a crate and stuffed that into the belly of the stove, along with a collection of miscellaneous debris. A blaze caught, spawned by the dying embers of the first fire.

After adjusting the damper on the chimney pipe—he could only hope there were no birds or mice nesting along its twisted length—he set to smashing the remaining furniture, which consisted of one broken chair and a bedstead. Then, when the chill was beginning to subside a little, he lay down beside Jessie again, wrapping the coat around both of them.

He was only human. He enjoyed it a little.

Damn. She was naked. He felt like a kid, peering through a hole in the bathhouse wall. He could feel her softness right through the legs of his trousers and the longjohns beneath.

He positioned her as close to him as he dared, reminded himself that he was a gentleman, and closed his eyes. Try as he might, he couldn't sleep. He just lay still, in a sort of dull-headed haze, listening to the wind and breathing in the scent of Jessie's hair. Even there, in that filthy, tumbledown shack, she smelled good.

Hours had passed, by his calculation, when he couldn't stand it anymore. She felt too cold, too still. "Jessie?" He patted her cheeks. "Hey, Jessie . . . wake up, will you?"

"I'm . . . awake," she said, in a sort of languid whisper. "Where . . . ?"

"We're in a shack," he reminded her. "Remember, I told you before. Just about the time we were both done for, here it was, like it was waiting for us." He glanced warily up at the rafters, which moaned with every snow-laden gust of wind. There was no telling how long it would be before it gave way, but he didn't plan on mentioning that. "Jacob and June-bug must be praying again."

She smiled, and the plain courage of that twisted something in Gage's heart.

"If anybody's praying for us," she said weakly, "I hope it's them." She sighed, and her lashes, thick and golden brown, fluttered against her cheeks.

"Stay awake, Jessie," he commanded and, still kneeling beside her, he drew her up onto his thighs and held her like a child. In a few minutes, he'd start walking her around the cabin in hopes of getting her blood flowing, but he didn't want to push her too hard. "Did the driver say where he was going?"

She frowned, as though it was an effort to remember. Her expression was dreamlike, and Gage feared that she might be losing ground again. They were by no means out of the woods.

He got to his feet, hauling her with him, and made her walk. "Jessie," he said. "Listen to me. I know you want to sleep, but that's the worst thing you could do right now. I shouldn't have let you close your eyes. You've got to keep moving."

"But . . . I'm so numb. . . ."

"Yes," he agreed. "When things start hurting, then you can lie down. Now, what did he say?"

She thought long and hard. "Who?" she asked, after all that effort.

At least she'd gotten that far. "Did he try to make it to Springwater? Jessie, I'm talking about the driver. Was he headed for town?"

She nodded, but not until they'd been around the inside of the cabin half a dozen times. "He said I'd be safer where I was . . ."

Gage hoped the poor bastard *had* succeeded in reaching the station, because he'd almost certainly be dead of exposure by now if he hadn't. The coach had broken down only about two miles from the station, and in good weather a man could walk the distance without undue wear on the soles of his boots. In a blizzard, it was another matter; there were a hundred ways to get lost, even if you knew the terrain, the way the relief driver surely did. He hoped the McCaffreys would offer up a few prayers for him, too.

"I have to lie down now," Jessica said.

"Not yet," Gage replied.

"I suppose we'll have to spend the night here."

He sighed. "We'll be lucky if we get out of this place in a week, Jessie."

She looked up at him with wide eyes. "A *week*? I'll be ruined!"

"You'll be *dead*, if you go out there before the weather clears."

"What will we do for food? For firewood?"

Her brain was thawing out; he supposed that was a good sign, though pretty soon her fingers and toes would probably start paining her pretty seriously. "You let me worry about the practical things, and just think about getting warm, all right?"

"But you must be cold, too. . . ."

He had been, but Jessica's presence had worked wonders. His skin stung and his bones ached, but except for those things, he felt about normal. "I'm fine," he said. "I could do with some whiskey, though."

She laughed, and if he'd had any doubts that he loved her, they faded to nothing right then. He wished he could tell her again, now that he was sure she'd hear, but he just couldn't bring himself to take the risk. If she rejected him, nothing else in his life was going to matter for a long, long time.

And so they walked, and walked, and walked some more. Finally, when he was sure it was safe to let her rest, he allowed her to lie down again, and she tumbled immediately into a deep and healing sleep. He ferreted around the dingy cabin and found some old gunnysacks to place over her in lieu of blankets, and listened with increasing dread to the shriek of the wind. Every new gust seemed to rattle the whole place, and a couple of times he really thought it was going to collapse into a heap, burying them both in snow, rafters, and rotten shakes. Worse, they were running low on firewood.

He didn't have much choice in the matter; they could freeze to death, or he could go out in the storm and see what he could scare up to stuff into the stove. As for food, well, they'd just have to do without that, because no sensible rabbit or deer was going to be out in weather like that, and the bears were all hibernating.

After making sure Jessica was covered as well as possible, he drew a deep breath, opened the door, and stepped over the threshold. The cold hit him with an impact that stole his breath and nearly blew him right back inside. He ducked his head and kept going.

Jessica was alone—she knew that before she even opened her eyes—and an awful sense of fear rose within her as she sat bolt upright. It was then that she realized she was covered in empty potato sacks and wearing Gage's long coat—with nothing underneath. She vaguely remembered him removing her wet clothes, but at the time she hadn't cared. Even now it didn't bother her half as much as knowing he was outside somewhere in that screaming storm, with nothing to protect him from the cold.

She sat up and tossed the potato sacks distastefully aside, only to pull them over her again when she felt the chill. The fire in the little stove was almost out, and she could see her breath. How long had Gage been gone? Suppose he was lost out there somewhere, wandering around in circles, as winter travelers were known to do?

She opened the stove door and prodded the embers inside with a stick she'd found lying on the floor. Then, awkwardly, she got up, holding the coat and the gunnysacks around her in a vain effort to keep warm, and looked about for a window. There was none. The small amount of daylight entering the cabin was coming in through a wide crack in one of the walls.

More for something to do than because she thought it would do any real good, she hunted around until she found more scraps of burlap. She wadded them into a ball and stuffed them into the gap, and when she did, the whole structure trembled and gave a long, low groan of protest. A shower of dust fell from the rafters.

Jessica gasped and squeezed her eyes shut, inwardly bracing herself, but by some miracle, the roof and walls held. Jacob and June-bug *must* be praying, she thought. It couldn't be her pitiful little "please" that was keeping that building up.

She was just beginning to panic again when the door opened and Gage came in. He looked like a snowman come to life, with his hair and eyebrows frosted and his clothes coated with gleaming white, but he was carrying an armload of wood.

Jessica pushed the door shut behind him, alarmed by the way he moved as he labored across the small room and dropped the precious branches and chunks of bark on the floor. He was stiff and slow as he opened the stove and began shoving things inside.

"Gage Calloway," she said, more out of fear than conviction, "you're a damn fool. Why, look at you—you're covered in ice from head to foot!"

He didn't say anything; he just knelt there, in front of that fire, willing it to burn. Finally the blaze caught, and Jessica could not be sure whether it was the warmth that drew her, or Gage himself. She got down on the floor next to him and began peeling off his clothes, just as he'd done with hers earlier, when they'd first found shelter, and he didn't fight her. She removed his shirt first, then his boots, then his trousers and longjohns. He was trembling, and his skin was an alarming shade of blue.

Instinct caused her to open the coat and enclose him inside it with her, and for a while, they shivered together. It would have been a mercy if she hadn't been so conscious of his nakedness, but she was. Indeed, she felt the contact with him in every pore and follicle. His member, which she had not been able to avoid glimpsing in the process of undressing him, took on a life of its own and pressed itself into the soft flesh of her belly, hard and growing harder with every passing moment.

"Sorry," he said. His teeth were chattering.

"Shhh," she replied, and they lay down together and slept, entwined.

When Jessica awakened again, the room was warmer, and Gage had gotten up and put his clothes back on. She was glad he couldn't know that she missed the feel of him, the strength and substance of him, pressed against her. She was careful not to look at him until the heat in her cheeks had subsided a little, even though the cabin was dark, but for the light of a single tallow candle.

"It's warm," she said.

"I tore up some of the floorboards," he replied. "And I found a jug of corn liquor underneath. Want some? I'm afraid it's the closest thing to supper we're going to get."

Jessica seldom took spirits, but this was surely a

time for exceptions. She nodded, and he brought her the jug, held it to her lips, and tilted it so that she could take a sip. It was like drinking kerosene, and she sputtered and coughed so violently that Gage felt called upon to slap her on the back, but the moonshine produced a spill of fiery warmth as it flooded down her throat and burned its way to her stomach.

"More?" he asked.

She shook her head and wiped her mouth with the back of one hand. "Let me recover for a little while first," she croaked.

He laughed and took an enormous swallow, hooking one finger through the small handle and supporting the jug on the side of his elbow and upper forearm.

She peered at him in the dim light. "What are we going to do?"

He considered awhile, took another swig of whiskey, and answered, "Wait. This storm has got to let up sometime, and when it does, folks will be out looking for us."

"We could get awfully cold and hungry before that happens," she said sensibly.

He set the jug aside and cupped her face with one hand. "They'll find us, Jessie," he promised.

Jessica didn't protest the familiar form of address; in fact, she rather liked it. She wondered if she'd ever be able to admit, outside her own heart and mind, that she loved this man. That she never wanted to be with anybody but him, in spite of everything.

He leaned his head down then and kissed her, softly at first, and then with a heat that made parts of her ache. When the tip of his tongue brushed lightly across her lips, she opened to him, and the sensations that followed left her speechless.

"Jessie," he said, when it was over, and she was still trying to recover her equilibrium. "I love you. I know I must sound like a damn fool, saying a thing like that when we've only been acquainted a few days—and spent most of that time arguing—but it's true."

She stared at him. Maybe it was shock that made her think she'd heard him say he loved her. Maybe it was the cold, or she was coming down with some sort of fever.

"Jessie," he prompted.

"Did you actually say—?"

"I said I love you," he told her clearly.

Tears filled her eyes. She'd almost given up hope of hearing those words, certainly had never expected to hear them from this particular man, but he'd said them all right, and apparently, he meant them. "I—I love you, too," she said, and just those simple, hesitant words took all the bravery she could summon up. Far more than surviving the storm had required, or traveling west alone, or taking on the raising of twins and the publication of the *Gazette*.

"Marry me," he said.

She swallowed. This proposal was distinctly different from the last one, which had been a mockery. "I have the babies to think of, and the newspaper. And then there are Michael's debts."

"We'll raise the babies together," he said. "With a

few of our own, of course. As for the rest, we'll work it out."

She shook her head. "No," she said. "We have to come to an understanding right now. I know Michael owed money to a lot of other people, not just in Springwater, but in Choteau, too. I won't let you take on my brother's debts, Gage, if that's what you're planning on doing. And if I'm going to reimburse the people he borrowed from, I have to make the newspaper pay."

"But you'll marry me? If I agree to your terms, I mean?"

She felt reckless and wild, as though she were careening down a snowy mountainside on a runaway toboggan, and she'd never been happier. "Yes," she said, and he kissed her again.

Come morning, the world was still and the sun shone on miles of snow with a blinding brightness. Jessica and Gage had slept in each other's arms through the night, but both of them had been fully dressed, their clothes having dried, and they had not gone beyond the kissing stage. Jessica might have given in, had he tried to persuade her, for he had awakened things within her that were as elemental as weather, but he'd said they ought to wait until Jacob had said the proper words over them, and she'd agreed.

Both of them had suffered for the sacrifice.

"Shut the door," Gage grumbled, when he awakened and saw Jessica standing on the threshold, one hand shading her eyes, gazing out on the landscape in a state of pure wonder.

Just as she was doing so, they heard a shout from somewhere in the near distance, and Gage nearly knocked her over getting outside.

"Over here!" he yelled, cupping his hands to his mouth.

Snow slid off the roof with an angry, scraping roar, loosed by the sound, and the little shack wobbled, but held. Jessica peered around Gage's broad shoulder, still bundled in his coat, and saw two men come over the nearest drift, wearing snowshoes. Each of them carried another pair strapped to his back.

"I told you they'd find us," Gage said.

Jessica raised her eyes heavenward and offered another silent prayer. *Thank you.*

The men were Trey Hargreaves and Landry Kildare, and they'd brought food as well as blankets and extra snowshoes. When they produced cold biscuits and jerked venison from their packs, both Gage and Jessica ate ravenously.

The trek back to Springwater was long and difficult, and there were times when Jessica thought for sure she would drop to her knees in the hard-crusted snow, never to rise again, but her pride kept her going. If the men could prevail against the elements, so could she. After all, they were all made of the same stuff—blood, bones, breath, and flesh—it was just arranged a little differently in her case.

All during the long journey, she waited for Gage to mention that he and Jessica meant to be married, but the conversation revolved around other things. Jack Arthur had gotten to the stagecoach station safely, though he'd nearly lost some toes and fingers in the effort, and he'd been the one to suggest that they look for Gage and Jessica at the cabin. Jacob had known the prospector who'd settled the place, and everyone had agreed that if indeed the two had found sanction from the weather, that had to be where they were.

It went without saying, of course, that if they *hadn't* gotten in out of the cold, they would surely have perished within a few hours.

Their reception in Springwater raised Jessica's flagging spirits a little—had she only *imagined* Gage telling her he loved her, proposing marriage, holding her throughout the night in an innocent embrace that had, all the same, left her branded as his, forever and ever?

June-bug McCaffrey threw a blanket around Jessica the instant she stepped over the threshold of the Springwater station, guided her to a chair next to the fire, *tsk-tsk*ing all the while, and thrust a cup of hot lemon juice and honey, laced with something a bit stronger, into her hands. She went right on fussing and fetching, murmuring prayers of gratitude, sounding as distractedly joyous as a mother hen who has just rounded up a pair of stray chicks.

Gage was welcomed, too, of course, but in a different way. Jacob brought out his special cider, and he and the other men sat around one of the long trestle tables, listening as the wanderer recounted his harrowing adventures. Jessica listened carefully with one ear, and there was not a word about the plans they had made together.

Had he forgotten? Changed his mind?

"I'd best get home," she said finally, when she felt she could trust her legs to carry her as far as the newspaper office. She made to lift herself out of that comfortable chair. "Cornucopia's been looking after the babies all this time—"

"Never you mind," June-bug said, and pressed her right back down onto the worn calico cushion. "Word's been sent to Cornucopia—Toby went right away. As for the babies, why, little Emma Hargreaves has been helping her tend them, and she knows what she's doin', too, what with those little'uns of Trey and Rachel's."

Jessica settled back with a sigh and accepted another cup of June-bug's wonderful medicinal concoction. Her eyelids felt heavy, and it seemed that every muscle in her body had gone limp all of a sudden. She realized she couldn't have walked even as far as the newspaper office; she was simply too tired.

She drifted off after that, and someone carried her to a bed—a blessedly soft, warm, clean bed. She was vaguely aware of Dr. Parrish leaning over her, his stethoscope dangling from around his neck.

"Am I sick?" she asked, unsure even as she uttered the words whether she was speaking aloud or simply thinking the question.

He smiled. "Just tired," he said. He sounded real, but he could be part of a dream.

Perhaps she was still in that freezing cabin after all, perhaps this delicious comfort, this cosseting warmth, was really a prelude to death. She'd read that it happened just this way. "Gage?"

"He's all right, too," Dr. Parrish assured her. "Get some rest."

She slipped beneath the surface of consciousness then, unable to stay afloat any longer, even if that meant she would never awaken.

When she opened her eyes again, the room was full of light, dazzling, snow-bounced light. And Gage was sitting on the edge of her narrow bed, grinning down at her. She blinked.

"I never thought I'd end up with a lazy wife," he said.

She blinked again. "Wife?"

"Jacob's agreed to marry us today," he went on, still smiling. "If you're still willing."

A great, jubilant shout of joy swelled within her, but she managed to contain it, and sat bolt upright instead. "What about the newspaper? The babies?"

He laughed. "We've talked about the newspaper and the babies, remember? We'll adopt the twins, and you can run the *Gazette* as long as it suits you. Just print a few favorable articles about the mayor now and then, if you don't mind."

Her mind was racing, but even at top speed, it couldn't catch up with her runaway heart. "But there's so much we don't know about each other, you and I—"

He kissed her forehead. "We've got a lifetime to

learn," he replied. "What's your answer, Jessie? Yes or no?"

She stared at him for a long while. "Yes," she said finally. As if there had ever been any doubt, from the first moment she'd laid eyes on him.

Jacob performed the ceremony that afternoon, in the little white church with the bell tower, and despite the deep, hard-crusted snow that stretched, glittering, for miles in every direction, the pews were packed with delighted guests. June-bug sang a wedding song of her own composition, high and sweet, and the women wept with joy throughout the whole service.

Trey and Rachel Hargreaves served cake and coffee in their decorous parlor when the ceremony was over, and at twilight, when the bride and groom finally took their leave, fat flakes of snow were swirling lazily down from a gray and low-bellied sky.

When Gage swept Jessica up in his arms, right there at the Hargreaves's front gate, a rousing cheer was raised by the wedding guests, gathered shivering on the porch to wave and call out good wishes. He looked down at her and frowned thoughtfully.

"What's the matter?" Jessica asked, still a little afraid he might change his mind about marriage. About her.

"You don't mind, do you? That I sold the house, I mean? I'd rather have one we planned together, but—"

Jessica thought her heart would burst; the love she

felt for this man was so strong that it brought tears to her eyes and caused her breath to catch. "No," she said, because she was too stricken with happiness to embellish her words. "I don't mind. I just want to be with you."

He kissed her, right there in the middle of the street.

Cornucopia had taken the babies to the store before the wedding, and the tiny apartment over the newspaper office was empty. A note left on the kitchen table said they weren't to worry; the twins were being properly spoiled.

"That woman in San Francisco," she said, "do you still care for her?" It was the first time she'd dared ask, even though the possibility had been pulsing in her mind ever since Cornucopia had told her what she knew of Gage's past. While she'd related the whole story of her experience with Mr. Covington while they were stranded in the cabin, he had said little or nothing about his own past.

He smiled, still holding her. Her skirt trailed on the floor, and her hair, like his, was full of snow. He sat down, without releasing her, in the rocking chair facing the empty fireplace. "No," he said. "That's been over for a long time, Jessie. Besides, she's married to my brother."

She searched his face. "But you're estranged from them, aren't you? Your grandfather, your half-brother?"

He sighed. "Small towns," he said.

She flicked at a stray lock of his dark hair with the backs of her fingers. "Make things right with them,

Gage," she urged softly. "Whatever happened, they're your family."

"You're my family," he said, kissing those same fingers. "You and the twins."

"You know what I mean," she insisted.

Once again, he sighed. "All right," he said. "I'll write to them. Extend the olive branch. But if they don't respond, there isn't much I can do about it."

She smiled, pleased. "What happened?"

"Could we talk about this later?" he was fiddling with her hair, watching her mouth as though it fascinated him.

"No," she replied.

He tilted his head back and closed his eyes. When he spoke, he seemed to be addressing the ceiling. "My grandfather told me that my father was dead, and I believed him. Hell, why wouldn't I? My mother remarried, had Luke. Then I found out that he'd lied—they all had. My grandfather had forced my father—his own son—out of the business, out of all our lives. Luke knew the truth, and he never told me. By the time I found out, it was too late."

"Your father really had died by that time?"

He nodded.

"And the woman?"

"She married Luke—my half-brother. As far as I know, they've been happy together."

Jessica was silent a long time. Then she laid her face against his cheek. "I'm sorry," she said.

He hooked a finger under her chin and made her look at him. "Can we start the honeymoon now?"

She blushed, then nodded, and he carried her toward the bedroom and the bed where she had expected to sleep alone for the rest of her natural life.

"It's not a very fancy place to spend a wedding night," she observed, a little ruefully. They were at the threshold of their room now, moving inexorably toward a fate that made Jessica's breath catch. He paused, looked into her eyes.

"It'll do just fine," he said. "Springwater's changed me, Jessie. I'm not the same man I was when I came here." He laid her gently on the bed and began to undress her, starting by unlacing her shoes and tugging them off. He caressed her ankles for a while, all the while talking in a low, melodious voice, describing the things he wanted to make her feel in minute detail. Finally, he unfastened her garters, rolled down her stockings, stroked her bare legs.

Jessica felt as though she were coming down with a fever. Tendrils of her hair were already clinging to her temples and her nape, and she couldn't seem to get her breath. The sweet, cold silence of the snow falling outside did nothing to cool her blood.

She watched, unable to speak, as he shed his coat, undid his string tie, worked the buttons of his fine white shirt. A tantalizing view of his chest greeted her eyes; she tried not to stare and could not help herself. He was more than handsome, more than magnificent, and he was hers.

"Jessie," he said, his voice hoarse. They were both bare of every garment and constraint, lying face to face beneath the fine quilt that had simply been there when the coverlet was drawn back. "You trust me, don't you? Never to hurt you, I mean?"

She swallowed and nodded. After what they'd been through together, she would have trusted him with her soul as well as her body.

He ran a hand down her shoulder and arm, brought it to rest on her hip, and left a trail of small, invisible sparks arching off her flesh. "I'll be as gentle as I can," he promised, "but sometimes—just the first time—if you want me to stop—"

She laid an index finger to his mouth. "I want you to *start*, Gage. And don't stop until I'm yours and you're mine."

He kissed her again then, gently at first, then with growing hunger. It was quite different, that kiss, from its predecessors—lying naked together in their marriage bed changed everything.

Over the long, languorous interlude to follow, Gage introduced Jessica to a variety of simple but soul-searing pleasures, exploring the planes and curves and hollows of her body, her spirit, and her mind, and sharing those same parts of himself. Long before they actually joined themselves together physically, they had formed a mystical bond that even death could not sever.

At long last, Gage raised himself over her—she was pleading by then, half delirious with wanting— and he looked into her eyes with such tenderness that she was sure her heart must have cracked within her like an eggshell, made forever strong by its weakness.

"Say yes, Jessie," he said. "Please, say yes."

She couldn't get a word past her constricted throat, so she merely nodded again, and he was inside her, in a long, unbroken stroke, filling her, exalting her, setting her ablaze. There was a suggestion of pain, but that was soon lost in a maelstrom of rising need; they flung themselves together, apart, together, faster and faster.

Then, in the space of a heartbeat, the universe splintered into glittering pieces, licked with flame, and showered down around them, bits of shattered sky, stars, and memories of stars. They were everything and nothing at all. They were themselves, and each other, and wholly separate. But some part of them, Jessica knew, even in those breathless moments when she was sure she could not survive such ecstasy, would always be one being, always live at the heights.

As they slept entwined, snowflakes pirouetted past the windows and blanketed the earth in a mantle of glorious white.

More to treasure from

Linda Lael Miller

ANGELFIRE

BANNER O'BRIEN

CAROLINE AND THE RAIDER

CORBIN'S FANCY

DANIEL'S BRIDE

DESIRE AND DESTINY

EMMA AND THE OUTLAW

FLETCHER'S WOMAN

KNIGHTS

LAURALEE

THE LEGACY

LILY AND THE MAJOR

POCKET BOOKS